Dragon Child

Book One of the Prophecies Saga

James R. Kitney

authorHOUSE®

AuthorHouse™ UK Ltd.
500 Avebury Boulevard
Central Milton Keynes, MK9 2BE
www.authorhouse.co.uk
Phone: 08001974150

First published by AuthorHouse 7/10/2009

ISBN: 978-1-4389-9659-2 (sc)

This book is printed on acid-free paper.

Acknowledgements

This book would not have been possible without the help and support of a number of people. To all those who have assisted me in any fashion I wish to offer my heartfelt thanks. I would also like to thank a few specific people for there help over the past few months.

To my parents, for their support and encouragement since the commencement of this project and to Victoria, who has been a constant source of enthusiasm and helpful suggestions in the final months of publishing.

Finally I would like to thank my cousin Catherine, for providing the artwork for the Kingdom's map at an extremely hectic time in her own life.

Without any of you this would not have been possible and you will forever have my gratitude.

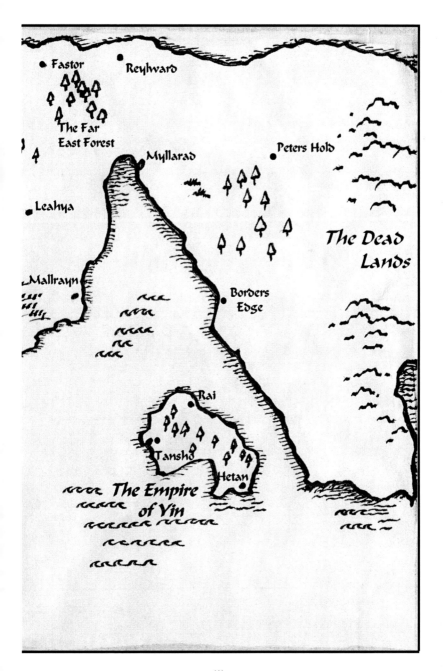

Prologue

A man awoke to the sound of movement out side his small house in the Far East Forest. There was always movement in this mass of trees, but something about this time caught his attention. He was out of his bed before he was thinking, and moved to the aged Longbow leaning up against the wall. Without thinking, he strung it with an ease that spoke of a great many years of use. He quickly put on hose, a tunic and boots, draped his great-cloak over his shoulders and attached a quiver of arrows to his waist. The man knew the woods and the sounds that emanate from them…. This was not such a noise.

He made his way down the old stairs that had belonged to his father and his father's father before him, and moved to the heavy oak door that marked the entrance to his house. Slipping the bolt back, he opened the door quietly and peered out into the long shadows of night. Nothing could be seen in the dark and so he took a cautious step out into the moonlight. He could not hear anything now, but knew that the reason he was out here had not left, and almost as sure it was watching him.

The man drew a cloth yard arrow from his quiver and nocked it to his bowstring. Again he heard the noise, this time from above him. He looked up to see a dark shape pass overhead, the sight astonished him, for despite his many years, he had never seen so large a beast, easily sixteen or seventeen

v

feet from wing tip to wing tip. As he continued to gape at this creature he heard the snap of a twig behind him. He spun and drew the heavy bow in the blink of an eye, coming face to face with a tall man completely shrouded in a grey great cloak "Be at peace, for I have not come to harm you." Said the man as he approached. "Nalas, are you always so jumpy? I would have you know, that if I was intending to kill you, you would already be dead"

"Who are you?" asked Nalas the fear in his voice obvious.

"Me? I am the one who takes people in the night, I am the Collector. The one who seeks out those worthy few who would die to serve the Great Master."

"The Great Master? Who are you talking about?"

"I'm talking about the one who shall rule this insignificant world and the rest of this Multiverse in time."

"Why have you come to me? Why the Collector?"

"I am called the Collector for that is my job, I seek out the Ones of Impurity and give them the chance to serve."

"And if they refuse?"

"Then they die. Enough of this," Said the Collector irritably, "I am here for you Nalas Draygin, will you serve?"

Nalas looked ill, he did not know what to think. Who was this man? Who were the Ones of Impurity? Why was he interested in *him*?

"Answer!" demanded the still unnamed figure.

Nalas paused, he did not know what to say, but he knew one thing was certain. If he answered incorrectly, his life became forfeit. "Yes I will serve." Came the slow and hesitant answer.

"Excellent. Come with me." The Collector looked up and made a strange cry. The dark beast that was flying overhead came crashing through the sparse greenery surrounding the cottage.

"Where are we going?" Asked Nalas still in a nervous voice.

"To the Masters realm, where you shall be initiated into his service."

Nalas mounted the strange beast that looked like a cross between a giant bat and a great hawk. It resembled a Graven, a beast of legend that was supposed to serve only the most powerful of the Dark Lords. He felt fear that rivalled anything he had felt before.

As the Graven circled high into the sky, a man in a rangers garb stepped from the trees and watched as Nalas flew to his death, wondering if he would have to face the walking corpse of that poor man.

He withdrew a small cube from his pouch and activated it. With a wave of heat and a gust of air he vanished from the clearing mentally marking another of the Ones of Impurity found by the enemy, and thinking that the Great War must be getting close.........

—

The demon raged. He had been awoken by one of his captives and his piteous cries. The fool did was unaware that his torture had not yet begun. Lumbering to the cage that held the trembling man, he slowly opened the steel door. The demon had had enough of the humans whimpering, and was easily convinced that he was hungry again.

Plucking the now screaming man from his cage, the beast proceeded to consume him in his powerful jaws, to the horror of the other captives bound in cages around the room.

The demon finished his meal and looked around. The castle once belonged to another of his kind, but he had made the mistake of not guarding his back. That was the most common way of advancement in the demon race, consume your superiors and gain their rank. The hulking form regarded his domain. Now he was a War Hand, and feared. In his regiment, he made a point of killing both the strongest and weakest once per cycle. He was resolute in the practice as it showed he would not let a weak demon fight for him whilst at the same time not allowing anyone to over step their bounds.

He regarded his kin through the high window that over looked the grey barren terrain. None had the faintest idea what the General had in mind ... No the War was coming and many would die. But not before the human Grey Mages were completely controlled by the demons. That was how demon kind would retake control of the world and how the humans would fall.

"Yes," the demon thought, "soon my time will come..." With that thought of glory, he walked back into the room, while outside the window the younger demons could hear the sound of their War Hand feasting on the humans that had been captured, their cries echoing through the castle as their bodies were consumed.

———

A gong rang loud in the hall of Elders as a column of men walked quickly to take their positions. The Lord High Seer took his place at the front of the great hall. He looked around the large room; on its walls were portraits of the great Seers in the history of the Kingdom. It was his hope that if the Kingdom survived the coming War, his own face would be upon one of these walls, for the portraits not only gave remembrance to great mages, but it reminded the current Lord High Seer of many lessons that can only be learnt with experience.

The gong rang a second time. All the other mages in the hall sat.

Silence.

A third ring of the gong and a small man in a white robe that matched the robe of the Lord High Seer, entered through the two large doors at the opposite end of the hall. He walked slowly to stand before the Lord High Seer, and then turned to face the rest of the hall.

"Dedicated magicians, the Court is now in session. Let only the truth be spoken today as the Lord High Seer has come to hear our concerns and to help put them to rest. May all who wish to address the High Seer make their presence now known in the usual manner observed among Magicians."

As the white robed man finished his address several other men all in similar white robes, lifted themselves a few feet into the air and illuminated themselves in a faint pale blue light.

"So be it. All who remain silent are deemed to have no news to bring forth today, please refrain from speaking other than to address the issues now at hand."

With that the speaker returned to the back doors and placed a white disk about five inches in diameter across the seam where the two doors met, and all in the hall could feel the working of magic as the disk flowed into the space between the doors and sealed them together tightly.

"None now may hear of what we speak. The Court has begun."

It was the formal way to start a court but many of the magicians gathered in the rows of seats knew the Lord High Seer by name as well as reputation. Jakrin Tiersing was a tall man, clean shaved, and with dark almost black hair. His eyes were the common green of the Kingdom yet they held a softer light than many. He was considered by many to be the greatest Lord High Seer of this century and many came to ask his advice.

Jakrin stood and with his arts changed the faint blue glow of a floating magician to a purple hue, denoting that this man has the right to speak in front of the assembled council.

The man who had just been given preference spoke in a loud voice. "Lord High Seer, Council of Elders, honoured Brothers. Now has come the Time Before. The signs all point to the rising of the armies of the Grey Mages, and The Rangers have observed the Ones of Impurity being sought by the Collector. What are we to do? We have all been informed that the Lord High Seer has been working on this problem for years, yet have we seen any results? No! So Jakrin, what is to be done?"

Jakrin Tiersing made himself erect, to be brought down in front of the council was one thing, but to be questioned about this subject in such a manor was close to insult. "I am aware of your worries Zyrich but as you do not seem to be in the City other than to question me, you would not have felt the magic that has been in creation for months now. Quiet your questions, for they are old and all have heard them."

With that the man named Zyrich descended back to his seat as the Court continued late into the night…

A pale skinned man with grey hair and a heavy grey robe, walked through the deep, dark tunnels that were only lit by the working of fey magic and guttering torches. Damp lined these tunnels and mould could be seen growing out of the cracks in the aged walls.

The tunnels were silent, they always were. No one would dare say too much here, a man could die by the misheard words he spoke and no one here really had any intention of dying yet. The robed man walked to a heavy wooden door and leant in to it. Slowly the door moved and from within the room a putrid smell emanated, the smell of dried blood mixed with the aroma of decaying flesh. The mage did not like the rituals that kept him rejuvenated but he liked less the thought of ageing seven lifetimes in the short space of a week before crumbling to dust.

Inside the room was a statue of a dark figure covered in a flowing robe, his face hidden in the folds of the material, but thin, clawed hands were visible from the sleeves holding the dagger that was used in the sacrifice that gave the mage his youth again and again.

In front of the statue was an altar of stone, around the altar were runes, these runes in themselves made the powerful man fearful, for they were what bound him to this life, a life of murder and dark deeds. They were an oath that one had to take before their first sacrifice, the oath of allegiance to the dark god.

Upon the altar, a man lay naked except for a loincloth, and still. The drugs that had been given to him would wear off soon and then the sacrifice would begin.

—

Jason awoke. He was on a cold stone slab, his captors had stripped him of all clothing and he was tied hand and foot to each end of the altar. He tried to scream but only a low moan emanated, as he realised that his tongue must have been removed while he slept. Jason now knew fear, fear as he had never felt before. His body shook as he tried to free himself.

Eventually he gave up and looked around hoping that perhaps he was simply to be left for dead. Maybe then he could get himself out of this.

What he viewed killed all hope and he began crying quietly. Kneeling on the floor in front of the altar was a group of about twenty men. All in grey robes and all chanting in deep voices that sounded very little like the human speech that he had been speaking all his life. At the front was a pale skinned man standing with a wicked curved dagger in his hand. His eyes were alive yet there was no hint of humanity in them. They regarded him like ice and felt just as warm.

This man was chanting louder and at a faster rate than the rest. He started to advance towards the altar, the dagger gleaming in the light that seemed to come from nowhere. As the man reached the altar he seemed to freeze, pause, as though he didn't want to go through with the murder. Jason felt relief, he may yet be safe. Thoughts of his family came to him as he thought he may yet see them again.

The dagger plunged.

Jason saw the mans eyes grow hard in that instant, and a fire a thousand times hotter than any smiths forge flooded through his veins. His sight began to darken as he saw the old mans face become younger, more powerful. Jason began to moan again as he knew with certainty that his soul would now be denied rest until this man was dead.

Jason wept as he died…

Chapter 1

Woods

Tal looked at the sky. His blue eyes focusing on the sun and noticing that it was too low for him to stand any chance of talking his way out of potential punishment when he finally returned home. The wind that gusted down the woodland trail blew his golden hair into his face as he hurried back to the small city of Dukeray, and the inescapable lecture from his foster parents. Tal walked quickly, carrying the last of the logs he had been sent to cut in his arms while the wood axe was strapped securely across his back. Broad shoulders held the logs easily after six years of logging, and although hard work, he enjoyed the open air and working out of doors.

His foster parents Jegar and Lynette Parnell while strict, were caring and understood Tal's love of the open air, and although it was guaranteed he would have some kind of punishment, he knew it wouldn't be too harsh.

Suddenly Tal realised that in his dreaming he had slowed to a crawl, and picked up the pace. The light was beginning to fade as dusk began to take its hold over the forest and Tal was beginning to feel like there was a need to be at home. Although the forest was generally a safe place to be this close to the city

Tal always felt somewhat vulnerable in it at night. His eyes began to scan the tree line as he walked, noting the way the trees reacted to the wind and the behaviour of what creatures were still out in the cooling night. Tal stopped as he realised that all the animals had gone quiet. He placed the logs on the floor as he tried to peer past the tree line and searching for what may have caused the abrupt change in animal behaviour. Tal was looking down the trail in the direction from which he had come when he saw a figure in a deep black cloak begin to take shape in the distance. The figure did not appear in a hurry, and so Tal was inclined to wait rather than run for the city.

As the figure approached, Tal could make out more detail about him. He was a tall man about the same height as Tal, though he didn't appear as well built, and the black cloak revealed a red ring running around the bottom hem along with a red dragon placed at roughly the same place the mans heart would be. He had green eyes and dark hair. The mans face seemed to be carved from stone and his jaw set with a hard edge to it. Under his cloak could be seen a sword, though of which variety Tal could not make out, perhaps if his friend Drew were here, he could say, but as it was Tal was drawing a blank. All this aside, the man did not seem threatening and Tal wondered why a man would be travelling alone through a wood this late in the evening.

As the man came within talking range with Tal he smiled and it seemed to change his face instantly. Gone was the hard fighter and in his place was an ordinary man, one that Tal wouldn't have thought twice about if he had seen him in town without the sword.

"Greetings lad." Said the stranger as he approached. "Could you tell me if I'm near the city of Dukeray?"

Tal paused at the direct manner of the man. "Yes sir, the town is about another half hours walk. I'm heading there now if you would like me to take you?" Tal knew that agreeing to take an unknown man that you met in the woods anywhere was a risk, but he wanted to know more about why a stranger would trek through woods in the night to visit a small city that had nothing special within its walls.

"Thank you lad, it would make it easier than if I were to try to find it myself." Said the man with a grin that knocked years of his age. "And in return perhaps I can help you with your load." He said with a smile as he looked at the pile of logs on the floor.

"Thank you sir, but its no trouble, really." Replied Tal as he started to pick up the logs from the damp ground.

"Its no problem lad." Said the man as he started to pick some logs at the young boys feet. Tal was impressed with the mans strength. Not many of the men in Dukeray could carry as much as Tal and yet the stranger seemed to have no difficulty with the bulky load. Once he held half the logs the stranger motioned to Tal, "Lead on then lad, I feel the need for a soft bed and the warmth of an inn tonight." Tal started to walk in the direction of the city as the mysterious man fell in beside him.

"So lad may I know your name, so I may know who was kind to a weary traveller?" asked the man after about a quarter hours walk.

"Tal, sir, I live with Jegar and Lynette Parnell above the lumber yard in the city."

"Living with them? As in not related to them? I take it you're an apprentice then?" asked the still unknown man.

"No sir, I'm an orphan, my parents died when I was very young."

"I'm sorry lad, I too lost my parents at a young age." He paused briefly before brightening again. "Pleased to meet you lad, I'm Layland Kendrik. My friends call me Lay, please feel free to call me the same." He said with another smile.

The two walked in silence for nearly the most of the remainder of the journey, until just before they left the woods Tal heard a noise behind them. He spun quickly to see who was there. Looking deep into the darkness but could see nothing.

He turned to face Layland to discover he was gone, the pile of logs placed where he had been standing. Tal became worried suddenly and turned to run home, when he found another man was standing in front of him with a drawn sword. "Give me what ever valuables you have kid and you walk away alive." demanded the ruffian. He had a scarred face that looked menacing in the dark light and was wearing tatty and hard worn clothing.

"I...I don't have any valuables, I'm only bringing logs for my father."

"Well then, I guess you're all out of luck aren't you?" Said the would-be robber, as he started towards Tal with an evil glint in his eye.

"I suggest you leave the lad alone friend." Advised a voice from behind the cutthroat. Tal looked over the mans shoulder to see Layland with his sword drawn and his cloak now open, revealing a coat of gleaming black chain mail with the outline of a red dragon on its centre. The man spun round to look at Layland with a nervous expression on his face. "Now don't do anything hasty mate, I just want the kids money. Nothing more."

"The lad said he doesn't have any, now leave. And don't let me see you around here again, or I'll see to it that you need several graves." Said Layland without the humour he had shown since Tal had met him earlier on that evening.

"Now don't be threatening me. I don't like it and I may attack, and you wouldn't want that."

"I think you should try friend." responded Lay, as the fellow looked at him nervously before running at him, sword held high.

Layland stepped back catching the mans blow with the edge of his sword before stepping to the side and bringing his own sword down with a speed Tal though impossible. The thief barely dodged the cut, getting away with only a slight cut to his arm. With a cry the man lunged at Layland, who with a flick of the wrist brought his sword up under the thief's knocking it away while putting his in line with the mans chest and stepped forward, pushing his sword into the scar faced mans heart. The man stumbled back and fell off of Layland's sword before falling still, to the ground.

"Come lad, you should not have to see the likes of this. Let's get to the city before it gets even darker." Said Layland as he cleaned his sword on the ground and picked up his pile of logs. Tal wasn't going to argue with that logic and so he started for the city at a quick pace. Layland kept up easily.

Tal and Layland arrived at the small city of Dukeray after what seemed like hours, when in truth it had only been about ten minutes, but to Tal it seemed like an eternity. The night's adventure arousing an awareness in Tal he had never thought about. He felt he could sense the presence of other beings without actually being able to see them. Tal looked down from the hill they were on, to see into the city. The walls were thick, a good twenty feet in width without the ramparts and the guards on duty were patrolling them slowly. Beyond the walls was the outer city, the buildings and streets built in a completely different fashion to that of the inner city, the inner city had its own wall surrounding it and had streets that were straight with nearly flat roofs. Clearly a city built for siege. The inner city was the home for the richer merchants and some of the duke's advisors who were not important enough to live in the castle. The outer city was not a bit like the ordered display of the inner city, but a mesh of intertwining streets that were built to cater for the constantly expanding population. The outer city was populated by labourers, poorer merchants and was also the chosen portion of the city for the temples. At the centre of this small city was the castle, its massive walls circling the keep and outer buildings such as the household guards barracks or the Dukes stables. The castle had stood for over two centuries without major repairs being needed and was undoubtedly one of the finest castles in the Kingdom.

As Tal and Layland walked into the city, Tal visibly relaxed. Layland smiled at the lad, he was clearly shaken by what had happened in the forest but had held his fear in check. Layland had also noticed the boys senses increase, he felt the lad reach out with his spirit and touch the forest, checking for disturbances in the dense woodland. *Could this be the boy I came here searching for?* Layland asked himself. And if so, what stroke of luck had landed the boy in Layland's hands so easily?

"Tell me lad, how old are you?" asked Layland, his purpose of being here being abruptly restored.

"I'm sixteen sir or will be in two months"

"Please lad, I said call me Lay." Answered Layland. Becoming surer by the minute this was the boy that he had been searching for.

"Sorry si… Lay." Answered Tal somewhat abashed.

"Don't be sorry lad," replied Layland. "respect for your elders is a wonderful thing, but between you and me, I'm not really classified an elder yet…Far too much impulsiveness in me for that." He laughed, the ever-present grin returning in a flash.

The two walked down the main street in the outer city that led towards Tal's home. Layland's clothes and sword causing no small talk as he passed. Visitors, while not uncommon to Dukeray, rarely walked around in such fine clothes or with armour and a sword. Clearly a man of wealth or so it seemed due to the weave of his clothes, and certainly an important man to carry a sword and wear such well tended armour.

As they arrived at Tal's home Tal entered, and was engulfed in the arms of Lynette.

Tal's home was above the lumberyard his father owned with the entrance up a flight of steps on the wall next to the yard, and was a warm home that no boy Tal's age would swap for another. A fire burned in the hearth and the smell of warm bread emanated from the kitchen, with a response from Tal's stomach that reminded him he was hungry.

"Where have you been young man? You know the woods are no place for anyone this late at night." The words were not angry just concerned.

Looking over Lynette's shoulder Tal noticed his friend Drew staring at him with an impish grin at Tal's suffering. Drew was not a short boy but stood almost a head shorter than Tal, and had dark hair cut short.

"Now young man I hope you have a good reason for being late. Your father has been going out of his mind with worry over you." Continued Lynette, seemingly without stopping for breath.

Layland seemed to just appear to Drew who hadn't seen him come in, yet also hadn't seen the man move to appear.

"Madam, perhaps I can offer a reason as to the lateness of your son."

Lynette seemed to jump at the sudden figure in the door.

"Who are yo…I mean, how is that sir?" Stumbled a shocked Lynette trying to regain her wits at the arrival of this man with Tal.

"You see Madam, I was making my way through the woods towards this city, and I noticed the lad struggling with his logs. I offered help in return for being shown to the city. On our way to the city I heard a noise behind us and went to investigate. When I returned it seemed that I had missed the man following us and he had found young Tal here all alone and had taken it on him self to relieve Tal of his money. When I saw this I stepped in immediately and tried to stop it, but there was a fight and the man is now in the presence of the Keeper of Souls." Finished Layland, referring to the god of death.

"Well sir, if your story is to be believed as it seems to be, I am in your debt. May I know your name then sir?"

"My name is Layland Kendrik madam." Said Layland bowing.

Tal looked at Drew who had been sitting in the corner with excitement clearly showing on his face. For Drew this must be like a story, he had always wanted to be a soldier, and of an age with Tal he would be looking for employment within the next few months. Drew was going to try for the Household Guard for service with the Duke, as he was well known in Dukeray as one of the finest swordsmen in his age range.

"Are you a soldier sir?" asked Drew, his eagerness clearly showing as he cut Lynette off from answering.

"Drew, manners now, this gentleman must have had a tiring journey and here you are pestering him with questions already!" Remarked Lynette as soon as Drew had finished.

"It's ok, really." Answered Layland as he walked over to Drew, the grin still on his face. Tal could see why he couldn't be called one of his Elders, to Tal, Lay didn't look that much older than himself, maybe early twenties in age. And with his always-grinning face, he seemed more the child than the man, though the way he had wielded his sword reminded Tal that this man was more than deadly.

Layland knelt before Drew so that they were at the same height.

"Yes lad, I am a soldier. But not the regular kind. You see I'm a…"

"He's a Dragon Rider." Came the remark from the door.

All heads in the room turned to see a man in the doorway. He was a well built man with light brown hair, and green eyes. He was clean shaven and had a powerful face. "Now what in the gods names are you doing with a Dragon Rider Tal? You haven't been raising armies of the dead have you?" Said the man with a booming laugh.

"And you must be Master Jegar." Said Layland walking to the man now identified as Tal's foster father, and extending his hand.

"I am sir." Said Jegar taking the offered hand and shaking it. "And you are?"

"I am Layland Kendrik." Replied Layland.

"Well, I'm pleased to meet you Layland." Replied Jegar. "Now, what brings you to Dukeray, if I may ask?"

"To tell the truth good sir, its Tal."

A silence clung to the room, it hung to everything within the house. Not even Drew who before this seemed to be constantly on the verge of asking another question, wanted to say anything. The reputation of the Dragon Riders was well established. They had fought in every major battle since the creation of the Kingdom and always remained undefeated. It was also common knowledge that the dragons that were taken into battle had magical powers that helped their riders, though the extent of the magic control the riders had over their mounts was always a topic of debate. A great many of the populace was sure that the Riders controlled the dragons, and it was the Riders themselves that had magical powers. The other side of the argument was a complete opposite, that the dragons were the ones fighting and the Riders were there only to let the dragons know if there was danger approaching from the sides or rear. Either way the Dragon Riders were a unit of warriors that commanded awe from the most arrogant of men, and here stood one, in the very room where Tal had grown up.

Jegar was the first to regain his wits, "What do you want with Tal? He hasn't done anything wrong has he?"

"No Jegar, he hasn't done anything wrong in the slightest. He is to become a Dragon Rider." Replied Layland smiling all the time.

"A...Dragon Rider?" Put in Tal nervously.

Layland walked over to Tal, "Yes lad. I came here looking for one who had the skills and abilities to become a Rider, and out in the woods after the attack you did something that told me it was you. Do you remember what it was Tal?" Asked Layland.

"No sir...Lay, I don't." Replied Tal.

"Tal, after the attack you became more aware. You didn't just look with your eyes, or listen for movement, you extended your mind to meld with the forest, and you felt the trees around you.

"You remember how I seemed to vanish before that man approached you? Well I knew he was gong to turn up by the same method. *That* is how I knew you were to become a Dragon Rider."

Tal looked stunned. He looked around the room and saw that his feelings were repeated through his family. Drew on the other hand, wore a different expression. He actually looked… envious!

"Master Layland," began Jegar, "I don't understand, how can Tal be a Dragon Rider?"

"Master Jegar, there is a certain type of person that can become a Rider. Few have the correct…skills, but when they are found, the Riders want to train them. You see the Riders do more for the Kingdom than most realise. They not only protect in the time of war, but they keep an eye out for danger from whatever quarter. This you must understand takes a great deal of men and women…"

"Women?" Blurted Drew before he could stop himself.

"Yes lad, the Riders are made up of women as well as men. Some of the women are even stronger than the men too." Replied Layland with a wry smile. "Anyway, I'm sure you can understand that we want as many trained Riders as we can get. But the question now, is does Tal want to become a Rider?"

Layland left the Parnell residence and walked through the streets of the now dark city. He had given the family much to think about, and was sure that it would take most of the night for them to come to a decision. Out of courtesy he had left them to discuss the matter in privacy, though the lad Drew seemed to have decided the matter for Tal already. He was going to go to the City of Dragons, become a Dragon Rider and have many a tale of heroism to tell his children when he finally left service.

Layland chuckled at the vision of children. Maybe he would have some one day, though not for many years yet.

As Layland walked through the streets his black cloak bellowed in the wind. Layland had a feeling on the back of his neck and quickly darted into a dark alley. In the alley he settled himself in a dark corner and let his mind stretch out. The technique was as old as the Dragons themselves and was a skill that defined the Dragon Riders. Layland pushed out further, closing his eyes he could see as though there were no obstacles baring his vision, shapes became substantial and insubstantial at the same time. A figure moved through the streets following his path. The dark figure approached the alley Layland had entered and paused at its entrance. Layland opened his eyes and let his hand slide to the hilt of his slightly curved sword.

The unknown figure entered the alley, still too dark to see clearly Layland waited as the figure approached. He moved closer Layland could see he was not a large man, yet there was a sense of speed about him. Layland waited as the figure moved within striking range, still encased in shadows the Dragon Rider waited for a count of three and jumped, drawing his sword, to come face to face with the figure. The lad jumped at the figure that just appeared in front of him, and Layland halted his attack in mid swing. Drew looked ill as he noticed how close to his head Layland's sword had come before stopping.

"By the gods will, what are you doing following me lad?" Asked Layland as he recognised the boy.

"I…I wanted to ask you something sir." Said Drew, stuttering out the reply.

"Well then lad, you had better ask me hadn't you?" Said Layland the grin returning as he sheathed his sword. "But not here. Tell me Drew, is there a respectable inn in the area?"

"Yes sir, there is one just two streets away." Answered Drew.

"Well then lad, lead on." Remarked Layland as he followed the young man through the streets, wondering what the Gods were lining up for him, and if he himself would be involved in this young lads fate.

Jegar turned to his wife, he had been trying to convince her that the opportunity to become a Dragon Rider was simply too good to pass up, and that Tal would become a more valuable citizen of the Kingdom. Lynette however was not so inclined, "No Jegar. I will not let Tal go soldiering off to the gods know where, and be put in danger like that." Tal didn't know what to make of it himself, he had heard rumours of the Dragon Riders like every other boy in the city, but also like every other boy, he did not know what the Riders were about. All Tal knew was that in times of great crisis the Dragon Riders took to the skies on their dragons and let fire, magic and death rain down upon their enemies.

Tal came round to the sound of Jegar's voice addressing him. "Tal, it's up to you. Neither your mother nor I can make the decision for you."

Tal looked up at his the man he had called a father for almost his entire life, "I don't know." He replied. "I think I need to sleep on it."

"I understand Tal, go up to bed then. We'll discuss this in the morning." Said Jegar softly as Tal stood and made his way to his room.

Tal woke to a sound out side his room. He got out of bed and slipped on a clean shirt. He didn't know what had awoken him, but that feeling was there again, on the back of his neck, telling him that trouble was close. He walked to the window and carefully pulled back the curtain. Tal looked up at the sky and noted it must be close to two maybe three in the morning. He scanned the street, looking for the source of his discomfort. Although he could see nothing, he felt it and that was good enough for him. Tal closed the window and got dressed, he grabbed a cloak from the peg on the back of his door and quietly left his room. He walked to the door of his home and quietly slipped out. He had an urge to be somewhere, though where this somewhere was he couldn't tell, he just knew a direction and a sense of distance. The attraction was coming from about two blocks away, and was pulling him towards it.

Tal left the cover of shadow and quickly walked in the direction he was being called from. He skirted the walls of houses all the way and ended up at the door to an inn called The Farrier's Arms. It was a well established inn, and the rooms were reasonably priced. The inn was three floors in height and had recently been repainted, looking up Tal could see a window open and knew that that was where he had to go. The inn was now shut and locked, all of the patrons at home or asleep in the inn.

Tal looked around, seeing no clear way to get to the window from the street he moved up and down the wide boulevard, looking for a way to the roofs. After several minutes of searching in the dark, Tal noticed a hole in the wall of a building. The building was the old tannery, a building not used in nearly five years. The previous owner had died one night by the stroke of a knife, and no one would come forward as relatives to take over the ownership of the business for fear of assassins.

After several tries he managed to bend his body in the correct way to allow him to squeeze through the hole at the base of the wall. As soon as Tal had entered the building he could feel the sense of wrongness again, stronger now. He knew he had to get to that room, and yet he was afraid. He knew that the wrongness -he could not think of a better word to call it- was also headed for that room and didn't want to be involved in it, but was somehow aware that his own fate was intertwined with whatever was within those four walls.

Tal knew fear. How had he suddenly gained this power to know what his fate revolved around? How could he suddenly feel danger? Tal put all these thoughts and worries out of his head as he moved up the stairs of the building, the smell of the

tannery still strong after five years. Tal reached the top of the
stairs and again looked up. Above the stair top was an entrance
to the roof, a small glass window that would allow the last
fading light in on dark nights. Tal looked around for something
he could use as a bunk to let him reach the window. In a small
room he found an empty chest and moved it to the hallway.
Tal climbed onto the chest and could just reach the window.
After many years of disuse the hinges on the window were
stiff and Tal had to put quite a bit of effort to get the window
open. Once it was fully open Tal jumped and pulled himself
through the window and onto the roof. Years of working with
heavy logs had built his body to a strength that not many in
the city had, especially at his age. Tal judged that he would be
able to move across the roofs to the inn and lower himself to
the room that he had to get to. He moved silently in the night,
taking care not to slip on the tiles that lined the roofs. When
he reached the inn, he leaned over and peered into the room in
which he was drawn to. It was pitch black, the moonlight only
just illuminating the first few feet inside the open window. Tal
lowered himself inside carefully, and felt something in the room
move. He was not aware of everything that happened, and as
a man in a black cloak emerged from the shadows, he again felt
the wrongness from outside the room get closer. Tal looked at
Layland and as he recognised him, he saw Lay draw his sword
and dive past him in one fluid move. As Tal turned he could see
Layland, his sword protruding from a mans chest, but what Tal
saw clearer than anything else, was that the other man also had
his sword buried in the Dragon Rider.

The would-be assassin dropped to the floor, Layland's
sword still protruding from his chest. Layland fell to his knees,
breathing heavily. "Tal," said Layland, looking at the boy. "Tal
you must become a Rider, take my sword and go to…. Damn,"
said Lay as his face contorted in pain. "…. go to the City of
Dragons Tal, go to the…" Lay coughed and groaned in agony as
a trickle of blood ran from his mouth "…the Palace of Dragons,

and ask to speak with Lord Rayburn, tell him I sent you, he will know what to do lad. Fear not for me, I know my lot, and I still have a part to play in the future, if not in this reality. Mortal death holds no fear Tal. Go now…" With his last words Layland fell to the floor his blood staining the old worn carpet.

Tal looked in horror. Layland, Lay, a man who had appeared without warning and had saved Tal's life twice, was now dead. Tal looked at the dead assassin, he was nothing like Tal had ever seen. He was tall and had dark hair. This was not uncommon but he had swept back ears and high eyebrows with a sharp angular jaw. The man appeared to be a figure of rarity. He appeared to be an Elf. Tal thought, what would an elf want to kill me for? Then Tal remembered, there was more than one race of Elves. The Dark Cousins were the darker twisted kin of the elves, driven by power and wealth. Though they were a close knit community that considered humans to be a plague, they would work as hired assassins for humans if they were paid enough. And usually they were very selective about their targets. Tal was even more frightened now than before, he knew the Elf was there to kill him, and had no where to go. He looked at Layland, the man had saved his life at the cost of his own. Tal took Layland's sword from the elf and sheathed the sword in its black and red enamelled scabbard, said a prayer to the Keeper of Souls for Layland and then left the inn through the open window.

When Tal returned home he noticed a light on in his parents room, and another in the living room. He moved to the door and listened, there were three voices that could be heard Jegar, Lynette, and a third unfamiliar voice. The third voice was deep and harsh, Tal could feel that shiver on the back of his neck again, a feeling of something evil inside the house.

Tal stepped back and drew Layland's sword, he knew that if he was going to save his foster parents he would have to kill this man, there was no other way.

As Tal readied himself he heard a noise behind him. He spun and saw Drew running up the street. Drew came to a stop in front of Tal and at a word kept quiet. Drew was clever enough to know that with lights on inside the house and Tal outside with a sword, something was very wrong. "Tal what's going on?" asked Drew in a hushed voice.

"Drew, what are you doing here?" Commented Tal at the same time. Drew's hand was gently playing with the long bladed knife on his belt.

"The room Tal, the room where the Dragon Rider was staying, there has been fighting, there was blood everywhere. The city watch are there now. But there are no bodies, and the Dragon Rider is gone."

"Gone?" Asked Tal. "He can't be gone. I saw them both die…"

"What? Layland has died?" Replied Drew, looking clearly confused by the whole situation.

"I'll explain later." Tal explained to Drew as his attention was again focused on the house.

Inside the house the third voice could be heard louder now, Tal was decided to what must be done, he readied Layland's sword and moved closer to the door. Behind him Tal could hear Drew pulling the dagger he always kept on his belt. Tal turned round, "Drew you don't have to get involved, I don't even know what's going on in there."

"Tal, you have a sword, I have never seen you with a sword, and to cap it all, that sword looks like the Dragon Riders. Put it all together and something is wrong. I'm not going to leave you to this alone." Answered Drew.

Tal returned his attention to his house, he knew Drew could take care of himself. Tal moved to the door and gently opened it, moving it as silently as he could, he peered inside. Inside his mother and father were being held against the wall by another Dark Elf at sword point.

"Tell me where the child is and you will live. This is your final warning and failure to answer will result in a painful death for both of you." Spoke the Dark elf.

"Well then you had best be about your business, 'cause we're not speaking." Replied Jegar with an expression of despise.

This was enough for Tal, never before had he felt the fire that was now coursing through his veins, it was a simple emotion, anger purified. Who was this man to threaten his family? With a cry escaping from his throat he threw himself into the room, swinging savagely at the elf. The elf spun at the unexpected entrance and barely deflected Tal's first blow. The surprise was soon lost however and the elf defended before he started an attack that forced Tal back towards the door. Tal was blocking from instinct, a series of reflex motions that held no hope of countering any of the Dark Cousin's strikes. Soon he found himself with his back to the wall when the Dark Elf finally stopped his attack.

"So the child returns." Mused the elf. "Well, I was hoping for more. I thought you would have been a challenge, but you're nothing more than an infant are you?" With a look of pure delight the elf raised his wicked looking sword. His look changed to one of surprise as the elf spun, Drew's knife buried deep into the back of his neck and with a gurgling sound the elf dropped to the floor.

The Dark Cousin was dressed in black with leather armour and a grey cloak draped across his shoulders. Drew glanced at the body and looked ill. Tal was in shock, he had just rushed into the house without thinking of the consequences and nearly died because of it. Jegar and Lynette were still standing against the wall.

Tal looked at his family and Drew, he wondered what he was going to tell them...

Chapter 2

Tests

Tal was up early the next day. He had explained to his parents and Drew about the events of the previous night, and his parents had agreed that perhaps Tal should follow the Dragon Riders advice, even if he did not join the Riders at least he may find out why he was being hunted and Drew had decided that he should go with Tal. Against the opinions of Tal's family and Tal himself, Drew was under the impression that this would be his break into the field of soldiery, though he did not seem to understand that the Dragon Riders were selective about who they let into their ranks, and that Tal himself might not even gain entry.

Tal was washed and dressed by the time Drew called for him. Tal was wearing a tunic of strong weave and breaches of tough material. Although not stylish they were comfortable and would stand up against the wear of the road. Over his shoulders was draped a great cloak of fine weave, a gift from his father, it was a deep green in colour, was warm and gave good protection against the wind and rain. Around his waist was hung a new belt with Layland's sword attached, and across his back was a bag containing food and water to last him to the City of Dragons.

Drew was dressed similarly but had no weapon other than his long knife. He looked expectant, as though he was eager to be away. Tal knew his friend had not told his family where he was going.

"Drew, how are your family going to react when they find you gone?" Asked Tal, concern showing in his voice.

"It's OK, I've written them a letter explaining it all. They won't miss me anyway." Replied Drew. Drew had never had a close relationship with his parents, spending most of his time with Tal and his family, and Drew's family cared little for what he was doing so long as he wasn't arrested by the city watch or causing a pain of himself where people would place their family.

Tal slowly shook his head. He found it amusing sometimes to watch Drew speak to his family, though for once he wished that Drew had taken something seriously and told his parents.

"OK well let's get off. I don't like what's happening here, and maybe the Dragon Riders can tell me what is going on." Said Tal.

"Now you be careful Tal," said Lynette, trying her hardest to keep a tear from her eye. "It's a harsh world out there and you're so young."

"I will, I promise." Replied Tal, hugging his foster mother tightly.

"Now Tal remember if you find yourself in trouble don't try to use that thing," said Jegar, pointing to the sword. "run if you must, but don't use that sword if your show last night was anything to judge your swordsmanship by." Jegar smiled and embraced his son in all but name, "take care Tal, come back to us."

"I will father." Said Tal.

Tal looked at his family once more before leaving the house. He looked at the family business he had worked in for three years of his life, and lived in for many more and knew that a new life awaited him now... one that may lead him to great adventures...or his death.

Tal looked down the long road stretching out before him. He had been walking for three days and was just approaching the ford that would allow him and Drew to cross the river that runs north of Dukeray when Drew suddenly stopped.

"What's the matter?" asked Tal. He looked at Drew, and saw the long off look in his eyes.

"It's nothing, I just realised that I've never been across this river before, never been this far from home..." Drew looked back the way they had come, his eyes distant.

"Come on Drew, we still have a long way to go." Said Tal reassuringly as he waded into the river, the water rushing past his legs was getting higher, to the point that it forced him to a slow crawl. Tal was holding Layland's sword above his head so as not to get it wet. He looked around and noticed that Drew was still on the fords bank. He motioned to him and continued on across the ford.

It took a further two weeks in the chill of late autumn to reach the City of Dragons. Drew had cheered up again after the first week of the journey, his spirits rising at the thought of the up and coming adventure, of the thought of becoming one of the legendary Dragon Riders.

At the gates to the city the boys looked up at the great palace that reared up above every building in the city, its great white spires and golden roofs casting shadows across buildings that were in themselves as awesome a sight as the boys had ever seen...pennants flying from the peaks of the towers, pennants from each of the cities regiments shown proudly in the bright sunlight.

The boys walked through the wide gates of the city, the guards casting only a glance at the two boys, young and travel worn these two lads were not going to be causing much trouble in their city. Once inside there was a bustle of activity that the boys had only ever heard of, street hawkers, shoppers and general traffic were all competing in the need to be heard over every one else. A cascade of colours and scents bombarded Tal and Drew as they walked through the streets; fine fabrics, the best silks, the sweetest breads, all being advertised by the shops owners.

Tal looked up at the palace, he could see one banner that stood out to him. On the very highest spire was a black pennant whipping in the wind, in a sudden gust the pennant was pulled out straight and in its centre was a red Dragon.

"The banner of the Dragon Riders." Said Tal softly.

"What?" questioned Drew, not seeing where Tal was looking.

"Up there, on the tallest tower, the banner of the Dragon Riders."

"Do you think that Dragon Rider was right Tal? Do you think we will become Riders? I know that soldiering was my calling, but, I just never imagined anything like the Dragon Riders could be my future…"

Tal looked at Drew and laughed out loud.

"What?" Asked Drew, confusion showing on his face.

"It's nothing," replied Tal "just that you are so busy wondering what your future may hold that you started to babble like farmer Gillon's geese."

Drew turned a light shade of red at Tal's remark, he realised that he had begun to babble and knew that Tal would torment him repeatedly if he didn't stop immediately.

"Come on!" called Tal, already running ahead of Drew, "lets get to the Palace quickly! I'm hungry for some real food and maybe we can scrounge some from the barracks!" Drew did not need to think about food for more than a brief second until thoughts of cooked meat came to him, within seconds he had caught up with, and moved past Tal, both boys now running towards the palace, their speed fuelled by the thoughts of food passing through their minds.

Arriving at the gates to the palace was like a vision from a dream, the high white walls towering high into the air, the black and red gates open, two of the Royal Household Guard at post beside them. Drew looked at the guards from across the street, they were in the silver chain and royal blue tabard of the royal family and were standing perfectly still, their swords sheathed yet somehow already in the hands of these elite guards.

The Royal Household Guard was a very small band of soldiers whose only purpose was the protection of their King. The Royal Guard were only considered second to the Dragon Riders, but only because of the ability the Riders had to control the mighty Dragons.

The two lads walked up to the gates and stopped, the guards were watching them, without a word uttered by the guards the boys had the sudden need to explain their approach to the palace. Tal spoke his voice a little shaky, "Er, we've been sent to speak to Lord Rayburn, Layland Kendrik sent us…"

The guards just looked at the boys, their eyes hard and penetrating, after several minutes one of the guards turned and walked briskly into the palace, the boys waited unsure of what to do, no invite was given and so they were forced to stand on the street. After what seemed hours the guard returned and motioned Tal and Drew to follow him into the palace. The boys followed the guard through corridors with highly polished marble floors and walls decorated with fine paintings, the ceilings were covered with priceless chandeliers giving off a light that seemed to leave no corner in the passages unlit. To Tal it seemed as though he was in a story, full of bright colours and expensive decorations. After several minutes they reached an area of the palace that was decorated with numerous Dragons of all colours and sizes. The small party ascended several flights of stairs and from a window, Tal could see one side of the City of

Dragons in its entirety. The city stretched off for what seemed like miles in every direction, the rich quarter and merchant quarters visible and the poor quarter behind them taking up just as much space and the first two combined.

The group arrived at the top level of the tower that they discovered they were climbing and from what Tal could remember from the City, this was the tower that had the pennant of the Dragon Riders flying from the peak. They arrived at a large oaken door which had two more guards outside, these were dressed in the Black and Red of the Dragon Riders. They had a look in their eyes that stated with pure fact that no one would get passed them without their superiors' orders.

The Guard that had escorted them all the way to the waiting room turned to Tal and Drew. His face changed for the first time since they had met him, he now wore a face that reminded Tal of his father when he was about to give Tal one of his 'life secrets'. "Lads this is important, Lord Rayburn is a good man, but don't lie to him, he will know immediately if you do and then he will get short tempered, tell the truth and he's the kindest man you shall meet…just bare it in mind."

With that he turned and walked swiftly back down the corridor to the flight of stairs which they had just ascended.

Tal looked at Drew and moved to the door, as they approached one of the guards knocked once on the door and opened it for the two boys. Tal stepped through to be greeted by a sparse office, though it was immense compared to his room back in Dukeray, it was still a room that had only the bare essentials. A desk was placed at the opposite side of the room in front of a large fire pit in which roared a chill killing fire. A large man stood by a window in the office, he looked older than Tal's father yet somehow younger and more energetic. Tal expected the man to be in casual clothes for work indoors like this, yet here stood a warrior in every sense of the word; he stood a good three inches past six foot, and looked resplendent in his black and red chain, his red cloak had two golden Dragons with one starting from each shoulder and meeting in the centre of the tall mans back. He had medium length black hair that was streaked with white, showing perhaps the pressure of his office, his short cropped beard nearly completely white gave a drastic counter balance to his dark brown eyes. He studied the boys closely looking them both up and down, his dark eyes seeming to penetrate to their souls. He looked at Tal, his voice strong, deep and clear. "I am Gareth Rayburn. And who, my young friend may you be?" Asked the man now identified as Lord Rayburn.

"I am Tal Parnell…er, my Lord" said a slightly nerved Tal.

"Then I am pleased to meet you Tal, I hear Rider Kendrik sent you to see me. I know the reason, I can feel the spirit within you, and I also know that Lay took a great wound whilst looking for you."

"Yes sir" replied Tal, a look of surprise across his young face at hearing how much this man knew while being many miles across the Kingdom.

Rayburn turned his attention to Drew, his eyes searching deep inside of him. "And what of your attendance here son?"

Drew looked at the old warrior, Rayburn's face showing no emotion other than curiosity. "I'm here to become a Dragon Rider…er sir" Rayburn looked at Drew, and Tal thought he could see a hint of humour in the aging mans eyes.

"Well son, I didn't know about you, and I'm not sure you'll pass the tests, but you've come this far, it wouldn't be fair to turn you away now would it?" replied a man bereft of emotion in his voice.

Drew looked at the Dragon Rider, not sure whether to laugh or be grateful for the opportunity he settled for a half smile and replied "Thank you sir".

"Well then," said Rayburn his voice becoming crisp and lively, "Lets get you two some food and a room for the night. We will begin the Tests tomorrow, so you will need to rest well tonight boys, tomorrows Tests are the physical trials, and they *are* hard, have no doubt."

With that Gareth Rayburn walked the boys to the door and gave one of the guards orders to get the two a meal and see that they get their own room for the night along with a hot bath.

Tal and Drew walked silently behind the Rider as they made their way to the soldier's mess, Tal considering what the future holds, thoughts of his family and thoughts of Layland, while Drew considered what the seasoned Rider meant when he said that he may not pass the tests.

It was night. Tal awoke and got dressed, Drew still slept on his pallet. He looked around the room. All the trappings from the walls had been removed leaving the stone bare. He moved silently to the door so as not to wake Drew and lit a candle that stood on a single table by the portal that wasn't there when he had drifted off to sleep. He quietly opened the door and slipped though. Closing the door again, Tal looked around, he was no longer standing in the palace but on a great mountain looking down over the countryside. A noise behind him caused him to turn to look into a large cave that receded into the mountain. Tal walked slowly into the mouth of the cave, his eyes slowly adjusting to the darkness lit only by his candle, a large form was hidden in the dark recesses of the cave and moved slowly towards the light. When the huge form became visible Tal froze in awe, it was a Dragon. It had a giant triangular head with an array of horns running up the side of the creature's face, and teeth that glowed in the light. Tal marvelled at the fabulous creature as it sped towards the open cave and with a beat of its mighty wings took off into the air.

Tal looked around. He was in a great hall that had many paintings of men and women on each wall, seats filled the room and at the front was a small stage. A single man in white robe walked towards him, he was average in height and had sandy coloured hair, and his blue eyes were kind with the look of a scholar about him. As the robed man reached him he extended his hands and placed the on Tal's temples.

Tal found himself in the midst of a battle, men and women were riding dragons, swords cleaving left and right, balls of energy and fire being launched towards an army thousands large and made up of …demons was all Tal could accredit them to. Men, women and demons were falling yet the numbers never seemed to give one nor the other an advantage. Hearing a roar Tal turned to see a demon bearing down on him. Tal reacted, not with sword or fist but some kind of psychic attack he could not place, the demon roiled and fell back away from him.

Darkness…and peace

Tal awoke. It was dawn and he felt like he had not slept at all that night. Drew woke at almost the same time, he did not look like he had the same trouble sleeping that Tal did, and looked ready for the day.

A knock at the door made the two get up and dressed quickly as a page told them that someone was there to take them to the Test. Tal and Drew dressed quickly and then followed the young page through the maze of corridors and pathways that led to the main courtyard that they had walked through when they first entered the Palace. There were soldiers lined up two deep and ten long. At their sides was the standard sword of the kingdom, and they were armoured as though for war.

Tal looked around the courtyard, there were several other boys about Tal and Drew's age and they were lined up in front the soldiers. The man in charge was dressed like a Rider, but unlike all the other riders that Tal had seen, this man was without the cloak and had only black leather on with golden studs across his shoulders. Tal wondered as to the relevance of this, but was quickly ushered into the line of boys by another Rider, this one in the full chain that Layland was dressed in when Tal met him. The Rider in the leather was a tallish man with broad shoulders and a look of steel, his hair was the deepest black and cut short, he had an age to his face that his seemed to contradict his youthful appearance and he stood at the front of the group as though not a thing in the world could possibly even phase him. At his side hung an evil looking sword, one edge was straight and sharp, the other was spiked in a saw design. This stopped the usage of a scabbard but the sword in its steel loop looked menacing enough to discourage even the most fool hardy of would be attackers in Tal's opinion.

"O.K listen up!" Called the man at the front that Tal now believed was some sort of officer, "Your all here because there is a belief you may be worthy of the Riders. This will be a hard day for all of you, there will be a great deal of physical hardness thrust upon you and you will be expected to cope, if you fall behind you will be pushed on by the other Riders that are out in the hills right now waiting for you." The man looked at the line of boys, some were looking concerned, and some looked openly frightened. "This is not meant to be easy," continued the man in leather. "I had to take the test, so did the Riders that will be pushing you today." His voice softened, "We are not trying to make your life a living hell today, we are just trying to find the best of the best. There is no shame in falling, only in quitting. My name is Captain Holbrook and I will be the officer in charge of your training." With a slight chuckle the man now identified as Captain Holbrook added "To make sure you don't feel hard done by, I will be taking every test that you take, eat every meal that you eat and sleep in the same bunks you will sleep in. But I'll be damned to hell if I will fail just to make you feel better." With that the captain called for the soldiers to hand the boys packs and weapons. Tal was handed a pack that weighed enough to make even his broad shoulders sag at the weight. He looked at Drew, and seeing the smaller boy struggle to place the pack on his back, Tal helped him to swing the bag over his shoulders. As the group of boys managed to get their kit together and lined up they saw the Captain throw a pack over his shoulders with little effort and call "O.K men, this is where we start, follow me and don't fall behind!" With that Captain Holbrook started a slow jog towards the main gate that lead to the streets of the City of Dragons.

Tal was breathing hard. This was one of the few stops that the Captain had allowed. The group had jogged through the main city and into the countryside where they had proceeded to move through the foothills that surrounded the huge city and continue to head west towards the Greenhome. They had been moving for four hours now and Tal was near exhaustion. Drew had fallen several miles back and had to give his pack to one of the Riders to be able to keep up, but he had, and although he looked like the Keeper of Souls was about to claim him, he pushed away the offer to stop and go back to the Palace. The group had already lost five of the original ten that had started that morning and Tal could see at least one more dropping soon. The Captain had remained cheery through the whole exercise, even offering encouragement to the people that were close to failing. But it did not seem to help, if someone was going to go, they did. And the Captain looked a little more disheartened each time one of the group had to return to the palace. Now they were five, and one almost to the point where he would soon need to be carried back to the city.

Tal had gotten to know the other boy that had so far managed to keep his pack. His name was Bradley Oswin and he was from Borders Edge. His father worked the shores as a fisherman and he had worked under his father mending the nets and selling their catch. Brad was short for his age, but stocky and well muscled, he had blonde hair tied in a tail with green eyes and a bold nose. Tal thought that if it came down to a fight between them, there would be no clear winner, and Tal was used to being able to over power almost everyone his age in the small city of Dukeray but here Tal thought he may have met his match.

Captain Holbrook called for them all to start moving again and Tal, Drew and Brad climbed to their feet. The other boy that was finding this hard was Marcus, Tal didn't know much about him as he didn't seem to be much for talking. He climbed to his feet but he didn't look like he could go much further. Marcus did however manage that much. Wayne tried to get up again but the pressure of the morning had finally beaten him and he fell back to the floor before anyone could catch him.

The party moved on while Wayne was carried back to the Palace by two of the Riders that were lining the route that they were taking.

Now there were three. The remaining few had been going only one more hour but Marcus had fallen. Tal and Brad still kept their packs but Drew was ready to drop. Captain Holbrook saw this and called a halt. "Drew, I think you should quit. You're in danger of causing yourself injury if you continue. You've done well, but I don't think you should go on any more today, go back to the palace and rest until tomorrow, there is still the weapons test to face yet." Drew looked at Tal who reluctantly nodded.

The scene faded into haze. A man dressed in a white robe turned to face a well built yet aging man, in the blue of the Royal household guard but this soldier had the red sash of commander hanging across his chest. He had jet black hair with only a touch of grey showing at the temples and a short well kept beard, his brown eyes were hard and spoke of a life in the army.

"Well Oren?" said the commander. "What have you called me here for? It is late you know."

The white robed man referred to as Oren chuckled softly at his old companion. "It is always late for you Denholm, now be quiet and watch." Oren lifted his arms and opened them before him. Between his outstretched arms began a replay of the first

Test, yet the vision tended to focus on a boy of medium build and dark hair that was cut short.

The commander of the household guard followed the day through to the point where Drew finally was told to quit.

"And this boy is not a Rider?" asked Denholm.

"No, just a boy. With the stamina he shows I thought you would be interested in him."

"Well, you certainly are not wrong there my old friend, he really is amazing. Who is he?"

"His name is Drew, more we do not know, he arrived with Tal Parnell to become a Rider. We knew he wasn't one of the Children but he seemed to have something about him that made Lord Rayburn put him in for the Tests."

"But what of the others? If Rayburn can tell whether someone has the gift why are there always so many that are entered into the Tests and fall?"

"Who knows why other than Lord Rayburn himself? But it is clear that here we have someone special do you not agree?"

"Yes Oren, I believe we do…"

Tal crawled back into the barracks later that day, his entire body ached as he collapsed onto the pallet that was his. He, the captain and Brad were the only people to finish the exercise that was set for them, the other Riders leaving one by one through the day as other duties called them or they took the people that fell back to the Palace. The soldiers that left with them broke of from the group just outside the city gates and left on their patrol of the cities limits.

Drew stirred at Tal's arrival. "You just got back?"

Tal looked at Drew, his eyes foggy with exhaustion. "Yes, we've been running with the packs all day. I feel my entire body is about to just fall apart."

"What time is it?" asked a sleepy Drew.

"Nearly dinner time I would guess, the sun is sinking and the smell of beef was coming from the kitchen as I came past."

"Good," replied Drew. "I am starving. Come on lets eat."

Tal groaned as he pulled himself reluctantly from the pallet and they both headed in the direction of the kitchen.

Tal sat at the table in the barracks. He was attempting to eat his food, fatigue making even that small task hard. Drew had no such problem, he had already finished his first helping of grilled beef and had gone back for a second plateful. As he sat down Tal looked at Drew's full plate and almost moaned, "I'm going back to the room ok? I'm still exhausted from today."

"Ok I'm going to finish this and be back too. I spoke to a Rider on the way back and he said that we have the weapons test tomorrow so I need to get some sleep so I can make up the points I probably lost today."

Tal said good night and headed of towards their room. Drew finished his food and returned his plate to the duty mess man, leaving the hall he decided to take a different route back to his room so that he could see more of the palace.

Drew had been walking for about ten minutes when he realised that the general decor of the palace had changed, where before there was no carpet, only hard polished floors and ornate weaponry hanging from the walls, now there was lush carpeting and pictures of men working great magic's. The general feel of the area was different too – there was a feel of un-naturalness about the corridors and there was a stillness that was not right for a palace that was so busy.

Men and women both rushed about down the long corridors, some servants, some soldiers, and some dressed in white robes that looked at Drew with no more thought to who he was than a common dog would to an ant.

Drew looked at the doors that he assumed separated the rooms from the passage. Each one held a collection of what appeared to be letters, but if they were letters they were not any kind Drew had seen before. They were all made up of straight lines and appeared to be actually engraved into the wood that held them.

He was convinced that he had moved from the military wing of the palace and into another. His thoughts were proven correct when after walking down a wide hall, he came upon a dead end, the only way beyond was through the two great doors that the corridor ended with. The doors appeared to be made of a heavy oak that screamed 'private' to him.

Drew paused at the doors and put an ear to the wood in an attempt to discover if there was anyone behind them. When he was convinced that whatever lay beyond the doors was clear he opened them and cautiously looked inside.

In the hall that Drew found himself looking into were rows of seats, capable of seating a great number of people and at the very front of the large hall was a stage with a stand to put any reference material the person speaking may need to use.

Drew moved slowly into the hall and shut the doors behind him. As he moved towards the front of the hall he noticed a feel about the room, one that he couldn't place. When Drew had reached the front row of seats he noticed a white piece of cloth that seemed to cover a doorway that lead from the hall. Drew moved closer to the portal and just as he was about to pull the drape aside the material was swept back by a tall man in an elegant white robe, his eyes focused on Drew quickly and without saying anything the man questioned Drew as to his business in the hall.

"I was just…erm…looking around…sir," stammered Drew.

"I see, and who may I ask are you?" Asked the tall man.

"My name is Drew sir, Drew Earemon." Supplied Drew

"Well Drew, this is the Hall of Elders. And I will be holding a meeting very soon. The Elder Council will be here shortly and I don't have the time to talk."

"Oh, I'm sorry, I didn't want to talk, I just wandered here." Replied Drew hastily.

"Then you had best go, I have work to do"

Drew turned and left the hall quickly, he realised that he had been wandering for too long anyway. He had to get some rest before the weapons test tomorrow. He was determined to be a soldier, a protector of his kingdom, nothing else would satisfy him.

Tal dreamed.

It was night again, a fire burned low on the ground. Tal looked around, the camp was made up of men and women, all dressed in red and black armour. They slept, but Tal kept watch, he had to stay alert, the Dark Cousins had been moving in force lately and Tal's party had already encountered two small groups of the elves while on their course.

Hearing a noise behind him Tal stood and took his sword in his hand. The bushes around him erupted in an explosion of leaves and branches as two Elves burst into the clearing. Tal wasted no time and shouted the alert. With the camp now bustling with activity there was only one thing left to do. Tal charged the Dark Cousins.

Blackness

Tal spun. He was in a baron place, rocks and dry earth surrounded him but nothing else. He was in a battle, his armour was worn but still displayed the symbol of the Dragon Riders. He was fighting alongside other races. Some were tall, fair skinned and sharp of features, they were dressed in green, they carried bows with long swords at their sides. At the very centre of the fighting were shorter figures, hardy, wielding great axes and wearing heavy armour. They were all fighting to the death but *who* they were fighting was not clear. The opposing army was made up of the same races but the looks on the faces of the combatants couldn't have been any less similar. The Dragon Riders army had grim determination painted across their faces, the opposition had mad and frenzied lust, their eyes alight with fire, their lips red with the taste of the foes blood.

Tal fell.

It was morning. The sun outside his room was bright and the cool air made for a chilly start. Drew was already dressed and had an eager look about him.

"Come on Tal, weapons day, finally I get to test on something I'm good at." Rushed Drew with a grin that stretched almost the width of his face.

"Hang on Drew, I'm still half asleep." Replied a weary Tal

"Why? Those are the best beds I've ever slept in I think!"

"I haven't been sleeping well." Replied an abrupt Tal

"Oh. Well you had best hurry up the Test will be starting soon." Said an excited Drew.

There was a rap on their door as a voice called through, telling Tal and Drew that they should meet in the main courtyard again and both boys replied that they would be there right away.

Once Tal had moved from his pallet and had thrown some clothes on he and Drew rushed towards the main courtyard and fell into the line of boys again, there were only eight now. Before Tal could enquire as to the location of the other two boys, Captain Holbrook called for the attention of the courtyard.

"Well we have two down before the final Test. This is the last, yes there are only two. You are to fight with the Riders around the courtyard until you have fought each. You will lose. We are not looking for someone that can beat one of our own, we are looking for something deeper. You will fight with knives, short and long swords, bows, pole arms, axe's, spears and bare fists. This will take most of the morning and you *will* feel like you are about to collapse at the end of it. Now move round until you are face to face with a Rider, take up a weapon and when you are told begin, if you do not initiate the fight, the Rider will."

Tal moved around until he was face to face with a Dragon Rider. The man was about average height and build, had the common green eyes of the Kingdom but had the same sense of lethalness about him as Layland had had. The Rider placed a bow in Tal's hand and pointed towards a target about fifty yards away, with that the Rider drew his own bow to full draw and released. The arrow sped true and hit the target centrally. Tal drew his bow, the arrow rested on his hand, he aimed as best he could, then loosed. The arrow sped towards the target but flew wide and high. The Rider handed Tal another arrow and told him to *feel* the bow, the arrow and the target. Tal focused what he could after the bad night he had spent in the barracks, and loosed his second arrow. This one sped truer and clipped the edge of the target before flying off into the distance. The Rider smiled at Tal and handed him another arrow.

Tall took the arrow and looked over to where Drew was fighting another Rider with a knife held in each hand, although he was being pushed back by the rider Drew looked like he was at least showing some skill, unlike himself Tal thought.

Each fight lasted about half an hour and by the end of the Test, each boy was sweating uncontrollably, the Riders were just as composed as they were at the beginning of the Test. Captain Holbrook walked to the centre of the courtyard and addressed the boys.

"You are to be congratulated. Few get to Test for the Riders, fewer last the Tests. That you have made it this far shows great determination and strength. Know that even if you are not selected for the Dragon Riders, that you are one of the kingdoms best men. Should any of you wish to go to the army, I know that you will lead a successful career.

"Now, go get something to eat, sleep and rest, tomorrow we will list the successful candidates."

With that the Captain turned and marched back into the palace. Tal looked at Drew. Both boys were sweating and exhausted. Tal motioned to Drew and suggested food then bed. Drew was in complete agreement with his friend and they both head off in the direction of the soldiers mess for something hot to eat.

Denholm looked in wonder.

Oren closed his arms and the picture faded. Denholm just looked at his old friend.

"Well this is quite...unique." said a shaken commander. "This boy actually pushed the Riders skill in the Test?"

"Yes, and what's more, he didn't do it with luck, this is skill Cyran. He will not be taken for a Rider, but you will have to move fast if you want him in your Guard. I'm pretty sure that with the display he put on others will want him too now."

"Yes my old friend I believe you are right. I will have to move quickly indeed."

With that Cyran Denholm, Commander of the Royal Household Guard bid his childhood friend goodnight and left the room quietly.

Oren Diarmid, a seer of the council and a magician of no small acclaim, blew out the candles that lit his room and moved to his pallet. The next few months could be very hectic and the mage was not in a hurry to lose sleep until he had to.

Yes the next few months could be quite hectic indeed he thought to himself as he drifted off to sleep.

Chapter 3

Unknowns

It was late the next day when Tal and Drew finally awoke from sleep. The previous two days had been exhausting and with the trouble Tal had experienced with sleeping he was not in any hurry to get up. There had been no page at the door to awaken them or collect them so they assumed that the Captain had let them sleep in today.

When they had both dressed and washed themselves in the bowl of water that was sitting by the door, they walked quickly to the courtyard. They did not know what they were to do, but thought that this would be as good a place to start as any.

When they reached the courtyard there was a single Dragon Rider practising his swordsmanship in the very centre. Tal and Drew watched the figure for several minutes. The skill that the lone man displayed was amazing. The Rider moved slowly, every motion precise and deliberate, every decision concise and thought out.

After several more minutes the Rider stopped the exercise and noticed Tal and Drew watching him. He quickly sheathed his sword and walked up to them.

"Hello boys, the Captain is waiting for you in his office, do you know the way?" Asked the Rider, his brow only slightly covered in perspiration from exercising.

It was Tal that answered the Rider. "No sir." He replied.

"Well then, if you head back to the Riders wing of the palace, you know where that is yes?" Tal and Drew replied that they did and the Rider continued. "Good. When you get into the wing, you will want to take the corridor that starts immediately to your right and has the two statues of Dragons on either side of the passage. The Captains quarters are the second on the left, you won't miss it, it has runes above the door."

"Thank you sir." Replied Tal and Drew together, and then they both set off for the Captains office.

After a short while Tal and Drew found themselves outside Captain Holbrook's office. The two boys found themselves pausing at the Captains door, neither wanting to be the one that knocked. As the boys waited a voice behind them made them start. "Trying to muster the courage too huh?" Tal looked around, behind him was standing Bradley Oswin, the other boy that had been Tested. Tal paused unsure of how to reply. "It's ok, I've been loitering around here for the past half an hour trying to do the same." Drew visibly relaxed at hearing this. Tal noticed his friend relax and did the same. Drew had never liked people thinking him lacking nerve in any way and this had come close to making him feel just that. Tal knew from experience that when his friend felt that he had been judged lacking courage he could go into a black mood and not talk to anyone for days. "Well then," said Drew in a voice Tal knew all too well. "I guess we should knock." With that Drew moved in front of the door and raised his hand. Just before Drew could knock, the door opened and the Captain was standing in the doorway looking at the three boys.

"Ah, boys I was just about to go looking for you. You three are the last I needed to see today and I thought you had got lost or spirited away by some dark beast." Said the Captain.

The boys stood there looking like they had been caught stealing from the bakery, their heads downcast and their faces red. "Don't worry boys, I drove you hard the last couple of days, being tired is no great sin to the gods." Said Captain Holbrook with a slight chuckle. "Well I suppose there is no point in delaying the news," he continued. The boy's faces became long at the sudden seriousness of the captains mood.

Tal thought back to what he had been through lately. The meeting with Lay in the dimly lit forest near his home late one evening, and Lay's untimely demise. The journey here, and the Tests he had been through. Tal simply could not imagine returning to his father and telling him that he had failed.

Drew looked as though he was about to collapse. He had been waiting his whole life for a chance to soldier with his kingdom, and now, at the very crest of his dream becoming true, he felt like his heart was about to be torn from his chest.

Brad, although not long known to Tal looked just as beaten as Tal felt himself.

The captain noticed the boy's faces and his own mood seemed to fade with theirs. "Well," said the Captain, "I will start with the more joyous news. Drew, I'm sorry to say you did not make the Dragon Riders," Drew's face showed no emotion but Tal knew inside he was crying completely to his soul. Captain Holbrook seemed also to notice Drew's mood and quickly pressed on, "But on the better side, Commander Denholm has personally asked for a meeting with you, now that can only be good news son."

Drew looked at the Captain in confusion, "Who is Commander Denholm sir?"

Captain Holbrook merely smiled slightly, a faint rise of the corner of his lips was all that was evident as he said, "Why, the leader of the Royal Household Guard son." Drew's face shone a mix of excitement, curiosity and wonder as to why he was asked to attend the Commander.

Tal was happy for his friend but could not forget that Drew's news was the good news. The Captain now looked at Tal and Brad, "well boys, I'm sorry to say that the Commander didn't request any audiences with you two, so I'm afraid that you get the rough end of the deal." Both boys looked at the floor once again, but in disappointment now rather than embarrassment. "You two are to attend Lord Rayburn tomorrow morning to collect your uniform, armour and arms. Well done boys, your Dragon Riders." All three looked excited, even if in Drew was slightly apprehensive at the same time.

Returning his attention to Drew, Holbrook said, "Commander Denholm wants to see you fist thing tomorrow morning as well lad. I suspect that tomorrow will be a busy day for all of you, best get some food then get to bed again." He said with the first true smile that any of them had seen.

Tal, Drew and Brad all gave their best salutes, that the Captain returned happily, then they all hurried for the soldiers mess to get some warm food before returning to their beds once more.

Tal and Brad were stood in Lord Rayburn's office as he sat behind his desk, in each of the boys arms was a new tunic, trousers, tabard and a list of weapons that were available to them. "Now boys. Most of the Riders fighting is done alone and not in organised squads like the army. For that reason we don't think you should learn this weapon or that. You are free to decide which weapons you will train with for your first few months as a novice.

"During this period you will be considered lower than low by those outside of our ranks, and you will have no more rights than the Pages in the royal court. You will be expected to take orders from anyone that holds an office within the Kingdom, even in the kitchen if it comes to it. You are the level of a normal army rat, don't however let this get you down. When we think you are experienced enough in weapons you become a fully fledged Rider, it is *then* that you begin to learn about the Riders as a unit, and at that point no one may give you orders except a superior Rider or the royal family."

Tal and Brad kept some semblance of impassiveness but it was clear that they were becoming overwhelmed by the amount of information that had been pumped into them so far today. Seeing this Lord Rayburn paused, chuckled softly and stood, "OK boys," he said, "I'm going to give you the secret to surviving the first few months here. It's simple really, salute any one in a uniform, say 'sir' a lot, and do anything anyone says." Neither Tal nor Brad looked too happy but they both nodded.

"Excellent. Then you should report to Sergeant Meldon for your new quarters in the Riders Barracks. Good day gentleman." Said Rayburn as he sat behind his desk once more.

Tal and Brad left the office of Lord Rayburn and put their new uniforms in their own rooms before heading to the Riders barracks.

After asking directions from a court Page, they found the impressive building, it was located at the back of the palace, almost next to the marshalling yard and was built entirely from white stone. The barracks stood several stories tall and looked as if it could hold over one hundred Riders. Tal and Brad walked to the main door and stepped inside. There was an atmosphere to the building that both could feel, as if something more than just people lived here. They were not sure what they could feel but nothing other than a 'rightness' could describe it to them. They saw a couple of other Riders walking through the entry hall to the barracks and asked them where they might find Sergeant Meldon. They were directed to quarters that were just like all the others save for runes above the door that read 'Sergeant Allen Meldon'. Brad looked at Tal who gave a small shrug and knocked on the door.

"Enter" came a voice from within. Tal opened the door to see a man of good build sitting at a desk looking at several sheets of paper. The look on his face showed clearly he wished he was anywhere but here. Tal estimated he stood about five foot eleven and he had short blondish hair, his eyes were a deep blue and he was wearing the red and black of the Riders.

Meldon lifted several sheets of paper and said "Ledgers, a Sergeant in the Riders and I'm sorting out Ledgers for the barracks food rations." At the last he added a theatrical sigh before brightening. "So what can I do for you gentlemen?" He asked.

Tal spoke up first after looking at Brad, "We just passed the Testing sir, we were told to come to you for Barrack assignment."

"Ah! New recruits!" Said Meldon, obviously forgetting about the figures he was previously calculating. "Marvellous, feel free to call me Allen when were not on duty, us Riders tend to be a lot less formal than the army! So you're looking for bunks huh? Well I have two that should serve, but they are on the top floor, that is not a problem for you two is it?"

When both boys agreed it was not a disaster Allen jumped up and took both Tal and Brad in tow. He led them up to the top floor and along a corridor until the reached what Tal believed was a corner of the building. He opened the door in the corner and told Tal that this was his room while he was stationed here.

Tal stepped inside his room and looked around. It was a simple room but being on the corner he got two windows, something Tal was pleased with since he had always enjoyed looking out at the sky. Against one wall was a simple bed with mattress and on the other wall a small table and wash basin. Under one window was a chest where he was told he could keep any personal items, and in the corner stood a wooden half manikin, where he was to hang his armour when he received it. There was a small wardrobe by the wash basin for his clothes and some draws for anything else he may need. Brad was shown his room and they were both told that they should begin moving their belongings in swiftly, as the quarters that they had been using would likely be filled again soon with others seeking to enter military service.

Both boys looked at each other and then went to run off saying "yes sir", as they hit their second step they both stopped and seemed to realise together that they forgot to salute. Both looked back nervously and made a poor attempt at saluting before Allen shoed them off, remembering his youth and how long ago it seemed to him now.

Tal and Brad had moved into their rooms that afternoon, and were told to report to Captain Holbrook the next day for equipment supplies. Tal only now was seeing what was really happening in the Palace, apart from Sergeant Meldon the officers had rooms and offices actually in the Palace while the standard Riders were in the barracks. At dinner that night Brad and Tal kept to themselves and turned in early so as they could get up the next day and be fresh for the Captain.

The next morning was chill, winter was pulling closer and Tal found himself reluctant to leave the warm blankets of his bed. When he finally dragged himself up from his slumber and had washed and clothed, he knocked for Brad to see if he was up, and when they were both ready they made their way to the Captains quarters in the Palace for their equipment assignment.

On the long walk round the palace Tal spoke, "So what weapons have you decided to learn Brad?"

"I think I'm going to chose the Long sword, Long bow and Knife for weapons. For hand to hand I think I'll use Boxing, and Wrestling. What about you Tal?" replied Brad.

"The Rapier has always been an elegant weapon according to Drew so I think I'll learn that along with the Short sword and Quarter Staff."

"What about hand to hand?" questioned Brad as they walked into the corridor that housed Captain Holbrook's room and office.

Tal started to reply that he wasn't too sure, when he looked up. A girl that Tal was positive could not be too much older than himself, walked from Captain Holbrook's office. Instantly Tal was struck by how attractive she was. The girl had long red hair that flowed down to the middle of her back. Her eyes were the most perfect shape Tal had ever seen, and shone deeply with a rich green that Tal could not believe was her true colour at first. She stood tall for the girls Tal had known at about five foot and ten inches in height. When Tal noticed that the girl was looking at him right back, he instantly decided the floor was also worth a good long look as his face flashed red, and he sped up to get past her before he found himself becoming even more red in the cheek than he already was.

Just as he got to the door of the office he turned to see the girl looking over her shoulder at him as she disappeared around the corner. "Tal?" asked brad, "Are you ok?"

"Yes…I'm fine." Replied Tal, his mind still focusing on the girl.

"Well were here, I suppose we should knock." Said Brad as he raised his hand and knocked politely on Captain Holbrook's door.

"Come in." Came the reply from inside.

Brad entered the office followed by Tal, his mind still on the beautiful stranger whose face was now etched into his mind

As they stepped into the office Tal shut the door behind them, Holbrook looked up and smiled faintly, "Ah gentlemen, I assume you're all settled into your new quarters?" Both boys nodded and the captain continued, "Good, well today you get the rest of your equipment and clothing, but first I need to know what weapons you wish to train with." Brad informed Holbrook as to his selection and immediately after Tal done the same. Captain Holbrook questioned Tal as to which hand to

hand he wished to learn after no styles were forthcoming from
Tal.

"I'm not sure sir, I don't really know which ones are which"
explained Tal.

"Well we can't have you making random choices that may
affect your future now can we?" Replied Holbrook, "I'll tell you
what, observe a few classes and come back to me when you have
made your decision, is that acceptable?"

Tal nodded and the captain grinned, "Now down to the
armoury."

Tal and Brad followed the captain through the corridors
of the palace and down into the very bowels of the estate itself.
Passing banners that hung from walls, paintings and statues
that lined the very walkways, the small group finally reached a
single metal door that had two Riders standing either side, both
were in full black chain with the red and black tabard of the
Dragon Riders and both carried their favoured weapons, the
first a curved slim sword that looked made to slice, the second a
square mace with a hook at the reversed end that looked quite
wicked in its way.

As Captain Holbrook approached, both guards snapped to
attention and saluted before opening the door to the armoury.
As Tal stepped inside, he saw rows and rows of weapons. Long
swords, short swords, rapiers, the scimitars that were favoured
up near the borders to the Lost Lands by the city of Sarafell,
pole arms of all kinds, bows and lances. There were entire racks
covered in armour, ranging from light leather to full plate mail
that Tal doubted his ability to even lift by himself.

Holbrook looked at the young soldiers and smiled ruefully,
he approached the armour racks and pulled off two pitch black
chain coats, and handed them to the boys. Each took their
armour and sagged under the weight of the newly acquired
requisition, and followed quietly, still in awe of the array of
weaponry and armour displayed in front of them even though
neither of them could completely understand what the majority

of the weaponry was used for. Captain Holbrook then handed Tal and Brad their selection of weaponry and again headed for the door.

"OK gentlemen, this is your equipment, take care of it well, because the weapons masters don't like students that neglect there belongings. After all what good is a trained Rider with a rusty sword? You can have the rest of the day off to familiarise yourself with the palace but tomorrow you will start your training and be expected to put all you have into it." With that the captain smiled and led them back through the palace and out to the grounds again.

When Holbrook had gone, Tal and Brad started to carry their new weapons and armour back to their rooms. They were just passing the mess hall that stood between the barracks and the marshalling yard when Tal heard his name being called. He turned to find Drew running towards him in his deep blue tabard of the Household guard, a sword hung from Drew's belt and he already looked the part of the soldier he had always wanted to be. When Drew finally caught up to them both Tal and Drew started speaking and laughing at once, and Brad said he would let the two of them catch up as he continued on to his room with his equipment.

"Look at you Drew! You look like a soldier already!" Exclaimed Tal.

"Tal you look dangerous with all those weapons!" Said Drew at the same instant. Both stopped and laughed at their forwardness. "Wow Drew you really *do* look the part of a soldier!" said Tal when they had both stopped laughing.

"I guess," replied Drew, "but it's not all glamour, weapons master Falkom is as crusty as they come, and he has definitely taken a disliking to me. I haven't been settled in for more than an hour before he grabs me, equips me and starts training without so much as even saying a word."

"Wow," said Tal, "so far things have been pretty good for me, the Riders I have seen have all been friendly and more than polite. I don't even start training until tomorrow as they have given me today to myself."

"Well at least you're having it easy. If we had come all this way and neither of us were enjoying ourselves I may have been upset by now." Said Drew with a smirk and a laugh.

"I never planned on becoming a soldier Drew, I never thought I could take the discipline, but this seems exciting and new to me. Like it could turn out ok, but its still a mystery." Tal chuckled, "but if I had *your* station I think I would have quit by now."

"No way by the gods am I going to quit and give that self important weapons master the satisfaction of chasing me home with my tail between my legs!" Said Drew with an air of stubbornness about him that lead Tal to believe that the contention between Falkom and Drew was going to get worse before it got any better.

Drew's face looked like it had been chiselled from stone, and Tal believed that he was going to stand there until the weapons master came to get Drew himself. Suddenly Drew's face changed to one of uneasiness as he looked over Tal's shoulder. Another man in the Royal Blue of the Household Guard came trotting up to Drew and grinned, "You had best get moving Drew, Falkom will have your head on his pike if your not around this palace another four times before he sees you."

"Around the palace?" asked Tal.

"Falkom's idea of discipline. I was late for weapons training this morning so I have to run laps." Drew sighed as he waved goodbye to his brother in all but name and jogged off across the marshalling yard. Tal suppressed a small chuckle and continued on to his room.

Tal spent the rest of the day getting to know Brad a little better. They wandered around the grounds of the palace that they both thought they should know, and shared a dinner at the mess before heading back for an early night.

James R. Kitney

They were passing the Barracks that they now knew held the female Riders and Tal noticed the same woman that he saw leaving the captains office earlier leave the woman's barracks and head to the palace in full uniform and chain. Tal thought to himself that she must be about to go on duty somewhere. He was about to look away when she seemed to look directly at him and stopped walking. They both stood their looking at each other until Brad noticed he had lost Tal and looked across the marshalling yard to see the woman from the palace looking directly at Tal and he looking just as fixedly back at her. Brad whispered into Tal's ear "I can leave you two to it if you want?" and made a grin any rogue would have been proud of.

"Huh? Oh, no its ok." Said Tal as he blushed furiously and looked away before continuing the journey to the barracks. He made one more look over his shoulder as he walked and noticed that the woman was still looking at him, though slightly angry now. "I think she likes you, even though she seems a bit upset at you not approaching her." Said Brad with another impish grin.

"You think I've upset her?" asked Tal, his voice a little uneasy.

"Man, you have it bad Tal." Replied Brad with a soft laugh. Tal just blushed and kept walking.

The days passed quickly for the trainees, and as they weren't in active service yet, they were given weekends off for themselves. Tal, Drew and Brad decided to go for a walk in the fields and hills that surrounded the city for a day of quiet relaxation. As they walked they talked about their first weeks training. Tal was quiet, he hadn't progressed like the others had, he simply could not get used to fighting with a sword. Brad had started to make progress immediately, and was one of the prides of his weapons master. Drew, even though he didn't get on with his weapons master was becoming quite the expert and although Falkom hated to admit it, he grudgingly conceded that Drew was a natural swordsman.

They had walked northwest for a few hours and were approaching the flat lands that were the beginning of the countryside stretch out before them. They decided to rest for a bit before heading back to the barracks and found a nice stretch of open land that had a few large trees scattered about. They leant against one and quietly watched the day drift away.

It was about an hour later, the sun had passed mid sky and the three friends were beginning to ponder if it was time to head back. They stretched and started walking in the direction they had come from. The day moved slowly as they walked, the cool air making the exercise pleasant.

On their walk back to the Palace, they noticed many farmhouses, their chimneys giving off trails of white/blue smoke from the fires to remove the chill from the houses. After some time the young men were passing one such farmhouse, about an hours walk from the main city when they noticed a man running with what seemed to be every ounce of his waking energy towards them.

Looking back past the man Tal noticed another figure following him, the man was screaming for help to the three friends, and Drew pulled his long belt knife, Brad pulled a dagger from under his shirt. Tal felt suddenly defenceless, as he had neither knife nor dagger. As Brad and Drew ran towards the man Tal stopped, he did not know the figure but he recognised the dress of him. Tall, dressed in black with a grey cloak trailing as he ran. Feeling fear grip at his very core, Tal sprinted down to his friends and the man just as they met. As he caught up with them Tal started them running towards the City. The frightened man needed no encouragement and was once more off as fast as his legs could carry him, Drew and Brad had to be pushed to flee by Tal before they would run.

"What is going on Tal?" questioned Drew as they ran towards the City.

"Don't you recognise the person chasing us?" replied Tal, putting as much energy into running as he could. "It's another

Dark Elf, like the one that was trying to kill me back home." Drew risked a look back. The cloaked figure was closing on the steadily. As soon as Drew recognised him he put even more energy into running, knowing that he wouldn't get a chance to sneak up behind this adversary. Brad, seeing a frightened man running for his life, the fear evident in Tal and Drew now realised that something was not right and decided not to hold back as he pushed forward ahead of the group. Brad may not be a tall lad but he had speed and was using it to full advantage at the moment. Tal called to Brad with what breath he could spare,

"Brad run ahead. Get help, any help!" Brad looked back. His face showed he did not like the idea of leaving his friends but saw the wisdom in Tal's instructions.

As Brad pushed further ahead, Tal glanced over to look at the man they were running with. The man was tiring and slowly falling behind.

Tal looked around for somewhere to they could put up or hide but the area around them was all flatlands and fields from the farms. Tal began to lose all hope as he was also beginning to slow. Drew noticed his friend and began to feel his own exhaustion. He looked around in desperation and noticed a field that was far from level ahead. He called to Tal and all three started to run with their last ditch effort. Maybe if the were lucky they could hide in the ruts in the field and regain their breath.

Tal looked back and the tall Elf was no more than a hundred yards behind them now, maybe closer, and started to feel panic rise within him.

The trio climbed the fence to the field. Running still, they tried not to leave a trail for the Elf to follow. They turned and found a fallen tree that had caused a hole in the earth to be created. Tal dropped to the floor, and Drew and the still unknown man followed suit. Hiding in the shallow rut, they unconsciously held their breath as the sound of Boots on the fence announced the Elf had also reached the field. Noise ceased from all quarters, both Elf and man, then the quiet hiss of a sword being drawn could be heard by the exhausted group. It seemed there was an eternity of silence, but it couldn't have been more than a few minutes before movement close by could be felt again, slowly creeping towards where they were hidden. The sound inched closer and closer until Tal thought the soft fall of boots was within his own head. Drew found he was holding his breath. Their companion was trembling slightly and Tal hoped he had the sense to stay put and keep quiet. The Elf must be close enough to touch them…

Madrik climbed the fence into the rolling field. The coward Yuril had not accepted the Great Masters offer and the Collector had sent Madrik to kill him. Though he had gained the nickname "Assassin" due to his power over peoples lives and their deaths, he rarely carried out that duty himself. None of the lesser servants knew his name, or even if he *had* a name, and his face was almost perpetually clouded. He had features, but no one could tell what they were. No, thought Madrik, he wasn't sure what his duties for the Great Master consisted of completely, but the rumours were that he took orders from the Great Master of the Grey Mages himself.

Madrik paused in the field, listening for any slight sound that would give away the fugitives position. Silence was the only reply he got, as quietly as possible he drew his sword and moved slowly, deeper into the field.

As he stepped further into the field, someone caught his attention. A dark figure was standing on the other side of the fence that Madrik had just climbed. A chill passed through the Dark Cousin, he didn't know what the Collector wanted with him, but he had been tardy with his contract and now there were witnesses.

Madrik sheathed his sword with a muted curse and began hastily putting his story together in his head as to why he had failed.

Tal breathed a sigh of relief at the sound of a sword being sheathed. Although he knew he was far from safe the sound of the weapon being put aside was a relief even in these circumstances. The sound of the Elf cursing could be heard now as he moved away from the small group of fugitives, the elf no longer bothered about keeping his movements silent. Tal heard a harsh voice from near the fence line, it was deep and full of authority.

"Madrik!" boomed the voice, "Why have you not slain him as you were sent to do?!" Tal listened intently, he could almost feel Brad returning, there were others with him, Tal was sure of it. *Maybe if they argue long enough, Brad and who ever is with him can capture them…* It was a slight chance though. Right now all Tal hoped for was to see his family again.

The man called Madrik replied, his voice quavering as he spoke, unusual for a dark cousin to be afraid of anyone. "I'm sorry, but he ran and took up with these boys. They ran into this field…I was about to finish the job, but I was…distracted…."

"Don't blame your incompetence on my arrival here. The Master has another job for you…maybe you may complete this small insignificant task. He is not pleased with your success to date, this *may* give you a reason to be kept alive. Head back to your chieftain. He will inform you of your orders." There was silence for several minutes and Tal risked a look over the depression that he was hidden in. He could see the elf clearly now on the other side of the fence, he was staring at a black figure as it strode away. Tal watched as the dark figure disappeared suddenly. The Elf cursed louder now, then made his way eastward. He moved at a pace that showed no sign of the previous flight across the countryside, and soon he too vanished into the distance.

Tal, Drew and Brad were in the antechamber of the great conference hall in the Palace and were anxiously awaiting the summons that was to come and call them into the presence of the king, his advisors and their superiors.

After the Dark elf and his colleague had left, Brad was quick in returning with a small company of the city guard at a swift pace. When the area had been secured the company returned to the city and quickly were made to report to their respective officers. From there it had been a quick progression on towards the conference that was being held now.

A page called the three friends into the conference hall. At a large round table sat six men. The king was obvious, he sat on a decorated throne that while regal and beautiful looked well used and comfortable. The king himself was wearing deep purple tunic with grey trousers. He had dark hair, almost black and his eyes were alight with worry. He was an old man yet the years had been kind to him and his stocky figure looked as strong as it had ever. Next to him sat his son and his daughter. His son was almost the complete opposite of his father, slim and lean, he had mousy brown hair and was wearing a blue tunic. His movements spoke of speed rather than power and his manner was kind. The Kings daughter was in a yellow dress and looked as regal as a princess should. Blonde hair and blue eyes set a beautiful face, yet a will as strong as stone was evident when she spoke and that was a gift from her father the Palace staff said. Next to the Prince was Lord Rayburn, his uniform clean and crisp. No armour yet he had changed from the man Tal and Brad had met before, he was now emanating a raw power and confidence that spoke of loyalty and love of the country. Tal and Brad could almost feel it. Strange Tal thought that he should feel love and loyalty for the country and yet nothing other than affection for the king and his family. Next to the Princess was a tall man in a white robe. Drew recognised this man as the one he met in the great hall. He was not so impassive this time and worry was also on his face. The man was introduced as Jakrin

Tiersing, Lord High Seer. Next to Lord Rayburn was a man dressed in blue with black hair and beard. Drew recognised Commander Denholm instantly. The Commander was also worried. The entire council was obviously at a point where fear was reaching a climax.

Before long the council had wrung all the information they could out of the three friends regarding the dark elf and the conversation between him and the unknown man. Tal had to recite the events that lead to him travelling to the Riders and in doing so reopened wounds that seemed to have vanished over the death of Layland. To the trio it seemed that everyone bar the Prince and Princess had asked for a complete narration of previous accounts a dozen or more times.

In time they were dismissed and each returned to their quarters.

"So Jakrin," spoke the King. "what does this mean and how long do we have until what ever is going to happen happens?"

"Amond, to be honest I am just not sure." Replied the mage to the king. "The Rangers have seen the Ones of Impurity being gathered by the enemy, and the man that now sleeps was to be another of their kind. The Brotherhood of Seers does not know how many of these devils there will be, but we have an idea of what they will be from the ancient tomes."

"You had best tell us then Jakrin. We need to train our men to fight them if there will be an army strong of them." Spoke Rayburn.

"I would not be worried about an army of them, they are more likely to be the leaders of the armies." Replied Jakrin uncomfortably. "They are liken to the nightwalkers from what the Seers can make out. Only able to move in darkness. Dead, with no soul but with mind and intelligence. They require living creatures blood to survive, yet unlike the nightwalkers who try to shy from people in fear of being hunted, they will probably be more powerful and not so worried about any human retaliation."

"How are we to kill them then?" questioned Commander Denholm.

"That we do not know, there are no records of that in the tomes here in the palace. The nightwalkers can be killed by daylight, fire, magic, or the severance of their head. But these 'Ones of Impurity' may require different methods to kill them."

"You paint a bleak picture Jakrin. What are these monsters to be used for? To lead an army you believe, but to what purpose?" Asked Amond.

"In truth your Highness, we do not know. I would advise a trip to Coladan, they have a much greater base of knowledge there. The university is immense and the scholars know more about the tomes and scrolls there than anyone else living. I'm sure they could help uncover more."

"Very well. What about the involvement of the Dark Cousins in all this?" Enquired the King.

"It is common knowledge that the Dark Elves are available for a price for any assassination mission. Perhaps that is all they have to do with this." Replied Jakrin.

"I think not." spoke the prince. Speaking for the first time that day, the council looked upon him. "What is your thought Rufus?" asked his father.

"The attack on the young Rider and his family, that I am willing to believe was a contract by the Grey Mages to stop another Rider being accepted. But this man, the one you have in stasis Jakrin, a dark elf was sent to kill him by someone or something called 'The Collector', or 'Assassin' the Dark Elves were once friendly with the demons of this world weren't they Jakrin?" asked the Prince. On the confirmation from Jakrin he continued. "Do you then not think that they are involved in some way with demonic plans here? This 'Collector', he certainly does not sound entirely human."

"This brings even more doubt to the situation my son. Nothing seems clear anymore. Only hazy and confused. Would the Grey Mages also be in league with these dark forces?" asked the King. It was the Princess that answered,

"I think not, they hate the demons as much as they are in turn hated by them." Jakrin smiled warmly at the girl who before his elevation to the rank of Lord High Seer was his pupil. "Well Kayla it seems that not all I taught you was wasted over the years." The Princess smiled back at the man.

"Then unless they have forged an alliance it is safe to assume that the two parties are unconnected in this.

"So what do you make of the fellow in stasis Jakrin?" asked Rayburn.

"I believe that he will remain a normal human being so long as he is not taken by this Collector. And so for this reason I think it best if we leave him in stasis. I don't know how these Collectors track their quarry but it may make it harder if he is outside of the bounds of time and space.

"We are also unsure whether there is simply one Collector or many. So far we have assumed there are several, but in all honesty we do not know."

The king now stood. He looked weary and the hours in council had passed slowly to him. His children stood at his side. "Then we send a party to Coladan, try to find out more about these Ones of Impurity and see what that leads on to." Declared the king.

With that the other men stood, Rayburn left quickly as did Jakrin, Denholm informed the King that he would inform the Generals of the Kingdom of the matter, and brief them to prepare the Armies of the Kingdom for war, before he to left to see to his duties.

The King looked at his children. They were still so young for war to be coming to his Kingdom. He hoped that fate may have spared them the sight of war. He had seen it himself barley thirty years ago, it was the war against the Grey Mages, when they had risen up and tried to take the Kingdom. The war had taken his mother and father from him and he had been ruling since. His wife and children were dear to him and he could not bear to lose them. He could not, would not let this happen to his kingdom. But there were simply too many unknowns…

Chapter 4

The Long Road

The morning came fresh and chill, autumn was past as winter was now settling in. Tal thought ruefully to himself that he would be turning sixteen in a couple of weeks and then he would be considered a man by those of the Kingdom. He sat in his quarters waiting for the day's drills, when a knock on his door made him jump. It was a Rider that introduced himself as Kelar Gwent. Tal was told that he was to make ready for the road. He was to accompany Kelar, along with Brad to Coladan.

Tal asked why he was going to Coladan, and was informed that at the council yesterday, the king decided to send a company of Riders and Seers to Coladan to seek more information about the strange occurrences of the past month and a half, and because of their involvement in these events Lord Rayburn had given them leave to travel with the company to aid in anyway they could. When enquiring after Drew, Kelar told him that he knew nothing of the placement of Drew with the company.

Tal dressed and packed what he thought he would need. He took his short sword, though he hoped he never needed to wield it and his quarterstaff. He was progressing with the weaponry but still nowhere close to rivalling Brad or Drew. He also took his armour, and uniform.

When he deemed himself ready he called on Brad. When Brad answered his door he was in full uniform and armour, his long sword slung across his back, longbow unstrung and in its covers, with his knife at his side. He looked the true semblance of a Dragon Rider and Tal felt suddenly foolish, he was going on a mission as a Dragon Rider and he wasn't even dressed in uniform. With a self-conscious moan he darted back into his room to change.

Shortly he was ready, and alongside Brad he walked out to the marshalling yard and saw twenty Riders, some with golden studs across the shoulders of their cloaks, all in uniform. He was glad he had called for Brad first now, he would have felt ridiculous without his uniform on.

Tal continued to look around and saw that at least eight of the Riders were women, and more than one had studs of rank. Brad also noticed this and smiled, he had been speaking to a Rider that had just been promoted from novice, and she was there talking to another woman of about the same age. Tal looked over at Brad and smiled, he knew about this fancy Brad had and thought it amusing. Tal suddenly stopped smiling and felt his throat dry out when he noticed that the other Rider she was talking to was the Rider with the red hair that Tal himself could not stop thinking about. The two boys walked over to the leader of the party who introduced himself as Captain Fen Trillar. He informed the boys that this mission was to be used to break the new recruits in, which is why there were so many inexperienced Riders and novices there and also why there were several Sergeants to make up the experience.

Tal thought about this and decided that the new Rider must have been Brad's friend, Cholla and the new novices, himself and Brad.

Brad started walking over to Cholla and although Tal deeply wanted to stay clear of this girl with red hair he was forced to follow. As the two friends joined up with the female Riders Brad and Cholla smiled and blushed slightly while the girl with the red hair gave Tal a slightly hurt look and Tal simply flushed red and looked elsewhere, only to result in an angry 'Hmmph' from the red haired girl. Brad and Cholla chuckled silently and Cholla introduced Tal and Wynhazel. To his surprise Wynhazel was only slightly older than Tal and had also just been promoted to the rank of Rider.

When the Riders had been assembled a further five men in white travelling gear joined them. Although they looked like they held authority, they seemed thin and retrospective in nature, the kind more suited for study than for soldiering. Tal was eventually informed that these were the Seers that were to accompany them to Coladan.

Midday came and the party set out at a steady pace on foot. The journey was estimated to take about two weeks to complete and Tal realised that he could turn sixteen whilst on the road. For some reason that thought upset him. Brad picked up on this and when he found out what was upsetting his friend he tried to reassure him, but with no real luck.

When the group had departed the city Tal noticed that all the Officers removed their studs of rank, and that almost all the Riders were jumping at each step, locating the source of any sound and muting it before they left sight of the city. Tal noticed that all the Riders now looked identical, all in their black and red chain, their black cloaks with red hem and dragon over the heart. He was informed that it is standard Rider practice to remove all badges of rank when on a mission. He accepted this and the group moved out into the world.

The party had been moving for about a week and were deep within the Greenhome. They had altered their course after a day within the forest so as to miss the lands of the Elves. Although the Elves of the Greenhome were not dark and twisted like their cousins they liked their privacy and more than once has a man found himself turned about without realising it.

That night at camp conversation was quiet. The company was aware that the Elves land was close and none wanted to bring unwanted attention upon themselves. The journey was taking longer than anticipated and it was now thought that the length of time to reach Coladan was going to be three weeks instead of two. Tal had come to accept that he would become a man with none of the normal celebrations that accompanied such an occasion.

They set out as the sun rose and shone down between the trees the next morning. It had snowed during the night and the camp was covered white. Each person awoke damp and cold, their spirits already low. Brad walked with Cholla and Tal walked next to Wynhazel. Over the past week he had become more comfortable with her around, even after the nearly fatal mistake of not shortening her name to Hazel – Wynhazel being a name out of stories and not very original according to her. He was still stumped for words when it came to starting conversation but at least now he could answer without his mouth drying out within the first few words.

Half way through the day Captain Trillar called a halt. Without signalling, two Riders moved into the underbrush silently, each had a knife drawn and was moving slowly. In a bare few seconds each was concealed from sight.

Tal thought back to what Layland had said when he met him, how he had felt his surroundings. Tal thought about the forest, he tried to stretch his mind out but could feel nothing. He was still trying when Trillar walked over to him and whispered silently in his ear.

"You learn fast Tal, but you wont feel anything here, it is hard to detect Elves unless you know what you are searching for." Tal blinked. He was unsure of what to say and just looked at Captain Trillar. At that moment the two Riders came back to the group. There were four tall, lean men with them. They were fair haired and sharp of features, each wore a leather jerkin and were dressed in greens and browns. All four carried a bow, a quiver of arrows and a knife. *Elves!* Thought Tal. The circle seemed to divide at that point, the older experienced Riders seemed to relax, the Seers seemed intrigued by the situation and the younger Riders and novices were in simple awe.

As the six men came to halt before the Captain, Trillar bowed deeply to the Elves then again to one in particular. Tal looked at this elf, he seemed of the same height and build, yet something in his manner spoke of a greater power. One of the sergeants leant close to Tal and explained that the elf in charge was Trail Lord, a very respected person, that only few Elves have the honour of being named.

"Trail Lords are Elves that are born slightly more in tune with the trees than other Elves lad. They train as regular Elven Warriors would until they have reached their peak with weapons, they then get taken into training by their mages and taught how to use their natural gift. When their training is complete they are given the title of Trail Lord. There may only be a handful in any one generation and they are charged with keeping the privacy of the Elves intact and intruders out. They can *speak* to the trees or as close to it as needed and the trees do what is bid to keep their glades safe. It is rare that any one who is not an elf gets to meet one, rarer still that one chooses to meet a non elf!"

Tal looked to Brad and Cholla, they were both looking at the Elves in what he could only describe as disbelief, Hazel was also looking on in bewilderment. He turned his attention back to Trillar and the Trail Lord who had finished their quiet conversation.

The Captain smiled and spoke to his party. "The Elves now know what we are doing and where we are going. Lord Arten has given permission that we may pass through the Elven Land

and he will guide us." At this news and because of the reaction of their Captain the whole group relaxed, if not visibly. The seers went as far as to murmur to each other and took a look of a physician examining a patient.

The Elves under the instruction of Lord Arten disappeared back into the forest and vanished almost instantly. He informed the group that his men would go to their King and inform him of the situation.

With that the group started out again under the guidance of the Trail Lord. It seemed that the density of the trees was increasing with every step and in a short period of time the company was being made to pick out the path from where the Trail Lord had stepped before. This continued for the best part of three hours with the only explanation from Lord Arten being that this was the fastest way to the Elven Glades. After the three hours the forest opened up slightly revealing great glades, full of colour and life. Birds sang openly and the small tree dwellers showed no fear of the company.

The small band walked through a tight clearing in the ring of trees surrounding the glade, and Tal inhaled sharply in amazement. Before him stood trees higher than the eyes could see, and amongst these were paths made from the softest of grass, this was the living city of The Elven Glades. Where the trees were not providing cover, there were great structures of wood that were supported by the great giants themselves, as if adopted by them to strengthen the landscape. Arches that stood high and lead into places of worship and houses that displayed leaves as a roof, no slate, just branch and leaf. Colours of all shades from browns and greens to reds and yellows, all mixed to increase the feel and appearance of an already impressive population.

On the ground were great stone designs that Elven children played around. Wooden structures that looked like storehouses. One elf walked from one such building carrying a selection of bows and arrows to a small gathering of Elven young that were to be trained as Trackers. Buildings that contained fruit and other foodstuffs were open to any who wanted and other buildings that contained tools were being used constantly by the tradesmen of the Elven Glades. The sound of voices sung loudly in the air, but it was no language that Tal had ever heard. It was akin to singing in the way it rose and fell, in the way sentences blended together. Fletchers and craftsmen worked in close proximity, producing arrows, bows, swords and repairing other metal works. The sound of the blacksmiths could be heard yet it was of a much softer nature than in towns and cities of men.

It was not simply the visual spectacles that amazed Tal, the feel of this place was that of magic and mystery. It felt like there was more occurring in ten minutes within these glades than had occurred to Tal within his entire life. Great works of nature mixed with magic. The entire atmosphere was almost too much for Tal, it was overwhelming to an extent that he never thought imaginable. He looked over at Brad, Cholla and Hazel. The girls were almost in tears and Brad was leaning against a tree in silent awe.

"Come." Said Lord Arten. "The King will wish to meet you. It is rare that man is allowed into these Glades and when they are the King would see them." He led them to the base of the greatest tree in the Glade, it stood higher than any of the company could see above the canopy of trees. At the base there was a great arch, actually in the trunk of the mighty tree, it led to steps that led up at a sharp incline in a circular path. The party followed the staircase up and up, many times they passed other exits from the stairs, leading to other parts of what could only be described as a palace of trees.

After what seemed an age of climbing they reached the top of the stairs. They opened out into a wide walkway, many feet wide and many more still above the canopy of the forest and the Elven Glades.

"Wary of your step so high. The few men that have come here over the years liked little the heights of our dwellings." Remarked Arten as they continued to a large portal. The door itself was immense and in turn was dwarfed by the size of the building that it allowed entrance into. The palace – for that is what Tal immediately recognised it as – was large, if not by human standards, by the amount of magery and love that had been forged into it when created from the trees themselves.

Arten gave hardly a push to the doors and they glided open easily. Inside the Palace were many portals that lead off from the main walkway they followed. At the end of the corridor stood a great gilded arch, coloured in gold's and silver's from the tree itself. The party lead by Lord Arten moved through the arch and into a grand hall. Inside there were twenty or so Elven Trackers and equally as many mages. The party walked through the hall in silence and up to the dais at the very front. Mounted on a throne of wood, sat an impressive figure. He was tall, even for an elf, his hair shone gold rather than blonde or fair, and trailed down to the centre of his back in a tail tied at the nape of his neck. His eyes were the green of the trees and his features hard and yet peaceful, like the trees themselves. He was wearing the same garb as the Trackers and the Trail Lord and yet the clothes seemed to become nobler on his frame. At his side sat a woman, beautiful in appearance she had the same golden hair, the same length as the King's but worn loose. She wore a dress as green as her husbands eyes and that of the trees, and her own eyes shone a clear deep blue that stood at extraordinary contrast to her dress. Each wore a slight circlet of gold upon their brow.

"My King, I present to you the party that was travelling to the human city of Coladan in search of knowledge. I introduce Captain Trillar of the Dragon Riders who leads this party." Arten bowed deeply to the King and Queen before moving to the back of the hall.

The king spoke his voice clear, commanding, musical and soft. "Captain Trillar, be welcome to the Elven Glades. I am Hanrial, King of these Glades, and this is my Queen, Lyria. We understand that you seek answers about these attacks by the Dark Cousins, and about the 'Ones of Impurity'. Maybe we can offer a little in the way of information about the Ones. But first, I would let you clean up from the road and rest. Food will be brought to you and tomorrow we can discuss these sadder tidings. There will be a feast later tonight. It is rare that man comes here, as I am sure you have been informed many times so far, and when they do, we celebrate. You are free to join us should you wish, and know that should you be weary from your travels then no offence will be taken should you keep to your beds." The King spoke the last with a slight smile.

"We thank his Majesty for his hospitality and will look forward to the feast." Replied Trillar bowing deeply. Hanrial inclined his head with respect to Trillar and called Arten to show them to the quarters that had been made ready for them.

The company was lead through the palace of trees and to a wing that had been set aside for their use. It was comfortable, more so than Tal would have thought possible for a structure crafted from living material.

The food was prepared and brought to them in quick order and soon Tal was feeling refreshed once more. He lay back on his bed and somehow felt as though this place soothed away all worry and eased all aches. It was not long before a call arrived for him in the form of Hazel. Tal found himself surprised yet happy that she was here. She was dressed in formal uniform, tight black trousers and tabard, with the red dragon over her heart and her black cloak. The formal uniform looked almost identical to the general uniform of the Riders, yet the quality and weave was much finer. She looked at him when he opened the door in astonishment, he had barely removed his travel gear.

"Tal, we need to be at be feast in five minutes and your not dressed! Get changed quickly and meet us out in the main corridor. Quickly!" As she started to turn away Tal stammered to reply,

"But I didn't bring my formal uniform!" he said, a trace of worry evident in his voice.

"*What!?* Tal what were you thinking? what were you going to wear when we addressed the University scholars? Your travel gear? You had better just put on some clean gear and hope no one notices. Hurry!." She didn't wait to see what his reaction was, she simply pulled the door tight and went to rejoin Cholla and Brad.

Tal, Brad, Cholla and Hazel walked into the large hall together. When Tal had met the other three he felt ridiculous, he was wearing slightly ruffled travel gear that he dragged from the bottom of his travel pack.

"You're lucky that our formal dress is so similar to our working uniform Tal." Remarked Brad as they all walked towards the feast. Already they could hear the soft music and Elven voices drifting through the palace. Tal merely nodded to his friend and continued in silence to the hall.

As they entered they were all astonished further to discover the feasts of the Elves were indeed feasts, tables upon tables were lined with food of every type Tal knew and some that he did not. The tables were arranged to make a large circle in the centre of the room where some Elves were already dancing.

Captain Trillar was talking with Trail Lord Arten and the other Riders were mingling with the Elves having conversations about everything and nothing. When they reached the main floor an elf offered them a drink made from what they thought was honey, yet it had a kick to it the like Tal had only tasted when his father had let him drink ale on special occasions.

Within a few minutes of talking to each other a couple of Elves walked over to them, and started to converse, discussing the differences between their societies. Tal was astonished to discover that they were still considered to be young amongst the Elves even though they were over a hundred years old. They had been talking for a few minutes when a more upbeat song started and the Elves asked to be excused as they made their way to the space in the centre of the tables along with other Elves. All the Riders present stopped what they were doing to watch the Elves that had assembled. They started to move in a synchronised way that Tal found interesting. They moved not in pairs or triplets as was the fashion in the Kingdom – as Tal could see it anyway – but divided. The females stood on one side of the floor, the men on the other. Each side then started to move towards each other with the music, their steps decorating the floor. They flowed through each other as they met, spinning and sliding past each other, a different partner every other step until they were again separated.

Tal noticed that Hazel and Cholla were looking on with great interest and that they kept looking at him and Brad. Tal felt he could see the way this was going and so pulled Brad over to the tables laden with food. Brad didn't seem happy at being parted from Cholla in such a manner but when Tal explained to him, Brad's face drained of colour.

"You think that they want us to do…that?" Asked Brad, looking towards the dancing Elves.

"I'm sure of it, I think Hazel has been trying to get me back for not talking to her before and this is her way of doing it." Replied Tal.

"But Cholla isn't angry with me, why should I have to do it?" pleaded Brad, openly starting to worry now.

"Because if you don't then I won't have to. If you go up there then they will make me also." Brad considered this, and why it made no sense to him, he decided not to put the theory to the test.

"Okay. Then how do we get out of it?" he asked.

"We say that we are tired and go back to our rooms." Replied Tal

"But then we miss the evening and miss out on talking with Elves." Countered Brad.

"Well you can stay here if you want but I'm going." Replied Tal, looking over his shoulder worriedly.

"What are you two up to? It doesn't take this long to get some food." Said Hazel as she walked up to Tal and Brad.

"Well we were just saying how tired we are, and how we were thinking of getting and early night." Replied Tal quickly before Brad was able to say anything that may put his plan in jeopardy.

"That's a shame." Said Hazel. "Cholla wanted to go for a walk with Brad in the Elven Glades while they had the chance."

"I'm sure I have enough energy for a short walk." Said Brad a little too quickly and got up and proceeded to walk over to Cholla. Tal watched him go and winced inside. How could Brad do that too him? And over a girl of all things?

"Well what are we going to do for the evening then Tal?" Asked Hazel, a smile ever so slight on her lips. Tal was looking directly at those lips and thinking that he would go for a walk too if he was asked before he caught himself and told himself to stop being so silly.

"To be honest Hazel, I feel tired and I think I might..." started Tal before he was cut off by Hazel.

"How about a drink? Why don't you go and get us another of those honey mixtures, then we can decide what to do." She smiled and Tal found himself agreeing without thinking about it. He moved to get them and spotted Brad and Cholla leaving the hall. He thought he owed Brad an apology. Maybe it wasn't his fault that he jumped when Cholla asked. He returned to Hazel with two full cups and after talking to her he found himself getting another round for them. He noticed that the room was beginning to spin and that noises were beginning to echo when he finished his third drink.

Tal woke up. His head was thumping and his mouth was dry and tasted horrid. He climbed out of bed and almost fell over. *What happened last night?* Thought Tal as he slowly washed in the basin that had been left for him, and got dressed. The last thing he could remember was that he was getting another drink for Hazel and his head was beginning to spin, or was it the room? He couldn't tell but he thought he liked it at the time… Tal ruefully remembered the only other time he had felt like this was when his father had left a bottle of wine out and Drew and he had finished it. He moaned when he realised that he probably made a complete fool of himself in front of Hazel in his drunken state. He left his room without even opening the heavy drapes that held out most of the sun and when he walked past a window he groaned at the sudden light. Tal guessed that it must have been almost mid day so he decided to call for Brad. Maybe he would know if anything had happened.

Tal knocked on Brad's door. Brad opened his door and let out a laugh at seeing Tal in his current state. Tal winced but followed when Brad left the door open for him.

"What were you drinking last night Tal? Cholla and I returned from our walk and you were dancing away in the middle of the floor as though your tunic was alight." Said Brad in near hysterics. Tal simply moaned. "I wouldn't worry though. The Elves thought it amusing and actually thought it was a dance from mans world. Some even tried to emulate it, though they just couldn't get the flailing right." Burst out Brad in a fit of laughter.

"Did Hazel see it?" Asked Tal in a pained voice that usually followed a haunted man.

"Yep, she sure did, she was dancing with you!" Replied Brad his laughter renewed.

Tal felt a little better on hearing that though he didn't think he could ever face anyone else again.

"Come on feet of fire, the Captain should have finished his meeting with the King and Queen and we should be moving on shortly. You had best get your kit together, Cholla should be seeing to Hazel about now." With that, he shooed Tal from his room as he started to get his own kit together.

It was early in the afternoon in the Elven Glades. The company of Riders and Seers was gathered near the edge of one of the Glades, Trail Lord Arten was with them again, to act as their guide once more. The meeting with the King and Queen had lasted most of the morning and whatever Captain Trillar had learned, he was not happy with it.

Alongside Lord Arten were the King and Queen, they had come to wish the company luck on their journey.

"I wish you luck Captain," Spoke the King. "There is a lot that rides on your uncovering more information about the Return, and I wish you the speed of the gods."

"Thank you Majesty. What you have told me only brings fear to my heart. I shall do my best to uncover more and send word when I have." Replied Trillar.

"Then we are in your debt sir Rider. Peace be with you and luck guide your journey. Goodbye." With the last words the King and Queen turned and slowly walked back towards the palace in the trees.

"Come then," Started Arten. "we still have a long way to go to the edge of our forest and the sooner we begin the better it seems." Lord Arten led the company into the woodland once more. The paths he was picking seemed incredibly tight and twisted yet he moved with great ease. The Riders had a little more trouble keeping up and the Seers were starting to lag behind when Arten looked back and laughed quickly. "I'm sorry, I forget that the Elves can move faster through woodland than man. I shall do better to pick easier paths for you." Arten then closed his eyes and the trees seemed to sing, Tal could feel energy round him and when he looked at his friends they too could feel it. The Seers stood frozen in awe as the trees themselves seemed to withdraw leaving an almost clear path running in a straight line north and west.

Lord Arten opened his eyes and spoke a few words that none in the company could understand. When he noticed the curiosity on the faces of the party he spoke swiftly before moving on. "I asked the trees to bear you an easier way, they obliged and so I thanked them. They do not mind shifting, but it is always polite to show appreciation." He smiled briefly at their amazement and then started out again. By the end of the following day the company had left the Elven Lands and were continuing through the rest of the Greenhome. Lord Arten still guided them and the trees still made a path for them. Every now and then Arten would stop and say a few words in Elven before moving on again.

That night at camp Tal sat with Brad, Hazel and Cholla. He was relieved to discover that other than the dancing, he had done nothing else that was embarrassing, and that Hazel was just as uncomfortable took some of the pressure off him. He felt that if she could face the group that he could too. Even if the jokes had not yet stopped and were not likely to for the foreseeable future.

The night was calm and cool, and there was a chill that seemed to touch nothing under these trees. Tal couldn't work out whether that was due to the thickness of the trees or the proximity to the Elven Glades. The food had been spread out and there was a stew of meats and vegetables. Lord Arten had given the cook something to be included with the stew that had added a pleasant spiced taste. Tal eagerly went back for seconds but was declined. Being told that until everyone had eaten at least once no person could come back for a second helping. Tal accepted this if grudgingly and went back to sit with his friends.

The night drifted by and Tal was to sit watch with one of the sergeants. The two moved away from the fire to relieve the man acting as guard currently. When the duty had been handed over to them, they stood away from the main group hidden in the trees. Tal enquired to this and was informed that unlike other armies, the Riders hide their lookouts in the hope that any enemy would make a mistake and reveal their position without knowing the lookout was even there. The hours started to drift by and Tal was beginning to feel hungry again. "Go get some food lad, everyone has had a turn now and if there is any left you will be more than welcome to have some." Tal started to move, eagerly wanting more when the lookout placed a hand on his chest halting him. "Wait a minute lad, I heard something out there." He whispered in Tal's ear. The sergeant drew his sword and Tal did likewise even though he hoped he wouldn't have to use it. Both men hid their weapons under their cloaks and moved further into the trees. Tal held back a little and could feel the man in front stretch out with his thoughts. He did likewise and was disgusted at what he could feel. Blackness, it was like he could feel four distinct patches of darkness moving towards the camp, one from each side. The sergeant looked back at Tal and smiled, before beckoning him back to the camp to raise the alarm. Although Tal did not like leaving one man out there with that shadow in his mind, he followed orders and was secretly relieved that he was not remaining. He returned to the camp and woke the Captain. Tal could feel Trillar Stretch out and slowly take his long sword. Tal then woke Lord Arten who awoke easily and took his bow before unhurriedly disappearing into the woods. Trillar woke two of the Seers and then the rest of the camp. At a point unknown to Tal, Trillar gave a signal to one of the Seers and he lifted an arm into the air and shot forth a searing bolt of light. The effect was that the entire clearing was illuminated. In the trees slowly making their way forward were three Dark Elves. Each had a sword drawn and was wearing the same gear Tal had seen them in before. The Sergeant that Tal had been on lookout with returned into the clearing, blood stained his sword but he looked unscathed. Within seconds one of the Dark Cousins fell to an arrow that sped from deep within the trees. The other two ran at the Captain seeing that their cover had been removed. One fell to another arrow that sped true from the trees and the other ran upon the sword of the Captain before he knew what had happened.

The light from the Seers flame died down and soon the company was in the relative darkness of the camp fire again. Lord Arten returned to the camp looking troubled. "They should not have been in this forest. That they are, and that they were sent as assassins only points towards the enemy knowing what you are about. And now you know that they want you dead. This means they can no longer use stealth. From now forth they will come in numbers if they come. It depends on how important what you search for is, that will force them into an open battle. The question that still burns though is who *is* the enemy?"

"I don't think we should wait here to find out." Replied Trillar. "Get your things together, we leave at once. I want to be at the edge of this forest by midday. Lord Arten we thank you for your aid but you should probably return to you King, I wouldn't make anyone walk for over a day to get home with these creatures abroad."

"I thank you for your thoughts Captain, but I am to accompany you to Coladan so that I may return to my King with news of the Return. And these bodies will be found by the Trackers before long and they will carry word to our King. For now my path lies with you." The Captain thought about this for a while and then replied.

"We would be honoured to have such a companion with us Lord Arten. Very well. But we must be swift now. Let us move." With that the company moved out. Lord Arten again took the lead, opening the trees before them and closing them behind.

It took until just past midday to clear the forest, but there were no more attacks and each member of the team was alert. Tal had been feeling sick the whole day. He had seen five Dark Elves dead, but he had never imagined he would see three deaths caused by conflict. There was an inner struggle raging.

He knew that it was their lives or his friends and his own that hung in the balance. But he still felt as though he had been party to some great evil. On asking Brad he found that his friend felt the same.

Hazel and Cholla told them that it was understandable but they should try not to think about it. That if they could quell the feelings down then it would help but never to stop feeling regret for taking a life. It was at that point that they would become as bad as the Dark Cousins.

The days pulled on, and soon a week had passed. Tal was sitting by himself that night at camp. He had not seen Brad, Hazel or Cholla that evening and he was feeling low at any rate. He decided that he would have been bad company anyway.

The Captain walked over to him and sat down.

"It's hard at first Tal. You were party to the death of a living creature. But be at ease. They are twisted by power and would have cut your throat in a second. What you done is what man has done from the beginning of time to stay alive. There can be no blame for that. Come now, there is something I want to show you." With that he stood and walked back to the main camp. Tal followed, wondering what the Captain wanted.

As Tal walked into the camp he was surprised to see the entire company there, each had a drink in hand and as he got closer they all raised their mugs and toasted Tal a happy birthday. Tal was speechless. He was a man of the Kingdom. Straight away a Rider started playing a small instrument that gave light merry feel to the air. The Captain came forward and offered Tal a present. It was customary that on a man's sixteenth birthday he receive a knife, but Tal received a Rapier. It was finely crafted and had the emblem of the dragon riders on the blade and sheath. The hilt was quilted in black and red and the guard was engraved with his name. It was a sword that was beautiful to behold yet could easily be used in a fight should it be needed.

Tal smiled and thanked each of the Riders for their gift. It had been arranged before they left and the captain had carried it the whole way, taking care not to let Tal see it.

The rest of the night passed without event and with much merriment. The Captain estimated that they would make Coladan in the next couple of days. They had already begun to see other traffic heading towards the city as they over took the caravans that merchants rode upon. The journey continued for two days.

Coladan was a city of scholars. It had large buildings that were of plain description, each one holding some kind of specialised library, made of stone and wood. The entire town looked practical. The streets were straight and the residences of areas identical. The Duke of the town held residency in a large house in the centre most of the city and although in past times it may have looked impressive it now looked like all the other houses in Coladan, strong of construction yet falling into disrepair as the owner gets deeper into his or her studies.

To the eastern side of the city was a great division. There was a wall that cut inwards from the main city wall to create a small town of its own. There were many entrances to this town and within there were many buildings, only some of which were used for housing. The majority of the great stone buildings were used to give lectures and undertake new projects. This was the University of Coladan.

Chapter 5

Coladan

The company entered the city through the South Gate and proceeded towards the Dukes residence. Arten had pulled the cowl of his cloak over his face and walked in the centre of the party. It was still a long walk to the city's heart and a company of armed men and women walking through Coladan was a strange, and worrying sight to the population without the added curiosity of the Trail Lord, and the City Guards were watching the newcomers apprehensively enough as it was.

Some of the City Guards seemed to grip their pole arms tighter and look to each other, satisfying themselves that backup was close by should anything occur.

The troop reached the Dukes house with little trouble but frequent stares, and proceeded to knock upon the door. A servant answered and stood gaping at the sight of twenty armed men and women in armour, five men in white robes and a tall man covered with his cloak. Captain Trillar introduced himself to the servant and requested an audience with the duke.

The servant seemed to stumble as though he was not quite sure what to make of the situation "He's up at the university sir, he will be for some time I expect. Should I tell him you called?"

"No my good man, it is ok. We shall head to the university and seek him out ourselves. Good day to you." With that, the Captain led the Riders and Seers away to leave the poor servant to wonder what was occurring.

The party arrived at the university wall and looked at the sign above one of the gates:

> *No weapon shall pass beyond this point,*
> *All such items should be left under the supervision*
> *of the guards, to be returned when you leave the*
> *University grounds.*
> *By order of Duke Whetal of Coladan.*

Captain Trillar walked up to the guard and handed over his long sword and knife. The guard thanked him and moved aside to let him in. When the guard noticed the number of people with weapons, he looked at his small station hut and wondered if they would all fit. The Captain chuckled under his breath as the guard took weapon after weapon from the company before allowing them in. By the time the group were assembled within the university, the guard could no longer fit comfortably in his little post and was forced to stand just inside the entrance to the small hut.

The group entered the grounds of the university, and Tal glanced at Brad. He, like Tal looked uncomfortable at giving up his weapons. The party passed through the main entrance and marched up to the man behind a desk marked as 'Information'. The man was clean shaven and generally nondescript and wore a plain brown robe. He looked up with a smile lining his face that vanished as soon as he realised he was facing a company of soldiers. His face moulded quickly to one of arrogance and disgust. "Yes?" Was all the man said in welcome.

"We need to see the Duke. Could you please tell us where we could find him?" Asked Captain Trillar.

"Why would you need to see the Duke? He has no time for your kind. He is an educated man and must put all his attention into solving the problems brought about by the likes of you." Replied the man behind the desk a sneer animating his face. Trillar simply looked at the man for a second before he lost his temper. In one motion, he reached across the desk and pulled the man from his seat, dragging him across the desktop to glare eye to eye with him.

The Seers looked to each other with raised eyebrows and amused expressions resting on their faces.

"To be perfectly honest I don't care what you think of 'my kind', we need to see the Duke and you are going to tell us where he is before you find out what I can do with bare hands."

The man shrank back without moving, he simply mumbled that the duke was somewhere in the Shannon College. Trillar dropped the man and his face became a picture of neutrality once again.

"Thank you." Was all he said as he motioned the party towards the direction indicated by the now fearful man.

As they crossed the university grounds Tal noticed the amount of people that wore simple robes and carried bundles of parchment. Not one person wore a sword or knife, and none looked particularly menacing. It was a completely different setting than the barracks and training grounds that he was used to now or even the slightly rougher city of Dukeray where he had grown up. Tal suddenly thought how he had changed in the past two months. He realised that he had started to look for weapons and the manner in which people moved to assess the threat they may hold.

Tal, Brad and the company, under the command of Captain Trillar found the Shannon College, it was a rather impressive building that stood in the centre of the University grounds. The captain pointed out that even though the other houses in the city didn't seem to be looked after too well the university seemed a different matter. The College stood several stories tall and was meticulously clean. The windows were all flawless and the walls were recently painted.

As they entered the college, the occupants gave rather disapproving looks and left quickly as though expecting trouble from the new comers. Just inside the entrance there was another desk occupied by another man in a plain robe. Brad leaned over to Tal and whispered in his ear, "there are more robes here than in a monastery!" He chuckled softly and continued to follow the pack.

Captain Trillar stopped before the desk. His face was still neutral but he seemed ready to drag another self important scholar across his desk to get an answer if necessary.

"Excuse me, we are looking for Duke Whetal. Could you tell us where he is?" Asked the Captain politely.

The man stood he looked quite nervous already "He is in a meeting sir, he should be out in about an hour if you would care to wait for him here?" Replied the man behind the desk, obviously intimidated enough to be polite.

"Very well. We will be outside. Please call us when he is finished, it is quite urgent."

The captain led the men outside and let them sit and rest. After the group had settled Trillar walked over to Tal. He pulled him aside from the rest and spoke quietly. "Captain Holbrook informed me that you have not yet chosen a hand-to-hand class. He also added that you should have chosen one by the time you get back and that I, along with some of the sergeants should get you started should any of us have studied your choice already. So, have you chosen a style yet?"

Tal froze, he had completely forgotten about the hand-to-hand classes. He thought quickly, trying to remember what Brad had told him about the different styles that were being taught in the palace grounds.

He remembered thinking he liked the idea of the martial arts and told the Captain this. He nodded at Tal's choice and called a sergeant over. The sergeant that reported was Kelar Gwent, the Rider that had collected Tal the morning before they set off from the City Of Dragons. When Tal and he walked to an area away from the main group Kelar told him that there were many forms of martial art, and that the Riders tried to incorporate all of them into their own form that each rider would then adapt into his own. He started by showing Tal the correct way to stand, breath and move. Tal seemed to pick this up quickly and so Kelar began to instruct him on the basic manoeuvres to stop an attacker from gripping and holding you.

The two had only been training for about half an hour when the man from behind the information desk of Shannon College came up to the captain and meekly mumbled something about the Duke being ready to see them in a conference room that was inside the college. As the man turned away to return to his desk, he noticed the instruction of Tal and shivered as he saw Kelar twist Tal around easily and throw him to the ground with no effort.

Duke Whetal was a short man, he was closer to plump than he was to stout and had brown hair with a beard that seemed to be oiled in no particular style.

"Good day gentlemen, and what can I do for you? I must say that it is not often that I get a company of Dragon Riders that wish to see me." The duke seemed quite reasonable and did not show any of the coyness or arrogance that had been shown by the other members of the city.

This time it was not Captain Trillar that came forward but one of the Seers, he was a slim man, like most of the Seers tended to be, he wore a white robe and had almost white hair to match. His eyes were a deep blue and shone with wisdom and a wit that Tal thought few could match.

"I am Oren Diarmid of the Brotherhood of Seers, I have come to speak with you of an urgent matter that has to do with the protection of your kingdom. Is this a safe place to talk?"

The Duke looked concerned now but nodded that this place was secure. Oren continued. "There is a possibility that we are now in The Time Before," at this, the concern in the Dukes face turned to worry and apprehension. "Good, you seemed to understand what is meant by that." Continued Oren. "However things have become even more confused lately. There is also strong evidence that the Grey Mages are planning something at the same time as their preparations for The Time Before. They are gathering the Ones of Impurity and the Rangers have noticed that creatures of dark legends are again roaming the lands. At least two sightings of Graven have been reported and it seems that the Dark Cousins are working for the Mages if not in alliance with them."

The Duke looked ill but spoke in the same manner that he had before hearing the news. "Of the Time Before and the Mage armies, I have some understanding, as do I know the legends of the Graven. But who are these Ones of Impurity? I do not believe that I have heard of them before"

Captain Trillar stepped forward before the Duke now. "Duke Whetal I am Captain Trillar of the Dragon Riders. We have passed through the Elven Glades to reach you. I have spoken to King Hanrial of the Elves and have discovered some information of the Ones of Impurity. They are, in some sense like the Nightwalkers, in that they exist by drinking the blood of the living. However they are more powerful. A Nightwalker may, in theory, be honourable and survive without actually taking a life, however the Ones cannot. They don't survive on blood, it merely strengthens them physically. They survive on the devoured souls of their victims. The numbers we can expect of them will not be vast as they will be the Grey Mages generals. A Nightwalker is a foe not even a Rider faces without caution, but not twenty Riders could kill one of these generals alone.

They cannot be killed by physical means alone, magic, weapons of power, and complete dismemberment is the only sure way to destroy them, and there are not many that I can think of that are strong enough in either way to fight one alone. One other thing, we have discovered that there are links to a demon army within the legends of the Time Before, but we cannot get any real proof of certainty to this."

"This is indeed grave news Captain. And I notice that there is an elf in your company. I will not pry by asking what your business with the Riders is good elf but I will ask how the demons and the Grey Mages fit together? If indeed they do?"

It was Oren who replied. "We are not sure that they do. After the last war with the Grey Mages they said that we would feel their power rise before the end of 'our' Kingdom and that this would be the Time Before. We have indeed felt their power rise. We know that a great evil of magic is being created deep within the Lost Lands, but every Seer or Ranger we send in fails to return. We have tried force and stealth. Neither has worked so we wait, watch from a distance and try to guess. We know that war is again coming to the Kingdom, but we never expected it from a possible two sides, that the demons might want to make this world theirs once more, while the Grey Mages simply wish to rule it. The Kingdom is sadly trapped between two swords and they are slowly closing in."

"You seem to know quite a bit already. What is it you wish from myself?" Asked the Duke.

"We need to know more about this war the Mages are bringing. Whether it is anything more than a simple war or if it is the start of a darker time to come. The Seers are creating defensive and offensive spells of their own in the City Of Dragons, but we do not have anywhere to start with this army, apart from marshalling the Armies of the Kingdom, and this I fear will not be enough." Finished Oren.

"Well I am afraid I can do nothing more for you than to let you use the libraries of the University. I will contact the librarians and let them know to give you all the aid that they can in solving this mystery. Do you have accommodation arranged yet?"

"We have not had time to rent it so far I am afraid, we came to see you as soon as we arrived. I fear we may also have upset the gentleman as the Universities Information desk today." Replied Trillar.

"Well I wouldn't worry about that. For some reason the scholars of this city try to belittle anyone that does not spend at least half their time buried in books and scrolls. I will find you accommodation in the city to save you the coin. You may start your search for information when ever you wish and I will send messages to each of the libraries immediately and they will be aware of your coming."

"Then we thank you Duke Whetal. Though we would appreciate it should you forget to mention what we are looking for. There will be enough time for panic throughout the Kingdom in the months and maybe years to come without it starting here today or tomorrow." Said Trillar as the Duke led the company from the conference room and arranged for them to be taken to inns that would accommodate them.

The Captain was informed of the locations of the libraries of the university and the city, then the Duke left them to settle and disappeared back into the University grounds.

Drew had been training every day since the order came from the Generals that the armies were to prepare for war without arising too much speculation amongst the population. The other soldiers of the Royal Household Guard informed Drew that this actually meant try not to let your wife or girlfriend tell everyone they know in less than a day.

Falkom had become even harder on Drew since the announcement. He had him training and running twice as long and twice as hard as the other recruits and whenever Drew slacked for even the smallest time he was punished with longer hours of exercise. Drew had come to the conclusion that Falkom was convinced that running made a good soldier.

The result of this treatment was that Drew had become broader of shoulder and fleeter of foot. His skill in weaponry was increasing constantly and he had been told by his instructors that he was by far one of their most adept students and a natural man at arms. Even with their comments though, Falkom would not budge with his treatment of Drew.

It was a cold, wet morning in the City Of Dragons and Drew was running laps of the marshalling yard again. This time for turning up for drills late. He tried to explain that he was late because of the late night he had running identical laps but Falkom was not having any of it. Every time he saw the Riders barracks just away from the yard he thought about Tal. His friend had been gone two weeks now. Brad had heard no news of the expedition and was still slightly upset that he had not been asked to go. When he had asked Falkom he was rewarded with the reply "Your part of the Royal Household Guard. What a great job you do if you would leave your King as soon as your friend leaves on a mission. Ten laps then go get lunch."

Drew finished his laps and stopped to catch his breath. He was gaining more stamina slowly but running in armour was not easy at the best of times. When he was satisfied he could continue with the training session, he returned to the training gym. There were seven other young men, aged between sixteen and twenty that had successfully gained entrance into the Royal Household Guard that were inside practising with the sword. The older privates, were transferred from other army units for showing skill and honour. These Falkom seemed to like, he never shouted and rarely criticised them. He once told Drew that they were *real* soldiers. Men that had seen combat and proven themselves, not boys that had gotten lucky on selection day or had the benefit of the Commander of the Household Guard put in a private word for them. The fact that he was surpassing even these soldiers in weaponry skill did little to abate Falkom.

As Drew entered he was greeted by smiles from the other privates and a glare from Falkom. Without thinking he approached the weapons master and saluted, reporting that he had run the laps and was ready to take part in the class when the weapons master was ready.

Falkom looked at him then nodded pointing to an instructor that was free. Slowly he moved over to the instructor and freed his sword in preparation to receive strike after strike. The practice swords were blunted so that they would not penetrate armour but if you were slow and a blow passed your block you would still feel it. The first time that he had missed the block, he had been pushed back so far he fell to the floor barely able to breath. To him at that point he thought he would never be able to move properly again.

The instructor asked his student if he was ready and when he was answered began the exercise. Drew blocked strike after strike, and still the instructor came. The man had been on the attack for several minutes constantly and showed no sign of slowing. Drew could feel the burn in his arms as he caught another blow with his sword. Then without warning another instructor was attacking him from his right. He barely caught the strike that would have beheaded him before the first instructor was striking again. Drew found himself being pushed back into a corner as both instructors hounded him.

Without thinking he took the first instructors blade on his and pushed back against him, locking the two blades together. As the second instructor moved in with a strike that he thought would send Drew flying, the young soldier stepped through his sword lock releasing the first instructor from the grapple and into the path of the second. The first instructor let out a cry of pain as he received a heavy handed blow to his ribs before collapsing.

Falkom stepped in then and stopped the fight without so much as a single word being muttered. He simply looked from Drew to the two instructors and nodded once before saying that there would be a ten minute rest period now while a new instructor was sent for to relieve the one lying on his side.

Drew left the training gym and walked to the mess to get a drink with the other privates. An older Private who had been transferred from the Kingdoms Eastern Front walked over to a tired and worn Drew. "I think Falkom is starting to slip. He would have thrown three instructors at you if he knew you could tackle two of them." The Privates all laughed softly. It was becoming a standing joke that Drew was the single person in the group that Falkom had taken a disliking to, and everyone was also betting that *he* would eventually get one up on Falkom. Today seemed to be the first glimpse of a success that Drew had seen where the weapons master was concerned.

It was the privates last week as trainees, as of the first day after the weekend the group would be given their watch details and orders. From then on they would have weapons drills twice a week and more free time. It was this news that had brightened the groups mood and had given Drew a reason to laugh again. Soon he may only see Weapons Master Falkom twice a week at most and sometimes even go for weeks without seeing him.

Drew and the Privates finished their drinks and returned to the training gym. Falkom was there along with Commander Denholm. He looked just the same as he had when Drew had reported to him after testing for a Rider and failing. His red sash instantly marked him and his build and posture gave no room to question who was in charge at that time.

"Ok lads. I wouldn't have done this in ordinary circumstances. But these aren't normal circumstances. Due to the increased security alert in the Kingdom, I am forced to train more guards and fast. To that end from this day you are fully fledged soldiers of the Royal Household Guard. Return to your quarters. On your door should be pinned your duties. They start from tomorrow. Oh and lads…well done." With that Commander Denholm smiled and left the gym.

"Ok boys, get your kit together and find out what your duties are. And none of you better foul up. If you do you will have me personally breathing down your neck." With that the weapons master turned and left the gym through the same door as the commander.

All the privates cheered once the weapons master left the hall. Each of them, whether sixteen or early twenties then sprinted from the gym back to their quarters to find out what duty they had been assigned.

It was dinner time in the Palace and Drew and the other privates were eating at their usual table. They had all been discussing what duties they had been assigned. Drew had been hoping for Royal Duty. Instead he had received battlements. It was certainly not the worst duty that one of them had been assigned but he was still slightly disappointed. He was to report to Sergeant Richardson at five hours past mid day, who would be his duty partner. He was the only private to be partnered up with a junior officer and Drew was unsure whether to feel privileged or as though he was not trusted to carry out his duty without supervision.

Drew had asked around and had discovered that battlements meant constant patrolling of the palace walls and grounds. He had been posted on the night duty which had added to his disappointment. Not only would his first duty be plain and routine but also at night so he could not see the city and palace shining in his new role.

After dinner the privates all turned in for their big first day and Drew was no exception. He awoke the next morning later than usual. He realised that he had slept in until about midday. This was the first time that he had the opportunity to do that and so he relished it. Drew finally got up and dressed about two hours past midday and went down to the mess to pick up some lunch. He wandered in and discovered it empty. He cut himself a portion of the bread that had been prepared for lunch and some cheese that was always provided for snacks throughout the day before moving outside to eat his breakfast. The air was cold and sharp and the sky was overcast. Drew thought absently that it may even snow. As if the weather could read his mind, a few minutes later the first flakes of snow came drifting down from the heavens. Drew thought silently to himself *'why me?'*

Five hours past midday was sounded on the Palaces bell and Drew was waiting in the guard post at the base of the entrance to the Palace grounds for Sergeant Richardson to arrive. Within minutes of Drew arriving another man dressed in the blue of the guards walked in through the door. He was a short man yet powerfully built. He had fair hair with blue eyes and was clean shaven. Drew estimated that he was about twenty or not far past that age from his appearance. He greeted Drew politely and said that after he had relieved the guards they were to replace they would start their rounds of the Palace walls.

Drew had brought all his weaponry along with him since he was unsure what he should have brought, and was told he would need would be his short sword and halberd. Drew neatly placed his long sword, mace, knives, and spear against a wall and breathed hard. It had been hard work carrying all his weapons here, especially in armour.

When he was ready he waited for sergeant Richardson to return and before long, the sergeant collected Drew and they began their rounds.

"So you have just been passed out from training eh?" Asked Richardson as they climbed the stairs against the wall that lead to the battlement walk.

"Yes sir, we received our duties yesterday." Relied Drew. His voice made it clear that he wasn't overly happy with his charge.

"Well buck up mate, for new guards this is probably the best duty to get." Continued the sergeant.

"Why is that sir?"

"Because mate, if there is any action that doesn't specifically involve the Royal family it is most likely to occur on this watch. That's why you are with me. Your friends are probably guarding the barracks or weapons stores or vaults deep within the Palace. No mate, this is the best place to gain experience, and the best place to become noticed for advancement if there is any action, if you know what I mean." Finished the sergeant.

"I hadn't thought of it like that before…" Admitted Drew, his mood brightening instantly.

"That's more like the attitude you need to work here mate, keep your humour and never let your guard down and you will thrive in the Guard. Now, we have some rounds. Try to remember the way because tomorrow I'm going to let you lead and I'll only step in if you can't remember the way. Don't worry I don't expect you to get it off the first night, you may take a week or so to get the route in your head. It took me that long anyway!" Laughed Richardson, remembering his first duty three years ago.

Drew followed and tried to remember the route that he would be walking for the foreseeable future, his mood bright and dreams of glory and valour re-igniting after thinking about what Richardson said. The night moved on and Drew was finally a soldier he told himself, finally a soldier.

Tal awoke. It had been about four weeks since he had left the City Of Dragons and about a week since he had arrived in Coladan. He had been spending his days outside with Kelar Gwent in the snow, learning the martial arts as best he could without the guidance of posted instructors. Nevertheless, he was gaining skill and progressing quickly. He had been informed by Kelar and some of the others in the group that he was a natural and after the problems he had with learning the sword and staff, this came as a welcome surprise and relief to Tal.

He left his room and as usual went to report to Captain Trillar. It was at this time he would discover any more information and find out his days plan, even if this just included sparing with Kelar.

The Seers and other Riders, aided by Lord Arten, had discovered little else about the possibility of an attack by the demons or a resurgence of the power of the Grey Mages. One of the few things they had discovered however was that a demon invasion had been prophesised over an age ago by a demon that had died immediately following the delivery of the prophecy. Human kind had only uncovered this when a younger demon attacked a village and the men of that village killed it after barely half an hour of it launching its initial attack. Before the demon had died however, it raged about the coming of their kind to the world as its rulers again, and that all humanity would die or be enslaved by demonkind. This mad rant had been written down on an old scroll by the priest of the village who was present at the creatures' death, and lost over the years before eventually finding its way to one of the libraries of Coladan. The scroll also said that the demons would be many decades in the preparation of this war. The Seers found this incredibly worrying as they had no idea how long the demons had been preparing, or if this was just the ravings of a demon about to die.

Tal walked to the house occupied by Captain Trillar and the rest of the officers and knocked on the door. On hearing the Captain call for him to enter, Tal opened the door and Trillar told him that he was to spend the day again with Kelar. Tal saluted then left. He knew that Kelar would be waiting for him outside ready to start the lesson. Tal didn't know how old Kelar was. He looked like Layland had, he could look both young or old but another feature he shared with Layland was that he always looked lethal whether relaxing or on duty. Tal considered this and looked at some of the other Riders as he walked to the garden of the guest house that the officers were in residency of. For the first time he noticed that all of the officers had this strange characteristic about them. It was as if their faces changed from moment to moment. One minute they were twenty, the next thirty or perhaps even older.

Tal was wondering about this when he met Kelar, and had asked him about it, though the only response he got was that life was strange at times.

The day moved on and Tal was becoming quick at disarming a foe with a weapon, with nothing other than his hands. It was lunchtime when Trillar walked up to Tal and Kelar, informing them that they were to take Brad and head into the heart of the city. There were rumours that a couple of people in the city had been taken from their homes in the night and stolen away on creatures that could fly. The Captain wanted them to go into town in their travel worn clothes, and see if they could find out anything to link these rumours with the Ones of Impurity.

Tal and Kelar went to get changed. Tal was to collect Brad from his room where he had been given the task of learning letters, and then return to meet Kelar before they all set off into the city.

Brad was relieved when he was able to aside his quill and parchment. He quickly got changed into clothing like the others had, a deep brown cloak and grey unremarkable clothes, and then he and Tal returned to collect Kelar. Each was to take one weapon and if asked they were to play the part of mercenaries that had hired themselves out to a merchant to protect his wares on their way from Leahya. Brad took his long sword, Kelar took a sleek looking sword, it was slightly curved and was bladed only upon one side. Its hilt was covered with what looked like leather and around that was material twisted so as to form a design on each side. Tal took his short sword though he prayed once again that he would not have to use it.

As they walked through the city centre they still received a few looks from the population but it was less attention than they had received while in armour and uniform. Kelar stopped and talked to them as quietly over the crowd as he could.

"We'll try the Inns, people with ale in them tend to talk more than those who are sober. Even if they do exaggerate a little."

The trio walked into a tavern that was little more than a room with an old wooden bar along the opposite side to the door with ale kegs lined against the wall. They received some quizzical looks from the patrons as they walked over to the bar and bought a round.

None of the people in the tavern said much. They all kept their voices low at first, but over a period of time when it became clear that the newcomers weren't going to cause trouble the mood relaxed and people started talking a little more freely again.

As a few people entered, Kelar looked to find anyone that may be willing to talk. Tal and Brad had followed Kelar's example of drinking little of their ale and letting most of it get spilled onto the floor or into the pots containing a few sad looking plants.

Eventually three men, already half drunk walked into the tavern and loudly ordered a round. Kelar nodded Tal and Brad and waited for the newcomers to finish their drinks. When they did Kelar emptied his tankard and returned to the bar. As he approached one of the three men looked at him, slightly squinting as though to help him see better.

"I don't think I've seen you or your friends around here before matey." Said the man with a slightly slurred speech.

"You're right on that boss. My friends and I have just finished a contract as guards with a merchant yesterday. So we're drinking away our earnings now before we gamble them away! In truth we also need a bit of healthy company that isn't interested in the price of wool! Can we buy you three a drink?" Replied Kelar already handing the tavern keeper the coins for the other threes drinks.

"Well seeing as you've already paid for them drinks it would be impolite to refuse now wouldn't it?" Said a second man, his speech less sleepy than the others but still quite a way from sober.

The four men walked over from the bar to the table where Tal and Brad were still sitting. When they were all seated Kelar opened the conversation, asking what there was to do in Coladan to relieve the boredom of weeks of guard duties. After a few suggestions of different bars and taverns Kelar started to shift the conversation slightly. He started by telling a story about some giant flying creature flying over head in the night and scaring the pack horses and the merchant. The three pub veterans looked uneasily at each other and when Kelar asked them if anything was the matter the three almost spoke over each other to tell their own stories regarding this monster.

"It was about a week ago now. I was the last of the three of us to see it, I was. I was coming home from the tavern as most do here, I'm not a common drunk I'll have you know, anyway I was walking home down the high street, and no more than fifty feet above my head went soaring this black monster. One minute it looked like a great bat, all black and sleek, yet when it turned I saw its head, it was like a giant bird, but it looked twisted in some way. It was giant, I would bet it wasn't less that thirty feet across!" Rambled the drunken man. He didn't seem to stop for breath the entire time he was talking and he seemed nervous again just recalling the sight of the thing.

Tal and Brad looked at each other then to Kelar, both of them slightly nervous, but Kelar simply looked like he sympathised with the man. After a sip of his drink that Tal and Brad both noticed never actually touched his lips, he asked the other two to tell their tales. They were both set on the same night, and both had almost identical details of a giant creature, yet each time it was mentioned, it grew in size.

Kelar finished his empty mug of ale and thanked the three for their company, before he led Tal and Brad from the tavern. They walked down the street for a few minutes then they ducked into an alley.

"Well, the descriptions they give match those of a Graven, even if the size has been exaggerated slightly. We will try a few more taverns and inns to see if we get the same type of story then head back to the houses." Said Kelar.

"What *is* a Graven though?" Asked Tal slowly.

"A Graven is a stead that the most powerful of the Dark Lords ride. In return for their service the Graven gets to have the riders life force. This way the Graven cannot be killed unless its owner is killed. Still, although it cannot be killed it can be beaten to the point of unconsciousness. However it is strong and fast. They are not a match for a fully grown dragon, but they could still cause nasty wounds to one should it not show proper respect."

"So does this mean that we need to get dragons now? I know we're Riders, but haven't seen a dragon yet." Continued Tal.

"I don't think you will have to wait long to see one Tal, yes I think we are going to need the elders for this one."

"The elders? Who are they?" Asked Brad stepping into the conversation.

"It is just what we call the dragons Brad. They are many, many years older than we, and will be around for a long time yet. So we give them the respect that they deserve."

"Respect? You mean they think?" Said Brad his interest perked.

"Indeed they do Brad. Unlike what the population thinks, we do not control them. They suffer us to help protect the Kingdom. It is from them that we gain our spell casting ability when we ride them. Although we cannot cast spells, they are powerful enough in the arts to use us as a catalyst. They give us access to their reserves and we use them as we would a bow, but with the dragons guidance. It is hard to explain but after you have been promoted to full Rider status and have gained a bit of experience in the field you will start to be trained in this ability slowly. But until then accept that it is the dragons that are in charge when we ride them. They simply listen to our suggestions. Oh, one other thing. You don't know any of this.

It is prohibited to talk to anyone of this, friends, or your past family. Is that clear?"

Tal and Brad felt completely awed. They had been fed information that they weren't expecting and they could do nothing but agree they would tell no one what they had learnt.

The three were leaving the last tavern they were going to visit that day late in the evening. They had spent hours moving from inn to tavern to try to get more proof that the Graven was seen here in Coladan. Even with half the stories being false leads, they had enough evidence that there had been a Dark Lord within the walls of the city on one night.

All three walked back along the high street and took an alley that was unlit to make their journey back to the houses quicker. There were few people in the streets this late and with the rumours circling about monsters. Half way down the alley Tal stopped and was pushed forward by Kelar who whispered softly to him.

"I felt them too. Keep walking I don't want them to know we've felt them. Just be ready to turn and fight."

Tal's heart was beating rapidly within his chest. Under the old cloak he was wearing he griped the hilt of his short sword still hoping he would not have to use it.

They continued to walk at a steady pace. Tal concentrated and thought that he could count six people that were giving off a dark, menacing feeling following them. As they left the alley, Kelar stopped and turned drawing his sword. Tal and Brad did likewise. Brad had his long sword in hand and looked prepared for whatever was to come. Tal felt awkward holding his sword. He never did like swords and he felt more at risk trying to use it than he did without it.

Tal, if you aren't comfortable using the sword, use what you have learnt this week.

Tal looked round. He thought he had heard Kelar talk to him but he was still standing at the entrance to the alley looking like he hadn't moved since he turned to fight.

At that moment Kelar turned and winked at Tal just seconds before eight men in black, armed with swords and clubs came running from the dark alley.

Kelar and Brad found themselves set upon immediately and returned the attack with just as much energy. Each had three attackers trying to reach them but each holding them off. Tal noticed that the would be murderers were hindering each other by attacking three on one. Brad and Kelar had their backs to one another and were doing an ample job at holding their foes at a distance.

Tal did not have much more time to survey the situation as the remaining two advanced on him. One was armed with a sword the other with a club. Tal thought about what he had learned that past week and re-sheathed his sword. His two opponents looked at each other uncertain as Tal took the stance that had become second nature to him over the last week of training.

The man with the club came closer to Tal as did the man with the sword. Tal slid to one side as the sword came slashing down past where his body had been, straight away he found himself catching the arm of the clubbed man so as to block the heavy wooden sap before it connected with his head. A second later Tal was twisting again, under the arm of his captive and turned the club to catch the sword with it. Tal kicked and caught the bladed man square in his chest sending him flying backwards into a wall. Again Tal twisted and removed the club from the remaining foe with one swift move. Without thinking he brought the club down on the mans head resulting in a loud cracking sound as the man slumped to the floor. Before he could regain his breath the man who held the sword was on Tal again. Now he was swinging blindly and Tal found himself backing up rapidly. Within five steps Tal's back was to a wall and he felt trapped. The mans face turned from one of anger to one of self confidence as his approach slowed and his sword came level to Tal's throat. The attacker paused briefly before thrusting, without thought Tal ducked under the blade and threw his shoulder into the mans stomach, carrying him backwards, and eventually to the floor. Tal panicked as he was suddenly pulled from the man and thrown to the floor away from the action but when he looked up he saw it was Kelar, he had pulled Tal from his opponent and proceeded to finish him before he could regain his feet.

Tal looked round to see Brad push his sword into the side of his last foe and pull it free. There were eight bodies lying on the floor in a dark street that had no windows looking down to it. The fight had taken less that five minutes but Tal was completely worn. Kelar cleaned his sword on one of the men's cloaks and Brad did the same.

"I take it you heard me back there then Tal? That's surprising, novice's don't tend to focus their mental attributes for a few years at least." Said Kelar.

Brad just looked at Tal who simply nodded.

"We had best get moving," said Kelar. "there aren't many people about at the moment but the city guard could already be on their way if someone heard the fight and I don't want to have to explain this. Lets get back to the houses quickly."

They all stripped their blood stained cloaks and left the street.

All three ran through the back streets and in the opposite direction to that in which they had came. They emerged onto a lit street again where there were a few remaining market stalls closing for the night. Kelar took time to be seen and even bought a new cup from one stall to make sure that they were remembered away from the scene and in no rush.

It was close to ten hours past midday when the three of them returned to the houses that were set aside for them by the Duke. Tal and Brad were told to go to bed by Kelar, he would go and report to Captain Trillar now. Both boys departed his company without needing to be asked a second time and fell asleep as soon as their heads touched the pillows.

Kelar knocked on Captain Trillar's door and was greeted by the Captain himself. Trillar saw the look on Kelar's face and asked him what had happened.

"This is bad Kelar. I don't think they were just out for your gold. Crime in this city is almost non-existent and they didn't offer you the chance to give them anything. I think they may have been thugs hired by someone to stop you finding out about the Graven, but hired by whom?. I don't know many humans that would work for the Dark Cousins, or that would work for the Grey Mages if not belonging to them. Do you?"

"No Fen, but neither do I know of anyone that would work for Demons. I like this about as much as you do. What ever the Mages or Demons are up to they aren't even taking too much care to keep it secret anymore. That hints that they are close to completing their preparation. And now with ordinary men involved it adds another factor to this mystery that we could do without."

"Well it can't be helped at the moment. I'll station a watch around the house tonight and let everyone know to be on their guard in the future. Go to bed Kelar, you look dreadful." Added Fen Trillar with a slight smile.

"Thanks." Replied Kelar with a sarcastic note to his voice. "One other thing though. Tal picked up a thought I sent to him today. He may be slow on weapons, but his mental abilities are growing daily and he is a natural at the martial arts."

"Did he now? Well that one seems to be an enigma if ever I encountered one. Goodnight Kelar."

"Goodnight Fen."

Chapter 6

A Line Is Drawn

Drew walked along the walls of the Palace that were covered in snow. He had become firm friends with Sergeant Akarn Richardson in the two weeks he had been doing the rounds of the Palace at night. He had found sleeping during daylight hard and still was not used to it completely. He had also found that he got every fourth day to himself when on duty, which he usually spent with the other guards from that watch in a tavern somewhere until the early hours of the morning.

It was half way through his shift and Drew was wondering how Tal was doing. It had been five weeks now and there was still no word. The armies of the Kingdom had been swelling in number. He had noticed that instead of the dozen or so trainees that were usually taken on by the guard over thirty were now on the roles. The regular army was also growing at about the same rate. Soldiers were being recruited from all over the Kingdom and sent to the north west borders as well as the eastern front. The Navy was recruiting seamen and stationing them on the Kingdoms war ships that were moored in Averlay. New ships were being constructed in the same city at the shipyards there, and the Merchant Navy fleet was running in extra steel from the Dwarves of Ulgon Du Yarin in the southern Kingdom of Mountains for the weapon smiths, armourers, blacksmiths, shipwrights and architects that had been hired to prepare the Kingdom for a war of unknown proportions.

Drew continued on to the next call point on his rounds. Akarn was beside him, he had taken to letting Drew do the rounds by himself and only stepped in if Drew came across a difficulty. As Drew approached the check in point, he saw the solitary guard standing there looking out into the city. As the two Guards approached the sentry, they noticed that something was wrong. The man was standing, but he wasn't moving. In fact, no breath could be seen in the cold night air and blood was visible, staining the snow on the floor.

Akarn ran up and examined his colleague. The soldiers' throat had been torn out and he had been propped up using his halberd to look like he was still on duty.

Drew and Akarn both ran as fast as they could back to the guard post and then back to the Household Guards barracks.

As they entered the building at a sprint, the guard on duty wasted no time in ringing the bell stationed inside the entrance. Within minutes, there were bells ringing on each floor of the barracks, and soon over fifty Guards were rushing around the Palace. Drew was taken by Akarn and, discarding his halberd, he took his long sword before spreading the alarm to the general soldiers barracks. They then left to take their positions inside the Palace.

Drew was to proceed straight to the servants' wing and join up with a party searching that section of the Palace and its grounds. Within half an hour, there were soldiers and guards covering every area the Palace. The King and his family had been awakened and were under guard in their royal suite by the best that the Royal Household Guard had to offer.

The patrol was joined by Drew as they were about to search the grounds outside the servants wing. They had made a sweep of the corridors and rooms and decided that if there was anyone in their section they would be outside.

The group split into sub-groups of three, each was to search part of the grounds. Drew and his partners split from the group and started searching the small garden that was used by the Palace staff in their off hours to relax. He walked along by the bushes, looking into the greenery, and where it was too dense, he thrust his sword into them to reassure himself that there was no one hiding within their cover.

Another guard came over to him and handed him a torch to help him see in the dark night. As Drew rounded a corner he saw a shape disappear over the top of a wall carrying something. He shouted to his party and gave chase. The wall was over eight foot in height and drew had to run further down the garden to get through a gate. When he ran up to where the figure had jumped down from the wall he picked up his tracks in the snow. They led off in the direction of the Palace boundaries and towards the city. Drew ran after the intruder as fast as he could, but he never seemed to gain on his prey. He finally caught up with his quarry when he saw the figure being closed on by five men of the city watch.

Drew saw that the figure was not carrying something, but someone. The man that they had been on the run with from the Dark Cousin all those weeks ago was thrown over the trespassers shoulder.

The intruder was wearing complete black. His shirt and trousers almost seemed to absorb the dim light given off from the palace lights and the moons that shone overhead. Around his shoulders hung a cloak that seemed to hang still no matter what movement the dark man made.

As the armed men moved in to circle the figure, it slowed down and without any noticeable action, three men of the city watch were sent rolling backwards to land in a heap on the floor, their limbs twisted in places that gave clear indication that bones were broken. The other two men rushed him with their spears. With one arm the figure took the end of a watchman's spear and twisted it so that the mans back was to his chest. The second mans spear already being trust at the figure, skewered his friend killing him, and proceeded to push straight through the figure and out his back. The intruder ignored the fatal wound and as he had done to the Guard on the battlements tore out the remaining spearman's throat. Drew almost gagged as the man shrouded in darkness tore at the man's neck with his teeth. The poor watchman's blood poured from the artery in his neck and covered the snow by his feet in an ever expanding puddle of steaming red lifeblood. The figure then pulled the spear out from his body and plunged it into the stomach of the watchman writhing about on the floor, his blood still draining from his body.

As the dark figure turned to continue his escape Drew saw a face that was as white as the snow, his hair was long and his eyes were a blazing red even in the dark of night. The figure snarled – if that was what it could be called – at the five dead men around it, revealing an array of fangs instead of teeth. With three steps, it ran towards the Palace border wall and jumped. It easily made the top of the ancient stone structure, even though it stood over thirty feet into the air, and disappeared over to the other side.

Drew stood in the Palace grounds as though he were a statue. He had never thought that anything like what he had seen could exist. To him it felt as though it was a scene from a nightmare. A creature, dark, foreboding and almost as though it did not truly exist, had walked into the Palace without trouble and kidnapped someone that was under the closest guard and magical protection, then left without effort through five armed men.

He was still standing there when the rest of his group arrived. They all stopped when they had seen him and asked him where the intruder went.

"Over the wall, after killing those five watchmen." Was all Drew said in response.

It was the following day when the conference was called to order. Yet again, Drew was waiting outside the conference hall in its antechamber, waiting to be called to replay what he had seen last night.

The door opened and again a page asked him to enter. In the room were the same people that were present five weeks ago. The King, Prince, Princess, Commander Denholm, Lord Rayburn and Lord High Seer Tiersing were in the same positions as last time but each looked a great deal more worried than previously.

"Come in Drew." Said the King. He motioned to the seat at the table they sat on.

"Drew, please tell us of the events that you witnessed last night. I understand if you don't want to, but this is something I'm afraid you will have to do." Spoke commander Denholm.

Drew had been in shock for most of the night he had barely spoken two words since he was found. It was nearly midday before anyone had finally managed to hold a conversation with him. It was now early evening and he was being asked to reconstruct in his own mind the traumatising events that had transpired the previous night.

It was early the next morning before he left the conference hall. People were still rushing about the Palace. Although nothing had happened since the previous night every soldier that was stationed in the City of Dragons had been assigned extra duties. There were not a group of soldiers that numbered less than ten on watch at any one time.

Rumours were spreading through the Palace like wildfire. The King was dead, or a devil of the night had cursed the whole city, no the entire Kingdom.

Some of the population had started to evacuate the city even though the palace staff and city watch were assuring them that nothing out of the ordinary was likely to occur.

Drew walked back to his quarters, he was wrung out and felt as though he had aged by twenty years in two days. Humour had left him and he found himself looking no further ahead than his next meal or sleep, even if that sleep would bring vivid images of an evil over and over again.

Looking up from the floor he realised that he had walked passed the barracks. When he turned, he saw more of the Guards rushing out in full armour. Without thinking, he ran to catch them up. His muscles ached yet he did not stop.

"What's happening?" called Drew to one of the Guards as he ran towards the Palace.

"The city of Peters Hold has been completely destroyed, two weeks past. Word arrived half an hour ago. The armies march for the East tonight."

Drew felt his legs stop. Those words seemed to strike him like nothing before had. *War.* Through his entire childhood he had wanted nothing other than to be a mighty hero and win honour in battle serving his King. But he was a man now. He would most likely get his chance at battle. Did he still want it? Fears ran through his body. Would he see his next birthday? Would he see Tal again? His family? In two days his childhood had been stripped away from him, his innocence gone. And now, in a matter of seconds, his entire life had been altered, and he knew not yet if that too was to be ripped from him and from this earth.

Legs, feeling like they were about to give way, somehow carried Drew to his quarters. Pinned to his door was a sheet of parchment folded and sealed with Commander Denholm's crest. Slowly, and with no small amount of apprehension, he opened the letter.

Guardsman Earemon,

> *You are to report to Captain Loytan at the main gates to the palace at midday today. You should take all necessary equipment for a swift journey to the ruins of Peters Hold.*
> *Your duty is the protection of Prince Allin. More will be explained to you when the rest of your company assembles*

at midday.

> *Take care. There may be many dangers on the road ahead of you. Remember your duty to the royal family and no matter what should occur you will maintain honour and courage.*

> *May the Gods look upon you with the favour you and the Kingdom deserves.*

Cyran Denholm.

Drew felt his legs start to buckle under him and caught himself before he fell. There were similar notes pinned to other Guard's doors, though what they contained remained a mystery to him. Wearily he opened the door to his quarters to find a new uniform folded for him sitting upon his bunk. It was the same cut as his uniform was now, but it was of stronger weave and thicker material.

Exhausted Drew collapsed on his bed as soon as he had removed his new uniform from his bunk and fell into a restless sleep.

A golden dragon circled over the ruins of Peters Hold. It's enormous frame casting a shadow onto the ground below. His mount had been called the instant that news had arrived of Peters Hold and now soared above the city. Nothing now moved within boundary of the collapsed walls. There was smoke billowing into the sky from buildings that were still smouldering.

Lord Rayburn looked down from the back of his ride, wondering if any man, woman or child survived the slaughter below. There were carcases littering the ground and areas around the city defences. Both human and demon dead cluttered the streets and decorated the remains of the walls, their blood collecting and mixing in depressions.

Almost as an afterthought, the veteran Rider once more surveyed the wreckage. He noted that there were no corpses of children anywhere to be seen amongst the carnage. Fixing it in his mind, he continued his search. From his mount came feelings of pain, anger and disgust all mixed into a complex ball of emotions. Absently he patted the great creatures neck in agreement.

There was now a feeling of evil over this place. It had once been a city garrison against any attacks on the Kingdom from the Dead Lands. Although there was little water in these lands, occasionally a group of marauders would locate a small spring and set up a camp there allowing them to strike against the Kingdom and then retreat without being followed. It was not a great concern however and there were only a hundred soldiers stationed there at any one time.

'Even though, there must have been a large number of demons to cause this much wreckage. And where did they come *from*? And *why*?' Thought Rayburn as he continued his investigation of the city.

That demons could attack a city was a thought of great worry and concern, and to most terror accompanied those feelings, but from the corpses that lay strewn round the scene, only smaller, younger demons had attacked.

Rayburn thought back to the lore he had studied in his younger days. The last known attack by demons en masse had been years past. So many years in fact that there were no details of the attack recorded in writing. The knowledge had been passed down from leader to friends to sons that became leaders and so on throughout the ages and from the tales the only reason that humanity had survived was the action taken by the mages of the time. They had created multiple tears in the fabric of time and space, forming a vortex of energy that pulled demons into a different realm while mankind hid beneath the earth in magically fortified caverns. This act had also unfortunately left the world in a desolate and unhealthy state where mankind was forced to struggle to survive.

There had been sightings of demons throughout his long life, but when a party of Riders had gone searching, there was nothing to be found. It now seemed that the demons had found a way to cross back into this dimension and that they were launching attacks. But why only the younger demons? There were certainly enough of them, but they posed no real threat until massed as they had been. Why not send in stronger demons and save their numbers? And where had the horde vanished to after the attack?

The questions gave way to no answer that Rayburn could think of. Dispirited he glided away from the ruins of Peters Hold and sped off into the distance on the back of his enormous mount.

In the darkness of a half collapsed building something stirred. Its dark shape bulky and heavily muscled. Fangs and razor sharp talons glinted in the shadowed light as it moved from its cover.

The demon looked in the direction of the dragon speeding away. It held no fear of dragons and their Riders, it told itself once again. With a snarl that bared the rest of its fangs and allowed a dark putrid liquid to drip from the end of each tip, it spun and disappeared into another building and down into the earth beneath.

Soon. Was all that ran through the creatures mind as it vanished from sight of the sun.

A knock roused Drew. He came to, and with an effort dragged himself from the bed to answer his door. Standing outside was Richardson, his kit already packed and ready to leave.

"What time is it?" Asked Drew.

"Close to midday. You had best get packed, there are people gathering at the gates already." Replied Richardson.

Drew just spun and wasted no time in discarding the creased uniform that he had been sleeping in, and changing into the new uniform that had been unceremoniously thrown across his quarters when he had returned from the council. Richardson chuckled softly to himself and started to help his friend pack.

In short time, both men were walking towards the main gates to the Palace and reporting in to Captain Loytan. Akarn Richardson moved over to a horse offered to him by a steward and placed his belongings to reduce the burden on the animal then jumped into the saddle.

Drew froze. Looking around he saw over fifty Guards. Each mounted. Another steward stepped forward and moved to give him the reins to his horse. Gesturing the groom to wait one moment Drew ran over to Richardson. He quickly and hysterically informed the sergeant that he didn't know *how* to ride a horse to the complete surprise of his friend.

"You weren't instructed in this during your training?" Asked Richardson puzzled.

"No, we were passed out quickly because of the troubles and I guess they didn't teach us that." Replied Drew becoming increasingly worried.

"Wait here a second Drew." With that, Richardson moved his horse over to where the Captain was now mounting his own ride. Drew saw the two talking and then Captain look over to him. He wanted nothing more than for the ground to open up and take him.

Richardson saluted then made his way back.

"Well, the Captain says that there is nothing that can be done now. Therefore, I'm going to instruct you as we move. Lesson one, if you cant do anything yourself, get help. I will help you get on the damn thing but next time you're doing it yourself ok?" laughed Richardson jumping down.

When Drew was seated on his horse, Richardson moved next to him and gave him the basics of riding. "Try not to worry too much, they are well trained and will do most of the hard work themselves. Just do as I do and by the end of the week you will either be competent or extremely sore…come to think of it you will probably be sore anyhow."

The Captain called for the group to form up and out of consideration for Drew, Richardson was allowed to ride next to him to keep an eye out. Looking round the group, Drew counted six men to a row, and ten rows of Guards and then the Captain at the front. At that moment, Captain Loytan called the company to attention. From the centre of the Palace grounds, Drew saw the Prince riding towards them. He was wearing a steel breastplate and leg pieces with chain protecting his arms. At his side hung a sword with a curved blade, much like those used to the north by cavalry units. Accompanying him were five other men. Armed and armoured likewise, they moved with a grace in the saddle that spoke of experience and their faces showed a lifetime of service in the company of weapons.

As they moved closer Captain Loytan saluted his Prince. The salute was returned and Prince Allin addressed the company.

"I know that there was little explained to you before now. For that I am sorry. But there have been many councils leading to this conclusion and it was a conclusion that we all hoped was not to be. We are at war. The small party of Riders and Seers we sent to Coladan has come under several small scale attacks from assassins and hired swords." Drew's heart stopped at hearing this. Thoughts of his friend came to him. The Prince continued. "Thankfully there have been no casualties among the party and they have discovered some useful information.

"Our task is to survey the ruins of the city of Peters Hold and from there, to move in which ever direction we believe the threat may lay and probe the situation. We move in armour for we know not the threat that may lie ahead. I do not know how long we shall be away, but I pray that it will be no more than a scouting mission. Now let us move."

Prince Allin, the second prince of the Kingdom of Dragons moved forward, the Royal Household Guard following behind. *I can take care of manual tasks father, I just hope the Seers can take care of the Grey Mages…*

The company left the Palace, and in time the city. They headed east and pushed at a fast pace. They expected to reach the ruins that were Peters Hold in three, maybe four weeks at the most.

Drew was riding next to Richardson, picking up hints and tips about how to keep his horse under control. He had accepted that he may be on the road for a long time, and so he tried to settle into a rhythm taking everyday is it came, at least that was his plan.

It had been just over a week. The company had passed the city of Leahya a day ago, pausing simply to purchase supplies before moving on again. It had been a hard ride and Drew was beginning to gain some measure of confidence on the horse. Akarn had been correct, it was well trained and easy to control when he stopped fighting against the unnatural feeling of being carried.

At the start of the journey, Drew had no real knowledge of an army life, but slowly he was becoming the soldier he had always dreamed of. After the struggle of learning to ride, he had begun to understand the true meaning of soldiering. He had been accepted by the others in the company, and he was determined to live up to all of their expectations.

The march continued apace and Drew had started to watch the other members of the company. Each person was handling the possibility of a battle in their own ways. Richardson had grown silent, his eyes constantly scanning the lands they passed, searching for an enemy that was hidden or maybe for an enemy that wasn't even there.

The Captain was ordering shorter breaks and the watches were double manned. Every slight lapse in the tasks that were set, was picked up on, and addressed within minutes.

The Prince was spending more time with the Captain during rest periods but away from the men. To everyone else he had simply become sombre.

Some of the soldiers were growing increasingly brash and jumpy, others keeping to a few friends and not leaving their company.

It was an air of tension that hung thickly in the company. and Drew was suffocating in it.

It took a further two weeks to reach the lands of Peters Hold. The march had been stepped up, even through the snow, after the company reached the Duchy of Myllarad. Rumours had been heard that the ruins of Peters Hold were occupied. By who or what, no person would say, but that the lands were being used for evil purposes was mentioned in every version of the tale, also that no man, either soldier or commoner would enter the lands surrounding the ruins was a cause for great concern for the Prince.

Drew had grasped the basics of horse riding and although his entire body was sore, he had started to enjoy the ride. About an hour from the city, the Prince called a halt.

"From here on I want no talking unless it is necessary, I don't know what to expect, but lets not give whatever, or whoever it is a chance know where coming." With that, he turned his horse and continued at a slower pace.

After thirty minutes, another halt was called. The Prince sent two of his personal guard ahead to scout the path on foot. There had been a feeling of disquiet in the company, growing every minute as they closed on the ruins, and the Prince wanted the area secured.

The scouts had been gone for approximately ten minutes when a member of the Household Guard drew his sword silently. Every member of the company followed his example as they heard the sound of metal clashing on metal a small way ahead. Within seconds, one of the scouts returned running flat out. A scream could be heard from ahead and the sounds of conflict halted. The scout took his horse and jumped into the saddle shouting the word 'Flee!'

The company wasted no time with questions and turned to retreat in the direction they had come. The Prince was pushed to the head of the retreating company, putting him furthest from whatever danger was following.

Drew was at the rear of the company and risked a look back over his shoulder as he rode. From the horizon came a sound of thunder. The snow underfoot was must have been muting the full extent of the noise yet it was clear to Drew that there was a great number of attackers following. His heart stopped when he saw what was chasing them. Cresting the horizon were enormous disfigured shapes. Great flying monsters glided up with enormous speed, overtaking bulky dark shapes running through the snow that was slowly being turned to slush. Some of the beasts were running on four legs, others on two. What Drew noticed most was the feeling of terror that was entering his being. The monsters that were running were closing on them, even if it was slowly, but the flying creatures were gaining on them fast and would be upon them in minutes.

Drew looked back ahead, he realised that he had slowed whilst looking back and pushed to catch up with the retreating company. He called to Akarn, telling him what was following and how soon they would be set upon. The Sergeant nodded, speeding his horse ahead. He moved next to his Captain and repeated Drew's observations. Drew risked another look back. The wings of the flyers looked beaten and full of holes, though their speed was not lessened for it. Their faces looked like grizzled, snarling, masks from a nightmare. Their claws black and razor sharp at the end of long muscular arms and legs.

Drew's heart was racing as he fled from the evil that pursued them. Great cries from the beasts echoed in the air around them.

He was praying to the gods that he survive this, that he could see his friends and family again. Another look. The creatures were almost upon them. Drew closed his eyes and hung low to the neck of his mount, the air rushing past his face. There was a smell in the air that could only have been coming form the beasts closing on them. Suddenly a searing heat could be felt by the company and Drew opened his eyes. Above them was a score of Dragons, their cries clear and strong. From their backs, figures in red and black were emitting blasts of white energy, while the Dragons themselves spewed forth great jets of flame. As the balls hit the flying creatures, they exploded into flames, consuming the demons in seconds. It took barely an instant for the others to realise that they could not best the Dragons and flew off in different directions, themselves now becoming the hunted.

Drew looked back again. The beasts on foot were still closing and the brief thought of reprieve fled as he realised that there were over two hundred still chasing the mere fifty guards.

Looking forward, he settled for pushing as much as he could, to stay alive and ahead of them one second longer. For the first time in the entire flight Drew actually focused on what lay ahead and he almost shouted in elation when he saw at least seventy Dragon Riders lined up ahead of them.

As the Guards reached the ranks of the Riders, the Rider in charge offered an invitation to join them which was enthusiastically welcomed by all in the company as they wheeled their horses and drew weapons.

Drew was trembling. Whether from excitement, terror, anxiousness or plain adrenalin he could not decide, but he stood next to Sergeant Richardson, sword drawn and ready. *For what?* He asked himself.

The Riders took up positions flanking the Guard, their array of weaponry an awesome sight. Riders with curved blades, straight blades, axes, maces, some with bows, others with knives. It seemed like there was no pattern to the arms that the Riders carried but Drew didn't care. He was simply glad that their number had more than doubled with the addition of the Riders, and whether they came armed with clubs or ballistae he was content that he may now have a chance of surviving this.

The Riders were wearing different armour as well he noticed. Some in the chain and cloak that Layland had worn when he arrived in Dukeray, others in black Plate Mail, and full helms.

Time had slowed for Drew and all sound had ceased, the demons were closing, but slowly. Each movement anyone made was extended and drawn out. The slightest shift in the horse beneath him lasted for hours, and the bead of sweat that left his forehead took a day to run the length of his face.

He looked sideways and saw the Riders and Guards rushing forward to engage the demons. The Guard was fighting in perfect unison, each person lined next to another Guard, slowing the advance of the demons. The smaller demons were falling quickly, the larger forcing the Guards back slowly. If a man fell, another instantly took his place in the wall of steel they had created. Sergeant Richardson was cleaving a path ahead of him. His clean armour now covered in black sticky blood. There was a gash in his left arm that seeped blood gradually yet he did not slow his slashing. The Riders were not in units or lines, instead they were spinning through the demons carving arms or heads from bodies before moving on. Several of the larger demons found themselves skewered by a pole arm from one Rider while another beheaded it. Both Riders would then disappear into the frenzy as though they had never been there.

Drew looked ahead and saw that a small demon was closing on him, the motions still long and drawn out. He raised his sword and let out a cry, bringing it down. The blade made contact with the small demons head, splitting his horse-like skull in two, spraying a dark blood in all directions. Time exploded with the blow, the slow drawn out battle had erupted into a cacophony of noise and visions. No longer was there time to sit and watch, no longer was there time to think. Everything was happening and it was happening now.

Sword in hand, rising and falling, slicing left and right, on and on it went. Without noticing it, he realised that he was now in the front row on the wall and was fighting with several other Guards to bring one large demon to his death. He felt a great pressure in his side and he realised that the Guard next to him had been de-horsed by a backhand blow from the demon, and had collided with Drew knocking him to the ground as well. Getting up from the floor, sword still in hand he suddenly appreciated the size of the demon he had been fighting. The beast must have stood a good ten feet in height and was built almost as wide. Without thinking, Drew rushed him from the side, trying to keep from being seen. He darted to the back of the demon and with one thrust, plunged his sword deep into the creatures' hip. With a speed that surprised Drew it spun swinging out wildly at its tormentor. Its blow collided squarely, and Drew was sent sprawling to the ground, pain exploding in his ribs.

From the floor Drew saw as the last few demons were dispatched by the Guards and Riders. So different were their styles thought Drew before the light faded from his eyes. There was no pain as darkness covered him.

Drew opened his eyes. He was laying in a tent on a trail bed and had been unclothed and bandages applied to his ribs. Looking around he saw he was alone in the tent and so decided to get up. As he stood, he felt a pain tear through his chest that eased off as he was fully standing. When he had dressed, he discovered that he only received any pain when he used the muscles or twisted his ribs.

Leaving the tent he looked round to try to get some understanding of where he was. It was drawing close to night and there was a modest camp, though very few people were to be seen. Hearing voices from a nearby tent he moved closer to try and hear what was being said but was drawn away by the smell of cooking meat. He followed the smell and found a small campfire with a couple of dozen men gathered around it. He recognised several of the faces as Guards that he had travelled with, while others he took to be Riders.

As he approached, he saw Richardson, his left arm in a sling, stand up and call out to him.

"Drew! Over here!" called Richardson happy to see him. Drew started to run over to the Sergeant only to be reminded of his condition and nearly fall to the floor in pain. Several of the men both Riders and Guards started to move towards him to help him when he waved his hand to halt them telling them that he was okay. As he got up space was made for him at the fire and food was given to him on a small plate.

"Did you know Drew, you're a hero now." Said Richardson a small smile of his face.

"What do you mean?" replied Drew still groggy from his wound.

"You struck the fatal blow to the leader of whatever passes as a squad to the demons. You're the champion of that little scuffle!" explained Richardson, still looking somewhat amused at the outcome.

"Did I? I thought the leader would be bigger than that." Said Drew.

"Slow down laddie!" said an older Guard at the fire. "That beast was big enough for me, I'd not want to see larger with all the damage that one did to us!"

"Old Gregory is right there Drew, he was big enough to kill several of us by himself. Let's not go inviting nastier to our table now." Said Richardson.

The thought of several Guards being killed brought back just how dangerous the situation had been to Drew. He let out a long, slow breath and gave quick thanks to the gods that he was alive. In silence, he ate the food that was in front of him, and only when he had finished and had time to collect his thoughts he asked about the dead.

"Eighteen Guards dead, eleven injured, two of those serious. The Riders aren't saying what their cost was though." Said Richardson looking across the fire to the Riders sitting with them who just smiled sadly and continued their slow eating.

"How long have I been asleep?" asked Drew.

"Just a few hours, you were carried back here by Dragon, though I doubt you remember it. The able ones had to walk though. Took us six hours and just as we arrive and eat, your awake. Most thought you would be asleep until the morning."

Drew nodded and sat there quietly, savouring the small warmth offered by the fire on a cold night.

Gareth Rayburn sat in his tent with Prince Allin and Captain Loytan. Explaining the situation as he saw it.

"We arrived two days ago. There was a feeling of evil in the area and the Riders decided to investigate. We have been scouting along the edge of the borders of the lands that the enemy now holds, trying not to let them gain knowledge of our presence. We were camped here when a lookout reported that there were Guards under attack by demons near the city. We came in the quickest time possible. Thankfully it was quick enough."

"Thankfully for the us, yes." Replied the Prince, "But how did you reach us so quickly? We're twenty miles from the battlefield."

"We have certain advantages for travel that few possess your Highness." Replied Lord Rayburn casually.

"Yes, I suppose you do. What is happening here Lord Rayburn? Where did all those demons come from?" asked the Prince

"We don't know Highness, only that they are here and multiplying in numbers. They have managed to turn Peters Hold into quite a nice fortress and are manning it sufficiently to stop us from retaking it at the moment. With the spring thaw starting I would not like to speculate on the numbers that will occupy that city before long. I dread to say this but I think this could be a long war. Maybe even the one that was prophesised." Said Rayburn.

"Prophesised?" asked the Prince.

"Yes, of course, you would not have heard. The Riders in Coladan have discovered that a prophecy from ages past claims the demons will return to seize this world as theirs once more." Explained Rayburn in a matter of fact way.

"So were battling prophecy now. This is looking worse by the day my friends." Said the Prince. His heart starting to sink in his chest.

"One thing is for sure Highness, the demons have drawn a line. What are we going to do about it?" Said Rayburn. The three men sat in silence contemplating on that thought.

Chapter 7

Discoveries

It was morning. The camp was awake and bustling with activity. It had been decided that a full quarantine was needed around the ruins that were Peters Hold. However, for that to be possible a much greater number of men would be required than was currently stationed around the city.

Drew had been relieved of duties until his ribs healed, or until he was needed, whichever the sooner. He was sitting next to Sergeant Richardson talking about the previous days battle, when Captain Loytan approached. He nodded to the two Guards and looked to Drew.

"I just wanted to see how you are. Make sure you are feeling ok after your stunt yesterday." Said the Captain with no hint of a smile on his face.

"I'm fine sir. Nothing that won't heal in time." Replied Drew.

"Good, see that you recover fast. We don't have the men to let you sit around for weeks on end." With that, he turned and left Drew looking at his back in disbelief. He had nearly died to bring down that demon and now he was being reprimanded for it?

Noticing the way Drew was looking at the back of the captain, Richardson leaned over to him, "Don't take it too hard. He is concerned about you but will not say it out right. That he came to see you shows that you have been noticed, and that is a good thing. I bet he hasn't gone to see the other wounded."

Simply nodding Drew turned his attention to what may happen next. A messenger had been sent to the City of Dragons informing the King of the situation and requesting troops to ring the city and try to stop the spread of the demon invasion of the Kingdom.

It was during this moment of thought that a call was made for all Guards to gather for new orders at Prince Allin's tent. Drew managed to get there himself even though it caused some pain and waited to hear what was to happen.

The Prince was waiting there for them as they arrived, he looked like he had slept very little the previous night, his clothes unchanged from the day before, his eyes shadowed black with a lack of sleep.

"A decision has been made. We are travelling to Borders Edge to organise the evacuation of the city." At this, there was an intake of breath from most members of the Guard though none actually spoke. "I know it may seem like an extreme action, but we do not know how the demons arrived here to take Peters Hold. Borders Edge is now out on a limb so to speak. To reach the rest of the Kingdom by land they must make a long journey, and so must the Kingdom to reach them should the demons press their occupation further. We will make straight for the city and get families moving as fast as possible. There we will remain until the army garrison stationed there can turn the city into a fortress, this we hope will allow fast access to the east by way of ship should the need arise.

"Those of you that are not fit to ride will be left here to rest. When you are able, you should return to the City of Dragons for further orders. Tarry not though, for the fate of our Kingdom may be in the balance at this very moment and your people need as many blades fighting for them as they can get.

"Get moving, we leave in two hours." The Prince looked worried. His voice lacked the energy it had the day before, it was now powered by urgency.

Drew looked round and saw his fellow Guards starting to return to their tents to make ready for the ride. Captain Loytan walked over to him looking at him in a way Drew could not quite define. "Will you be joining us Drew? Or will you be staying here?" asked the captain in a neutral voice.

"I will come sir, my ribs can't get any more damaged by riding can they?" Replied Drew, hoping that he wasn't going to cause greater harm to himself by the horse.

"Stout lad. You may make a Guard yet." Said the Captain before saluting and leaving to make his own equipment ready.

Now completely confused by the man, Drew simply left to gather his kit together. Walking across the camp he ran into Akarn who had already packed his equipment and was making his way to the horses.

"You coming then Drew?" Asked Akarn, a smile on his face.

"Yes, I wasn't sure if you would be though, your arm looks pretty messed up." Replied Drew.

"It will be fine, could leave a nice scar as a trophy too." Continued Richardson.

"You want a scar?" Asked Drew in amazement.

"Not really, but if I'm going to have a demon tare into my arm, I want something to show for my bravery to the ladies back home." Supplied Richardson winking as he continued towards his horse.

Drew could not help but laugh even though it hurt him to do so. *Is this what comes of years of service in the Guard? May the gods help me!*

He found carrying his pack hard work, and was relieved when he had it strapped to his horse. Richardson offered to help him into the saddle but when he let out a cry as pressure was placed on his bad arm, causing Drew to fall and cry out with the pain in his ribs, they both decided that using a mounting block would be the simplest answer to both their predicaments, much to the amusement of the remaining Guards.

The Guards now numbered thirty six men plus the Captain, the Prince and his four personal guards. The rows were reduced to six men in width and the strongest were placed on the outer ranks. Drew found that riding with broken ribs was no easier task than packing the horse, still, he was not going to quit, he felt he had a duty to his Kingdom now and nothing was going to stop him from carrying that out.

It had been five weeks since he was attacked, and there had been no further attempts on the Riders since. Tal had been training vigorously with Kelar every day after the attack. He was now more comfortable without a weapon than he felt he ever could be with one. This aside however he found that when he was using a curved, light blade, he could incorporate it into his movements with relative ease.

They had discovered little else about the prophecy regarding the demons. Only that there was a single event that would mark the completion of the demons preparation and the start of the war proper. However what the event was, had not been uncovered.

The small party had been recalled to the City of Dragons with all available speed and Tal had thought that would mean a forced march. He had been surprised and elated however to discover that it in fact meant travel with the aid of Dragons.

When news arrived of this, he had been counting the days before they left, and every second spent in the company of Kelar had lent towards Tal probing him about Dragons.

The day before they left, the Seers reported that they had their own ways of travelling back to the city and would not require the aid of Dragons. Personally Tal wondered why anyone would give up the opportunity to be carried by a Dragon, however the Seers left that day, and had not seemed too upset that they would not get to see the fabled creatures of legend.

The Riders packed up their equipment and made their way from the city of Coladan. As they left, they stopped at Duke Whetal's house and thanked him for the use of the houses that had been acquired for their use while staying in the city.

They left Coladan to the same suspicious looks they received when entering the city. The small company marched for one day before calling a halt. They set up a camp that would do them for a single night but were informed that they were not to settle in too well.

Tal had grown more comfortable around Hazel, and Brad and Cholla seemed inseparable these days. They all sat together around the fire that night, talking together. Brad had become acceptable with pen and parchment and was beginning to record the events that were transpiring on their trip. Tal had also started to learn though he was not even close to the level of Brad, he found himself asking how to spell words repeatedly.

They were still talking when a great gust of air swept through the camp. Tal looked up to see several dark shapes converging on their position. Each member of the company smiled to themselves. They could *feel* the Dragons, feel the rightness of them and how they fit into the universe.

"Ok people, get your kit together, we're going home!" called Captain Trillar. Each Rider was ready within five minutes and the campfire was covered with soil. Tal found himself being urged towards a giant black Dragon. Upon its back was a Rider with the most studs of rank he had seen yet. They seemed different to the others he had seen also, they were not simply gold studs that were pinned to the shoulder, but crescents that were made of silver. Each Rider that was seated upon a Dragon, looked ancient yet youthful all at once and each looked battle tried and tested and tougher than stone.

The Dragon itself was immense. Its huge head seemed friendly almost, even with great fangs shining in the moonlight and green eyes that pierced the darkness. The horns that lined its head seemed pure white in a beautiful contrast to the deep black scales that covered its body. Measuring the size of him, Tal guessed that he was at least thirty feet in length and again that in wingspan.

He saw that upon the back of the Dragon was a seat for the Rider to position himself in, but the other Riders on his back simply sat behind the older Rider along the Dragons spine.

As Tal was given a boost onto the Dragons back, he saw that he was riding with Kelar. Each Dragon took two of the company before lifting themselves into the sky with one great beat of their wings. Tal had expected that he would need to hold on tightly to avoid falling, but there was not even a feeling of movement as their ride took off.

Tal thought he could sense amusement from the Dragon and chuckled softly to himself at his foolishness. *How can I sense what a Dragon feels? Its ridiculous.*

This time Tal thought he could sense the great creature correcting him and started to doubt his own sanity. Kelar leant over to him and explained that this was how the Riders communicated to the Dragons while they were being carried. He also informed Tal that it was rare that a novice could communicate with a Dragon, let alone understand what was being said.

Tal felt an agreement from the Dragon and began to feel out of his depth. A reassuring feeling came to him from his ride.

As they continued to ascend into the sky Tal asked Kelar when they would start to move towards the city, in response Kelar simply replied "Wait and see!"

The Dragon and its passengers continued to climb for a few more seconds and Tal was glad that it was night so that he could not see how high they had flown. There was a slight feeling of being pulled back and air rushing past their faces before the comfortable feeling returned.

Tal looked around and thought he could see the landscape below – or what he thought was the landscape – blur as it sped past. In minutes, there was a light on the horizon which quickly became a glow of lights from a city speeding towards them. As they sped closer to the lights Tal noticed the Dragon slow down almost instantly, and then saw the City of Dragons ahead of them.

He was in complete awe. He had never thought that travelling could be done so fast without the aid of magic. *Who said magic* wasn't *involved?* He asked himself.

They flew over the walls of the city from a height that Tal never thought possible, though he didn't feel scared of the distance off the ground for one instant. They glided steadily over the city until they reached the Palace and then slowly, and in large circles glided down to the great marshalling yard where the Dragon allowed its passengers to climb down.

Feeling totally awe struck, Tal tried to thank the Dragon for letting him ride, there was a friendly feeling given back from the creature before it spread its large wings and took to the sky again to let another land where it had just been.

Tal and Kelar left the marshalling yard and walked to the Palace to report to Captain Holbrook. When they knocked on his door, they were called in and found themselves in the company of several other officers that Tal had not met.

"Hello Kelar, Tal, I'm sorry to say this but you will be leaving soon. We need a force of Riders to travel to Peters Hold. We already have a small band there, but there is going to be a complete quarantine to prevent the demons leaving if possible, and we need as many Riders there to lend support as we can get. You will be carried by Dragons to our camp in the east and from there be under the command of General Cristof. There will be a number of Seers there as well though most of the numbers will be made up from the regular army. You are to keep a low profile, I don't want to have to be explaining why there are so many Riders interfering in the army's business.

"Oh one other thing. Tal I have been informed that even though your progress in weapons is slow, you have made excellent progress with your hand to hand and mental abilities. Keep up the good work son, if you can improve your weapon skill you could be made up to Rider quite soon. There are few novices that have seen what you have of the Riders and have the natural ability you seem to." Said the Captain with a slight smile on his worried face.

"Yes sir!" Replied Tal enthusiastically as both he and Kelar saluted and left the office.

When they were both outside, Tal asked Kelar, "What is this about demons?!" He said, now worried.

"While we were gone the city of Peters Hold was completely destroyed by a host of demons. A detachment of the Royal Household Guard was sent to investigate and they were attacked. Several were lost but there were a few dozen Riders also investigating the area who went to their aid and together they managed to fight their way out. Where they came from, and what they want we don't know, other than it may have something to do with that prophecy" Answered Kelar.

Tal thought of his friend. Was Drew sent to Peters Hold? Was he still alive? Pushing unwanted thoughts from his mind he continued. "What did the Captain mean, I was progressing with my mental abilities?"

"Well, for a Rider to progress through the ranks of our order, it is not simply enough to be good with weapon and quill. The reason you are a Rider and not simply a soldier is because of a natural gift that Riders seem to be born with. We all have the ability to use our mind to feel the terrain we are in, to sense the enemy approaching before we can see them as it were. We also have the ability to communicate with certain animals. Possible Riders are sought out by our order and invited to attend the Tests.

"The Captain was referring to your 'conversation' with the Dragon. Mental attuning is taught later in your career, once you have been made up to a full Rider. You seem to have gained the use of this gift very early on in your life and with no training.

That is rare indeed. Captain Holbrook was trying to get you to knuckle down with your weapons and get made up as soon as possible so that you can progress. He believes that you may be a very powerful Rider when you are trained to your full potential." Said Kelar as though it was obvious.

Tal considered this and just accepted it without trying to reason it out. He was too tired to try now. "So how long do novices train before they become Riders?" he asked, regretting the question as soon has he had asked it.

"It's different for each person, you have been a novice for how long now? Three months? There have been novices that have been promoted to Riders in half that time, and others that have not made Rider for years. The length of time as a novice does not limit your chances of promotion since you will be promoted because of your level of skill, not how long you took to get that skill."

Tal simply nodded, it was a strange feeling that he was talking about his future prospects as a Rider when earlier in his life he had only been concerned about that moment, that portion of time that he existed in at that very instant.

The next day Tal was again packed and ready to go by midday. Kelar met him outside the Riders Barracks with his own kit. During the night he had learned that the man they had rescued from the Dark cousin had been taken from the Palace whilst in stasis by some devil or other of the night. It was simply another thought that he did not want. Tal stood still as he looked toward the sky. Out of the glare of the sun descended several large Dragons, each one different in colour but each magnificent. No few of the servants in the palace openly gazed at the animals of legend. Their faces showing awe with a hint of fear. To them, seeing these creatures was something out of the ordinary and exciting. Though they have seen the Riders leave by such means before, it was not a common occurrence and to see so many Dragons at once was not only exciting but worrying, for what could trouble the Riders so much that they needed so many of their most powerful allies to overcome? Between this and the city Guards increasing their patrols, the palace staff were becoming increasingly frightened at the prospect of some unknown conflict.

Tal was shaken from his reverie by Kelar who pushed him towards a Dragon which was deep red in colour. Upon its back sat a Rider with the same silver crescent studs of rank on his shoulder. Kelar climbed up first and then helped Tal up and fixed their gear into place behind the Rider whilst Tal made himself as comfortable as possible upon the Dragons back. The Rider asked if they were ready and when Kelar said they were, the dragon lifted into the air. Up and up they rose upon the dragon until again they were at such a height that the city below looked almost small in comparison.

"Since you seem to have some attuning mentally as it is, it would be a shame to waste the opportunity to expand upon it." Said Kelar as the Dragon stopped climbing.

"What do you mean?" questioned Tal.

"What can you hear from our host?" asked Kelar. Tal tried to concentrate but could discern nothing from the great creature. "Relax, your thinking about it too much." advised Kelar. "Empty your mind if you can, don't think about listening, or hearing, or sensing, or whatever you believe you should be doing, just relax."

Tal tried but with no success.

"I can't feel anything." Said Tal finally and in almost defeated tones.

"Don't worry about it. You have the ability, you showed that the other day. It will come to you in time. To be honest it is almost unheard of that a novice can communicate with Dragons at all. That is one of the last things you are taught after danger awareness and environmental assessment." Replied Kelar in a sympathetic voice. Tal nodded, but felt disappointed inside. He had communicated once with a Dragon why shouldn't he be able to now?

The Riders, carried by their host moved forward. There was the same pull back and rush of air that Tal had felt the first time he had been transported by Dragon, and again shortly afterwards the comfortable feeling returned and he could see the earth passing below faster than he could estimate any speed for. In a short time a flat field could be seen and to the east of that a devastated city reared into the distance. There was movement from within but it could not be made out significantly at the speed they were travelling at. In the field, there was a camp, and as the Dragon slowed to descend, Tal could see other Riders there, some in the chain he wore, others in plate.

"How many Riders are stationed here Kelar?" asked Tal.

"Its hard to judge. There may be two hundred in this camp but there may be other camps." Replied Kelar.

"Two hundred? I didn't think there was that much room at the barracks." Questioned Tal.

"Well remember that the City of Dragons is only one city. There are barracks all over the Kingdom that Riders are stationed to. In addition, some of these will be female so you need to add the ladies barracks to your total. Then there is the number of Riders that are not attached to any city and are out in the world. There are thousands of Riders all over the Kingdom at any one time Tal. As a Novice, you are in the City of Dragons learning. Once you are made up, you will learn about the enormity of the Riders as a whole." Said Kelar, and again Tal felt he was getting out of his depth. Before he had thought that although there were a fair few Riders, that the number was relatively small, now though he wondered where else Riders were and how many there are in any one place at any time.

As the Dragon touched ground, Tal felt as much as saw a shimmer around him. "What was that?" he asked of Kelar as they were dismounting.

"You felt that? That's surprising, but a good sign of your abilities. As we were approaching the area, our ride concealed us from sight. Did you feel that as well? It would almost be the same type of feeling." Replied Kelar.

"No, I didn't notice it. So we were invisible?" Continued Tal.

"Wouldn't it be safer for all of us if the demons in Peters Hold didn't know we were here?" came Kelar's reply.

"Well yes, but I didn't know they could do that." Said Tal.

"They can, and they do." Said Kelar smiling. "There was a score or so of Dragons waiting above the City of Dragons when we left but you couldn't see them. If they were visible then the entire city would start to panic."

Tal was even more in awe of the power that the Dragons had, and as they walked towards a tent that was larger than the rest, Tal tried to clear his mind once more. As they entered, they were greeted by a group of six men and two women. Three of the men wore the black and red chain of the Riders, as did the two women, one wore the black and red of the Riders though in field plate mail and the remaining two men wore the white robes of the Seers.

The tent was sparse of furniture that most would have expected to find in the tent of a General but it more than made up for the loss with the ample tables covered in maps, ledgers, orders, and reports.

"Good afternoon gentlemen," said the man in the plate armour. He had short brown hair and was clean shaven. His eyes were a deep brown and his face was set with an angular jaw that looked as hard as any slab of ebony. Powerfully built, he was not towering in height, being almost a head shorter than Tal himself. "I am General Cristof. These are my senior officers and advisors in the camp. Let me give you the basic outline of what has been occurring here. There have been raids out of Peters Hold made by small parties but no real heat so far. The small band of Royal Household Guard that was here initially with Prince Allin has moved on recently to try to evacuate Borders Edge and there is a good size detachment from the Kings army on its way from the surrounding cities to quarantine this area. They should be here early next week and until then, we are here to assess the situation. When the army reaches its position, which I assume will be close to this current camp we want to have faded out and no sign left that we were here. There for I ask you to be sensible about rubbish and the likes.

"Tal, you were friends with a Guard called Drew Earemon weren't you. He was here just a short while ago, in the conflict that first alerted us to a continued Demon presence here. Don't panic lad, he's safe and he's made quite the hero of himself if I understand things correctly. Though not without a few broken ribs." The General finished the last with a smile that seemed to take years off his dark face.

"Go get unpacked. Then see Captain Trillar. He volunteered for this position and since you are all familiar with each other, it is probably best if you are under his command as you are still a Novice." Finished the General.

"Yes sir." Replied Tal and Kelar together, both saluting before being dismissed to seek their Captain.

It was late afternoon. The two Riders had unpacked their gear and reported to Captain Trillar. They were assigned to a watch of eight other Riders that were to patrol the area north of the city and to report should demon activity spread. As they were waiting near a fire for the patrol to return, they ate a light meal of camp bread and roasted meat. The thaw had started to move faster and now the air was warmer and the days of rain were becoming less as the land moved into spring.

It was late in the evening before the party they were to join returned, and Tal and Kelar had explored the camp and memorised the places of importance before moving onto more hand to hand training and some weapons practice. They introduced themselves and quickly discussed the way the operation worked.

"We leave in the morning and split into two groups. Those groups then take half the area to be covered each. They spend the morning on patrol and return at midday for some food before setting out again. After lunch, we take some food and swap areas. This way should anything slip past on team on a patrol, with luck it wont slip past the second later in the day. We then patrol for most of the remainder of the day and return late evening. Giving a verbal report to Captain Trillar or, should there be any evidence of movement from the demons, we would submit a written report.

"So far, there hasn't been any movement from the city that we can see, inside or out. We only know there are demons in there because of the war parties that are sent out. These are not uniform in time or size, so we can't guess as to their plan. Anyway, we track them down and destroy them as fast as possible once we are aware they have been sent out. Should any demon get back to the city then they would all be aware of our exact position rather than just being here." The speaker was another sergeant named Samuel Drey. He was a short man and slight of build, but there was a speed about him that Tal could see by the way he moved. He possessed blonde hair tied in a tail at the nape of his neck, much like Brad possessed, and light blue eyes that seemed to notice all around him.

When Kelar had informed Samuel – or Sam as he insisted he was called – of his rank, it was commonly agreed that Kelar would take charge of one group while Sam maintained command of the other. Tal would stay with his tutor and learn what he could about the work of the Riders outside of a study environment. Though on learning that Tal was still a Novice, Sam appeared apprehensive about his presence on the field, reminding Kelar that Novices are usually kept under supervision in the City of Dragons until they are made up to Rider.

Kelar shrugged this off saying that Tal had already been out of the City on his first mission nearly three months ago due to his involvement in the events leading to this moment in time.

Sam did not seem convinced but nodded and said they were going to eat, then get some sleep. Before the group dispersed and the night watch took over, Tal and Kelar were told to be ready to leave at sunrise.

Kelar left to go get some sleep but Tal felt a nagging in the back of his mind. He wondered where Brad and Cholla were now, more importantly he wondered where Hazel was. After he left them outside of Coladan, he had heard nothing from them and now he was miles from the City of Dragons and possibly a Kingdoms length from Hazel.

He looked up and realised that he had been walking without knowing it, and was now outside Captain Trillar's tent. One access flap was pegged back informing that the Captain was still awake and so Tal entered, knocking on the wooden board placed outside.

"Come in Tal. What can I do for you?" said the Captain.

"I was wondering sir, do you know where my friends Brad or Hazel are at the moment?" replied Tal, a little nervous that he was asking such a question in the current situation.

"Call me Fen when were alone or off duty Tal. I'm sure you have been told were not as formal as the regular army with rank. Anyway, Brad is now back at the City of Dragons continuing his studies Tal. As for Hazel, I assume you mean Rider Jensook. She has been assigned a duty in Sarafell, the Grey Mages are still up to something, and we can't ignore them just because of this demon invasion." Tal nodded. He would have liked for Hazel to be here with him but realised that was not possible.

He thanked the Captain and left the tent. At least he knew that Brad at least was safe in the City of Dragons. He eventually got back to his tent after walking around for what seemed an eternity thinking about Hazel and how stupid he felt all the time she was in his mind.

The morning was bright and slightly warmer than it was the previous day, even though that still meant it was cold enough to see their breath. The team of five Riders under the command of Sergeant Kelar was sweeping the area to the north of the city. They were in uniform with one difference. Their cloaks had no red on them, they were plain black and although in contrast to the landscape done a good job of hiding them in the shadows created by the rolling land.

The five of them were spread out in a search pattern with one scout, two flankers and Kelar and Tal following behind in an arrowhead formation commonly used in the small units of the Riders. It was nearing lunch when Kelar called the other Riders back by a method Tal could neither see nor hear. Kelar said he would explain it to Tal as they returned to camp and they set off on the return leg of the patrol.

"What I did Tal was to think about myself and then project it outward. It's an egotists dream really, but the effect is that with the Riders sense of the environment they can pick up the thought and know they should return to me." Said Kelar explaining the technique.

"It is a lot easier to sense it that it is to produce it, believe me there!" said Kelar chuckling softly. "Try to focus your mind on the world. What can you sense?" asked Kelar.

Tal focused and he could sense the birds that flew overhead, he could feel the worms in the earth below. He could feel the direction of the wind as though a wind vein had been erected in front of him, and knew that the air was being blown from the North Sea. He was also aware of Kelar next to him. Not just his presence but his sense of the area as well. There was a feeling of the other Riders ahead of them and a sense of surprise and approval of Tal's sense joining with theirs was returned.

Kelar smiled at his pupil. Although Tal had been away from the training grounds longer than any Novice that Kelar had known, he had somehow by shear ability managed to progress at a very fast rate indeed. *If only I could get him up to speed on his weapons.* Thought Kelar, *Tal doesn't know how close he is to being made up to Rider.*

Slowly they made their way back to the camp when they arrived the other group was already there eating. Kelar and Sam went off a distance to discuss the mornings patrol and the others including Tal got some soup from the make-do galley and ate it gathered around a fire that tried to keep away the slight chill of the day.

Tal was surprised to learn that the other riders could sense him from a distance of over five miles away. In itself, that was not an unheard of feat for Riders, though to reach that distance, Tal's senses should have filled the other Riders sense in his party, stopping them from sensing anything else that was occurring. That he had managed to reach so far without 'deafening' his team members was an astonishing thing for Riders.

Kelar and Sam returned shortly and there was a mission de-brief before the team took some bread and cooked meat and headed out to continue their patrol.

It was early afternoon. Tal and Kelar were patrolling in the same formation as in the morning. As they moved through the landscape Tal was searching with his mind. Kelar was still instructing him on how to focus his energies to get a more accurate picture of what was around him. Tal was now able to sense the exact position of the other Riders as they were searching in their formation, and when he linked with them, he could know their senses almost as well as he knew his own. He was informed that the Riders called this the 'Joining', when a group of them focused on each other to enhance their own senses.

The hours were passing and there was nothing new that could be sensed. Kelar called his group back to him and informed them that he wanted to swing closer to the city to see if they could detect what was happening inside its quiet walls. They set out in a close group, no more than twenty feet from each other.

It was late afternoon when they got close enough to the city to sense anything within their walls. It seemed deserted, there was nothing that could be felt except for the death and carnage that occurred not two months past. Tal felt nauseous, his stomach was turning and he had to stop sensing within the city walls before he could regain control of his belly. Kelar was disgusted, as was the rest of the party. The strength of the death they felt could only have been caused by a gruesome conquest. Many people had died in the most horrific way for the city to be stained so badly.

Kelar told Tal not to try to sense anymore. The group moved in closer to the city, and the Riders faces became hard. The more they sensed the greater their pain. Kelar held up his hand, and the group stopped.

"What is it?" asked Tal.

"I'm not sure," replied Kelar, "there is a large presence of… energy, close to the centre of the city. I'm not sure what it means but we should report this to the General as soon as possible. Come on, let's get back to the camp."

Tal did not argue, he had seen as much of these ruins as he cared to and being so close it seemed that he could still feel the pain and suffering that stained the city.

Chapter 8

War

Tal was waiting outside General Cristof's tent. Kelar had been in a council with the leading members of the camp for the past few hours. Night was passing and it was cold outside. The air had been warming slowly as the days past, but Tal still felt summer was an eternity away.

Kelar emerged from the tent. He looked tired but showed no other emotion.

"What is happening?" Asked Tal.

"A pair of Dragons are going to be sent with their Riders to sweep over the city and see if they can pin point the source of the energy. There was a lot of talk but with no definite answer as to what this energy could be a proper course of action could not be decided upon.

"The Seers have tried to use their arts to unravel the mystery, but they have been blocked by the demons. Or that is their best guess anyway. All they could say was that the magic was not of human fashion." Replied Kelar.

"So what are we to do?" Continued Tal.

"The same as we did yesterday, patrol. Our orders have not changed." Finished Kelar. With that, he turned and walked away from his pupil.

Tal was worried. He had been with Kelar for many weeks now, and he had never seen him this way. Usually Kelar was open about anything Tal asked him, though now he seemed closed, guarded. With nothing else to be done tonight, and the morning patrol growing closer Tal retired to his tent. He was going to have another long day tomorrow and some sleep would be of use.

The night drew in again and the party returned from their patrol together. Meeting as both groups returned they decided that returning in close formation would be safer as they had stayed out longer than usual trying to get some idea as to what the demons were planning inside the city.

The patrols had been going on for a week now. The past plan to have left when the army arrived had been altered in light of the energy source being discovered. The Riders however had left the camp and had spread out over miles of land. No more than five Riders in any group and to be constantly moving their camp with a watchman at all times to alert the others should the regular army get close. They slept in cold camps and ate rations of cold meats and bread.

As they grew close to the small camp that held the General, the highest ranking Seer – Tal had not yet worked out how their system of rank worked – and the Riders most senior officers, Tal noticed something was wrong. They were waiting for the patrol to return outside the tent.

When the group was close enough, the General ushered them inside and asked them all to sit on make shift chairs.

"We have a problem. We have been trying to get information on this energy emission for the past week using Dragons and Seers, but there has been only one advancement in our knowledge. The location of the power. It is within the main citadel that was once the sole settlement of Peters Hold. It may be that this is where the demons are holed up which would explain why it appears so calm outside. The tunnels and rooms under the citadel can hold hundreds, thousands of men in the case of a prolonged siege. They could lie in wait there and without going in no one would ever know. That is why I am asking you to try to get as close to the citadel as possible and hope you can get some more information. Your new orders are to enter the city. How far you go is up to you. Do not risk yourself needlessly, we need as many swords as possible in the coming war I fear.

"Tal, I know you have been following Kelar from the moment you took your first mission, however this is beyond your skill and experience I am afraid. You will stay here and await your parties return." Said General Cristof.

"Sir, I have been told that I am further advanced than any Novice…"said Tal starting to protest, but was cut off by the General.

"It is correct that you are further along in your mental attuning than *most* Novices. But the point of the matter remains that your skills with a weapon are still substandard than that of a Rider, and should a situation evolve where weapons and force are necessary it is more likely than not that you would be a liability to the team rather than an asset." Said Cristof firmly yet not unkindly.

"Yes sir." Said Tal. He did not like the order but he had to follow it, no matter what he wanted.

"Good. Now let's go over the plan. Tal there should be a free tent prepared for you outside. Go get some sleep, you will be staying with us here until Kelar and the others return." Continued Cristof.

Sam and the rest of the party looked at Tal. Although they had only known him a short time, they had grown to think of him as a Rider. Although he was still young, he had been working as though fully ranked and now they were reminded that although his mental abilities were approaching theirs, he was still a Novice.

Tal saluted and left the tent. His mood was dark, he had grown used to being treated as a Rider, as one of the group, and now he was back to being different.

He found his tent but sleep was slow to cover him that night.

Kelar crept forward, armoured by chain on his legs with his arms and chest covered with plate mail, and a black cloak covering his body. The city was dead. The buildings were torn apart. Blood still stained the walls, streets and doors. His team was working their way towards the centre from the north, Sam's team was making their way from the south. Kelar was attempting to sense his surroundings, but it was hard to stay calm and keep the ability going when his entire body was filled with the deaths of every man woman and child that had been slaughtered here.

The team was walking down a street, keeping to the sides and hiding in what shadows they could find. The sun was high in the sky now, nearing midday and there was a tense feeling in the air. A fifth member had been added to the team to replace Tal and the four Riders were aligned behind Kelar, two each side of the street with Kelar ahead almost invisible to the others but for them sensing him.

Bryant was the parties second in command. He was a veteran Rider who looked in his thirties, short of stature and build, with dark hair and blue eyes. He was wearing complete black, with chain arms and legs but his chest was protected with solid plate armour. A black cloak finished his attire and he carried a thick curved blade. Behind him followed Shan-Yin, an ex Imperial Guard to the Emperor of Yin. It was custom to bestow only the brave and devoted with the honorific 'Yin' after their name. He was dressed similarly to Bryant but carried the same thin curved blade that Tal was beginning to favour. He was also short with dark hair pulled into a tail at the nape of his neck and dark eyes, yet he had a speed that few possessed and was hardy of nature.

On the other side of the street were Matthew and Martin Ilan. Twin brothers that looked almost identical. Both had scars on their face and looked battle hardened. Both had shaved heads and green eyes, they moved almost identically with the large broadswords, almost cat-like despite their large stature. All five Riders carried bows slung across their back and a quiver full of arrows at their waist.

The group could see the citadel looming over the wrecked city. Its age worn walls were now dark with years of service. The air was heavy with the smell of dried blood, and rotting flesh. The thaw was slow this year and the result was that the decomposition of the bodies was slowed slightly. There were the bodies of demons here as well, though most of them were young. The demons that were here had horrible cuts and broken limbs. *Even the young are hard to kill*, thought Kelar, stopping the thought from reaching the others in his team.

They continued through the streets slowly, not wanting to end up a meal for some undetected demon. There was a thought that came from Shan-yin to the others,

Where are the children?

The team looked around. As noted, there were none visible. Kelar wondered on this briefly but quickly stored it in his mind to mull over later, there were more important things to worry about now.

An alien feeling smothered Bryant. A city man born and bred, the silence that smothered this city unnerved him and this feeling was received by all in the party, until he could isolate it from the Joining.

They approached the large square that separated the city from the citadel. This point would be the last stand if the city was attacked from without and the exterior walls had fallen. The large gap was designed to give archers from the walls of the citadel clear shots at anyone who charged their position. It would be a killing ground. Nevertheless, it was almost clear – the city had been attacked from within. That was the only reason that Kelar could give for why there were no demons lying here.

The group closed up to the position where Kelar was standing.

"How are we going to do this?" asked Bryant quietly.

"I'm not sure. If there is anyone on lookout duty, there is no way we can get any closer without being seen. I suggest that we find a building that is half hospitable and just monitor the situation. Maybe we can see if anything happens regularly. Who knows, we may even see what we need without going in." Replied Kelar just as quietly. "Spread out, don't go too far but look for a building that is set back enough that we are covered if we need to leave and walk about, but close enough that we can see the citadel as clearly as possible."

The others nodded and moved out slowly, disappearing into the shadows of the growing afternoon so that soon, the only contact Kelar had with them was through the Joining.

It was about half an hour later when Matthew gave a call to the others to go to him. They found him at the entrance to a house set three back from the citadel with an entrance set away from the enormous structure and a view straight up a street opening into the square around the citadel. Not surprisingly, Martin was there before anyone else.

"Good job." said Kelar. "Well this is our new home for the next few days lads so lets go make ourselves comfortable. We will start watches this evening, until then lets try to get the lay of the land. I want to know our fastest escape route out of here and our best defensive spot should we need one."

The team left in five different directions. They kept a constant check on the others to make sure they were connected mentally at all times, and so the day progressed until afternoon evolved into evening and they regrouped at their base. The fastest route out was as suspected almost straight down a main road, though some of the buildings had collapsed and several small detours would need to be made. The best defensive position in fact proved to be their base. As a taller building it gave the advantage of longer bow range and at the same time there was only one probable direction of attack as most of the other buildings had crumbled to some degree, leaving only the road up to the citadel free of any real obstruction.

They settled down for the night, Matthew and Martin to take the first two watches, followed by Shan-Yin, then Bryant. Kelar would take the early morning watch.

Night passed slowly, the hours dragged and Martin was relieved by Shan-yin.

The weather was calm, but cold. The stillness of the air belied the time of year, where the winds should have been whistling at the windows and rain should be pounding at the tiles on the roof. The quiet of the city was almost made thunderously loud by the lack of motion that was evident.

Shan-Yin extended his senses and settled in to wait. He could reach into the centre of the citadel and the same range all around him. Nothing stirred. Only the energy emission reminded him of why they were there.

He wondered silently if the other team was doing the same as they, or if they had dared to enter, or if they had turned back when reaching the square. He berated himself. This was not the time. He should be constantly thinking about his duty. His mind wandered to his family back home. Back where his home was, years ago. He assumed his family was dead by now. The years had been long for him, even though he looked barely in his late twenties. Again he berated himself. In past years he could have been punished physically if he was caught in such a preoccupied state while guarding his Emperor.

He again focused on his surroundings, extending his senses outward. Something was wrong, there was someone or something within the vicinity that was not there before. Cursing himself for a fool, he moved silently over to Kelar, waking him gently.

He quickly explained the situation and through constantly monitoring the newcomer, he could tell that it was making its way towards them and that it was human.

Kelar woke the others. He decided that whoever was out there was coming to them and knew they were there. Going to them would do nothing but take their edge and defence should they need it. Quickly, Bryant strung his longbow and moved to the next floor up. He positioned himself at a window facing the direction the stranger was coming from. The others with Kelar at the front lined themselves up, two at each ground floor window, bows ready, swords close to hand. The figure was now only a street length away.

In the darkness, they could see what they now thought of as a man. He was keeping to the shadows and moved carefully in the night. He was slowly making his way towards them and was carrying a sword under his cloak.

The figure halted halfway down the street alerted to the risk somehow. He ducked further into the shadows. The Riders could still track him and knew that he was still now, not moving.

Kelar moved back slowly.

"Where are you going?" asked Shan-Yin quietly.

"He isn't coming to us, I'm going to him." Replied Kelar, quietly placing his bow on the floor and taking his sword. He crept over to the window on the side of the house and nimbly jumped through. He took a wide sweep moving in the darkness around the house the unknown man was hiding in the shadow of. He separated his senses from the rest and reduced the sensitivity. He hoped that if the newcomer could sense them that he would be focusing on the other four and not notice him moving around. He noticed the others increase the intensity of their senses and smiled. They had the same idea and their powerful senses would cover his reduced sense should the other person know how to feel them somehow.

Creeping around the building Kelar ducked behind a broken wall. Ahead of him, no more than about twenty feet was the man he was searching for. He was covered in a black cloak and hiding in a doorway, his position only given away by a slight movement for his sword.

As though he sensed Kelar, the figure spun quickly moving out into the light.

"Tal?!" Said Kelar, his surprise causing him to speak louder than he anticipated.

Tal jumped. Kelar quickly joined his sense to the others and informed them what was happening.

Kelar felt the others confusion but also felt them put up their weapons.

"What in the God's creation are you doing here?" he said almost incredulously. "Did the General tell you to come get us? Why didn't he send a Rider? Was there a problem, is the General o.k.?" The questions flooded out before he could stop himself. Suddenly the situation they were in seemed to impress itself on Kelar as he cut Tal off before he could answer and ushered him into the house.

They had settled in once more and Shan-Yin was again keeping his vigil of the citadel. Kelar had fed Tal and given him some water, before questioning him on his presence here. He had snuck away from the Generals camp and had followed the group here. He had followed their sense right to the building they were hiding in, but when he felt them draw weapons he thought he might have gotten it wrong and maybe he was following someone else.

Kelar then asked him what he did that stopped them from identifying him as they sensed him. Tal said he had tried to do the opposite of stretching his feelings out. He withdrew them inside and smothered himself, hoping that it would shield his identity should others be searching for him.

It struck Kelar with a force that was like a hammer blow. This skill a Rider possessed after long training only. It was like a runner switching events and becoming a swimmer. It was hard to realign the mind to do something different when it is attuned to one thought. Tal had managed to just switch as if it was like changing clothes.

The sun was rising by the time they had finished talking. Kelar was not prepared for this but decided that Tal would probably be safer staying in the house until they left the city rather than try to travel back by himself.

The day was spent with Kelar continuing to train Tal with a sword while the others maintained a vigil of the citadel. Kelar was slowly teaching Tal to use the weapon with some skill, but it was hard going. Tal could grasp the basics but could not quite put them together. It was as if the sword just went in a different direction than which he wanted. When he used his lighter blade, one almost identical to Kelar's, though not as finely crafted, he found he could manipulate it slightly better though still not as well as Kelar would have liked.

Tal had become more than satisfactory in the martial arts, there were few that could best him one on one, and his mental abilities were without question above the level required by a Novice before being made up to Rider. Kelar was almost despairing about Tal's predicament, so close yet so far. How could someone so adept in studies and fighting in one style be so clumsy in other fighting no matter how much they train?

Night drew close again and the watches continued. Nothing new was felt or seen, that night or the following night. Kelar decided that one more night was enough and if nothing were to happen then he would risk attempting to enter the citadel.

The fourth night was the same. The hours past. The silence endured. The sun rose. The days remained structured of watches and training. And as night fell the party was ready to move. Each member was armed and armoured, Tal wearing only chain armour, as he was not issued with the plate chest as the others were. Each had their weapons ready for action and their bows slung over their backs again.

They left the relative safety of the city and moved up the street, towards the dark citadel, illuminated only by the planets two moons.

It seemed strange to Tal. For days they had monitored the citadel, and for days nothing had been seen. But as soon as they were moving towards it, the tension increased a hundred fold. All of a sudden he was not going into a silent defence structure, but to war.

Moving slowly, they approached the edge of the buildings that lined the square outside the citadel. Kelar paused, as though judging one final time if it were safe to enter or if he should turn back here.

Without a word he darted forward. Running swiftly, his cloak billowing behind him he reached the walls of the citadel. Hiding in their relative shadow he waited. Seconds seemed to last decades. Suddenly Shan-Yin was sprinting. His slight figure almost fading into the night as he ran.

He was followed by Matthew and Martin who, together, ran from the shadow of the building to the shadow of the fortress. Bryant told Tal he was to go next.

Tal took a deep breath. It seemed that they had been standing there for centuries now if the seconds between each run felt like decades. With a final breath he ran, as fast as he could, to meet up with the others at the walls of the citadel.

Bryant followed and soon all six were lined up along the wall. They crept along until they found the main gate. It was mostly closed, a small gap between the doors the only space showing. The portcullis was still raised and secured inside the wall. Kelar again used the strengthened sense from the group to search as far into the citadel depths as he could for a much more accurate picture. Still sensing nothing but the energy, he looked through the doors. Nothing moved, but a thought gripped his heart. *What if the energy is covering the demons presence?*

The moonlight shone on the stonework creating an eerie presence. Kelar slipped inside the doors and crouched behind them. The others followed and soon they were inside the citadel's outer defences.

This side of the wall held no shadow and they were open to anyone who happened to glance their way. Quickly they looked around, the citadel seemed enormous from the inside as much as out. The huge defences cast broad shadows across the citadels ground.

The group quickly sprinted into the cover of the citadel. The shadows quickly covering them from sight once more. Lined up against the main structure of the citadel they again waited perfectly motionless. They stretched out their senses once more and Tal instantly felt the horrid murders that took place in the city flood through him again. The stomach-turning feeling returned and he wanted to turn off his senses, to retract them into himself again.

Within the walls there was nothing moving, nothing living. Further down they could sense the energy. It was being emitted from deep within the earth. One of the stores cellars was the guess of the party. But there was something else. Focussing their senses upon that area there was something new, a movement. There was something down there, and it was alive. They continued to search the area. Slowly they found more life signs. Their search routines lasted about half an hour, their bodies remaining still their minds floating from room to room.

Tal now, with the help of the others knew the layout of the entire citadel underground. They estimated that there were about thirty beings down there. Some larger than others.

"What now?" Asked Bryant casually.

"We go in for a closer look." Replied Kelar just as offhandedly.

The party took a deep breath and nodded. They all knew the possible peril of entering, but there were some risks that had to be taken, no matter what the outcome may be.

Searching the edge of the keep, they found a hole through the wall that lead to some non-descript room that had long since been destroyed. They entered, Tal in the middle of the group and spread out forming a circle in the centre of the room.

The party now drew their weapons. Pulling something from under his cloak that looked like a bottle, Kelar quickly pored a black powder onto his blade, he smeared it carefully with a cloth he was carrying and then passed it to Bryant who did the same. The bottle was then passed through the group until it was eventually given back to Kelar.

"What is this?" Asked Tal.

"It blackens the weapons so that no light will shine from it. It would be a bad thing should we be discovered for some chance gleam of moonlight to betray us on our own weapons." Said Matthew as he applied it to his broadsword.

They moved out of the room, keeping low and against the walls of the wide corridors. They made swift progress, the group scanning ahead to ensure there were no surprises waiting for them. Passing along corridors and through large rooms, they headed towards the stairs leading down.

"Hold up." Said Kelar quietly at the final corner.

"What is it?" Asked Shan-Yin.

"There is something round there." Replied Kelar in a whisper.

Slowly he looked round the corner. Crouching in the darkness was a figure. It was large and powerfully muscled. It was a demon. Its body was covered in a leathery looking hide with horns down its face and arms. It's eyes were a deep red, their glow piercing the shadows around it. The creatures' teeth were jagged and the upper fangs extended over its lower jaw.

The demon was as guard. It was stationed at the head of the stairs barring any way down. Kelar stretched his senses further down the stairs to try to determine if there were any other demons around. He found nothing.

Nodding Kelar closed his eyes and his body seemed to blur leaving only an outline and a shaky distortion where he was standing. Tal saw him slip round the corner and waited.

It seemed that time was no longer running, that the gods had somehow halted existence. Then in a horrible moment, Tal could see through the eyes of Kelar. He could see the demon become aware of Kelar's presence and in a heartbeat Kelar had swung his sword decapitating the creature. Dark blood squirted into the air and the body fell, lifeless to the floor. The others moved round the corner to back up Kelar should there have been a demon that they had missed, but there wasn't.

"How did you do that?" Asked Tal of Kelar as he met up with him at the top of the stairs.

"You will learn it in time, it is similar to the ability of the dragons, however I am nowhere near as powerful as they, and can only blur myself to blend in with the background." Said Kelar.

Tal simply nodded. In the few weeks he had been with Kelar he had learned so much, yet he was now becoming painfully aware that there was still even more that he did not know.

They descended the stairs slowly, scanning ahead. At the bottom they spread out in a defensive formation with Kelar at the head. They were now deep underground. The stairs had been long and this was clearly designed as a last stand position. The doors had been reinforced and used to be capable of being bared from the inside. Though now they were torn from the walls and lay broken on the floor. Opposite the doors was a wall that had arrow slits in it, reinforced it allowed the defenders to spray death at their foe if they broke through the doors and stay protected.

It was quiet, the air was rank and stale. There was a smell of blood and rotting flesh that hung heavy in the air. The closest life form they could sense was further down the passage behind the wall. The corridor lead further down in a spiralling form, again this was designed in a defensive mind. The curvature of the passage disallowing the use of bows, and the breadth of the passage allowing no more than two armoured men to stand abreast at any one time, even though the walls had collapsed in some places and earth had now been dug out for wooden supports to be placed. They followed the passage down and came to a locked door. They could sense a demon standing on the other side of the door and two rooms further back was the energy source.

What do we do now? Thought Martin for the others to sense.

I'm not sure, we can't stay too long or they will discover the body upstairs and realise we have entered the Citadel. Any ideas anyone? Thought Kelar in reply.

Where is Sam's Group? Said Tal. *Could we get him to create a distraction and when they go to find out what is happening we could slip in?*

If he is within the grounds of the Citadel then possibly, answered Kelar, *but if he isn't we wont be able to reach him.*

But Tal might be able to. Remember his range on patrol? Threw in Bryant.

The party looked at Tal

Do you think you could Tal? Asked Kelar.

There was a pause in the mental dialogue. *I will try.* Was all that came back from Tal.

The party could sense that Tal was stretching out, though they could not make out what he was saying. It was about five minutes later when Tal spoke to them again.

Sam is just outside the Citadel limits. He was pondering entering, he was also a little surprised that I could speak to him from down here. Anyway, he said he would create a distraction in a few minutes.

Well then, lets get out of sight before demons start running through here. Said Kelar backing up the passage until they found one of the dug out support holes. The group huddled in and Tal was ushered to the back where he covered himself in his cloak. The others blurred themselves into the background, and so they waited.

It was a further five minutes before anything was heard when all of a sudden a great thudding sound could be heard from overhead followed by a second and a third.

Kelar and the group could feel movement in the rooms below. The thunderous eruptions overhead continued apace.

Well Sam did say he was going to cause a distraction, I never thought he would lay siege to this place to do it though. Thought Shan-Yin with slight amusement.

The was the sound of bolts being slid back and a sharp blue light flooded the passage as the door swung open ahead of the party. Demons poured out in single file, a group of about twenty, each one larger than a well built warrior. Inside the door Kelar saw the source of the energy and felt fear within himself. There were several…doors was all he could think to call them, leading to a rocky place. Lava seemed to run as water in rivers and monstrous castles could be seen in the background, though this is not what scared Kelar. In front of the two doors that he could see, were massed thousands of Demons, large or small each looked capable of killing many humans.

Lets go, we have seen what we must. And Kelar lead the group out, following the hurrying demons up as the door shut behind them and the light faded into darkness again.

They paused at the top of the stairs as the Demons discovered the body of their fallen guard and spread out to search the area. A smaller demon was sent back to down the passage to inform their leader, or so Tal assumed, but as he rounded the bend, he was met swiftly with Kelar's blade and fell victim to the same fate as his comrade above.

The other demons quickly left the room at the top and spread out to discover the source of the explosions. Kelar and his group followed, leaving the depths of the Citadel and stepped into the night once more.

Tal looked up as they left the fortress and saw huge boulders crash into the outer wall. Even though he shouldn't find it funny, he couldn't imagine how five men could hurl boulders that size at a wall. Quickly the group followed the demons that left the citadel through the same doors the group first entered by.

The demons quickly entered the city towards the source of the boulders and the Riders disappeared in a different direction. Kelar quickly sent out a thought to Sam's Group telling them about the approach of the Demons. Sam replied he was barely a city block away now and fading into the depths of the city.

Kelar followed Sam's lead and vanished in the jungle of concrete and steel that was Peters Hold.

It was the following day when the party found General Cristof's new campsite. The General was waiting for them as they returned.

He greeted Kelar and his group and offered them warm food and water before their debrief. When he reached Tal, his face was like a thundercloud.

"I am not used to being disobeyed young Novice. I will let it pass this time, as I understand the mission could not have been a success without your aid," At Tal's confused look Cristof explained that Sam's party had returned earlier that day. "but should you disobey another of my orders then I will see you punished. This is not a game we are playing. It is war and if we lose discipline this kingdom and possibly this earth may be lost."

"Yes sir." Replied Tal, his face downcast and ashamed.

"Right, now go eat, we will reconvene in half an hour." Finished the General a bit softer.

"Doors?"

It was a startled question that came from Cristof's mouth.

"Yes my General. There were several of them that I could sense though I only could see two. Each one had thousands of demons lined up behind them, either training or in units. It looks like they are planning to start an invasion." Said Kelar.

The meeting had been going on for a few hours now. The seers had been using their arts to draw a picture of the scene that had been observed by Kelar and the others in the air. Though they had no idea where this other land was, they knew that if it was on this planet it needed to be further away from their own lands than any traveller had ever been.

"I'm afraid this news is not the only bad news I have heard today." Said Cristof. "The Grey Mages have begun openly attacking villages around Sarafell. They have been using armies of the dead apparently. Always at night, and always lead by the Ones of Impurity. The Kingdom has lost several villages to these armies already and the others have all been abandoned. The Kingdoms armies have been marshalled and have been sent to bolster the defences around Sarafell and Coladan. The portion of the army that was here has been stripped to a minimal level, just enough to keep an eye on Peters Hold.

"Riders are doing all they can up near the border to The Lost Lands, picking off smaller bands of skeletal warriors or ghouls, however the times that they have attacked any band with the Ones in, they have had to retreat after barely a skirmish. The Ones are powerful indeed, and no one Rider has the power to tackle him during the night."

It seemed to the party that their entire world had been turned upside down.

"What are our orders sir?" Asked Kelar.

"Sleep untroubled tonight. Or as untroubled as you can be after hearing such grim news. We will talk again in the morning and I will inform you of your orders then." Replied the General.

The party left the tent and Tal suddenly felt a stab of fear in his heart. He stopped abruptly and Kelar looked confused.

"What is it Tal?" He said.

"Hazel, she was stationed in Sarafell, I have to know if she is alright!" replied Tal.

"I don't think the general would know Tal, you will have to wait for a while to learn this I think." Said Kelar.

"But I need to know!" insisted Tal.

"Tal! You need to learn patience." Said Kelar firmly. "You have great talent, but unless you curb yourself you may not make the next day after a battle. You are a Rider, act like one. Hazel was a smart girl, she won't get herself into any trouble she can't get herself out of. Now concentrate on your duty and let others concentrate on theirs."

Tal nodded, he had been put down twice today now. In addition, he realised that he was impulsive and that he rarely stopped to think about others when he wanted something. He felt ashamed once more and decided to do better. To follow orders and do what was required of him, but never to stop thinking about his friends.

He dreamt that night. And it was a dark and terrifying dream. His home destroyed, and his friends and family gone.

He wouldn't let that happen. He would die first.

Chapter 9

Conflict

The sandy earth shook.

Hazel ducked behind a mound of earth and sand previously deposited by a One, as a ball of magical energy impacted into the space she had lately occupied.

"Damn." Was all she said before her Sergeant gave the order to fall back.

They had been tracking a group of skeletal warriors across the Lost Lands for two days now, and they thought they might be able to discover if there was an army massed, or if the units that struck the villages were just that. However, as they moved further north they were confronted by a One of Impurity.

It struck in the night, while the camp slept as well as it could in the harsh land they were in. Before anyone could raise the alarm, there were two Riders on the floor, their blood seeping from their neck. When the distress was realised and the camp was awake, it took little time to assemble the Riders into a defensive formation. The One was as formidable an opponent as Hazel had ever seen, and the group Captain was dead saving a newly promoted Rider. The result was a break in the command structure that was quickly seized upon by the

One as is killed a further two Riders. When Sergeant Erikson had taken command, the remaining group had managed to hold their own, forcing the One to retreat though there were now several wounded Riders to show for a Nightwalker with a few small cuts.

Slowly the party withdrew, the One having now turned to leave. It moved faster than any of the Riders could have thought possible, blurring as it left the conflict.

The Riders were having no real trouble in fighting the skeletal warriors or the ghouls created by the Grey Mages, but they were out matched by the Ones. How many of them there were, the Riders couldn't estimate, they never got close enough to notice any real difference from one another, though the Ones seemed to be everywhere the Riders were in the Lost Land.

However, if the Dragon Riders were having trouble with the Ones then the regular army was having more, whenever the army came into contact with them they were almost completely wiped out unless there was a Rider unit with them or they were very lucky and better skilled than their comrades.

The company stopped their withdrawal when it was evident that there would be no further attack upon them.

"Other than the Captain, how many were lost?" Asked Sergeant Erikson.

"Four. Harrison, Teller, Yates and Michaels." Replied another Rider. The Sergeant shook his head, there had been too many Riders lost to the Ones, and unless a way to fight them was discovered soon then there may be irrevocable damage to the Order.

"Who here is injured?" questioned Erikson after a short while. A further six spoke up, showing various wounds from gashes in the arm to broken ribs or nose. When the injured Riders had been seen too as best as they could be out in the open the company headed back to the camp.

Another failed track, more Riders dead and no more information. What are we going to do? The thoughts must have been echoed throughout the company assumed Hazel from the feelings she was getting through the Joining.

The only time she could remember anyone besting a One in combat was a small band of ghouls attacking a well held position. The ghouls were quickly dispatched but the One took longer and several Riders we dead before the Nightwalker had turned and fled with no few small wounds. *Still he wasn't killed.* The thought rankled.

"OK people lets get moving. We can do no more here, and if we stay here we may end up in another conflict." Said Erikson, his voice not quite hiding his anger and frustration.

The patrol set off south again after pausing briefly only to bury the bodies of their comrades. Moving quickly, they headed south across the cold desolate planes that formed the Lost Lands.

It was two days again before they made their own lines. They had seen no movements of the undead nor did they have any further encounters with the Ones of Impurity. The camp was as they remembered it, earthwork defences reinforced with barbed wire and wooden stakes. There were catapults and ballista at strategic points along the lines, and Riders, Soldiers and Seers were on constant guard along the length of the fortifications.

The ground between the Lost Lands and the Kingdom was pitted and churned up. There was a scent of dried blood on the air and a pyre was burning off in the distance, the bodies of the fallen being cremated.

As the patrol approached, there was a call from the watchmen and they were taken instantly to the command tent. Inside Sergeant Erikson retold the events that lead to the attack by the One. Hazel was stationary listening to the recap of the saga. She did not know the name of the General that they were reporting to, for some reason she was unable to remember any of the names from the regular army.

The General seemed worried, they had been stationed there for a week now, and had been under almost constant attack, but when any company was deployed to track the retreating horde, the fleeing army always turns to fight before any clue can be gained as to the main army's whereabouts. When the undead retreat they never took the same route, there seemed no pattern to their tactics.

"We need to change tactics gentlemen." Said the General after the patrol had finished their report. "Any ideas?"

There was a silence in the tent. They knew what needed to be done but the risk such a measure meant could not be over looked.

"I'll say it then, we need to attempt to capture one of the enemy."

Hazel looked at the General, he noticed her and spoke. "You have a question Rider…?"

"Rider Jensook sir. We could catch a skeletal or a ghoul without any real trouble, but they feel no pain, how are we to get any information out of them?"

It was not the General, but one of his Captains that spoke.

"That is a stupid question to trouble the General with at a time like this girl, remember your place."

"My place…?!" started Hazel before Sergeant Erikson stepped in.

"I'm sure she was just curious as to how we were to get words out of a dead person that does not *want* to give any information. I'm sure if it is such a simple question, you can answer it for her. And as for her place, Captain you have no authority over her, and I'm willing to bet that for combat with a blade or fist you have little skill over her either."

The unknown Captain looked close to drawing his sword there and then to settle the argument, his hand gripping the hilt of his weapon, but the General held up his hand and the tent became still.

"Captain Reynolds put up your sword and stand down. Rider Jensook's question was appropriate and I am also willing to lay a wager on her skills in combat as well." Reynolds looked close to outrage as he sheathed his sword and stepped back. Hazel locked eyes with the man, if she ever had to fight alongside this man there would be trouble, she was sure of it.

"As to how to get information out of a dead thing, the Seers have assured me they have ways of getting the information out of anyone brought back, providing that they reach here still animated. Now it is late in the day and I still have much to do. Sergeant Erikson, thank you for the report and I mourn the loss of your Captain and comrades. Go and see Lord Rayburn, he is newly arrived and has taken command of the Riders here, I'm sure he will have your next assignment."

The Sergeant saluted and left the tent, his Riders following him. Inside Captain Reynolds was in a dark mood, his body tense from the way he had been spoken to and put down by his own General.

"With all respect sir, you give far too much freedom to these Riders. It is not a woman's place to fight in an army, much less to question the strategy of her superiors!" Remarked Reynolds in an almost violent outburst.

"Be at ease Captain, that 'woman' if not already will soon be more battle hardened than yourself and twice as important to the war effort. Don't glare David, it is true. You have no idea of the job the Riders do, in war, and in times of peace to protect our kingdom against forces you aren't even aware exist."

Captain Reynolds merely saluted and left the tent in quick haste. He would be damned in the eyes of the gods before that woman had any authority over him.

The General shook his head sadly, his Captain was a great strategist, but he would get no further than his current rank, for Reynolds sake, the General hoped that he would let his dislike of Riders slide for the benefit or his kingdom and for his own skin.

Lord Rayburn was in his own tent and on his arrival, Sergeant Erikson was admitted hastily.

"Sergeant, you are hereby promoted to Captain, congratulations, though it is indeed sad circumstances leading to the event.

"Let me fill you in on more details. The kingdom is fighting a war on two fronts, with two different enemies. It is a dire situation I'm sure you understand. The Demons are pouring into this Kingdom by means of doors situated in the depths of the citadel in Peters Hold. They are trying to enforce their prophecy it seems. Meanwhile for the Grey Mages it is the time before, they see themselves as Masters of us and they are now making moves to ensure that *their* prophecy will come to pass.

"However it is not all bad news, neither has yet launched a major offensive, each side willing to dig in and secure the area first. We have been trying to gain information, to get the upper hand in the conflict, but so far, we only know the Grey Mages have an army of the undead, and the demons are preparing for invasion from whatever hell they come from. So as you can see, detail is something we lack.

"Your team now has a new mission Erikson, get a captive, get a ghoul but get him back alive and still animated. We need to know where they Mages are attacking from and when they plan to launch their full attack on the Kingdom."

Captain Erikson, newly promoted Rider, saluted his lord and in grim determination left to gather his team.

Hazel was dressed and ready; her black cloak billowing over her chain, the long sword at her side well used and cared for. As the team set out into the desolate waste once more the regular troops stationed in defence of their camp shivered. As the Riders proceeded into the dark, their line looked like wraiths as they moved, their forms almost blurring into nothing as their cloaks camouflaged them with the deep of night.

As soon as the Riders were a mile clear of the camp, they quickly made their Joining, using their combined senses to explore the area around them. They numbered twenty, one

Captain, one Sergeant and eighteen Riders. Erikson was a careful man by nature, he insisted on taking point himself and was always the first to explore any unknown area before letting his group follow.

Hazel shivered. To her this was new, they had never gone to capture before, always to hunt and destroy. If the Captain had a plan to capture their prey, he had not yet informed the company of it. There was a feeling of anxiousness throughout the Joining, a welcoming for action that would see them out of this chilling silence and a nervousness that always followed at the thought of an encounter with a One.

Night turned to day and again back to night as the company pressed further into enemy territory in silence.

Wait. Thought the Captain.

He had sensed the movement of large numbers two days previous and the party had taken to ground. They had now been in the field for over a week. The harsh winds of winter had now moved on past the thaw, and spring would be in the air back home. Here all the turn of the seasons meant was the winds subsided to be replaced with humid weather that never seemed to ease.

In the distance there could be seen a large number of figures lined up, marching directly towards them. Quickly the group was on the floor, their cloaks covering their form that hid them in the shallow light of the moons.

Counting, Erikson thought there must be over ten thousand skeletals and ghouls making up their number from what he could sense. In the front could be seen a group of figures numbering between fifty and a hundred he guessed, each one a black shape that seemed to draw all the light from the area. He could not see the back of the procession, but he imagined that there would be others.

The gods curse us, it's beginning! Came the thought from Erikson through the Joining.

We have to get back and warn our lord. Came the thought from the Sergeant.

Quickly the party got up, it would not be hard to beat the advance back to their front, but to get there in time to give sufficient warning would be the real challenge.

With haste, the party set out south towards their own lines. Their speed was dictated by their need and to Hazel it felt like they were moving too fast to sustain the pace for long.

In contradiction to Hazel's belief, three days later they arrived back at their camp. Dust covered, sweating and near exhaustion, the patrol of Riders came running through the gates with the news of the attack. They were met by Lord Rayburn before they could move too far into the base, and before they could finish their report, runners were already sent to ready the settlement for battle.

It was silent for the next three days. Everyone was going about their tasks in the studied silence of apprehension. The walls had been reinforced again, pit traps and stakes had been set throughout the desolate waste that was leading into the heart of the Lost Lands. The traps from the previous attacks had been reset and any weapons that were available were placed in easy reach of the defenders.

Night had fallen. In the distance, thousands of fires sprang up, illuminating the horizon in a false impression of the rising sun. Slowly the fires crept forward, torches being carried by foot soldiers making a snake of fire across the wilderness. In the sky came shrieks from beasts that only legend remembered clearly, the Graven. Sixteen feet from wingtip to wingtip, its tough leather body resembled that of a giant bat while its head belonged to an eagle, its giant beak razor sharp and snapping at the air. On their backs were carried the most powerful of the Grey Mages. The Dark Lords that had shunned mortality and had incurred the dark arts of necromancy to immortalise their body at the cost of their very soul. They feared nothing and worked towards an end unknown. The Rangers had heard talk of the 'Great Master', but whether this master was one of their own or not no one knew.

At the head of the army was a wall of darkness. In the distance, it was outlined by the torches of the ghouls who lacked any real perception and relied upon the light given off to see. As the army advanced, the Seer's Mage sight allowed them to see further than the rest, almost in unison they whispered prayers to the gods and started to gather the energies they used to cast their spells.

The tension in the air visibly increased. At the sight of Mages alarmed and readying themselves, the rest of the armies gathered their weapons close and peered into the darkness.

Riders stood silent and ready in their units gathering their own powers, their bodies shimmering, almost vanishing into the background. The Royal Guard detachments in veteran discipline held their lines steady, guarding the Royal officer they were attached to and refusing to let themselves be shaken.

And so the night passed, the enemy's army advanced and the tension grew.

The attack did not occur the following day, for hours the Kingdom armies stood watching the opposing force in readiness. For hours, the opposing army did nothing but stand in their lines, moving not a single inch. The most powerful Seers were using their arts to see into the camps of the war host gathered against them. There were tents that held the Grey Mages. They were working on spells of their own, spells to strengthen their army of necromantic soldiers. Their Dark Lords flying overhead on the backs of the dreaded Graven, looking down on the undead army as it stood to attention unmoving. The day progressed, the sun rising and falling, protective spells were wrought and swords, spears and axes were sharpened, but still there was no assault, no release from the deafening silence that stretched across the miles of lines that stood ready to fight.

The armies of the Kingdom were tired. They had been sleeping in patterns of four hours since midday. No one knew when the attack would come, and so men and women tried to get sleep if they could.

It was close to midnight and Hazel was asleep. Outside in the camp there came a shout that jolted her awake. Quickly it was followed by another. Hazel calmed her mind and instantly felt her *Danger Awareness* set alarm bells ringing in her own head. Instantly she was up and donning her armour and belting her sword round her waist. She threw open the entrance to her tent and froze at what she saw. The opposing army had grown, the skeletal remains of the fallen had been animated to join the ranks of the undead as it now marched towards the camp. Hazel made a quick prayer to the god of war and made a dash towards the defences.

As she neared her station, the other Riders where there, ready with weapons drawn. There were Seers amongst their ranks, waiting for the opposing army to close enough that they could use their mage skills most effectively.

As the shambling horde approached, they fell victim to the numerous traps that had been set for them by the kingdom troops. Hundreds of the enemy had fallen into pits deep enough to break limbs with sharpened stakes at the bottom to ensure any who fell would not climb out again. But the enemy continued to close, their vast numbers not appearing to be depleted. They hit the second wave of defences, the large ballistae hurling their great payloads into the host that continued to approach. Again hundreds were torn apart in the first volley. Still onward they marched, their pace not slowing for their fallen. They approached the line that archers could use their bows. At three hundred yards, the army appeared too close for comfort as the arrows pin cushioned the ghouls, slamming them to the ground. The arrows were all alight with pitch so as to consume on impact and the trails of smoke hung heavy in the air.

Closer the army came and in an instant there were hundreds of lightening bolts, fireballs or plasma surges heading into the front ranks of the enemy as the Seers brought their arts to bear on the undead creatures.

Hazel stood still behind the wall and the stakes in the ground that pointed towards the enemy that still advanced. Behind the makeshift wall, which was all the protection offered, stood six thousand men and women of the Kingdom armed and ready to defend their country with their lives against an army that outnumbered them nine thousand to six. Bodies were torn apart and smoking on the ground but still they came. One hundred yards off they drew weapons and the first explosion hit the defenders.

A magical attack that sent a hundred men of the Kingdom Army flying in all directions as a hole appeared in the wall, created by the spell-craft of the Grey Mages from the protection of their camp. At such a range the attacks that would be used would be weak in comparison to that unleashed by the Seers against the invading army, but still visual enough to shake the defenders confidence.

The Seers own mages that were more skilled in the arts of defence withdrew from the front lines to start the counter spells that would attempt to stop any more attacks from the Grey Mages.

There was a screech from overhead as the Graven flew threw the dense smoke rising from the earth. Their riders unleashing fire attacks of their own. Seers and archers redirected their attentions on the new arrivals with varying success. Though the archers were numerous, the arrows did little hurt to the enormous creatures, and their riders were protected by the Graven's bulk. The Seers caused more damage but their numbers were less and fewer still actually hit their speeding foes.

Hazel cleared her mind, or at least tried to. She quickly found the minds of the other Riders close to her and entered the *joining*. She suddenly felt someone familiar, and looking to her left she saw Cholla, smiling back at her, bow in hand as she let loose another cloth yard into the advancing horde.

Hazel smiled back as Cholla dropped her bow and drew her sword. Almost in unison, the Riders who could, all shifted their appearance using their arts to blend into the background. The undead army reached the stakes barely twenty five yards from the wall, a few of the slower ghouls were impaled on the gigantic poles, their comrades barely halted as they tried to push past the inconvenience.

The wall the defenders stood on was barely four foot high and was more to give the defenders a solid line to defend than to give any real cover. As the first ranks of the undead host came within striking distance, the defenders let loose all their anger, fear, and zeal against them. Lightning buzzed through the enemy as the Seers continued to wreak havoc amongst the attacking host. Riders, blurred and dealt a swift death to anyone they came across on the other side of the wall. The army using spears repelled the enemy as best they could but were taking losses as much as they were inflicting them.

There was almost a thunderous explosion as the horde of undead finally reached the wall in numbers. Their bodies crashing against the hastily constructed stone defence.

Regular soldiers, Royal Household Guards, Riders and Seers deployed their arts, the enemy falling crushed, cut, pierced, burnt or electrocuted. At points along the line, men and women were trying their hardest to hold against the attacking mass of undead bodies and the relentless assaults from the Graven and their riders, inflicting great losses to the defenders number.

Hazel and Cholla were fighting in unison, each guarding the others flank. On impulse and from a feeling of dread that came from Cholla through the *joining* Hazel leapt to her right and nearly knocked over another Rider as a Graven's claw sliced through the air in her previous position. Swinging at the leg of the beast, Hazel made hard contact between the Graven and her blade, the beast shrieked in protest. As the giant creature pulled back, Hazel looked at the leg that should have nearly been severed, yet in disheartened realisation she discovered that there was the barest of cuts to the Graven's leg. As it wheeled, she noticed the Dark Lord that was riding it focusing on her, the human that had inflicted hurt to his pet. His pole arm came swinging down on Hazel who, this time was not quite fast enough. The blade cutting her shoulder as it parted the chain armour protecting her.

Hazel felt the heat pulse through her body as the blade bit, her scream came out as a low groan as she tried to clear herself of the fighting to see how badly she had been hurt. Cholla cried out as the feeling of pain flooded through the *joining*. Closing herself off from it she pulled Hazel away from the front, the Graven now circling higher away from the melee. As soon as the gap appeared, another Rider filled it to stop the flood of skeletal warriors that was waiting for the line to break.

Away from the main confrontation Hazel slumped to the ground, Cholla looked at her arm and winced. "It isn't pretty Haze," she said "we need to get you to a medic and get you stitched up before you lose the arm." Hazel merely nodded numbly as she tried to stand up.

Cholla lifted Hazel up and supported her using her good arm. Slowly they made their way across the camp that was in turmoil. Soldiers Riders and Seers running back and forth, no one without blood staining them, their own or others, shouts and orders mixing with screams and moans. Eventually they made it to the field hospital, wounded scattering the ground outside as the surgeons assistants tried to apply some sort of order to the masses waiting to be seen. There were cases of cut arms, torn off legs and slashes to the chest. Hazel looked at the waiting lines and saw Captain Reynolds sitting on the floor, his leg suffering a minor slice that still stopped him from walking.

As Hazel sat, one of the hospital assistants came over to her and inspected the damage done to her shoulder. Immediately she was lifted and taken into the tent much to the disgust of

Reynolds who grabbed at Cholla's wrist as she walked past. "What do you think your playing at girl? Others were here first, me for one." He nearly spat at her. "Hazel is hurt, badly. More so than you, she could lose her arm. I thought by now you would be aware of the way field hospitals work. The urgent get seen first." Replied Cholla, her voice steel as she matched gazes with Reynolds.

"Pure favouritism. You Riders get the best treatment because you're *so powerful*. It hasn't helped that upstart of a girl in there has it!?" he spat back viciously.

Cholla took the hand holding her wrist, and lifted the Captain of the floor and planted him down again face first, her boot pressing squarely on the lesion in his leg.

"Talk to me like that again you dog of a man and I'll see to it that you're a private again digging latrines… if I don't kill you first." She stormed off past the other wounded leaving Reynolds fuming in the mud.

Inside the tent, Hazel was placed on a make shift table, her armour and top removed and she was cleaned as best as was possible. The surgeon came over in a blood-covered apron. Though he looked exhausted he still had a genteel look to him that showed sympathy for a patient. Quickly he gave Hazel a sedative that made her drowsy, and set to with needle and thread. It seemed an eternity to Hazel, the numb fuzzy pain shooting through her arm seemed to be a continuous slow burn as the surgeon worked. She slipped further away into blackness, her only sense left, hearing. She could still hear the screams of dying, the roars of graven overhead and the clash of steel mixed with the sharp smell of magical energy. At the last she heard the call for all wounded and non front line personnel to fall back to Sarafell itself. Blackness followed and so did blessed oblivion.

"The hospital and a company of the Royal Household Guard are evacuating the wounded now sir." Reported a colonel to Lord Rayburn sombrely.

"Good get the Riders ready to retreat, if we can call any dragons do it, I don't know what they are up to but lets hope they hear us in time." replied Rayburn. The colonel saluted and left to follow out his orders. Gareth Rayburn started to collect his maps and files together, handing them to a secretary who quickly stowed them in a wagon and steered the horse team away from the conflict. He looked around his tent, his armour weighing heavily on him as he reached for his great sword. It had been a long time since he had felt its weight in his hand ready to fight. There was an almost comforting feeling, reminding him of a simpler time.

With determination, he left the tent and placed the plate helm squarely upon his brow, walking deliberately into the melee. Within seconds, he was shimmering and blending with his background. Skeletal warriors surrounded him and with little thought he took one swing with his great sword and beheaded them all in one three hundred and sixty degree arc. Stepping over the fallen remains of the undead warriors, he quickly joined the defending line that had broken, stepping straight into the centre of the gap. Enemies fell before him, his speed with the blade unnaturally quick, the blade glowing slightly giving it a ghostly appearance as it sliced and hacked through his foe.

Slowly the gap was closing around him, the defenders line was gradually strengthening. The Riders were now rallying around their Lord. Their zeal, passion and courage renewed, they fought like demons dealing death to any that stepped within their reach. Gareth paused in the brief reprieve as the final ghoul was cut down before him. The word was being passed down the line, they would be falling back in formation covered by archers from the rear.

Slowly and on Lord Rayburn's command the line of Riders started to retreat, slowly walking backwards, watching the mass of the enemy staggering after them. The defending army must have lost two thousand men, the undead must have lost twice that, still the defenders were outnumbered.

Gareth looked up, *where have the Graven gone?* He thought silently. As the undead reached the wall the Riders and army had been defending the archers let loose a thunder crack of bows, their broad-head arrows arching in a line of steel towards the enemy. Ghoul's fell, skeletal warriors were spun and toppled over before climbing back to their feet and continuing their slow march towards the Kingdom army. Another rain of arrows and more ghouls pinned to the blood soaked earth. The Seers that were still with the army gathered their energies and linked hands. Gareth could feel the magics being worked in his skin. A low chanting began within the ranks of the Seers and the ground started to tremble. No few of the attacking army started to lose balance or topple to their knees the skeletal warriors began to lose their animation, collapsing to piles of bones on the floor as the trembling became shaking. With a great crash of sound and a white flash of light the earth beneath the undead horde erupted skyward.

Bodies flew up, fifty feet into the air and more. With one rush of air, the remaining undead army seemed to spasm before collapsing unmoving to the earth.

"What happened?" asked a Rider looking shocked.

"I don't know, I think the Seers must have broken the spells of the Grey mages but I don't understand how." Replied the Lord Commander of the Dragon Riders.

"The loss of a slave under a mages spell is like the feeling of putting your feet up after a long days work. Multiply that feeling by a thousand fold and you would probably pass out with the relief. That is what has happened. Unfortunately most of us have also passed out." Replied a hard looking man in white robes. His eyes were a pale green and his dark hair matted with sweat.

"Jakrin! You're here?! You should be back at the palace guarding the King!" replied Rayburn shocked, pleased, and yet confused at the arrival of the Lord High Seer at the front line of a battle many leagues from where he was supposed to be.

"Fear not my friend," commented Jakrin, "I am returning now."

"You have the power left?" asked Gareth Rayburn with genuine concern.

"I do, but I must not linger, the King is not aware I…slipped out." Replied Jakrin with a slightly mischievous grin.

"Then go, and thank you." Said Gareth as the magician nodded in reply and vanished with a gentle rush of air.

The Kingdom Army arrived at Sarafell, the spirit of the soldiers was almost broken. They had barely survived an attack from the creations of the Grey Mages and were only spared in the end by the intervention of the Seers and Jakrin Tiersing. Gareth Rayburn walked through the North Gate of Sarafell close to sunset and looked around. The city was in a state of disarray, the occupants either battening down or evacuating their families. Any builder was being employed to reinforce the walls and carpenters were working with engineers creating siege engines and defences.

Rayburn walked over to a Rider, his armour was still covered in the dirt of war, his expression dark with loss. On noticing his Lord, the Rider saluted crisply but was waved off by Gareth.

"Enough of that lad," said the Rider Lord. "where are the Rider wounded and new command post being set up?"

"Over by the watch tower sir, there is an old town watch building that is solid and has enough space to hold the senior officers and personnel. The wounded are being treated in the market square, it has been cleared and a field hospital has been erected there for general use." Replied the Rider.

Saluting, the Lord thanked the young man and continued towards the square.

He had walked half the way through the crowded and busy streets when he heard his name being called from somewhere behind him. Looking back, he noticed a liveried servant of the city's mayor trying to push through the throng of people towards him.

"Lord Rayburn! Sir! The mayor would like to talk to you! He says he must know what is happening! No other officer in charge has yet arrived but his entire city have either fled or locked up. He is in a terrible state and demands you explain what is occurring to him at once!" puffed an exhausted servant, looking slightly nervous.

"Tell the mayor I will see him after I have seen to my wounded and have established my command post. Should he have evacuated before then he would be a wise man." Replied Rayburn in a sombre voice as he wheeled on the spot and marched off through the densely populated streets.

Though night was closing in, lamps had been lit to enable the defenders to continue working. Like ants, the city's remaining inhabitants and soldiers scuttled passed each other in a bid to accomplish their tasks before they were unable.

Rayburn approached the market square, the entire space was now dominated by an enormous field hospital. Men and women were lying on makeshift beds outside the tent – an ominous indicator that inside was full with the wounded. Passing through the beds and making his way to the main entrance, Gareth Rayburn Lord of the Dragon Riders stopped where he could, to give his best wishes, his commiserations and some chance of hope to those he could. There were dozens of Riders lying in beds near the entrance, none too badly hurt. All would be able to rejoin the war effort in a few weeks hopefully. Holding back a silent tear, Rayburn saluted his men before entering the tent to find his Order's final toll.

Inside, his breath caught deep in his throat. Wounded men and women laid everywhere, the few camp doctors that were here were trying their best to see everyone. All the Riders were in one corner of the tent. There must have been over fifty inside the sparsely outfitted hospital estimated Gareth, these poor warriors were in worse condition to those outside, some he judged to be near to the final release that would end this life.

He wanted desperately to turn and leave, to just work in numbers lost, yet he knew he could not. Though the faces and names here would haunt him forever, he owed his soldiers something, anything to help them, whether it be a joke to help them recover, or a kindly face to give their sacrifice meaning. Knowing what he must do he squared his shoulders and slowly walked over to his fellow Riders.

Every one of them knew his name. He had promoted each and every one from Novice to Rider at some point in the past. Whether it was twenty years past, five years or one hundred and fifty. *Nearly two normal lifetimes and wiped out in one day of fighting,* thought Rayburn looking at a young Sergeant he remembered promoting over a century ago. At his approach the more able bodied, managed to salute with one or the other of their arms while those who were unable, apologised in heartfelt honesty that burned him to the heart.

He must have spent a couple of hours within the tent, trying to cheer up his comrades, before he finally left into the cool night. Slowly he walked to the main watchtower where his command post should have been set up.

Entering the building, the Generals and senior officers acknowledged Rayburn and set to debriefing him of the action.

"We had six thousand men and women from the Army, Royal Household Guard and Riders. Of that, we lost two thousand, one thousand one hundred of the regular Army, six hundred Household Guard and three hundred Riders. There are more as you have seen with the wounded. We managed to inflict quite a bit of damage considering. Most of the undead they sent at us were destroyed and whilst not physically hurting the Grey Mages, we must have reduced the size of their army considerably." Remarked General Peterson.

"Then we may have bought some time, but let's not count on it." Commented Rayburn still worn and tired. "We should continue to reinforce the city and try to convince the rest of the population to evacuate. We now have four thousand men at arms defending this city. That should be more than enough to hold the place should we come under siege. We may lose the land to the north of here, but we evacuated all the villages between the border and here so an army can't pass us and leave their back exposed. So we hold. Moreover, we can now concentrate – if that is the right choice of words – on the quarantine around Peters Hold."

The night stretched on, and plans were set, broken and reset again.

Chapter 10

Tactics

Tal awoke, he had been training the past few weeks since the news of the marshalling of the Demons. He was improving with sword and letters, though slowly, however he was beginning to excel at the martial arts, no longer needing to be trained. This fact fascinated Kelar beyond words. Many an evening he had watched as Tal took on challenges from any willing, and many an evening he had taken money from several colleagues in wagers.

Word had filtered back via Dragon Riders, that the line holding the border to the Lost Lands had fallen. The new front to the Grey Mage War as it was coming to be called, was now Sarafell. Reinforcements had been slowly arriving at the Riders camps throughout the Kingdom, and Tal waited anxiously for the list of fallen to be approved. He had no word of Hazel, and worried for no reason he could fathom. Yes, she was a friend, but she was also better trained than he, and stronger in many ways. He should not feel the need to fret so much, should he?

Brad had recently arrived to Peters Hold and had heard that Cholla was well and had distinguished herself in battle. He had been swanning around with a daft grin on his face ever since he had been told. Coupled with the fact he had been promoted Rider last week and not a thing in the god's creation could dampen his spirit.

Tal was up and dressed before most others in the camp. He walked outside and again found Kelar sitting on a barrel waiting for him.

"You're always waiting for me when I wake Sergeant Gwent. Is this another skill that will be taught at a later date?" Remarked Tal with a rueful grin.

"Maybe," said Kelar smiling back "but in truth I have the night watch wake me an hour before they turn in, I'm surprised you did not work that out for yourself"

Tal looked at him in disbelief, surely this warrior of might and mysticism would not stoop to such low tactics to impress? Kelar was grinning still as he watched Tal struggle to come to an answer.

Yes, he would stoop to such a level if it made sport of me. Thought Tal as he let out a soft laugh and slowly shook his head.

"Any news from Sarafell yet?" He asked of Kelar as was becoming his morning tradition.

"No. Though try not to think of it, you are progressing steadily with your studies, Brad was made up to Rider and he is not too far ahead of you on weapons and writing. It would be a shame for you to hold up your own promotion."

Agreeing Tal took his curved blade and followed Kelar to a clearing in the woods. So far, there had been little activity from Peters Hold. However, that would not last forever, and Tal had made a promise to himself that he would face whatever coming storm approached as a Rider, not as a half trained Novice.

Kelar bowed to Tal and swung a violent slash towards his head. Tal ducked as if his life depended on it – he doubted Kelar would actually let it strike him, but it was best not to test that theory – the sword passed over his head with a hiss of air being cut. Tal made a thrust towards Kelar, however the veteran Rider blocked it easily and stepped in with the hilt of his sword to hit Tal with it.

Spinning Tal caught his wrist and spun him away, increasing the distance between them again.

"Well done," said Kelar "now try this." Before he had finished his sentence, Tal was being pushed back, a series of high and low cuts was thrown at him. Barely able to deflect the attack, Tal made no pretence of finery as his sword moved faster than he could think, in the desperate attempt to block Kelar's lightning attack.

Eventually Tal could not hold off any longer and a misstep took his legs from beneath him as he fell backwards.

"You're doing a lot better Tal, I think I should get a different Rider for you to spar with." Commented Kelar, helping Tal back to his feet.

"Why?" asked Tal, a strange sadness in his heart and a look of uncertainty on his face, "I can't keep up with you, why would I do any better against someone else?"

"You have trouble keeping up with me, because you are too used to me. I have taught you all the defensive forms I can, some you have benefited from, others you have not, but you can learn no more from me. Another Rider would increase your experience and might know some tips or tricks that you will find useful."

Tal nodded, he did not want his mentor to place him with another. He had come to think of Kelar as a friend as much as his sergeant.

Kelar was just about to say something more when a Rider came running from General Cristof's Tent. He spoke quietly enough so as not to let others close by hear, but it was still loud enough for Tal to make out the vague idea of what was being said.

The Rider saluted as Kelar nodded and then left, moving to another Sergeant close by. Feigning ignorance, Tal asked what the quiet discussion was about.

"Nothing that requires you attention Tal." Said Kelar with a smile on his face. "Rider Shan-Yin Hito should be here soon. He is an excellent user of the same blade you prefer, and you know him. So that should do away with the awkwardness of a new trainer. I want you to wait here for him, and then follow any instructions he gives, understand?"

"Yes sir." Replied Tal as Kelar smiled then turned and walked off towards his tent.

Shan-Yin arrived less than five minutes later, and stood silently as Tal finished his set of forms. "That is well done, young Tal. Kelar has done very well in instructing you in the forms. However, he seems to struggle to make you *feel* the blade. You remember the moves but do not truly believe them, moving from one to the other because you have been told to, rather than because it feels right."

"What do you mean sir?" Replied Tal.

"Watch. Make ready Tal." The two faced off, sword tips touching each ready for the other to attack first. Shan-Yin struck in perfect attack to the first form. A high overhead blow followed by a slash from Tal's left to right at hip height. Tal made the first block then had to stumble as the second blow nearly slipped behind his hasty deflection.

"Stop there Tal." Said Shan-Yin as he pulled away. "Now show me your first form." Tal readied himself, and then started. The high block became a side block, he then twisted, and faced the other direction with his blade above his head ready for a blow designed to cut a mans head in two.

"Stop. Now again, slowly, and with me."

The two men faced each other. And as Tal started his form, Shan-Yin began his attack. The first blow met with Tal's first block, and as Tal moved to the second block, steel once again struck steel. Tal spun and found himself behind Shan-Yin, his sword poised ready to make the fatal blow.

"Do you see now why you should believe the forms Tal?" asked Shan-Yin

"Well yes, but only if the opponent does what you want him to do." Replied Tal.

"That my young friend is the real trick. Come, start the forms from number one, with me." As the two fought slowly, Tal began to get a feeling for the moves that were to come next, and by the end of the forms, Tal and Shan-Yin were moving smoothly and together, a theatrical play, performed slowly and in perfect unison.

As the final blow was "struck" by Tal, Shan-Yin bowed, "you have done well this morning Tal, and now have much to think and practise upon. I will leave you to the rest of the day."

"But how will I know what blow will be struck next?" asked Tal again.

"Practise this first Tal, your answer will come in time. Trust me." Shan-Yin bowed and then withdrew, leaving Tal to practise alone and in peace.

An hour passed and Tal was beginning to grow sore, his arm started to ache when he swung. Looking to the sun he estimated the time to be nearing mid day. He sheathed his sword and moved to the camps mess area. There was bread and a vegetable soup on the menu and Tal set to it with a ravenous appetite as though he had hardly eaten for days, for in truth he had eaten little while awaiting news of Hazel.

Finishing his last mouthful of bread after mopping the bowel with it, he noticed Kelar moving with a full pack towards the command tent, closely followed by Sergeant Sam Dray. Both wore a very serious expression that seemed to sit uneasily on their faces.

His interest piqued, Tal laid aside his bowl and began to trail his Sergeant at a respectable distance. He noticed the speed at which both men walked and the determined set to their shoulders. As they entered General Cristof's tent, Tal crept closer. He could hear mutterings as he waited to the rear of the tent, but not the full briefing. Slowly he pieced together some details but could not work out what they pertained to.

Something about a mission into Peters Hold, a full company of Riders, and a quick withdrawal. He could not work out what else, but as he heard the tent door slap back, he quickly made his way back towards the row of tents that surrounded the command centre.

Kelar and Sam emerged from the tent, a new bag was slung over their shoulders. They started a forced march towards the city side of the camp. Their cloaks hiding the field armour that each wore.

Reaching the edge of the camp, both Kelar and Sam started to blend in to the background, their forms blurring as if the trees around them were behind an intense heat. The latest campsite that the general had selected was in a dense wood that stretched right up to the south side of Peters Hold. Tal followed only by his sense of them, for as soon as they entered the tree line, keeping them marked by eye was useless. He continued to track them for most of the afternoon, until he spotted them approaching a clearing. Kelar Gwent and Sam Dray, now visible moved to a group other Riders, numbering over a hundred.

Looking at the group Tal saw both move to a woman and salute, as they stood at ease something was obviously discussed, something that troubled both Kelar and Sam for they both seemed ready to speak a complaint until a hand movement from the woman silenced them. Nodding they moved off in two directions as indicated to them, joining up with a separate group they seemed to take command, each group had ten to fifteen people in it, and Tal saw that each of the other parties had a sergeant in command. Without a spoken order, the legion moved off into the woods again, all of them blurring into a wavy nothingness, and moving in the direction of Peters Hold.

The trees whispered in the winds. The bushes rustled, and the light that was fading shot down through the canopy offered by the trees. The city was no more than an hours march but the specific orders stated that it was only to be entered by night.

Slowing their pace Kelar, brought everyone to him through the *joining*.

"We will wait here until the sun is setting, then move on the city." Said Kelar as he removed his pack to check the contents were still there. "If anyone needs some sleep or rest, you have three hours.

"Bryant, do you have the Seer's devices?"

"Yes, they are in my pack. Can you tell us what they are for yet?"

"I'm sorry, no. We do our job, place the devices at the requested points then get out and I smash this vial. Should I fall before that point, you, as second in command will take this vial and leave the city, when you are safely clear by thirty minutes hard march, you will smash it, and so on through out the company. More than that I cant tell you, believe me, I wish I could, but should any of us get captured, the fewer who know what is occurring, the better."

The group simply nodded. A few took the opportunity to rest, but the four that had seen service with Kelar recently stayed alert. Shan-Yin, remembering the way Tal had snuck up on them refused to let his vigil relax again. Walking up to Kelar he spoke quietly.

"What will happen with Tal? I left him practising his forms, he has no idea where we have gone."

"Don't let it trouble you," said Kelar. "when he cannot find you tomorrow he will probably go to one of the remaining Captains and will be assigned another Rider to follow."

Nodding Shan-Yin, simply returned to his survey of the woods.

Martin and Mathew seemed almost frozen, standing at Kelar's back, they appeared as immovable boulders at his shoulders. Their broad swords an imposing sight strapped across their backs.

Time passed and so did the light, the party was formed up and slipped into the trees once more. Creeping through the underbrush, the Riders made their way slowly towards the ruined city of Peters Hold. In the darkness, each of the Riders relied upon their senses not to trip on an exposed root, or slip on wet moss. The tension clouded the air around Kelar as he moved, almost having to push himself through the suffocating atmosphere it caused. Bird calls, the rush of a fox at edge of the *joining*, the unexpected hooting of an owl, all did their part to increase his heart rate, and blood pressure.

From the *joining* Kelar heard a snap of wood ahead and to his left. The response from the other Riders matched his own. Stillness flooded through him. The sound was amplified, but originated from outside the range of their joined senses. It might have been a wolf padding around looking for his next meal, but a wolf would be light footed enough to avoid braking branches. It may have been another Rider, from a different party out of position, but they would have been easy enough to spot with both party's senses out stretched. No this was something not native to the forest, and something that was no Rider.

With a mental command, Kelar called his company towards him silently. They moved like water over grass, without sound. When they were within twenty feet of him, they moved together towards the sound of the breaking wood.

As they approached, Kelar could see a fire burning. Wondering who would let a fire burn here, they continued to approach until they heard a guttural snarl. Halting instantly, and hot fear coursing through his blood, Kelar commanded his unit to wait. Building his courage, he slipped forward alone. He needed to know what was here, and how many there were.

As he neared a small clearing, he hid behind a bush and gently parted some of the sparse leaves. He counted eighteen demons, mostly small in size, however there were three that towered over him, and one that towered over them. A low moan emanated from a cage that rested behind the fire. Unable to see what caused the wail due to the flames, Kelar waited and watched. The larger demon turned his attention on the captive, his large red and black eyes seemed to struggle to focus in the flickering light. When they did seem to locate the captive, a torn lip raised, bearing uneven fangs. His entire face was leathery and full of scars and cuts, and his arms bore the same marks, whether from swords, or the same type of claws that he owned was unknown. The beast snarled something at the cage, but its occupier simply cried. With a speed that seemed unlikely from such a large creature, it stood and moved over to the cage in what Kelar could only describe as a rage.

Howling louder, he uttered something else in his vile language, but the crying from the cage simply increased in desperation. With a snarl, the beast reached between the bars, his claws gripping something within. With a howl of pain from the cage, the demon pulled his arm back, a grisly tearing could be heard under the screams from whatever it held. Kelar nearly vomited as he realised that the demon was holding an arm, torn from a man. Opening his mouth he took a bite, rending the flesh and swallowing it without so much as chewing. With a look of disgust, he threw the arm in the fire letting it burn to blackness before removing it and consuming the rest of the meal.

Kelar watched in silent horror, the cage became silent. The occupier dead, or passed out from pain or lack of blood. On a growl from the giant demon, the others piled in to tear parts from the man lying in the cage.

Backing away, Kelar returned to his company. When he returned he noticed the sick look they all possessed after witnessing the spectacle through the *joining*.

What do we do? Asked Bryant.

We try to go round them, we don't have the numbers to guarantee we silence them all. Turn east and we will give them a wide distance, I don't want anything to cause complications to our mission.

Sensing the agreement from his party, he turned to the east and started to flank the demons still feasting on human flesh. The party slowly moved through the bushes and trees, not wanting any misstep to give away their position. Kelar tried to stretch out his senses further. The Demons had not stirred from their meal. The scent of burning flesh was heavy on the cold night air as the Riders made their way past the gruesome spectacle.

Behind Kelar there was a snap of a branch. Regret, dread, and apology flooded through the *joining* to the party. Bryant had slipped in wet mud and in trying to right himself had put his foot against a root he thought was sturdy.

No fault of his, everyone in the party knew it could have just as easily been them. Senses outstretched they tried to discern if the demons had been alerted to their presence.

Nothing.

The Demons were not moving…but they had stopped eating. In silence, the Riders waited. Minutes passed and time seemed to halt its passage. Breath caught on the cool air. But then it sounded, a guttural growl came resounding through the trees, and echoed through their hearts.

Get ready, circular formation, and camouflage yourself, get ready to support each other. We have to take them all down before they get suspicious and send for reinforcements from the citadel. Ordered Kelar to his party, drawing his sword and fading back to a gentle blur against a tree.

They waited, silence only broken by the sounds of eight demons, that could be sensed, moving towards them, breaking branches as they forged forwards. No pretence of stealth, their sheer size and bulk all the defence they needed.

Mark your target when they move inside our lines. Move swiftly, do not linger within arms reach of these creatures. Commented Kelar to his company.

The first Demon entered their circle, medium sized for a demon it still stood at a good two feet taller than the tallest man and was easily twice as muscled. The thing had claws like a thing from nightmares, and his eyes glowed the red and black that seemed common amongst their kind. Naked of clothes, the only protection to the skin was tough scales that glinted a putrid rotting brown colour. His face was elongated into a snout that had chipped and broken fangs protruding over the lower lip, a black slime clinging to each serrated tooth.

Hold. Wait for the others, we can't afford to let any get back to the main camp.

And so the Riders slowly moved their circle with the demons. Slowly as each of the eight entered the circle, the Riders composed themselves. On an unspoken command the battle was joined.

Blurs wove in and out of the Demon ranks. Slashes appeared and demons dropped, three were down before the others could react, but when they did it was devastating. The larger of the eight stood still, and as a faded Rider slipped past him, the fourth demon falling to his blade, the creature lashed out, his claw gouging the air with a whistle as red life blood arced from the neck of the now visible Rider.

The other Riders lost their camouflage as the backlash from the death spread through the *joining,* causing another Rider to take a gash to her arm before they could blend in to the background again.

Five Demons were now down, one Rider dead, and the remaining beasts were circled by the remaining fourteen humans. It was a stand off, each side waiting to see who would make the first move. Shimmering shapes slowly circled the Demons as they snarled to themselves.

The night was drawing on. Kelar looked at the sky, it was nearly midnight. Half the night gone and they were still not at the city. Lack of time forced his decision. If he delayed any longer the demon camp would send more of their kind to look for the security patrol it had sent out. If that happened they would lose the advantage of surprise that they would sorely need to take down the rest of the invaders. And if that was prolonged the knock on effect could detrimentally affect their main mission.

Acting on impulse, Kelar stepped forward when one of the remaining smaller demons had its back turned to him. One slash and the foul beasts head was rolling on the floor, black blood fountaining from its neck. Quickly before its colleague could repay the compliment, Kelar hurriedly stepped back into the line of his own side. Two were left. The larger of the beasts snarled and tried to tear his way through the line. four Riders instantly formed a barricade, denying it the possibility of fleeing. The other remaining demon snarled helplessly as a couple of Riders that had stepped away from the main battle sent cloth-yard after cloth-yard arrow into his chest, back and face. On the sixth arrow the scaled creature fell and started to crawl towards its larger ally, three further arrows were required to stop the thing from moving further.

The last creature fell to the press of twelve Riders darting back and forth, hacking off parts of its body in an effort to best the creature as quickly as possible.

In the silence that now seemed to deafen Kelar and his party, the Riders shed their camouflage and stood looking at the Demons that littered the floor. A single Rider lay on the ground, his neck torn from him.

"Carry him, we will not leave a Rider here to rot." Ordered Kelar as two Riders collected their fallen. "How is your arm Rose?" He asked walking over to the wounded Rider.

"Its ok, it was only a glancing cut, not too deep thankfully." She replied.

"Good, lets get Michael laid to rest away from here. Then we have to kill the rest of those creatures before they send someone back to the citadel."

The funeral took less than two minutes, laid beneath the budding shoots of a bush, a swift prayer to the gods, and a silent farewell from his colleagues, Michael passed from the earth and into eternity.

The fire was burning low, there was no human left to eat. His nine minions milled around waiting for the return of their companions. He did not hear anything, but the chittering of his second was grating on his nerves. So he agreed to send an octate in search for this phantom snap and grunt. They should be back soon then they can get on with the patrol. So far they had found two different patrols of humans, each had been slaughtered with some taken for food, but his three octate strong force had been whittled down to just over two. He wanted to get back to the city, his placement here was nearly finished. He had seen the first attacks and taken the citadel, but now longed for the warmth of his home world, this one was too cold and unpredictable with its weather. No, he was due to return home, and he welcomed it. He had progressed his position here, and had gained muscle and strength. He may even challenge his tribes Force Hand – the second in command – to a dual for the position.

Yes, things were looking up for him. He grinned a fanged smile, where was that cursed fool he sent out? He lifted his snout to the air. He could not smell the Octate, but he could smell something - Blood, and human sweat.

Lifting a lip he started a snarl to tell his Patrol they were moving when a whistling and rush of air sped past his raised ear. He heard a growl and a yelp of pain as the Demon behind him fell to the floor. Turning he saw the creature twitching on the floor. The humans had used arrows. Singularly they posed no real threat, but in numbers they could be fatal, and the weaker Demon was stuck with seven of the things.

Around him the remaining eight started snarling and looking to the trees for any sign of the attackers. There was the scent of fear and anxiety all around him, he could not use his sense of smell to pin point a target. His eyes struggled to focus as the light from the dying fire flickered and cast deep shadows across the woods. More whistling and snarling. Growling he turned to see another of his tribe fallen to the floor, his black essence spilling onto the wet mud.

Then he saw it, a blur moving through the trees.

With a snarl he launched himself at the shape. He landed where he thought it was, but it had already moved on. Growling and snarling he turned looking for another target. Not a leap from him he saw a distortion in the air and charged. The figure slipped away from him but dealt him a cruel slash with its steel claw. With a howl of rage, he charged again, the ground speeding past him as his prey darted behind a tree after slicing a deep gash in his right arm.

Looking around, he saw his tribe's warriors all falling to these hidden humans. There was only himself and one Octate Hand left standing

"Retreat! Fall back!" he growled in anger. Never before had he withdrawn from a battle, but how could one fight what he could not see?

As he made a break in the direction of the city he heard a growl and a thump, he knew the Hand was down. Not looking back, he continued his four limbed rush back to safety, breaking branches and pushing bushes aside. How would he explain this to his superior? It was a simple mission, patrol the woods to the south of the city and kill any human found. He was dishonoured, but maybe the knowledge of invisible humans would be enough to spare his life.

Maybe.

Tal watched from a distance, although not *joined* with the other Riders, he could hear the silent command almost shouted by Kelar. They cannot let this demon escape them. Following the track, he ran through the retreating woodland as they approached the City, after barely two minutes he only just stopped himself from bowling Bryant over. Slowly retreating from the Rider, he watched as Bryant let his focus on the running demon sharpen. With a snap of a bow string, an arrow sped true through the sparsely scattered trees, the bare branches moving as the arrow flew past close by.

With a satisfying thump, Tal saw the demon carried forward by the arrows momentum as it struck. The following Riders were quick to swarm over the beast and end the chase.

Pausing only to take stock of the situation, Tal saw the Riders check each other for unseen wounds, then blur again. Slowly they slipped towards the City, each of them knowing that the night was too far progressed. Tal in his ignorance simply following at a safe distance. In the back of his mind, he wondered what the camp had made of his disappearance. It wasn't overly large and someone would have noticed his absence by now for sure, if not one of the other Riders, then by Brad at least. But Brad *was* a Rider now, and maybe off on a mission himself. It could not be helped. He had a duty to Kelar, and that had to come first. He would apologise to anyone he had to and take any punishment like a man. Even if it was ejection from the Order.

Kelar estimated that there was only about three hours of darkness left as they approached the walls of the city. Though they were fast running out of time, he made sure that he put as much effort into scanning his surroundings has he could. Leading his patrol into the hands of the enemy would not be something he would allow to happen.

After what felt an eternity standing at the edge of the tree line of southern Peters Hold, he motioned his party forward. They sprinted silently across the open area in front of the City and into the shadows of the wall. Crouching, they all silently stretched their senses out into the city.

There were dozens of Riders within, most of them making their way from the centre to the outside of the city. Kelar assumed they had laid their packages and were retreating to the safety of the woods. Signalling, he motioned the rest of the party onwards. As they approached the gate Kelar halted the company, there were shadows departing the city. *Riders* was who he sensed, and so continued. When they moved into visual distance, the other party stopped and greeted Kelar's with a nod of their heads. Query was passed through the *joining*, but when they saw the cuts and dried blood on Kelar's clothing, they simply nodded sadly and turned to leave, allowing the battle weary company to continue their mission in peace.

Tal watched as Kelar, Bryant, Shan-Yin, Martin and Matthew made their way into the city followed by the other nine Riders that remained in the party. The city walls were dark and foreboding to him. Standing intact yet somehow emptied of the majesty that he was sure once inhabited the mighty stonework. Tal looked upon the blackness of the walls that he must once again pass through. He remembered what had been discovered the last time he ventured into the vastness of Peters Hold, and he was loathe to enter again.

Building his resolve, he stretched out his senses. He could not make out much past the wall but what he could sense was neither alive nor moving. How much easier it would have been if he were *joined* to other Riders, their power added to his allowing them to sense further. For the first time he began to appreciate the focus and guidance of Kelar. Field-tested and trained, he had a much greater grasp of their powers than he had acknowledged before, and now that he was alone and heading into a known danger, he was stating to feel young and inexperienced. Would this be how he felt when he was promoted and sent off on a mission alone?

He thought back to Brad. He must be back in the camp now. Either on sentry duty or asleep. Did Brad have this feeling of ineptness? Shaking his head, Tal cleared these thoughts from his mind. He had to get into the city and he was not going to get there by thinking disparaging thoughts about himself.

With a final check, he ran full sprint to the walls. His eyes closed against the unseen watchers imagined on the other side. Opening his eyes at the last moment he stopped under the darkness and cold stone of the wall. Regaining his breath, he slowly made his way towards the gate, previously used by his former companions. At the entrance he drew his sword, it shone faintly in the murky light of the moons, cursing he wished he had some weapon black. Looking around he could do nothing about it except wipe some wet mud onto the blade, it was better than nothing but would not last long.

Breathing deeply he stepped round the wall and entered the city proper. He did not know what to expect, but nothing was certainly not it.

The buildings stretched forward, not a person nor demon moving. The silence was deafening to him, he was expecting a pitched battle or an army of Riders ready to storm the Citadel, but emptiness was all that surrounded him. He cast his senses out and felt two troops of Riders, one heading into the city, one heading out, almost on reciprocal courses. Moving forward he clung to the shadows of the abandoned buildings as he followed the sense of the patrol moving further into the city.

Tal stopped five hundred meters inside the walls. The patrol he was following was splitting up after a brief pause. Slowly creeping forward, he tried to pick up Kelar with his senses. It took him a while to recognise his friend, there were too many other Riders in close proximity at first, but as they slowly dispersed, he managed to locate him in a building close to the citadel.

As he slid up to the building he saw Kelar, he was placing a small round object at a corner of the building and covering it with dust to conceal it. When he appeared satisfied with his work, Tal saw him stand and move in darkness to another building, three down the street. There he stopped to place another orb and again with about eight other buildings. Tal quickly worked out that there must have been one thousand of these items placed around the city if all the Riders he saw in the clearing placed ten.

Wondering what they could be, he started to catch up to Kelar, but without any warning, a clash of steel caught his attention. From half way down the street, he saw a Rider clashing steel against the claws of a demon. One demon was dead on the floor next to him but the Rider was still struggling on his own against the creature towing over him. There was blood trailing down an arm hanging limp at his side as he fended off blow after blow levelled at his head.

Kelar turned and looked at the spectacle. With only the briefest second pausing to assess the situation, he placed his pack on the ground and drew his sword, rushing to the aid of the flagging Rider.

The demon was suddenly assailed from another side and was quickly dispatched by a slice across the throat from Kelar. Tal watched as Kelar spoke softly to the injured Rider. At a nod and handing over of his pack, the injured Rider saluted then moved swiftly towards the main gate of the city.

Kelar returned to his own pack and retrieved it. He quickly sheathed his sword and set off in the direction that the injured Rider came from. Tal could sense that Kelar was tense and that he felt time was short, though why he could not guess. As he followed Kelar he spotted a couple of Riders laying their orbs and then heading towards the gate, one he thought he recognised, short but well built he moved in a way he recognised. It was Brad! What was he doing here?! He had only been promoted to Rider recently. He should be doing sentry duty not raids into the city. Tal began to run over to him but before he could get there a roar sounded from the building near Brad. He turned drawing his sword but a demon that stood twice his height burst through a broken wall in the side of the city and with a wave of his powerful arm sent Brad flying through the air to crash into another building and slump at its base not moving.

Tal froze, he saw Kelar draw his sword once more and charge, the Rider who was leaving also did the same, swords raised they started to push the demon back. Tal stood still, his shock doubled as he recognised the Rider fighting alongside Kelar, it was Layland.

The world reeled as he saw him. Layland was dead, run through by one of the dark elf assassins. But he was here, fighting with Kelar to defeat a Demon twice their size. As quickly as these thoughts ran through Tal's mind, the beast moved faster. An arm swung wildly and caught Kelar across his chest sending him sprawling across the road, Tal was scared Kelar was in the presence of the Keeper of Souls but felt great relief when he saw him move. Drawing his own sword, he darted into the fray. He heard Kelar call his name in surprise and terror, and noticed Layland turn to look at him, also confused. None of it mattered to him as he ran straight to the demon that had attacked his friends. Layland tried to put himself between the Demon and Tal but only managed to receive a full-clawed gash to his chest that flung him over to where Kelar was struggling to stand.

Tal looked over in horror, expecting to see Lay cut open, but he was wearing plate armour that had taken the claws, and though it was heavily gouged, Lay had only taken a throw across the street.

There was a sudden jolt as Tal realised he was in the grip of the Demon and being raised over it's shoulder. His sword was lying in the dirt and well out of reach, and trying to struggle simply brought a backhanded blow to his head, sending his senses reeling. Trying to focus on what was happening he saw the demon throwing Brad over his other shoulder before turning towards the citadel and running towards its main portcullis. He felt dizzy and could no longer keep his mind on what was happening, he saw Brad start to stir but was barely conscious and lapsed into unconsciousness himself as he watched Kelar and Lay falling behind.

Chapter 11

Captivity

Kelar struggled to stand. His chest felt like he had taken a chariot square on at full speed. Wincing, as he moved ribs that were fractured, he surveyed his position. He had been thrown across the street by the Demon, his companion still fighting on. Looking for Brad he saw him move, even if it was barely, at least he was alive. Turning back to the fight he saw something he could not believe.

Tal was rushing the demon, sword drawn. Calling his name in warning, Kelar saw Kendrik turn to look at him, and when he recognised Tal, he darted to the space between him and the creature. With a mighty swing of its limb, a claw gouged at Layland's chest. The pain in his ribs burning, Kelar tried to move towards the demon as Kendrik came flying towards him. Kelar watched as he saw Tal standing before the towering hulk of the Demon.

Tal was looking at them, disbelief plain in his eyes, he did not even notice the demon close on him and reach out. With powerful arms, the beast took Tal and lifted him over his shoulders. Tal's sword dropping from his hand at the shock of the sudden jolt of being lifted from his feet.

Kelar's eyes began to stream as he forced himself to move, the foul creature was moving to Brad. Stumbling and falling to the ground, his chest screaming at him, he pulled himself along the ground. He must save Tal and Brad. They were more than just students and fellow Riders, they were friends.

Grief eating at him as a scavenging cat tears at a dead animals stomach, Kelar let out a tortured scream as the Demon turned and ran back to the Citadel.

Layland approached him from behind, helping him to his feet with his one good arm. "We must go. There is no more we can do for them, as soon as that creature gets back, it will tell everything it knows and our advantage goes out the window. We must get away."

Nodding slowly Kelar accepted Lays arm and support as they gathered their kit. He sent out his senses and contacted the other members of his party. As soon as they arrived, Martin and Mathew supported Kelar and they all headed for the walls of the city. Layland had met up with his group, and was also swiftly leaving the city. Both sergeants were down heartened, but both also knew their duty. On leaving the city, they quickly smashed their vials and made for the thin tree line.

"So can you tell me what those vials are for now sir?" Bryant asked carrying both his own and Kelar's packs and weapons.

"I'm sure you will find out shortly so lets not hang around." replied Kelar motioning his party forward. They had not got ten minutes from the walls when the first explosion sounded.

Drew awoke to the sharp sounds of thunder. Getting up tenderly dressed, weeks had passed since his ribs were cruelly fractured, and though he was getting back to his old self, if he rushed a movement he still felt a twinge of pain.

He had been in Borders Edge for five weeks now, the populace had been evacuated and the first regiments from the regular army were setting to making the city a fortress. Drew had been pulling light duties due to his ribs and though he had only been assigned guard duty, he was now feeling more content with his lot. Though he had been wounded, he found his fellow Guards were starting to treat him as one of their own. No longer was he a boy that wore their colours, he was now a Royal Household Guard.

Leaving his barracks quietly so as not to wake his fellows, Drew moved towards the command post. It was in the upper rooms of the small keep in the centre of the city. Not an overly large military city, it still managed to hold back the infrequent raids from the bandit tribes that somehow survived in the Dead Lands. Approaching the keep, Drew waved at the Guards standing post at the entrance. As he got close enough he called out to them, "What are those explosion sounds?"

"We don't know yet, they started about half an hour ago, all hell broke loose and a meeting of generals was called; about a quarter hour gone a Seer arrived looking very pleased with himself and the doors have been locked shut since."

"Thank you, mind if I wait around? find out what is going on?" asked Drew.

"Knock yourself out, its your down time your missing." replied the sentry with a shrug.

It took until well past sunrise before the doors were finally unlocked, and the gossip spread quickly. There had been a raid into the ruins of Peters Hold, the Riders had entered under the cover of darkness and placed orbs created by the Seers at pre selected positions and when they had departed, the Seers had ignited these orbs bringing down every building in the city – including the citadel itself.

Drew was at the market square to hear the news from Prince Allin himself.

"The plan was to collapse the citadel on top of the Demon Gates, and thus slow the advance for as long as possible. There were some losses to the Riders, but they acted nobly and the mission was a complete success. There is to be a continuous quarantine around Peters Hold with the main military base stationed here at Borders Edge with regular patrols between us, Myllarad and Reylward."

Drew stood in stunned silence. The speech delivered by the Prince flowed over the heads of soldiers, sailors, shipwrights and Seers. The entire crowd seemed to hold their breath, waiting for more. News of the assault, the number of demon dead, the kingdoms plans to fight back, but no more followed. Prince Allin simply instructed the Guard to speak to their commander and receive their orders.

Moving out of the square, his head hanging, overwhelmed by the news received, Drew tried to come to terms with what he had heard. The Kingdom had never struck back before. He had fought when attacked, and held quarantines, he had taken part in recognisance missions and guarded lines, but he had not heard of an offensive manoeuvre against the Demons or Mages before this. As he looked up, he noticed he had navigated the streets of the town and found his way back to the barracks without even noticing.

Captain Loytan was standing at the entrance with papers in hand. Calling out names, he was assigning new duties to his Guards. Some of the soldiers appeared happy with their lots, others seemed disappointed, others still looked angry at their assignment.

"Drew Earemon!" called the Captain.

"Sir!" replied Drew approaching his senior.

"How are you feeling lad?" asked the captain, his voice that tone of pure neutrality that always left Drew unsure on how to answer."

"Fit for any duty you assign sir." He replied carefully.

"Good lad, your on patrol. Join up with Sergeant Richardson and get your kit ready we leave in an hour."

Drew smiled. He had feared puling guard duty for another two months. This trip would be just over two months and would be something new. Racing into his billet he collected his gear and then made a move to meet Akarn.

He too was ready, kit packed and ready for the road. His arm had healed well with the aid of a helpful Seer, no bones had been broken so he was able to aid the soft tissue in repairing itself. Unfortunately for Drew, bones were beyond the skill of the Seer that had had been available to help the wounded.

Moving back onto the street Drew cringed. A company of twenty men – all on horseback – was preparing to leave. He secured his kit behind the saddle and loosened his scabbard before gritting his teeth and pulling himself onto the horse. Akarn smiled as he saw Drew stop himself from groaning by sheer force of will. Shaking his head slowly, he too mounted and moved beside Drew.

"Perhaps you're not ready for active duty just yet?" he said softly.

"I'll be fine, just a little sore, that's all." Replied Drew breathing slowly to let his chest return to a normal state.

"Just tell me if you can't go on ok? No need to be a hero - again." He said with a wry grin.

Nodding Drew turned his attention to his Captain. The last Guards had arrived and mounted as the Captain was outlining their route. They would be taking a curved passage to Myllarad so as to move closer to Peters Hold, then on to Reylward crossing through the Far East Forest.

When everyone was ready, they moved off through the northern gate of the city. Drew looked around, the countryside was another world to him. He loved every moment of it, he had grown up in Dukeray, a rough city that gained its strength not from practise with swords or pikes, but with bow and work gained from the forest. The country and the outdoors was where Drew felt most comfortable. He had been here all his life and felt rejuvenated after sitting in a town for five weeks.

Breathing as deep as his chest would allow, he pushed on, into the countryside and the chance of soldiering once more.

A week into their patrol, an outrider crested a verge and came back into sight of the main company. The weather was becoming warmer, and the ground drying up as spring became dominant over the winter. The sun was bright in the morning air and the slight breeze had a warmth to it that most had forgotten in the long and cold winter.

Drew was riding next to Akarn, talking about his childhood in Dukeray, how he had always wanted to become a soldier in the defence of his Kingdom, and that it was only when a Rider appeared to pick up his best friend that he had actually done something to follow his dream. Richardson smiled, remembering his own sign up to the army four years past. Then two years ago, he was transferred into the Royal Guard. A year after that he had been promoted to Sergeant after controlling a riot at the local jail when *his* Sergeant had been knocked unconscious by a drunken protester.

The two friends were sharing a joke when Richardson noticed the expression on the approaching outriders face. It was one of seriousness, no light banter would be shared only a professional report on something he had discovered.

Halting the party, Loytan awaited the news brought by his scout.

"Sir, there is something you should see, half an hour from here." Said the scout breathing heavily, his horse likewise fatigued.

"What is it? Explain while you lead us there." replied the Captain, his voice sharp and clear.

"Prints in the earth sir, horse like, only larger. A lot larger."

About thirty minutes later, the company pulled up where a scout was kneeling on the ground. Captain Loytan dismounted and walked briskly to stand next to the scout.

"What have you found?" he asked, concern audible in his voice.

"This sir." Replied the Guard, indicating the tracks in the soft mud.

The prints were large, larger than that of any creature Loytan had seen before, yet they were outlined like a hoof, like that of an enormous horse. There were several sets of tracks here, moving eastward, moving towards Peters hold.

Looking at the tracks, Loytan guessed that they were no more than a day old. Were they heading towards Peters Hold? Or, was this just a patrol stationed somewhere else and moving in that direction simply because it was their route?

If it was another stronghold for the demons, then it would need to be found and soon before they could get a foothold somewhere else in the Kingdom. Thinking quickly Loytan calculated his options.

He could organise a search now, get his trackers to follow the trails in each direction to find the demons stronghold or main party. But that would mean splitting his company only ten Guards in each team, not enough to confront the amount that passed this way let alone a larger party. Alternatively, he could simply follow the prints in the same direction and hope to catch up to them. But that would let any other parties to go undiscovered. No, he would send riders ahead to Myllarad and back to Borders Edge to organise a more detailed search. Calling Richardson and Drew over to him he outlined his proposal.

"Richardson, I want you to take Drew and head straight for Myllarad. This cannot be ignored, but neither can my duty to continue the patrol. When you get there, pass on a message to whoever is in command there. Tell them about these tracks, they can be no longer than a day old and if they herald another stronghold in the demons fortifications we cannot let them remain there.

"When you have passed on the message you can either join a patrol heading north or wait for us, which ever you feel would be most beneficial to the Kingdom. If I do not see you before, I will see you back at Borders Edge in one month."

Saluting, Richardson and Drew turned their mounts and headed off at the best speed they could manage.

Loytan watched them leave, wishing them the gods speed he turned and called two of his other Guards. Within fifteen minutes the word had been sent out. All he could do now was to take his remaining men and continue the patrol at a steady pace. However, he would now be twice as alert, nothing would slip by him, not if his country was at risk.

Drew came within sight of the city of Myllarad. Looking more like a building site than a city, Myllarad had scaffolding visible on almost every building of note, with workers moving through the streets in an organised fashion, it was a hive of activity that Drew had never known in his life.

It had been three days since he and Akarn had left their colleagues and they had hardly slept. The horses were breathing hard as they entered the city through the main gate.

Asking directions to the commander's headquarters, the pair moved as quickly as the crowded streets would allow. Dressed in field gear, and weather worn, the two soldiers caught the eye of every person on the streets, and none looked overly trusting of the newcomers.

Although this was to become a main post to protect the Kingdom, the decision had only been made twelve days ago and it would take another two weeks before any sign that the city was marshalling its forces to become obvious to the local population.

Arriving at the Ducal Keep, Richardson introduced himself and Drew to the gate watch and waited for permission to enter.

"Do you think they will believe us?" asked Drew.

"Why wouldn't they mate?" asked Richardson his ever-present grin holding only a slight hint of worry to it.

"Well it sounds a bit far fetched, demons still walking around after all the destruction at Peters Hold." Replied Drew.

"Just remember Drew, those tracks were a clue, not an answer. We don't know if the tracks were another force of demons strengthening their position, or if they were a scouting party caught outside of Peters Hold before the citadel was collapsed. We just want the Dukes advisors to hear us and organise a search of the surrounding area, nothing more, even a group of twenty could manage that so it wont come as too much of a hardship to the duke no matter much he complains."

Nodding Drew simply waited in silence. Eventually a guard in Myllarad's yellow informed the two Guardsmen that they were to follow him immediately for an audience with Duke Teele.

Cholla awoke an hour before her watch began. The mornings were becoming warm again, and normally she would have been enthused by the light and warmth of a new day. But she had lost her best friend. Hazel had been among the lost when evacuating the defence to the Lost Lands. The entire hospital she had been treated at had vanished during the transport to Sarafell. There was a search and rescue party launched on discovery of the number lost, but only a handful were recovered, a few more than this were found dead, and the rest had simply vanished.

Hazel had been among the missing, and no one had the slightest clue where they could be. The scouting parties sent back to the line had discovered nothing of the missing casualties, nor of the Grey Mages. Their army lay decomposing where they had fallen, the Ones vanished completely, the few that had fallen had been removed from the field of battle.

In the silence of her tent, Cholla could hear Hazel's laughter, quick comments about her hair, and her pondering of Tal's behaviour. The half of the tent that was given to Hazel seemed cold and bare, as if she haunted it even in death.

Death.

It seemed impossible to Cholla that Hazel had passed to the Keeper of Souls. She should have felt something, felt Hazel being freed of her life. But she felt nothing, only a bitter emptiness.

If the war were to take from her then she would take back from the Mages. All her pain and loss would be given revenge by her blade, and then and only then would she say farewell to her friend's soul.

Strapping her chest plate over her chain and wrapping her cloak around her shoulders, she discarded her usual fine blade and took up a heavier long blade. Determination set her face as she strode purposefully from the tent, straight towards Lord Rayburn's command post.

She passed several Riders on her march, each moved out of her way as they saw the rage clear and present in her bearing.

"I need to speak to our Lord Rayburn." Cholla said to the sentries stationed outside Rayburn's command post.

They looked at her face and nodded slowly, one entering the town watch building to pass on her request.

The minutes passed slowly for Cholla before the Rider emerged and held the door open for her. Entering the relative darkness of the building, it took her eyes a couple of seconds to adjust fully. Gareth Rayburn was standing, stooped over a map of the immediate area with his senior staff. On it was marked the positions of all the Rider units on patrol, along with sightings of the enemy and skirmish sites.

As Cholla entered, Rayburn looked up.

"You wanted to speak to me Rider Redfurn?" asked the commander.

"Yes I did sir. I wanted to ask a favour." Replied Cholla, her heart beating rapidly at the thought of the question she needed to ask.

"Well go ahead Redfurn." Said Gareth, his staff listening intently now.

"I want to go into the Lost Lands and find the base of the Grey Mages sir."

There, she had said it. Rayburn paused.

"A mission like that would take at least ten Riders for the safety of the patrol, and would last an unknown period of time. If I were to sanction such an undertaking, I would also need to set up contact points regularly to provide the unit with food and water to continue the search. There would need to be a Sergeant in charge and nine volunteers for a search like this.

"I'm sorry Redfurn it is not possible at this point." Rayburn gave his decision kindly, yet firmly. Had Cholla been in full control of herself she would have accepted this and departed. However, the loss of a friend does not allow for rational thinking nor does it allow prudence.

"Sir, please, I must do this. I cannot rest until I have avenged Hazel, and our progress so far is slight. What must be done will come at great risk, and I am willing to take it. Let me go sir." Implored Cholla.

"Give me a week. I want to seek out volunteers, not pressed men for this task. If at the end of that time I do not have the number, then the mission will not take place. Now, go about your regular duties." Stated Rayburn flatly.

As Cholla departed the command post, Lord Rayburn turned to Captain Erikson.

"What do you think Marc? Is the idea credible?" asked Rayburn.

"It could be, though it should be correctly planned, not just a killing spree for the sake of revenge."

"Organise it. We will need a sergeant and eight other Riders. Only Volunteers please. Ask quietly, I don't want Cholla's hopes getting dashed if we cant get the numbers." Stated Rayburn, kindly. Erikson nodded and left his Lord to continue his planning. Outside the building, the sun was warming on Erikson's skin, his uniform and armour weighing against him in a comforting way, the bulk adding heat and safety.

Looking around the city, Erikson noticed the changes occurring. The walls were becoming reinforced. Ballista and Catapults were being positioned against the walls and behind them where they were judged to be most effective. A trench was being dug wide enough to be difficult to cross and far enough away from the wall to stop ladders being leant against the wall to bridge it. In effect, it was a crude moat, small, but should still make reaching the walls troublesome enough should the Grey Mages push that far.

Canopied fortifications were being added to allow Seers to have some modicum of defence against physical attacks while wielding their magics. A city was becoming a fortress and fewer and fewer commoners were seen on the streets as they came to the realisation that their home was rapidly becoming a war zone. Most had already evacuated, and those that had remained were quickly warming to the idea of life in a city closer to the heart of the Kingdom.

As he slowly walked thought the city, he came across several patrols of Riders. If one had a sergeant, he would call him or her aside and make some discreet enquiries.

Quickly, he had more than enough volunteers from among the ranks of the Riders, but he was still lacking a sergeant. All those he had spoken to, had too much to do, or were directly in charge of areas of the defence and could not be spared. Still, it was only the first morning; he had the rest of the week to find someone yet. There was still a great deal to organise, and to do that he must get to the collection of maps and charts for the Lost Lands that were kept in the command post.

Hazel woke up.

Her shoulder was healing slowly, a Seer had reset the bones and started the tissue healing before the evacuation of the hospital had begun. She could now move her arm, and move around without any sharp pain darting through her.

Looking around, she took her surroundings in one more time. A grey cell with one window only just big enough to let some light in, a stone bed and a heavy studded door that blocked her escape. This was her world now. She did not know how long she had been here, but she knew that she wouldn't have too long left if she didn't escape. There were three others in the cell with her at first, but slowly they had vanished, being dragged out into the night and not returning. There were other cells close by, she could hear the wailing from the injured and those that had lost their minds. The sounds of their cells being raided for the captured echoed throughout the night and on especially still nights she could hear chanting and screams from somewhere under her cell.

She had no weapon, and was dressed only in the smock the hospital had given her before the withdrawal. All she possessed now was her training. Calming herself, she tried to stretch out her senses, but there was some kind of field around the cell, stopping her skills from penetrating.

Thinking, she probed the boundary of this field, and found that it encompassed a larger area than just her cell. From her estimates, she guessed that one field surrounded the whole of the prison. Were there any prisoners left alive?

Yes.

There were eight left other than herself. How could they escape? Where *were* they come to that?

It did not matter, she must get the others and escape. How? It kept coming back to that. An idea struck, but it was dangerous and could spell her death should luck not be smiling upon her.

For four nights now she had been left alone, every night she had stayed alert, sensing out constantly until the morning light. Two more prisoners had been taken. Their screams echoing from beneath her, seven now remained, Hazel included. The days passed in troubled sleep, the nights dragged on in tortured silence, broken only by the sounds of a haunted soul, being tortured, killed or the gods knew what else.

Two more nights passed and no more captives had been taken. Hazel sat in a focussing trance. Her senses stretched out as far as they could – which was the extremity of the prison. The emptiness was swallowing her, she paid no attention to the soft wails that accompanied her nights, nor the gentle despair she could feel emanating from the other six inmates. She waited, she felt. The walls were mapped out in her mind so well now that the ten cells with their grey, damp and ancient stone walls were almost displayed as a map in her mind, even when she was not thinking of them. Tonight was different.

The door at the end of the corridor of cells opened. The change almost made Hazel jump out of her skin. They were coming. Two men walking deliberately between the cells, passing the other prisoners, moving towards her.

Quickly, Hazel retreated to the dark corner of the cell, lay down and turned her back to the door, feigning sleep. There was no jingling of keys, no creak as the door swung open on rusty hinges, simply a quiet rush of air as the great wooden barricade glided open.

One of the men walked into the cell. He approached Hazel, the other following him.

Hazel did her best to keep her breathing slow, she needed to be ready. The two men stood either side of her.

"I hope you have made your peace." Said the one of the men as he reached down and started to haul her to her feet. In one smooth motion, Hazel used his strength to heave herself to her feet and with a strike faster than he could believe crushed his windpipe. She didn't wait after felling the first, she needed to act quickly to silence the final guard. Before the second heartbeat she levelled a kick at his stomach, sending him reeling. He hit the floor hard and rolled, coming to his feet. Hazel stood her ground ready to take his attack, but none came.

With a cruel smile the guard motioned her to attack, happily she obliged. As the first punch flew towards his head, Hazel turned it to a feint and cut her other fist into his stomach. He blocked easily, laughed, and with one punch sent Hazel flying across the room, she hit the rear wall but didn't fall. Something was holding her fast to the cold bricks, *magic*. She focussed and with all the energy she could focus sent a pulse at the magician.

Not expecting a retaliation the spell snapped and hazel dropped to the dust covered floor. She rushed him, now desperate to escape, but he had recovered. With a snarl from her assailant, Hazel was lifted into the air, bound tight, her hands at her side and unable to move.

"Well what do we have here?" Growled the Magician as he looked to his colleague lying prone on the floor. Hazel gave no response but spat at the unknown Magician.

"No matter, we can get the information we need without your assistance."

The cell blacked out, the last Hazel knew was the Magician in the dark clothes was studying her as she slipped once more into that blackness of oblivion.

When she awoke, Hazel tried to look around. Darkness enveloped her; she was blindfolded and bound.

"Do not fret, you are safe… for now. How long for, depends upon your cooperation. Think carefully because you are in a highly fatal position. There are a lot of hungry Mages here that think you should die for what you did to one of us."

"Who are you?" asked Hazel quietly, not trusting herself to speak any louder.

"Who am I? You are not in a position to ask questions *Rider*. However so you are aware of just how precarious your position is, I will humour you. I am a Dark Lord. For now, you require no more than that."

Hazel sensed her surroundings, there was a dark and evil presence that was in a medium sized room with her, but she could not sense outside of her immediate prison.

"You will answer our questions. If you do then you might be allowed to live in captivity for the rest of your life. You might even be offered the chance to join us if you are extremely helpful. However, if you do not cooperate, then your soul and life energy will be used by one of us to regenerate ourselves. Which would mean your knowledge will be ours anyway.

"Think on it. When we next meet you will have your only chance." The raspy voice finished as a door shut.

Hazel tried her bonds, her hands were tied behind her back, her feet tied but not together. Using her shoulder, she slipped the material covering her eyes off. Obviously, they had not intended for her to stay blindfolded continuously.

Looking around, she took in the room. It was not a cold dank cell this time. Thought there were no windows and she was sure that the room lay below ground level, it was furnished to a more than acceptable standard. There was a bed, a desk, candles for light and rugs and tapestries. There was also a single book laid out centrally on the desk.

The title read, 'Magic and Black Magic – Is There a Difference?' Cringing at the use of a book possibly designed to lull her into a false sense of security, she turned away. Sitting on the floor, she slipped her hands below her feet, bringing them round to the front. Using the candles, she managed to burn her wrist bonds and break them then untie her legs.

Wondering what she was to do next Hazel waited. The time seemed to drag, with no reference from the sun and her senses cut off by the ward placed around her cell, she didn't know what the time was, nor how long she had been sitting on the bed before she picked up the book and started to read.

Existence was a blackness, heat, growls, a rotting meat smell, and a shoving of his shoulder.

Tal came to looking into the face of Brad who was smiling sadly at him.

"Glad to see your awake. Now I can have my break down with a friend." He said to Tal.

"Where are we?" groaned Tal leaning up on his elbows.

"In hell Tal, we're in hell." Brad moved back and Tal looked around.

There were bars around a cage, a cage that they were in. Looking through the bars Tal examined the large room. It was almost a cave, with the walls all natural rock, and windows cut from it. If there wasn't such a view from the large opening in the wall Tal would have thought they *were* in a cave. But Tal knew exactly where they were. They were in one of the giant castles that Tal had witnessed looking through the portal in the depths of the ruined citadel of Peters Hold.

Outside of the window, the red sky was filled with guttural roars, black sulphurous smoke columns rising into the sky and flames spilling over the rim of several volcanoes in the distance, their hot, spitting and fast flowing lava running into larger rivers in the base of granite valleys. Brad was right, if there was indeed a hell, Tal felt he was in it.

The week had passed faster than Erikson had thought possible. He had planned a search strategy of the Lost Lands, organised re-supply points, and all units involved would be given maps of the area. All had been set, but there was one hitch. No Sergeant had volunteered for the position, and if Erikson was completely honest with himself, he couldn't blame them. He now needed to explain to Lord Rayburn that Cholla could not make her desperate search. How would she take it?

Cholla was on duty, she was patrolling the walls of Sarafell, waiting for the noon bell to chime, to signal that her watch was over. She looked out to the countryside, the hills rolling off into the spring day. Her wait was up, it had been a week since she had seen Lord Rayburn. Should she go to see him? Or would he summon her?

"Rider Redfurn?" The voice made her jump. She turned to see a young page standing behind her.

"Yes?"

"Its Lord Rayburn, he wants to see you…err ma'am." The boy looked slightly nervous talking to one of the legendary Riders.

"Thank you." Replied Cholla, she tried to be kind to the boy but could not keep her anxiety out of her voice completely.

As the bell tolled noon, Cholla approached the command post of Lord Rayburn. She needed this quest, it might give the kingdom the intelligence required to stage its own offensive against the terror of the Grey Mages. More importantly, it would give her a channel for her grief, let her find a way to avenge the loss of her best friend.

She was lead into her audience with Gareth Rayburn. He was standing over an array of maps and ledgers with his staff, which was all he felt he did these days.

"Redfurn, please come in." Said Gareth looking apologetic already.

Cholla entered and waited. Rayburn was finishing up with his captains, organising some small scouting parties to go beyond the previous border north of Sarafell, and see if there is any activity from the Grey Mages.

She waited patiently, not liking the apologetic tone he used to address her.

Eventually the meeting had finished, the officers departing to issue orders, make plans and set off into enemy territory. Rayburn wasted no time in broaching the news to Cholla.

"I'm sorry Cholla, we got the soldiers, but no one to lead them. Marc couldn't find a Sergeant that would volunteer for the duty. We can't put the resources into this now. I won't press anyone to go that deeply into the Grey Mages land with no backup."

"There must be a way, what about the Riders that have already volunteered? Surely with the last offensive, there must be an opening of Sergeant that one of them deserves?" Cholla was begging, but she didn't care. She felt se had to get this mission, knew it would help the war effort and would yield results.

"I'm sorry, I can't in good conscience let you go. I would want you all to come back, to ensure that I would need someone with a little more experience to go with you. We cannot find any volunteers so no. Take a couple of days off to come to terms with things, then back to duty, understood?"

She had no idea what else to do. Saluting, Cholla turned and left the building.

Marc Erikson looked at Rayburn, then followed her out the building. "Cholla, wait a minute.

"Don't start to lose yourself over this. You're a good soldier, and you have a good future, but not if you burn out so young. There will be a lot of people that lose close friends through this, please remember you are not alone." He gripped her shoulder, a small comforting gesture, but something real none the less.

Night was settling in.

Cholla was sitting in one of the taverns frequented by Riders in the city. It was a dark place, wooden floors, beamed ceiling and a large open fire pit in the centre of the room with a boar on a spit rotating slowly. The tables were rough wood and the seats plain with out any cushioning, it was the kind of place where no one pulled rank or pretended to be better than anyone else, those who wanted a quiet and refined drink went to nicer places. The two musicians standing on the small stage were regaling the patrons with bawdy and slightly obscene ditty's. In short it was right where Cholla wanted to be. Here there was life, she wanted to forget the death and loss of the previous slaughter.

Cholla tried to convince herself that getting blind drunk would be the best course of action, get it all out of her system, wake up hung over, recover then get on with her life. If this was her great plan, then why was she still nursing her first ale after two hours?

Of course, she knew why. She didn't want to be here, in this city, in this den of life, of greed, of debauchery and opulence. She wanted to be outside, in the Lost Lands, tracking down the home of the Grey Mages. Not here, locked in Sarafell, a prisoner in the confines of a gigantic jail.

Captain Marc Erikson was in the private office of Lord Rayburn. He had followed Cholla when she left the barracks, and had sat watching her, from a dark corner of the bar for an hour while she sat looking into a half filled tankard.

"What do you think Marc? Will she hold it together?" Asked Rayburn.

"I don't know sir, she is trying but she is still green, and Hazel was her closest friend. It is very hard for her."

"Will she be a danger to herself or other Riders?"

"I really can't say sir, do you want me to post someone to monitor her? make sure she is ok?" asked Erikson.

"Yes I think that is best. It really is a shame we couldn't send her on that mission, it would have helped her and us. I have had the Dragon Riders and Dragons searching the Lost Lands for the base, but its too well hidden. Either hidden with magic or just so well concealed that top down observation is impossible. Either way we need someone on the ground.

"Just keep her together Marc, we have lost too many people already to start losing to aftershock."

"Yes sir."

Chapter 12

Strangers

Brad's pick axe bit into the rock in front of him. He had been working for what seemed like hours. His long blonde hair was dripping with sweat, his bare back taught as his muscles sung under the strain of the work. All his strength had only yielded a rock the size of a tomato to break from the wall of the cave.

They had been in the strange land, the strange *world* for just over a month now. Within a day of Tal waking up, they had been taken from the cage and put to work with over a hundred other humans carving great caverns into the mountains and cliff faces in the red desolate world. Both Brad and Tal had quickly discarded their chain mail, working only in their uniform trousers. They had only completed one cavern in the entire month, and this was now being used to house a small army of demons.

Tal returned to the cavern breathing heavily. He was dragging a litter along the ground behind him, several minutes ago he had left the cave to get rid of the remaining rubble that was gathering on the floor of the new barracks. Tal had received the easier of the jobs two weeks ago when he got the gist of what one of his captors was struggling to tell them.

It was a quick lesson learnt. If you did not grasp what was required of you, then you became lunch. Tal did not know how it happened but in a split second, he had gone from only hearing guttural grows, to getting a sense of what was demanded. The revelation had saved himself, Brad and several others from becoming the main source of sustenance for the next couple of days.

In the following fortnight, Tal had gained some idea of what was happening. It did not matter how far from the creature he was standing. If he focused hard enough, he could almost read the mind of his subject. Not in any detail, but with enough images that he could get a good firm idea of what the being was thinking about. Because of this he had become the sight foreman, if such a position existed here in this hellish world.

Food was scarce, and he had got some images from his jailors, that the meat they were being fed on, was from some sort of giant rodent, not dissimilar from the rats that inhabit their world. What the demons ate was unknown and Tal thought that it had best remain that way.

The short supply had caused several arguments within the demon numbers; often Tal had sensed an urge for blood, for a fight, then a great satisfaction and a hunger abated. Did they eat their own? Were they cannibals? He tried not to think on it too long.

The other useful piece of information he had gathered was that a days walk from here, in a direction he had labelled South, was the only other gate, portal, whatever it was called, that could return them to their own world. The only catch was that they could not get away, had no real idea of where the gate was and that it was guarded.

Oh, and they did not know exactly *where* it would bring them out on their own world, Tal reminded himself.

They were stuck here for the present, but the longer they stayed, the greater the chance that they would incur the wrath of the demons - and that would mean a very painful trip to the kitchens.

Tal smiled at Brad, it was a weak smile, but it seemed to give his friend some sort of comfort. The pickaxe swung again, more chips of stone fell to the floor.

An army was building. Tal did not know why, but if it was for an invasion it did not seem to be gathering momentum, in fact it seemed to be gathering size but without any obvious purpose. Nothing Tal could sense gave any idea as to their mission, in fact, in most cases, he only sensed confusion, and on the rare occasions it wasn't confusion he only sensed frustration and eagerness.

Eagerness for what?

Night was creeping closer, the red sun was level with the horizon, and Tal and his workers were being herded back into their cells. The cage doors were shut and a heavy bar was positioned so as to stop the door from opening. They had tried each night to lift the bar, but they were not strong enough.

"What are we going to do Tal?" asked Brad as they sat there, eating their dried meat.

"Why are you asking me? *You're* the Rider here" said Tal with a smile.

"Maybe but you are the one that has gained this sensory gift, not me. Besides, I'm not a very good Rider am I? I failed my very first field mission."

"Well you got captured, that is not failing it, and you said the gate was blocked after we came through. I'm guessing that was the mission, so congratulate yourself, you succeeded, in a twisted, failed, sort of way." Tal gave a twisted smile.

"Ok, but you can't pull the *'You're a Rider and I'm not.'* routine anymore. If you were slightly better with your weapons you would be a Rider by now too", said Brad as he lay on the floor trying to sleep.

The cage door swung open on rusty hinges. The pot containing the slightly sulphurous and stale water was placed at the entrance. Enough to maintain life, but not enough to quench the thirst of the prisoners. Tal, through his ability to sense the desires of his captors, had become the best chance of staying alive, and so the group of workers in his cage had pushed on him the position of their leader.

It was a position that Tal did not want. The people he was locked up with numbered fifteen and himself, and was the largest number of prisoners left alive in one group. The number consisted mostly of normal men, taken from the city of Peters Hold.

There were a couple of Soldiers in their number; they had been knocked unconscious during the fighting. They said that children had been taken too, but none knew where they had gone.

They shared their usual conversation in the morning, what was known? What were they eating? – Tal hadn't been able to bring himself to tell them they were eating giant rat – What was the probable plan for these demons? How would they get home?

Every morning the same questions were raised, no answers were given, and before they knew it the door was opened again by a demon that would take them to their day of slavery.

That was every morning up until today. For the first time in just over a six weeks, they were sitting in silence, without anyone coming for them.

It was halfway through the day when a beast the size of a horse came to collect them. The door was swung violently open, and a blood-curdling growl was emitted from its jaws. Something was different to Tal's senses, this was no ordinary demon, this one was more coherent, Tal could almost understand it.

"Tal?" Asked Brad uneasily. The call brought Tal back to the present.

"He wants us to follow him, said he was the 'Force Hand' to the Razor Claw Tribe. I don't know what that means but it seems like some kind of rank. We should go."

They all followed the giant creature, he was leading them out of the shadow of the castle they were usually under, and down a trail, a trail heading *South*.

"There was something different this time Brad." Said Tal quietly as they followed the bulky Demon.

"What do you mean?"

"I mean I could almost understand him coherently, I heard him like I would hear someone from Yin if they could only speak to us in broken tongue."

"So what did he say?" asked Brad.

"I told you, just to follow him."

"Well what is he thinking?"

Tal focused on the beast, he was full of anger. He did not agree with his superior's decision to take these humans so close to something. To what?

The beast's thoughts wandered for a while, to food and his position, how he could advance his rank. The thoughts so clear, Tal wondered why?

Why risk placing them near the Gate?

The thought exploded into Tal's mind. It was so sudden that he almost tripped and fell, his only saving grace was Brad, who caught him before he fell to far.

"He is taking us to the Gate, Brad. Pass the word, I don't know how long we will be there, but as soon as we get a chance, we need to get back to our world."

The large red sun crested the mountains, shedding its harsh light and heat on the rocky world. They had been walking the all of the previous day and stopped only for three hours rest as the night grew cold.

A trail led between two great mountains, a pass that disappeared into the distance. They were pressing ahead at a gruelling pace and the prisoners were all tired and feeling drained.

It was nearing mid day when the captives turned almost one hundred and eighty degrees round a pile of broken rocks, the sight that met them was one of shocking familiarity to Tal.

An opening in the air with a room the other side, an altar was visible and men walking in dark robes in procession. There was someone tied naked to the cold surface and Tal watched as a wicked looking dagger was held over the person by an old man. In an instant, the dagger plunged and a black sickly mist left the wound and crawled up the old mans arms. He seemed to be struggling to hold the dagger as his weathered old face grew younger and stronger. The body on the altar convulsed twice before becoming still, all colour had been drained from the limp body before the dagger was removed and the body carried from the by the watching robed men.

There was a growl from the Force Hand that caught Tal's attention.

"We need to go to that cave and start digging it out." Said Tal to the group. They had all seen the same as Tal, and all looked worried. Slowly, they moved to the cave, inside there were a several pickaxes and the same construction of litter that were back at the castle.

Without any comment, they started to swing and slowly expand the cavern.

Several hours later, they were herded up and slowly marched into another cave, there waiting for them was a cage much like the one they had been housed in previously.

Tal knew the drill, the others were marched inside, he was the last to enter. The door was slammed shut and was locked, but not by a heavy bar. It was secured with a crude padlock. Committing it to memory he decided to get some sleep, their nights were short, for as soon as the sun appeared above the horizon they would be woken, and have to get ready for the coming physical day.

Although their geographical position had changed, their situation was startlingly similar. Day after day, the group was collected by one of their jailors and taken to their cave, they collected their tools and started chipping away at the walls.

Tal would then lug a collection of rocks down to a river of slow flowing lava and tip them in, watching them break up and disappear under the surface. He would then carry the litter back to the cave and start to load it again.

The days wore on and eight weeks had now passed. The high-pitched clink of pick axe meeting rock resounded over and over. Brad's already heavily muscled body was getting broader, Tal joked he was becoming more dwarf than man, his width nearly equal to his height.

He raised the axe above his head, and just as his shoulders tensed to bring the point back down a great roar from outside the cave could be heard. Tal came running in, his litter nowhere to be seen.

"Get back inside the cave, stay in the shadows!" called Tal as he threw himself through the entrance.

"What is going on Tal?" said Brad nervously, backing against the wall.

"There is some sort of fight going on, the Force Hand that brought us here is in a stand off with three others. I'm not sure what over but it concerns the Gate."

From outside came a horrible sound of flesh tearing and roars and growls. A squeal broke the air, then more growls. A demon came lumbering into the cave, snarling at the prisoners.

"Everyone just stay quiet and follow me." Said Tal as he nodded to the hulking beast and followed it out of the cave.

They followed a trail that lead away from the combatants. There was now only two demons facing the Force Hand., the third laying in a heap on the ground his throat ripped out and its black blood oozing and pooling on the hard unyielding ground.

One of the men with them started to choke at the sight, Brad put his arm under the man's to keep him moving.

They were led back to the cave that their cage was held in, the door was opened and the captives ushered in, a growl from the demon was translated by Tal.

"If we want to stay alive, don't make a sound. I can't make out the rest of what he wants to say, he isn't as coherent as the Force Hand." The others shrank back and a couple whimpered softly to the disgust of the demon.

Another growl and snarling match from outside made the demon turn away briefly, there was another squeal and the beast let out a soft purring sound. A deeper groan however made him turn violently and roar himself, he slammed the gate and left the cave.

Tal turned to Brad, his face almost white.

"I don't like this Brad. These things aren't very friendly to us, and now it doesn't look like they any friendlier to each other. Either way, this really looks bad for us."

"True, but there is one this that is looking up." Said Brad, a little hesitant.

"What?"

"When that thing left, he forgot the padlock."

Tal spun, the cage was shut but it was only when he walked up to the door he noticed that the padlock was lying next to the bolt, and not in it.

"Ok people," said Tal "our chance is here, we have to go if we want to get home." He tried to make himself sound confident, whether it worked or not he did not know, but he certainly didn't feel confident.

The others in the cell stood up, some looked determined, most looked frightened. One just sat huddled up in the corner of the cage.

"We have to go, this dispute won't last long, and they will not forget to lock the cage again." Said Tal, putting as much comfort and reassurance into his voice as he could.

"They will look after us, as long as we work they will keep us alive, they need us!"

"But for how long? Until we finish these caves for them? Until they get hungry? Until we misunderstand one of them and they lose their temper? We have to go" said Tal. "I am going to get us home, but I can't risk everyone else for you, are you coming?"

The man nodded and stood up. He appeared shaky but Tal could not worry about that. Getting everyone ready at the mouth of the cavern, he looked round to see what was occurring with the demons. There were now two main groups; the Force Hand had a group of sixteen demons behind him, but the initial protagonist had a larger company of twenty four. Something struck Tal about this, why was everything here organised in multiples of eight?

It did not matter right now, he had to move. There were now two dead demons and what looked like a promising scrap about to take place. The gate was behind the possible combatants, so he would have to circle around them and hope they wouldn't see them.

Slowly Tal stretched out with his senses, he felt Brad join him. The *Joining* felt good, it had been so long since he had used it he forgot how clear a picture of his surroundings it gave him. Sensing all the demons to be standing around the two opposing gangs, Tal gave a silent order to Brad to follow him. He led the people behind a series of large boulders, moving the captives in small groups so that they could hide behind them.

It took much longer than Tal had hoped. He was only half way round the perimeter when the fight kicked off. Tal had seen brawls outside the local taverns in Dukeray before, and he had seen organised riots pitched against the local guard, but this was mayhem, it was pure violence, there was no fighting in unison, just each demon tearing chunks out of others, only stopping when they were dead, not slowing a beat before then.

Tal needed to hurry; he got his people moving faster from boulder to depression back to boulder again. He had sent Brad on ahead to guide them and stayed at the back himself. Brad was at the last boulder, a short run was all that separated him from his world, and even though it led to a place Tal would rather not go to, he would prefer human foes to demons any day.

Brad stood still, the battle between the two factions was raging not fifty yards from him, a look at the wrong time would condemn them all to death. There was a deep red pulsating light that skirted the edge of the Gate, giving it an ominous appearance. Looking through the portal, Brad surveyed what he could of the room, it appeared empty, but he was unsure what his vantage point was.

Looking back at Tal, he sent a silent question back to him.

Do I send them through?

No, you will have to lead them through in case there is anyone in the room you can't see. I will send them as I can to you.

Brad accepted, but grudgingly. He counted slowly to ten and then ran head long through the Gate.

Tal saw his friend run at the slightly smoked room then disappear out of the field of vision. Two minutes later Brad walked past the Gate and nodded to Tal, indicating the room was safe for the prisoners.

"Wait here," said Tal "As soon as I give you the signal, run to me, do not come out from the cover until then ok?"

The five prisoners remaining with him nodded, including the one who previously curled up and refused to leave.

Tal ran, hunched over to the remaining prisoners. One at a time, he sent them running through the gate to Brad, who ushered them out of sight. The fight between the two factions was wearing down to duels, the Force Hand and his group had the distinct advantage now.

Tal sent the second to last prisoner through the Gate. He was left with the one scared prisoner, hiding behind the last refuge before his home world.

"Are you ready?" asked Tal.

"I cant. They will see me, I don't want to die like this." Whimpered the man pitifully.

"If you stay here you will definitely die." Countered Tal.

"You go first, I will go as soon as your through, I promise." Replied the man.

"No you go first, I have a better chance of getting through without anyone watching my back."

"No, don't make me. Please." The mans voice was getting louder, the sounds of battle were falling quiet. Tal found himself having to attempt to quiet the man, but with very little success.

"Be quiet! They will hear!" whispered Tal urgently.

"I cant go, if they see me they will catch me, kill me, *eat me!*"

There was a growl coming from what was the arena the other side of the boulder. It was the Force Hand, Tal could almost understand him, he knew something was wrong. Reaching out with his senses, Tal could sense that there were three Demons heading their way.

"They are coming but not this way directly, you can still get out if you go now." Said Tal.

"No they will find me, I have to get out of here!" the man was hysterical, he started creeping away from the boulder, away from the Gate and away from the carnage.

"Come back!" whispered Tal, but it was no good the man was now running. Tal shut his eyes took a breath and run, straight for the Gate. He opened his eyes just as he reached the view of his world, he was getting away, would be there shortly.

A scream pierced the air as the man was caught by the demons, Tal could hear him begging for mercy as he stepped through the door back to his own reality once more. The sound of tearing and screams, then silence was all that he could hear as he hit the ground, falling through the Gate.

Hazel was pacing her comfy cell. She could not forget the man with the raspy voice and his warning.

"*Think on it. When we next meet you will have your only chance.*"

She did not know how long she would have left. Nor what time of day it was, nor how long she had been in that room. She was stuck, she had no way out. Knowing that she was no match for a Dark Lord, she only had a couple of options. She could give in and give him any information he wanted, or she could withhold it, try to stall him for as long as possible in the vain hope an opportunity to escape would present itself.

'Magic and Black Magic – Is There a Difference?' – the book lay closed now, she had read it from cover to cover. Although it made a good show of making the two look similar if not compatible, it was easy to lose yourself in the book, and believe that Magic and Black Magic were simply two sides to the same coin; if you were not in constant contact with users of magic, be they Seers, or fully fledged Dragon Riders.

She guessed that she would have to wait for the time to arrive, before she knew what she would do when confronted with the simple choice. *Time*, she must have been locked up for weeks, but had no idea how many. As with all the important things in life, it came down to time in the end, it always did.

She was asleep when the shouting started. It seemed that there was always some kind of voice raised in this living cemetery, but this was something new. It was not a voice of anger, or pain, but several of them, all with alarm evident and a great deal of fear present.

There were sounds of confrontation coming from a short distance away, Hazel stood up and moved behind where the door would open, she waited silently, ready to react to anything that happened.

Screams mixed with shouts, explosions soon followed and the ground and walls seemed to tremble. There was a tingling feel to the air, the hairs on the back of Hazel's neck stood up and a shiver wracked her body. Magic, the field that surrounded the room was wavering. Hazel tried to sense outside the walls of her prison. The blanket that enveloped her was fluctuating, but not enough for her to get a good idea of what lay outside.

She occasionally got senses of life; black, dark smudges that walked halls, some in groups, others alone. There was a group of ten, maybe more moving upwards from somewhere below her, but again her senses were cut off before she could get any sort of real information.

Hazel breathed slowly, her eyes closed. She did not need to see, she could feel the air in the room, each piece of furniture any small bit of dust that floated under the door. Her chest moved deeply, slowly, relaxing so that she could react in an instant.

The barricade came down, she could sense again. There was magic being used outside the room, strikes against something, *nothing*. There was a blankness in her senses, and it was moving. There were Grey Mages surrounding it, striking out at it. The wall came back up, her sight restricted to her cell once more.

Time passed, she did not move. Her senses still trying to see beyond the walls. There was a sudden jolt, her vision swam, and she fell to her knees. Breathing hard, she stood slowly, her legs shaky. Stretching out, she felt for the unseen blindfold, but it was not there. No wavering of power, no half seen, split second feelings, but the whole area. Whatever was supporting the barrier had been disabled, or whoever it was, had been killed.

She felt for the emptiness that had been moving previously but could not find it. There were no groupings of Grey Mages, in fact there seemed to be little around locally at the moment. There were still sounds of fighting echoing through the corridors but nothing clear, nothing definite.

Moving to the door, Hazel tested the handle. It was locked, but the door did not seem too heavy, this room was not meant to be a cell. Looking at the hinges, she thought it might be possible to break down the door even though the hinges were not designed to bend back on themselves.

Bracing herself, she gave the latch a solid kick - nothing gave. Again and again, she tried to force the door but nothing gave.

Moving to the chair she sat and waited, there was nothing else she could do.

It was the movement outside her door that caused her to start. The sound of a latch opening brought her to full awareness. With her senses fully available again, she instantly push outwards, attempting to discern who was on the other side of the door.

Confusion ran deep through her entire mind and body. There was shear nothingness that was stationed the other side of the wooden barrier.

The door opened slowly, Hazel stood up and backed away. With no idea what was entering, she did not want to be too close when it came into view.

A tall pale man, walked into the room. He moved slowly, fluidly. There seemed an ethereal presence about him that cowed Hazel in a way she had never known. Through the battle north of Sarafell, Hazel had seen some terrible and terrifying creatures, but there was something cold and calculating about this man. That in itself made Hazel more wary than anything she had fought previously.

The figure looked at her, he was over six feet tall, pale skin but bright blue eyes. He had long brown hair that hung loose to his neck, and was dressed in a long brown robe. Though she could not see his build beneath the flowing material of the garments, there was an air of power about him that came across to Hazel so very obviously.

"And who are you?" It was a simple question, asked so very softly, yet it held as many promises and threats as there were drops of water in the Purple Sea.

"My name is Rider Jensook. My rank is Rider. I will give you no more." Replied Hazel, her voice slightly shaky.

"As you wish Rider Jensook. Nevertheless, if I want more I *will* get it, no matter how much you try to avoid it. Why are you here?"

"You tell me! You and your Mage friends brought me here!" Hazel snapped. She had been subjected to too much for too long, and her composure had just shattered. The fear and anger at her position, the worry about her friends, the anxiety about the war effort, all had combined to break her resolve.

"For a prisoner, you have been given a very luxurious cell." What did this man want? Was he making a point that her lot could get worse if she did not co-operate?

"I am not telling you anything, the Kingdom is mine to defend, and I will do so with my life if necessary, so best kill me and get it over with." Hazel squared her shoulders. She had done it; all the worry about whether or not she would cave in to questioning was now over. She had kept any secrets about the Kingdom she could, and she had recaptured her backbone. Better dead than a traitor.

"The Kingdom, oh how noble! But which one?! The Kingdom of Dragons or this self stylised Kingdom of Mages?" Snapped the ominous man, with the first words Hazel had heard that were slightly emotional.

"Who *are* you?" asked Hazel, the edge of her fear being blunted by her curiosity. Whoever this stranger was, he might not have anything to do with the Grey Mages.

"Who am I? My name is Vorlin Mansford, though in truth that man died several hundred years ago." Said the ghostly man, only just loud enough for Hazel to hear.

Hazel tried to edge further away without it becoming too obvious. "*What* are you?" she asked, her fear surfacing above her curiosity.

"Among my kind, we are called *Seicolantrai*, but humans call us Nightwalkers." The man looked deep into Hazel's eyes, his agelessness now obvious and reminiscent to that of the Dragon Riders. Why hadn't she noticed this before? Well that was easy, she was not looking for it. But what did she do now? This man fed of the blood of the living, she had a duty to kill him, it.

Moving as quickly as she could Hazel, launched herself at the foul creature. Her foot landed firmly against the stomach of the Nightwalker, but where the beast should have given way, it stood planted to the floor. Falling hard on her side Hazel felt the wind get knocked out of her. The man bent over and picked her up by the front of her hospital smock.

"Humans, you hear stories whispered in the night, and never try to learn the truth. It does not matter that there are two factions of *Seicolantrai* you just assume the worst and try to kill us without learning who we are first."

"Who you are? You survive by killing other humans, by drinking our blood! How can there be two factions?" Retorted Hazel trying to free herself from the man's grip.

"The two factions are quite simple Rider. One will kill a human to feed, the other will leave the human alive. But that doesn't bother you does it? as long as you can exterminate a race you don't like. Think about it Hazel, humans feed on cattle and poultry. I don't kill what I eat, which is more humanitarian?

"I am going, you have a choice, come with me, or stay here." He let his grip loosen, and Hazel fell hard to the floor.

"How can you fight your way out of here? It is a stronghold for the Grey Mages. And come to that, what are you doing here in the first place?" there were a hundred questions that Hazel wanted to ask, but she knew that her time was limited should she not go with him.

"I cannot keep answering questions here girl, but to humour you. Firstly, I can handle anything that is here right now, the Dark Lords are out somewhere doing whatever evil they get up to, and only the Mages and Necromancers are around. Secondly, I needed to check something, so I knocked but no one would let me in, so I let myself in. Now, are you coming?" without waiting for her, he turned and walked out of the room.

Hazel was confused, scared and angry. She could either stay and wait for the return of the Dark Lord, hoping that she could keep her composure and not reveal anything about the Kingdom. Alternatively, she could follow the stranger, trust that he didn't kill humans and hope that he could get her out.

Swearing, she climbed to her feet and moved to the door. Looking up and down the alleyway she saw him disappearing round a bend. She left the room and followed him as quietly as she could, keeping far enough behind so that hopefully he would not notice.

Tal was hauled to his feet.

Brad looked around, the remaining prisoners were gathered in the corner out of sight of the demons the other side of the Gate.

"Where are we, Brad?" asked Tal, looking around the room. All he received was a barely visible shrug from his friend. The room was dark, lit only by candles. The walls were carved out of the rock and Tal absently wondered if this cavern was dug by slaves, just as he had been forced to do so recently. There was an altar in the middle of the room, it was made from a darker stone to the rest of the chamber, and now he was closer he could see there were some sort of Runes engraved into the head and the foot of the solid table.

Turning round, he looked back to where the Gate was positioned, or at least where the Gate *should* have been located. There was only the room.

"Brad? Where is the Gate?" asked a confused Tal.

"It is there, we just can't see it. When I waved, I was just waving in roughly the right direction. We appear out of the air, but we cannot go back through, it's a one way door. It would probably also be a good idea to get out of the line of sight, just in case they are watching, they could come through at any moment if they want to silence us."

Tal agreed and both Rider and trainee moved back to the group they had brought through the Gate to their own world.

"Where do we go from here?" asked one of the prisoners.

"I don't know, but we have to move." Replied Tal before anyone could argue. "We are going to head up, the temperature and dampness of the room, it is like we are underground, so for now we head up. The first thing then is to get out of the room. So let's go, Brad take point I will follow up behind again."

Brad nodded and motioned everyone to follow him; he stretched out with his senses and began to feel the area around him. Almost at the same time, he sensed Tal link to him, once more creating the *Joining* and extending their area of awareness.

There was no one in the local vicinity, so Brad decided it was as safe as it was going to get. Moving to the doorway he motioned the others to follow quickly and get out of sight of the hidden Gate. As Tal made it safely to the alleyway Brad clapped him on the shoulder and moved out again, taking the lead and heading in the only direction available, up a long flight of stairs, disappearing into darkness above.

They had been climbing for several minutes, the dim stairs lit only by sporadic torches attached to the walls. They seemed about half way up, looking back they could just see the base of the stairs, looking ahead they could just make out the outline of a door.

From above them, a sudden explosion and shouts of alarm were heard. Turning to Tal, Brad gave his friend a questioning look. Merely shrugging Tal motioned them onwards.

Their *joining* was starting to reach the areas of population, they could sense the black smears of Mages rushing round their subterranean lair - so they were in a Lair of the Grey Mages. At least one question had been answered - Their movements seemed ragged, gathering in groups then rushing off towards an area they could not yet reach with their minds. The shouts soon became screams, the explosions did not stop but increased in frequency. The few Mages that could now be sensed were running in the opposite direction than they were previously.

"Let's go, before whatever is scaring the Mages reaches us." Said Brad continuing to move upwards.

A few minutes later, they were at the door. It was large and made from a deep red wood. Bound by heavy iron it would make a strong barricade should it be required. Brad stopped next to it and listened. There were sounds of fighting reaching him clearly, and with himself and Tal *joined* they could sense the fighting now. Black smudges were swarming over a point of nothingness, but as they got to a certain distance from this nothingness, they vanished, their lives being wiped out.

"We have to get out of here." Said Tal, slightly worried.

"Easier said than done." Replied Brad turning the latch, the door remaining firmly closed.

"We have to break it down Brad. We don't know what is killing the Mages but whatever it is, we can't assume it will be friendly towards us."

"Then get up here and help." Replied Brad as his weight slammed into the door for the first time.

Tal added his weight to the push but the door held firm. Over and over, they tried to break down the barrier, but it did not give. There was suddenly a scream from directly outside the door, followed by a choked gurgle and the sound of a body hitting the stone paving.

Brad urged the group back down the stairs, he and Tal remaining in front of them, ready to see what happened.

The door opened to the sound of a key.

Light spilled round the edge of the sturdy wood, growing brighter as the door continued to open. As the barring wood finally came to rest on the extremes of its hinges, Brad openly laughed at the sight that greeted him.

Standing with light illuminating him from behind, like a hero in a bards tale, stood a sight both Tal and he had doubted they would see again. A Rider in chain mail, his black cloak caked with the blood of the fallen, but looking surprisingly happy with himself, stood at the head of the stairs sheathing a strange looking sword.

"Well this is unexpected." Was all he said as he laughed openly and motioned them to follow.

Chapter 13

Escapes

Tal nearly fell.

He stumbled to the doorway as quickly as he could, not wanting to lose sight of their rescuer. Brad was left to round up the rest of the survivors and follow Tal.

At the top of the stairs was the body of the man they heard dying from the other side of the door, running round the far corner at the end of the corridor Tal disappeared from sight as Brad tried to link with him. Feeling the familiar presence of Tal in his mind Brad was grateful that he had the foresight to open himself up to him before running off.

Where are you going Tal? Asked Brad as he got the survivors running towards the fleeing presence of Tal.

This is a test Brad, he is seeing if we can follow him all the way out of here. He even mocked me, asked me to 'keep up if you can' before he ran off! Now hurry up! He is getting away! Replied Tal as he moved further from Brad.

The survivors who had been poorly fed and watered for the past couple of months were struggling to keep up with to two fitter members of the Rider Order.

Tal we need to let up, the others can't take the pace. Thought Brad as he slowed them down. They had been running for only

235

a couple of minutes, but to the fatigued and totally drained group it felt like they had been running their whole life.

We're stopping, the others cant take the pace and I wont leave them alone now, not after so long looking out for them. sent Tal to the rapidly departing Rider.

A sense of acknowledgement was returned but nothing else, and Tal felt the Riders presence disappear somewhere above him. Realising that the Rider had shielded himself from his senses, Tal stopped to let the others catch up to him.

In no more than twenty seconds the others reached him, breathing hard with the exception of Brad.

"What's happened Tal? Where did he go?" Asked Brad while the others caught their breath.

"He has shielded himself from us, were on our own now." Said Tal, more than slightly despaired. He had hoped that his job as dictated leader was finished with the arrival of the Rider, but luck had not favoured him. Instead, his would-be saviour had abandoned him and the group to their fate in the Grey Mages lair.

"Why would he do that? He should have stayed and helped us!" raged Brad, his own temper finally snapping.

"I don't know but were ok for now, I cant sense any Mages anywhere near us, we passed some sort of battle a few intersections back, but I couldn't follow what was happening, there was a nothingness that was killing the Mages, but I haven't felt anything like that before. Was anything told to you when you were made a Rider? Anything that would explain a nothingness like that?"

"No, its not some enlightenment that occurs when you're made a Rider, Tal. I was told it just meant I could be trusted not to kill myself with a sword and that my senses are up to par, the rest; blending, dragon sense and mind strikes, that comes later with experience, so don't worry Tal, you are just as equipped as me at the moment." Said Brad, looking round nervously, not liking being so open to attack.

They were standing at a cross junction where the corridors were lighter than they had previously been. Still cold and slightly damp, they were now carpeted with tapestries hanging from the walls, some artwork showed gruesome visages of men being tortured or killed with powerful magic in battle. The wide corridors were well lit by wrought iron chandeliers and torches attached to the stone walls.

"Which way from here?" asked Brad, he only got a broad idea of which way the Rider had gone, being too far behind to have placed the Riders route with the layout ahead.

"We take this corridor," pointed Tal to a slightly wider alleyway. "it carries on for a couple hundred yards then there are stairs up, that should leave us only one level below ground. From there? Your guess is as good as mine, that's where he shielded himself."

They set off, not contemplating what would happen should they run into a Mage. Moving slowly now, the group nervous after their run into the heart of the enemy's base. In the fast pace of the pursuit, the party had forgotten about the precarious position they were in, but now they had slowed the realisation of their threat had taken hold once more.

They crept along the corridor, hugging the walls as if the tapestries could conceal them. Tal and Brad's *joined* sense searching ahead for the trademark blackness that denoted the Grey Mages.

As they reached a corner, they could sense the stairs that led upwards just round it, but they could sense something else too, there were two Mages at the top of the stairs.

Motioning their group to silence Brad sent his thoughts to Tal.

What now?

They have their backs to the stairs, I can shield myself and try to sneak up on them, as long as they don't turn round we might be able to take them? said Tal not sounding over confident in Brad's mind.

If they do then we will all die. Was all that Brad said, his warning and concern obvious to Tal.

I know.

Brad nodded slowly to Tal and gave instructions by hand to the group to wait.

Tal took a deep breath and closed his eyes, again trying bring his own sense into himself, as he did so long ago when sneaking up on Kelar and his party.

Brad felt Tal start to disappear in his mind. When he had completely vanished from his senses, Brad tapped Tal on the shoulder, nodding to his friend.

Steadying his nerves, Tal again took a deep breath and stepped round the corner. He tried to keep to the wall for support as he silently placed one foot in front of the other. Creeping forward slowly, he mounted the bottom step. He could hear the Mages talking. They were discussing the assault; two intruders had infiltrated the base, killed dozens of Mages and took off with a prisoner.

Climbing each step as though it were made of paper and might give way any moment Tal made himself as small as possible, wishing himself invisible or at least blending in to the background.

Brad could not take any more waiting, he had to see how far Tal had moved up the stairs. Leaning round the corner, he watched Tal ascend at a snails pace. Forever had passed and Tal was only a third of the way up the stairs, each step costing dozens of breaths and a hundred heart beats. Brad watched intensely as Tal continued his slow and agonising climb.

He was half way up the stairs when Brad started to notice something strange about Tal. His friend was starting to become insubstantial, beginning to fade to Brad's sight. By the time Tal was three quarters of the way up the stairs he was almost invisible against the background, only a slight blurring where he stood could belie his position.

Brad took a sudden gasp as he realised what had happened – Tal had managed to blend. It was a skill that he was due to start learning in a couple of months, but the war had put that on hold. And Tal had managed to pick it up somehow.

The gasp made one of the Mages start, and look round behind him. Brad ducked back behind the wall, praying he hadn't cost Tal, and all of them, their lives.

Looking over his shoulder, the Mage squinted his eyes, looking to the base of the stairs. A sound like a rush of air had made him jump. The stairs were empty, it must have just been a draught in the carved corridors of the fortress. With the assault by the outsiders still a danger, his nerves were shot and he was feeling more on edge than he should. Gradually he slowed his breathing and turned back to face the entrance of the hidden lair.

Tal hugged the wall for his life, willing himself invisible. His heart racing, his breath held to the extent that his chest was burning, he forced himself to open his eyes and look to the guards.

They hadn't stirred, one was looking right past him, but the other had not even turned round. Eventually the more alert of the guards turned back to maintain his vigil of the entrance. Tal was barely ten feet from him and the Mage hadn't noticed.

Taking his first breath for what seemed an eternity, Tal tried to relax his very tense muscles. His legs were trembling and he had no real want to attempt to move, he didn't even trust his legs to make it one more step before giving out under him.

As the moments passed, Brad started counting to himself, when he reached five hundred he took a deep breath and leant round the corner once more. The blurry outline that gave away Tal's position was still in the same place he was when Brad nearly gave them all away. *Come on Tal. Move.* Thought Brad to himself, willing his friend to move again.

After a further count of two hundred, Tal moved. Slowly, Brad watched the outline of his friend start to climb the stairs again, moving closer to his deadly prey. In five smooth steps, Tal had gone from a timid mouse hiding in the shadows, to a stealthy assassin.

He reached the top so quickly Brad's eyes hadn't followed and when they finally caught up, he watched in disbelief as Tal came back into focus. In a single sweeping move, Tal wrapped an arm around one Mages neck and snapped it quickly and cleanly. He then spun, and with a forceful kick sent the second Mage falling backwards down the steps. It all happened so quickly that the Mage was taken by surprise and had no time to fashion a spell before he was propelled painfully by the kick.

Brad jumped at the sudden action of the attack. As the Mage tumbled hard down the stairs his resolve hardened, the instant the man hit the ground in front of him, Brad landed a vicious blow to the side of the mans head. He blacked out instantly, lying prone on the cold deck.

"Let's go, someone may have heard that." Said Brad to the rest of the group that stood, looking shocked at the sudden display of violence.

Brad started running up the stairs, the others followed out of fear of being left behind. When they reached the top, Tal was stood waiting for them. There was a long steady rise that led to a door that had been blown apart, bare splinters hanging from the hinges was all that was left of what was once a strong gate, outside, it was night. The warm breeze drifting down the tunnel was almost refreshing to the survivors.

As they ran up the tunnel a figure stepped round the edge of the smashed up door. He was dressed in the black and red of the Riders, and was smiling broadly.

"I knew there was something special about you, I didn't even have to help you at the end here. Well let's go, the night is almost out. Don't worry there is no need to hurry, the Mages are going to be busy for a few minutes yet, and after, they won't have the enthusiasm to follow." Laughed the man as he turned and walked away from the entrance.

Tal looked at Brad, neither were sure what was going on or where they were. They knew from their sensing earlier, that they were in a Lair of the Grey Mages, but where was that?

Somewhere in the Lost Lands, but that was a large area and other than heading South, they had no idea on the way home.

Deciding that for now they had best follow the strange Rider, they led their companions out of the Lair and caught up with the man retreating slowly into the night. Tal was not sure where they were heading, but he would get the answers he sought eventually, he was sure. Grim faced and determined he walked, and tried to persuade the Rider to reveal who he was, and what he was doing in the Lost Lands.

The man in the black and red of the Riders talked a lot, yet for all the words and stories Tal received on their trek, no answers were given, not even clues.

Hazel was following closely the Nightwalker called Vorlin, they had made their way upwards and Hazel sensed they were close to ground level again, only a couple of floors to go and she would be free.

Vorlin had encountered several Mages on his way out of the compound. Hazel watched in dread fascination as he withstood magical onslaughts that would have destroyed powerful Seers. The man – if he could still be called a man – stood his ground, all the magical attacks seemed to hit an invisible barrier a foot around him and disperse into nothingness.

His form of reprisal shocked Hazel too. He was lightening with his body, movements so fast that Hazel struggled to follow them. Moving from Mage to Mage, he would break necks, backs, tear throats from others letting them bleed to death, others he would drain of the life giving substance, leaving them white and unmoving on the hard floor. Vorlin Mansford seemed detached the whole time, his speed in shocking contrast to his facial expression.

The way he carried himself in battle, his demeanour and his expressions gave a view of distaste for killing but a resigned acknowledgement that it was necessary.

They were moving up to a final flight of stairs, the fluid movement of the Nightwalker almost wraith-like.

"I know you're following me Rider Jensook." Spoke the Nightwalker to the emptiness around them both.

"Then why not talk to me?" returned Hazel not wanting to get too close to the lethal creature.

"Because you have not asked me anything." Said Vorlin as he reached the stairs. Mounting them, he glided up effortlessly. "You have no need to fear me Rider, I will not harm you.

"Looks like someone beat me to this one." He said, stepping over the body lying on the floor, his head bent at an impossible angle.

Hazel reached the bottom, and looked at the Mage stretched at her feet. She could sense the life of the man still within him, he was just unconscious.

"This one is still alive." She stated bluntly. Not truly bothered if the Nightwalker came back to finish the job.

"I know, he is just unconscious, but he won't come to for another ten minutes or so yet." The reply was fair and while not hostile, there was still the brevity that masked a lack of interest towards his temporary shadow.

"You're just going to leave him alive? He could come after us." Said Hazel cautiously.

"So, you have decided to follow me after all. Good, you're more likely to stay alive that way. And as to the poor creature on the floor, he does not pose me any threat, and killing people is not the reason I came today." Vorlin turned and continued walking towards the entrance, not looking to see if Hazel was following or not. She was tempted to finish the man herself, he had taken the lives of some of her friends and hundreds of others she was sure, he had dared to invade her home, and she could end his evil right here and now.

Looking up she met the eyes of Vorlin. He was regarding her in a completely neutral fashion, but her skin crawled causing her to shiver. She stared back at the prone body on the floor, a deep breath got her anger under control once more and she stepped clear of the man, walking up the stairs. Vorlin turned and continued walking away, not giving any clues as to his approval or not of Hazel's actions.

Leaving the shelter of the Lair, Hazel saw the sky for the first time in a couple of months and the sight rocked her physically and mentally. The immensity of the universe made her feel awe for the Creator, the Father of the Gods. She felt exhilarated, wanted to soar among the stars, and yet felt helplessly small and insignificant, a grain of sand in the hot and dusty Lost Lands which she now wandered.

"I have heard that the universe can have an effect upon Riders, though I have never seen it before." Admitted Vorlin as they walked.

"What do you mean?" asked Hazel confused. It was a strange statement to come from nowhere and even more so from a Nightwalker.

"Your eyes, I can see how you are affected by the sky. It is not uncommon for people to shy away from it when locked up for a long time, but you seem, hypnotised, by it. In wonder of it. I have heard of the same happen to other Riders in my long life, but have never witnessed it before." Vorlin had only looked back briefly as he spoke and again led the way without pausing to talk to Hazel. She wondered if she was supposed to reply or if the conversation was deemed complete with the observation made.

She followed him in silence for a couple of hours. He neither looked round nor offered comment as to where they were going. They walked across the dry and sandy ground, cresting dune after dune. Hazel was trying to sense her surroundings, but there was no one within a fifteen-minute brisk march.

"It will be dawn soon." Observed Hazel. The sun was already starting to illuminate the horizon to the East.

"Yes. It will." Replied the Nightwalker. His reply as distant as ever.

"I had always believed that you could not survive daylight." Said Hazel, trying to get some kind of conversation from him, to get some kind of clue as to his personality.

"We can't, for long. There is a shelter not far from here, that is where we are heading. I will be asleep long before the sun crests the earth." Again statement and no conversation.

What is it with him? Does he have some aversion to speaking? Thought Hazel to herself as she followed the tall man into the trough of another rolling wave of sand and dirt.

It was a further twenty minutes of swift trekking later when Hazel saw a pair of iron doors set into the ground. It was almost horizontal with a solid stone surround that supported it just above the sand. As they approached the portal, Hazel noticed a design on each of the two doors, a clawed hand shaking what looked like a human hand. There were strange symbols around the motif that she could not place, certainly she had not seen the like before in any of the books or parchments she had studied back at the Rider Barracks.

"What are those symbols?" asked Hazel when they were almost at the entrance.

"It is writing, at least it is a form of writing. It dates back nearly fifteen hundred years."

"What does it say?" asked Hazel

" 'Never forget, once we were allies' " was all the reply she received from the mysterious stranger.

He reached out with a hand as they arrived, and placed it an iron disc positioned centrally over both the doors. As he touched the dull metal, it started to glow, first orange, then red and finally white before a loud click was heard. He reached to the iron rings that were the handles and pulled, opening the heavy doors.

There were stairs inside that led sharply downwards and Vorlin hastened into the entry. As he did torches in the stairwell lit by themselves, showing that the vault descended about thirty feet before levelling out.

"Close the doors behind you," said Vorlin as he disappeared "they will lock by themselves." Hazel did as she was instructed, a metallic clunk echoing down the stairs as soon as the doors met. Once more, she was encased by torch lit alleyways, the dank smell of subterranean constructions and the company of a devil.

They moved to the bottom of the stairs and Vorlin opened a further door, this one made only of wood. Inside was a room, luxuriously appointed with furniture that looked ancient, golden candlesticks and chandeliers, rich wooden tables and fine pieces of art.

"What is this place?" asked Hazel as Vorlin sat on one of the rich sofas.

"We call it a Crypt, though as you can see it is far from a place of rest for the departed." He paused and offered Hazel a seat. She sat down, relieved to finally let her aching muscles rest. "Crypts can be found all over the Lost Lands, and even the Kingdom. They are part of long forgotten history, but they give us a means to travel great distances and avoid human contact should we wish. The locks only open to the touch of one of the *Seicolantrai*, and there are magical wards that are placed around them to discourage mortals from coming too close. Nothing harmful," he stated quickly, noting Hazel's distaste at the word 'discourage', "but it turns the human, *or Rider* away from the entrance subconsciously."

"But what about the Dragons? Surely they are not mortal? How have they not come across them?" questioned Hazel.

"You are young, girl. The oldest Rider must be nearly two hundred years? The oldest Dragon must be close to five hundred. Yes the Riders and even the Dragons gain longevity, but both are still mortal. I, personally have seen over seven hundred winters on this world, and there are *Seicolantrai* older than I."

"Then who are you? What are the two factions you talked about?" pressed Hazel in an attempt to get more information from her strange saviour.

"We will discuss who we are when we get back to the Coven tomorrow night, until then I will rest. You are free to do what you wish until then." Motioning to two sets of doors Vorlin continued, "Through those doors is a bedroom, you are welcome to the use of it. Through the other set is a store room, there are clothes and some weapons there, you can dress and rid yourself of that hospital smock, and chose a weapon that suits you if you wish, you may have need of it before we get you back to your own border." With that, he turned and walked to a third set of doors. Opening them, he stepped through and shut them gently behind him, leaving Hazel to wonder what twist of fate had brought her to this place.

When Vorlin had disappeared, Hazel moved into the storeroom. It was a good-sized room, with piles of clothes and wracks of weapons neatly placed against the walls. She quickly stripped out of the dirty and coarse hospital garment, and dressed herself in some faded black trousers and tunic and pulled on a serviceable pair of brown calf high boots. She equipped herself with a simple but well made long sword and practised a few basic swings to get the feel for it.

After about half an hour, Hazel realised she was feeling tired and hungry. A quick search of the stores revealed no food so she tried to put the feeling of hunger aside and went to the second bedroom. If she couldn't eat, then she could try to sleep at least. She felt like she was safe, after a fashion and it was the closest thing to relaxation she had felt for months. As soon as her head touched the soft pillow, she drifted into a deep and desperately needed sleep.

A knock on the door awoke her.

"Rider Jensook, it's time to get ready. We leave for the Coven in a few minutes."

As she climbed out of the bed she stretched and realised that her muscles we not taut for the first time in what seemed like a decade.

She strapped the sword belt around her waist and left the room. Vorlin was waiting at the bottom of the stairs, still dressed in the brown robes he was in the previous night. Looking into his eyes she had to remind herself what he was and not to trust him too much, he was still a Nightwalker and until she was safely back to her own lines she would not relax completely.

Nodding to him in greeting, she asked him where they were going.

"We head South and West, the Coven will be about six hours from us if we move quickly." And move quickly they did. Hazel was struggling to keep up with the pace set by the Nightwalker. It was closer to a jog than a brisk walk, and the tempo was not slowed once through the night. The warm gusts of wind kicked up the sand and dry earth that made the Lost Lands so difficult to track in, and blew it straight in their faces. Vorlin appeared not to notice, but Hazel found her eyes streaming with tears from the stinging attacks of the wind.

At one point Vorlin stopped and looked up to the sky, tilting his head slightly.

"They are hunting us." Was all he said before pushing on at the same gruesome pace once more.

"How do you know that? I can't see or hear anything" replied Hazel as she panted along behind him.

"My hearing is substantially better than yours, I can hear the Graven crying back in the distance. The Dark Lords are upset by our attack it seems."

"*Our*? Who else came with you and where are they now?" asked Hazel, using the conversation to keep her mind from the thoughts of food and bed once more.

"A friend and I decided we needed to know what the source of energy was in the bottom of that Lair. He found out so we left."

"Why didn't he stay at the Crypt today as well?" came Hazel's question.

"Because he does not have to worry about the sun, he pressed on to the Coven and is there now probably."

"Who is he?" Hazel wanted to keep him talking, it helped her to keep moving, but Vorlin had decided she did not need any further answers apparently and remained stoically silent.

A further two hours passed uneventfully when Vorlin turned suddenly. He reached back and grabbed Hazel, dragging her to the floor. Letting out a surprised cry Hazel found Vorlin's hand covering her mouth as he pulled his robe over them both.

Trying to remain quiet, and not to let her fear get the better of her, Hazel slowly reached up and pulled Vorlin's hand away. It was cold to the touch, in sharp contrast to the warm summer night.

As he pulled his hand away, a shriek was heard in the distance. Hazel froze, she had heard that sound before. On the wall defending the line north of Sarafell, the same sound had followed from a mighty swing at the beasts leg, only the slightest cut had been left on the winged creature, and the meeting had left Hazel with the scar on her shoulder.

Each successive call from the Graven came progressively closer. Hazel was trembling softly, Vorlin placed a hand on her shoulder in an attempt to comfort her, but it was no use. He could sense she had a history with the creatures and he could understand her fear. If he came face to face with one of the Dark Lords, or Assassins as some of them preferred to be called, he could not be sure he would walk away alive, indeed the odds would be in favour of the vile Mage. If the Graven were to join the fray, he knew he would stand no chance.

The sound of giant wings grew louder as the monster got closer. Eventually Hazel could hear clearly the wings, the shrieks and the disturbed air directly above her as the foul thing flew above them.

They stayed perfectly still, Hazel could hear Vorlin whispering something over and over but dared not interrupt him. The Graven and its rider seemed to circle them again and again, causing Hazel's heart to race. She started to feel the urge to run, to get up and run away as fast as possible and hope the

Graven could not catch up to her. Vorlin held her tighter, his strength pinning her to the floor, stopping her moving.

Her breathing increased in intensity and she recognised the start of hyperventilation, her vision started to swim and she felt nauseous. Just as she thought she might pass out, a shriek resounded that carried with it a note of frustration. The wings beat powerfully and the creature sped away to the East, the sounds of it growing fainter until they had vanished into the warm night.

Vorlin stopped his chanting and pulled the robe off of them both.

"Are you ok?" he said simply standing and helping Hazel to her feet.

She forcibly stopped herself from taking rapid breaths and slowly came back to herself.

"What happened? Why didn't he see us?" she asked in the end.

"I shielded our presence from him, and in the night my robes and the disturbed sand hid us from them visibly." Replied the man quietly

"Were you casting a spell? All the Seers I have seen practice their arts only needed to recite the spell once for it to work, why were you chanting repeatedly?"

"Riders have an innate ability to blend in or shield themselves from people. Mages or Seers have the knowledge of spells to do it for them, but they also need a base ability to do so. I was once human, I had no ability and mage-craft and was not one of the Children, that is those who are born into the legacy of the Riders. But when I was turned, I gained certain abilities over my surroundings and people. The catch is I need to focus hard to carry them off. Chanting what I want to do is the way I focus my mind on the task, it was how the Dark Lord back there could not find us."

Hazel merely nodded and brushed the sand and earth from her clothes as the Nightwalker set off once more for the Coven.

"My name is Hazel."

The statement came from nowhere after a further half hour of walking.

"Why do you tell me this now?"

"You saved my life. Twice, and that is without the Mages you killed in getting me out of that lair. I felt you deserved to know my first name."

Vorlin stopped. Turning to her he bowed, "It is a pleasure to have met you Hazel, and thank you." With that, he turned and continued to move towards his home again.

One hour later, they approached what looked like the entrance to another Crypt. Again, it had iron doors set almost horizontal into the ground, and again they were framed in stone. There were the same motif and writing emblazoned upon each of the doors and the entrance appeared as foreboding to Hazel as had the entrance to the Crypt.

Vorlin stretched out his hand once more, the colour of the locking disc changed from orange, through to white before allowing the couple to pass into its shadowy interior.

Hazel closed the doors behind her and followed Vorlin down the stars. The further they descended, the more lavish the place began to look. Carpets and paintings adorned the floors and walls, chandeliers gave more and more light the further down they travelled.

At the bottom of the stairs, there was a further lock that Vorlin opened in the same manner as that of the first. The door swung open by itself, and he entered a well-lit room. Voices could be heard inside and Hazel felt slightly uneasy as she followed him. She had become too relaxed around him and now fears that she was being led into a trap flooded through her mind.

There were about ten people inside the room and it hit hazel hard who they were. Half the men were in the same type of robes that Vorlin was wearing, some with cloaks and cowls.

The other half wore the black and red of the Riders; on their shoulders were the Silver Crescents that denoted the ranks of the Dragon Riders as opposed to gold studs of the general Riders.

"What is all this?" asked Hazel as she saw the strange gathering of warriors and Nightwalkers.

"Ah, welcome Rider." said a short man wearing eight closely spaced silver crescents on each shoulder. He was nearly white of hair, powerful looking yet not as ageless as most of the Riders that Hazel had seen previously. There was no doubt that the man was aged by their standards, but he also appeared sharp and in control of himself.

He walked over to her and clapped a hind on her shoulder. "I must admit, finding a Rider here in the depths of the Lost Lands, especially in a Coven was the last thing I would have wagered on before now, but here you, and not alone either."

"What do you mean not alone?" asked Hazel, pulling back slightly from the man's touch.

A door opened from across the room and the conversation halted as all turned to view the new arrival.

"Hazel?!" it was a shocked statement that came from Tal. Hazel looked at him in disbelief, forgetting the strange situation, she ran across the room and flung herself on him, holding him tightly. Tears ran freely down her cheek as she kissed him firmly.

"I thought I would never see you again! What are you doing here? You were posted to Peter's Hold weren't you?" she asked refusing to let go of him.

"Yes but Brad and I were captured in an assault, we ended up on the demons world and have been held there for the past two months, we only returned back last night after escaping." He replied, enjoying the secure warmth of her against him.

"You were captured?! How?" she said forgetting her own troubles, her tears drying up at the realisation he had been in danger.

"There was an assault on Peter's Hold. The Riders took several small units into the citadel and planted some type of explosive devices fashioned by the Seers. We got captured during the mission. The Riders managed to bring down the citadel and render the Gates in the foundations of it, useless. The only other gate that could get us home brought us out into a lair of the Grey Mages. We were saved by Dragon Rider Risce, he just appeared and led us here without us having any idea of who he was or where we were going. But Khris has answered a lot of questions, and filled us in on what has been happening here over the last couple of months."

"I wasn't even told you were made up to Rider, congratulations, even though it seems the promotion led to a hard time for you." Said Hazel hugging him again.

"I haven't, I mean I'm not a Rider yet." Said Tal, his eyes down cast and his voice trailing off.

"Then what were you doing on that kind of assignment?!" asked Hazel, amazed at the commanding officers decision to send a trainee on a dangerous mission.

"I tagged along, no one even knew I was there until I was being dragged off by a demon. Kelar and another Rider, the one that sent me to the City of Dragons, tried to save both Brad and me, but had been beaten too sorely to get to us in time."

"You rock-headed fool!" shouted Hazel pushing him away. "Why would you do something like that? Don't tell me you did not know it would be dangerous!"

Tal looked hurt, he had no idea what to say in reply and so he simply turned round and walked back into the room he had come from.

The room was silent, Hazel was in a state of disbelief. When she turned back she noted that everyone was looking at her in silence. Eventually, Vorlin spoke.

"Down that corridor there are rooms, the first four have been taken but after that you may use any you choose." He spoke in his usual quiet voice. Though this time it seemed as if it contained a tension she had not heard before. Nodding she walked away from the congregation of high ranking Riders and Nightwalkers and decided that a good long sleep would settle her nerves, and calm her anger.

Tal closed the door behind him. Brad looked up at his friend.

"So was it a warm home coming? I heard you speaking to Hazel, what is she doing here?" he asked as Tal moved to his bunk and sat down heavily upon it.

"I don't know, I didn't get a chance to ask. When she found out I had followed Kelar to the Citadel she flew of the handle, lost it with me. I know it was a silly thing to do, but I think I have made up for my mistake, don't you? Why are girls always so confusing?" moped Tal, his head hanging as he threw his legs up and rolled over onto his side.

Brad didn't know how he should reply. He desperately wanted to go speak to Hazel and ask about Cholla. He had heard there had been a pitched battle that the Kingdom had all but lost, and he wanted to find out if Cholla was safe, but the chance had passed, the raised voice of Hazel had kept him from going after her, and Tal certainly was not about to go and get a second portion of abuse.

Patience. He wished he had more of that great quality, but as he lay there, he could not stop his mind from replaying possible worst case scenarios about the battle and the chances that Cholla was ok.

As he drifted off to sleep slowly, his thoughts were filled with the blonde girl with the blue eyes that so easily made him feel comfortable. It had been too long, he needed to see Cholla again soon, he had to tell her how he felt.

Chapter 14

Revelations

Tal awoke.

His head felt heavy and as though it was full of lead, not surprising he supposed, considering what sleep had managed to get was tormented by Hazel's anger towards him.

Stretching, he pulled himself from his bed, and walked quietly to the washbasin so as not to wake Brad. He wet his face and ran his damp fingers through his hair. Pouring himself a drink from the pitcher full of water that had been left for them, Tal walked to the door.

Opening it only slightly, he slid out so as not to let the brighter light of the main reception room flood into the dimly lit bedchamber he and Brad shared. Sat around a circular table to one side of the room, was the collection of Riders and Nightwalkers that Tal had been introduced to when he first arrived at the Coven. It had been a shock at first, but Khris had been very reassuring that all was well and said that when he was refreshed in a couple of days, all would be explained to him and Brad.

"Good afternoon Tal," said Khris, smiling as usual. "how did you sleep?"

"Not too well if I'm honest." He replied, remembering the hot, uncomfortable and restless night.

"That's not surprising, you got quite the chewing out before you went to bed." Said the overly friendly Dragon Rider. "I take it there is a history between you two?"

Tal paused, not sure what to say. Was there a history? If so to what extent?

"Yes, there is. We became close on a trip to Coladan, but that seems so long ago now. Nothing has really happened between us, I'm not even sure where I stand with her half the time."

"Ha, well your not the first lad to be confused by a girl, I remember when my wife and I first met, even after a decade, she still confused me at every opportunity." Said the Dragon Rider in good humour.

"Your married? I wasn't sure if Riders were allowed wives -or husbands- or not. I mean I have never heard anyone talk of their wife or husband before."

A tall man with lose shoulder length hair and the brightest blue eyes Tal had ever seen, pulled out a vacant seat for Tal. Sitting down Tal thanked the man who simply nodded. There was an air of power about him that Tal could sense immediately, he was a Nightwalker, but what did that mean now? The line between good and bad guys was blurring and Tal didn't know where people stood in regard to it any longer.

"I *was* married," continued Khris, his smile fading ever so slightly. "she was a fellow Rider, I was a young Captain, she was my Sergeant." The room fell into silence, though all here knew his story, something was different this time, Khris wasn't just giving them information and telling jokes, he was delivering his story.

"We were on a routine patrol, the Kingdom was a different place back then, there were brigands roaming the countryside attacking at will. The Dark Cousins were not restricted to the Dark Forrest as much as they are now, and there were some civil feuds that were destroying cities slowly.

"We were moving my company between Greymarth and Farstor, there had been sightings of elves roaming the countryside between the two small towns -as they were then. The idea of the patrol, was to discover if there were actually Elven forces in the area, and if there were, to discover if they were our allies, or if they were Dark Cousins. We had been moving round between re-supply points for a month, and were beginning to think there were no forces other than ourselves, after all, if there were, they were Elves and how could humans track them?

"We carried on like this for a further two weeks, finding nothing other than our own shadows. With two weeks left before we were to head back, we had relaxed too much. We were skirting the edge of the Dark Forest, hoping to draw out these phantom elves so we had something to report when we got back to Greymarth. I made a mistake with that decision; I had underestimated the Dark Cousins. They hit us at sunset, taking out the sentries without us knowing, and then continuing to kill half the company before we could organise a defence.

"My wife had a small group of Riders prepared and started a sweep of the immediate area, trying to flush out the Dark Elves into our company so we could eliminate them man to man."

It was obviously hard for Khris to disclose this about himself, especially in front of Tal, whom he did not know that well.

"She was a tough woman, my wife. And to give her credit, she dispatched a respectable number of them before she was forced out of the woods. She was the only one of the group of ten that entered the trees to force out the enemy that got out alive, and when she came out I was beside myself with joy, it may have been wrong of me, but though my company was falling around me, I was only happy my wife was still alive.

"I called to her, and she smiled and came running towards me. It would be ok, somehow we would get out of there and make it back to civilisation. Then head back with reinforcements and make them all suffer for the losses we had suffered.

"As she reached me, she threw her arms around me, and held me tight, I did not realise it immediately, but the reason she was holding me, was because she had a cloth yard arrow buried in her back." Khris was talking quietly now, tears appearing on his cheeks.

"She died in my arms. I was distraught, and as I laid her on the cold ground, I felt a rage that had not surfaced in me before. I became possessed by the desire for revenge, and I welcomed it.

"I stood, held my sword tighter and walked straight into the woods. I blended myself into the background and I killed as many Dark Cousins as I could find.

"The sun had set, and still I was fighting and killing. My entire company had been slaughtered by this time, and all I was worried about was revenge for the death of my wife.

"I found myself surrounded, and without hope very quickly. You see the force we were sent to find had found us, and they were a great number. More than my company could handle, and as I was all that was left, failure was about to become absolute. Then a saviour arrived. His name was Vorlin Mansford. He killed those that surrounded me, and managed to get me away from the rest of the Dark Cousins to a local Crypt. He brought me back to sanity slowly, and it *was* a slow process.

"That is why you do not find many Riders that have husbands or wives Tal, not because we are forbade it, but because it can be far too painful.

"This all happened about two hundred and seventy years ago now. I am not telling you this as a simple story Tal, I'm telling you my soul destroying history so that when we tell you what we are about to, you can take it as the truth and hopefully, give it the weight it deserves."

Khris stood up and gathered himself again. The door to Tal and Brad's room opened and Brad entered the gathering.

Sensing the mood in the room, he moved to Tal in silence and nodded to the others around the table.

"I was just giving Tal the story of my late wife Brad. Do not worry, it is not relevant to the current state of the world. I just wanted Tal to understand that not all things that are thought to be evil, are."

"What do you mean sir?" asked Brad quietly, the mood in the room still oppressive.

"It is common thought that Nightwalkers are evil creatures, shying from the world of man other than to feed and kill. However, this is not nearly the complete truth.

"As you are aware yourselves, the group here are quite friendly, and not a throat has been chewed since you arrived. This is because there are two types of Nightwalker, or as they call themselves *Seicolantrai*. The first is as you believe, strong, ferocious, and kill for the pleasure and for food, but these are not the original. No, they are the rebellious children of the fathers. Those you see here follow the *Honourable Path*, that is they will not kill to feed, indeed they hunt much like you or I would, and deer or fowl caught provide them with the blood they require for survival.

"In a previous time, *Seicolantrai* and man lived side by side, literally neighbours in some towns. As time passed the race became divided, the impetuous young decided that they were set above humans, they were stronger faster, immortal should they be careful, why should they not feed off humans like humans feed off cattle?

"There was an uprising against the Elders of the Nightwalkers, the Elders and their followers demanded the same relationship between *Seicolantrai* and Human that had always existed. The young wanted to dominate us. In the end, as is always the case when dealing with creatures that have emotion, the disagreement dissolved into violence, and though the Elders and supporters loyal to their way of life were stronger due to their increased age and wisdom, they were also outnumbered.

"Eventually there was a stand off, and the humans worried about what would happen should the younger Nightwalkers win, decided to take matters into their own hands. They struck out at all Nightwalkers, whether pro human or not, and drove them all out of the towns. It is true that ignorance leads to fear, which in turn leads the human heart.

"Those that still followed the *Honourable Path* went underground and continued their way of life in secret, those that wanted to feed on humans did just that, they hid in the close proximity of towns and fed on those that ventured out at night. The whole race of Nightwalkers however took the bad reputation of the young as that is what happens, one bad apple and all that.

"Over time however, the number of those following the Honourable Path has dwindled, there is a war being waged you see, and for immortals, what is the point in agreeing to disagree? You have eternity to put your side across after all.

"There are about ten Covens left my friends, and that is all, however the numbers have stopped decreasing recently for one reason, and *that* is what all this has been about.

"Have I missed anything out Vorlin?" asked Khris, his ever present smile returning.

"I do not think so, but it is the next part that should be stated very clearly, the message needs to get back to the King without misinterpretation." The Nightwalker was as quiet as ever. His voice never seemed more than the barest whisper.

"Very well. Ok boys here is the important bit.

"There is a truce between the two warring factions of *Seicolantrai*, though they have been fighting for over a thousand years, now they help each other – though they still disagree about their food. The reason for their sudden truce is this; the human race, the *Seicolantrai* race, even the Grey Mages, all face extinction should the demons regain control of this planet. You see, this planet exists because the Gods wish it to. Because the world was set up by the eternal creators, it *must* survive.

"That is the whole crux of this war lads, not the Kingdoms survival, not the survival of its people, but the survival of all life." Khris paused, waiting for the thought to take root in the young Riders minds.

The past two months had been physically draining, and intimidating, the previous couple of days had been mentally stressful. Now Tal was trying to take in that the whole world is in danger of extinction. It seemed a lot for a sixteen year old to come to terms with, but what about a Rider?

"How can they kill all of us? Surely even in the worst-case scenario, some of us would escape? And what is with the Grey Mages? Why is there a Gate to the demon's world in the sacrifice chamber of their lair?" Brad seemed to be having trouble coming to terms with the situation as much as Tal was.

"To answer the second point first," replied Khris "the Grey Mages are being deceived." Such a flat answer to such a confusing question. "The demons fashioned two Gates, one in Peters Hold, the other in the basement of one of the Grey Mages lairs. The Mages are self important and egotistical. They actually believe they are destined to be the rulers of man. Their blind belief has led them into the claws of the demons. These dark creatures manipulated the Mages into reading the signs that this was The Time Before. Whilst their puppets attack man, they would too. But their ultimate plan was confusion. With two different wars, mankind would be in confusion, it would be that much easier for them to reclaim this world as theirs, and *that* is when we all die."

Tal's head was starting to hurt, the entire Grey Mage invasion was nothing but a ploy to split the forces of the Kingdom, to give their own invasion that much more chance of success.

Khris still had not answered the first question posed by Brad though, and Tal feared that answer would be even more terrifying.

"As to why we will all die if the demons gain supremacy here, well that is a little harder to explain, but I will try to make it simple and hope you trust me.

"This world must continue to exist, if it fails to do so, then the gods will would have been negated and that is not possible, so in their wisdom they made a fail safe system. To ensure that the world continues to exist, they made it adaptive. Should demons become the predominant life form, the world would adapt to house them, if it did not, they would tear it apart so *they* can survive. By becoming demon friendly, for want of a better term, it would become human *unfriendly*. Where the demons are now is limbo, it is a world that exists just to house life forms. It is not a comfortable world but life *can* survive there.

"Thousands of years ago, demons were the predominant life here. The atmosphere was made up of different gasses that would kill you instantly. Eventually another race emerged, they arrived by means unknown, at least to humans. This race was that of Elves. They are long lived and at the time could survive the gasses that made up the atmosphere. The demons did not resist the arrivals as the new race provided a new source of food that was not their own kind. Eventually the elves grew to such a number that the planet started to adapt, slowly the gasses mixed with what we now call air. The demons started to get upset but could not understand why this was happening. Then came the biggest blow to the demon race, humans arrived. We have spoken to the Elves and they will tell us nothing of those days, but they did tell us that when humankind arrived, it pushed the balance of the atmosphere against the demons. They were forced to flee, to find a limbo world where they could survive and plan how to regain their world. If we fail to stop them, they can open more gates, they can have unlimited numbers with which to rotate until the atmosphere becomes acidic enough for them to return here permanently.

"So you see, it is a dire situation. The oldest dragons were not alive when man and *Seicolantrai* lived in peace together, and many of the population would not believe there are any honourable Nightwalkers. This is why only the highest echelons of the Rider Order are aware of our pact with those you see here. All five of our pale skinned brethren here are the most powerful *Seicolantrai* left alive. The Riders here are all ranked Dragon Rider, some of higher status than others, but all heavily involved in the hidden war that is being waged.

"Vorlin and I will lead you and your refugees back to the lines of the Kingdom, and from there we will head to the City of Dragons for an audience with the King."

Tal felt like his legs would never work again. He placed his hands behind his head and breathed a heavy sigh.

The Mages were being manipulated and the world would slowly change into an inhospitable planet should the demons return in any numbers. Looking at Brad, he saw his friend looking as stunned as he felt, and could sympathise with the young Rider.

One of the doors opened and Hazel walked into the room. Everyone looked up and caused Hazel to stop still mid step.

"What?" she said hesitantly.

It was Vorlin who spoke, quietly and with his usual simplicity.

"We are heading back to the Kingdom. Get your gear together if there is anything special you wish to take. We leave when the sun sets."

Drew awoke, he had been back in Borders Edge for a week now and was on refresh duty. He was working lunch and diners so that the ordered watches could get food without needing to rush back to their posts. The advantage of this routine was that it gave Drew some time to himself that was usually unknown to the common soldiery of the army.

He and Richardson had received their audience with Duke Teele of Myllarad who was worried to hear about the events occurring in the countryside. It had taken a couple of days, but the result was worth it. A company of twenty of the Dukes personal guard under the supervision of one of the senior sergeants was to be guided by one of the Rangers, one of the secret army of the Brotherhood of Seers.

They had returned to the position where the track had been sighted, and the Ranger had been able to sense the direction the pack of demons had set off in, even though there were no physical tracks any longer. Drew was in slight awe of the tracking abilities of the Rangers, seemingly able to pick up tracks where others could not. It was a day later when he told Brad that the Rangers had certain Gifts granted to them by the Seers that allowed them to follow tracks that no longer existed.

The tracks led back towards Peters Hold but when they got back to the destruction there was confusion, some tracks led away from the main group while others seemed to pace. When all the routes had been followed they all met back with the main party and they had all set off once again westwards, close to the same track that had led them to the demolished citadel.

The party had caught up with a group of seventeen Demons two days later, walking slowly and without caution. Sergeant Richardson and the Dukes senior sergeant decided that an ambush would reduce the number of demons significantly enough that the odds would be heavily with the Humans.

In a small wooded area an hours walk in front of the isolated demons, a group of eight archers and the Ranger were stationed in the trees ready to send as many arrows into the demons as possible. The rest of the company hid themselves as well as they could in the foliage surrounding them.

It took just over an hour for the large creatures to come bounding close by the copse of trees. On a hand signal from the senior Sergeant, the nine bowmen let loose with their arrows. Two demons fell straight away with arrows piercing their throats, another three were knocked to the ground and rose very slowly to their feet, arrows protruding from their chests or limbs. Another flight of arrows left the trees killing two more, the three that already were slowed by the arrows were writhing on the floor in agony, beginning to look like pin cushions. The remaining ten demons were struck head on, Drew doing his best not to find himself on the wrong end of one of those razor sharp claws again.

The battle ended quickly once the first few demons fell, and they quickly returned back to Myllarad to report success to the Duke.

That had been a while ago however, and Drew was now safe in the confines of Borders Edge once more.

Safe, it seemed a strange word. He was safe from physical attack and harm here, within the reinforced walls of Borders Edge, but he was not safe from memories. Every night he found himself back amongst the battles he had fought, the fear he had felt once more coursing through his veins as he struggled to survive. He had asked Richardson how he coped with it, the Sergeant simply smiled sadly and replied that eventually he would see enough action that no single memory would overpower another and his dreams would stop, though the memories would always be there, that was a soldiers lot.

He was getting dressed for his breakfast duty when a knock interrupted his reminiscing. Opening the door to his room, he found one of the privates that was serving as Captain Loytan's messengers.

A summons for him to present himself to Captain Loytan, ready and equipped for a field assignment of unknown length was given to him by the private who appeared to envy Drew his assignment, obviously not content with staying within the safety of the walls.

Drew packed some clean uniforms and placed a chain mail shirt on his shoulders, his long sword was strapped round his waist and two knives were attached to the sword belt.

Hefting his pack containing the uniforms and weapons maintenance gear onto his back, he left the small room that had been his home for a week and headed to the command building that Loytan was stationed in.

It would be good to be doing something again he thought. He felt it was the lack of activity that was causing his mind to wander back to the battles and horror of the demons. Yes, he decided it was definitely time to be in the field again, away from the quiet, safe, and distressingly haunting nights.

Arriving at the command post, Drew looked at the rising sun. It's warmth made the morning pleasant, and the soft reddish yellow glow gave the building an almost angelic appearance.

Reporting to the sentry outside, he was escorted into Loytan's presence and offered a seat.

"Drew, good morning. I trust you are recovering well after your last assignment?" Drew said he was, a little curious as to what was causing his Captain to act so curiously. A private was very rarely offered a seat when receiving orders.

"You have seen more action that most of the Guard in your very short career to date. So I have decided to be generous, or at least I hope you see it that way.

"The ruins of Peters Hold have been quiet since the Riders assault. That does not mean that the area is safe however. I am tasked to take a field tested group to the ruins, accompanied with a small contingent of Engineers and Seers and to secure the area around the city. It should be a very dull and uneventful assignment and will last an unknown length of time. I have selected sergeant Richardson's unit to accompany me along with two other sergeants and their people. I trust that is acceptable to you?"

Drew sat still unsure how to handle this situation. Confusion held his tongue and silence was the Captains answer.

"Guardsman Earemon?" supplied the Captain.

"Sorry sir, if I may ask, why am I given the option?" asked Drew, his confusion spilling over at last.

"Because Prince Allin has been impressed with your efforts in tracking down the party of Demons, and so wanted you and sergeant Richardson to have the option of returning to field service or not at the moment."

"The Prince has offered me the choice?" asked Drew completely shocked that any Royal would have noticed a private soldier.

"Yes, but I have asked you a question and expect an answer Guardsman." Said Loytan firmly but not harshly.

"Sorry sir," replied Drew, his soldiers discipline taking over once more. "yes I am ready for duty sir."

"Excellent, you will be briefed tomorrow morning by myself. Go get some proper rest, someone else has been assigned your duties so you have the day to yourself, make the most of it, it may be the last day you have for some time." Captain Loytan gave Drew permission to withdraw and turned back to his own duties.

Leaving the building, Drew walked slowly through the streets. The city was slowly becoming a giant fortress. Buildings being torn down to provide clear views of the walls, nasty traps being set into the ground in specific positions, walls being reinforced and siege weapons being placed along the length of the defences.

It seemed that everything Drew had come to rely upon growing up was slowly being torn apart. The goodness of the world that had seemed so obvious when Tal's parents explained it to him, was slowly dissolving into chaos and carnage.

Stopping at a crossroads, Drew took a deep breath and looked up into the sky. No matter what happened here on earth, the sky always seemed blue and infinite, always clean, no matter how rough the weather got, there would always be a blue sky that followed. Would the human race be the same?

Looking left he glanced up at the now imposing keep of the city, to his right he could see all the way to the docks, ships were lined up waiting for pilotage into the harbour. They were bringing in soldiers from the west of the kingdom, construction materials from the mines of Ulgon Du Yarin, and orders from the King that could be carried by sea for swiftness but did not require the attention of the Seers to transmit them instantly.

He found it strange that he had lived close to the sea for most of his life but had never really noticed how endless it seemed.

Moving to the docks he found a tavern that was still operating and entered, there were the usual types he would associate with such a place, sailors, soldiers and the poorer of the remaining populace that could not afford to leave the city and needed to drown their sorrows.

Ordering ale, Drew took a seat next to a sailor from the Kings Fleet and asked if there was any gossip.

Sarafell was preparing for war, much like Borders Edge and Myllarad was. Other than that, the main population of the Kingdom knew something was wrong but remained ignorant to what it was. The few that had managed to get the story out were being called crazy and storytellers, other than that the kingdom was still at peace.

Drew spent the rest of the day drinking ale slowly and making casual conversation with anyone that cared to talk. He may not have achieved much, but it was relaxing, and it was nice to simply talk to people without worrying if he was going to have to fight his way out of a situation soon.

All too quickly, the sun was once more rising above the horizon. Drew was prepared for the road, and had been briefed by the Captain. He was sitting astride a horse with twenty-nine further Guards waiting for the signal to depart for the ruins of Peters Hold. A group of six Seers and twenty Engineers emerged from the Seers temple together, the two groups openly talking and in good spirits. Drew relaxed as he saw his superiors laughing, surely this could only mean that things were going smoothly.

Captain Loytan saluted the Seer that appeared to be in charge of their group and then shook hands with him vigorously, a large grin spreading over his face. Speaking up, the Captain introduced Master Oren Diarmid, one rank below entry into the Brotherhoods Elder Council. Oren was an ex Household Guardsman that joined the Ranks of the Seers when it was noted he had the ability.

"It is a boon that Master Diarmid has been sent to guide us, he was a great Guardsman, and as such knows our ways well. This will make us all work easier with each other. Should any of the Seers require anything, please help them if you can. Ok get ready, we leave now."

Richardson's squad was positioned at the rear of the column, the Engineers of the company were next up the column preceded by the Seers and then Captain Loytan and Sergeant Kestar's Squad. Sergeant Wynters squad were acting as scouts, both advance and along the flank of the column.

"How long have you been serving?" asked an unknown Engineer to Drew as the man

He had not thought about it, but it had been almost a year, all bar a couple of months. How could a life change so dramatically in such a short time?

"You look like you have seen some action?" continued the Engineer.

Drew realised that he had not answered the man's first question, snapping himself back to full concentration he apologised and replied to the middle aged man.

"I have been in the Guards nearly a year, and yes, I have seen some action, all with demons."

"That is a hell of a start to a career my lad. And I do not envy you, though I'm sure it will lead to fast promotion."

"Thank you, how long have you been with the Seers? I was not aware there was an official group of Engineers attached to the military.

"There isn't we are civilian, but when Peters Hold was lost, and the Mages started to push towards Sarafell, our Guild asked for volunteers to join the Kings forces. I raised my hand

and here I am. Last year I was constructing machines to allow better irrigation of fields, now I am constructing ballista and hidden traps. Strange life huh?"

"Yes." Drew fell into a silence, his eyes watching the edge of the roads, his mind searching what he saw for any sign of an attack, but his heart was silent. Some hardness had smothered him and he felt cold inside himself. For the first time in his life, he could not find any humour in his existence.

It took three weeks to get within sight of what was once Peters Hold. Over half of the walls surrounding the city had fallen, and within them was nothing but rubble. There was the occasional building that still stood, but the majority of it was piled bricks, stone and wood.

The company stopped an hour's march from the boundary to the destroyed city. In silence, they bowed their heads and prayed to whichever god they held dearest for the souls of those who died within that city during and after the initial attack.

The next morning they moved closer to the city, their camp was set in the woodland to the south of the ruins, and that would be their base of operations for the foreseeable future. The Guards along with two Seers made a complete circle of the city, and on finding no evidence of activity from outside the boundary of Peters Hold, decided they would make one patrol inside the walls to determine if there was any evidence of the Gate within the destruction of the citadel.

It was taking a lot longer to navigate the fallen buildings that littered the city. The Seers in their flowing white robes were struggling with climbing the mountains of brickwork and collapsed walls. Drew and the Guards were trying to pick the easiest route that could be found but were not having much success and the going was indeed slow.

It was nightfall when the small party eventually returned to camp.

"Did you find anything?" questioned Loytan to the Seers as they all sat in the main command pavilion.

One Seer, a greying man of slight build answered in a soft but strong voice.

"There is still an energy source where the citadel once stood, but it is weak."

"Because of all the debris?" asked Loytan, looking very concerned as he heard the news.

"No, rock and stone does not impede my skills. The reason for the weakness I believe is that when the citadel collapsed, it effectively swamped the Gate. As the surroundings fell about it, it is inevitable, that an amount of the building would fall through the portal. Everything that passes through uses the energy of the Gate. There is so much around the Gate that it is constantly using its energy and cannot keep up with the drain, shrinking in on itself until it is unusable. This renders it harmless as it is too small for anyone on the other side to clear the entrance. As long as the city stays as it is, nothing can pass through it, however there will be a constant link to the demons Realm until whatever is holding the Gate open is destroyed, or killed."

"Well, at least that's something. We should get some sleep, tomorrow the Engineers and the Seers will start to lay down traps and place warning spells to give us advance notice should anything leave the city that is not human. Thank you all, good night."

Drew had been at the site of what was once Peters Hold for a week. Explosive spells had been placed in the direct vicinity of the Citadel, pit traps were placed at random points all the way to the border of the city. At that point a ring of wards were placed to ensure nothing other than humans crossed either way without a group of dedicated Seers being alerted.

"What is going to happen now?" Drew asked Richardson as they sat eating a lunch of bread and cheese.

"I suspect that we will head back, and there will be a patrol this way each week to ensure that everything is ok here."

"That's it then? Back to routine duties?" replied Drew, not sure whether he wanted to return to a simple duty roster life or stay in the field.

Richardson was about to reply, a grin spreading that made Drew think that the next sentence would be a shot at him, when the Captain emerged from the command tent. Conversation around the camp stopped as Loytan was joined by Oren.

"Gentlemen, Oren and I have been in contact with Prince Allin, and the King. It has been decided that the threat of an open portal to the Demon realm is too great to be left unchallenged.

"Therefore, we are to be stationed here for the coming few weeks to allow the Seers time to study the Gate without being interrupted by anyone. Sergeant Kestar," said Loytan looking over to the named man, "you and your unit will travel to Myllarad and return as soon as possible with stores. I will write up notes of requisition for you now, that is all."

Turning, the two men walked back into the tent and the campsite seemed to settle back into life without so much as a pause.

"I guess that is that then. What do you fancy for dinner Drew? I hear the bread is a little stale, but the cheese is good." Said Richardson with a wry grin.

Drew nodded, exhaling slowly as he took a bite of the dry bread.

"Just a little stale?" he said grimacing once more and washing the taste away with a long drink of water. "We have six Seers including a Master here, yet they can't keep bread fresh?"

Chapter 15

Retaliation

Lights blazed in the city of Sarafell. Tal could only make out the glow of the city on the horizon, the illumination from the lights standing out against the bleak night sky. The party consisting of Tal, Brad, Hazel, Khris and Vorlin, along with the slave party from the Demon realm had left the safety of the Coven and travelled as fast as they could towards the Kingdom, stopping only at dawn for the safety of Vorlin.

"You seem nervous Tal." Said Khris coming to stand next to him.

The party had halted short of the city a couple of hours shy of dawn tonight. This was on request of Vorlin who wanted to arrive in the city with the greatest possible time left for the night in case of inquisition.

"I am." He said, "I will probably be dismissed for disobeying orders again. My parents had pride in their eyes when I left to become a Rider, how can I return after a dishonourable discharge?"

"Try not to worry yourself overly Tal, you may have disobeyed orders, but no one was hurt through it, and you have done an amazing thing in recovering information from the

Demon Realm, and leading the escape while keeping all those slaves alive. I'm sure you will be punished, but I am just as sure you will not be dismissed."

Tal looked less than pleased with the thought of punishment, but his heart was lightened by the confidence of the veteran Dragon Rider.

"Thank you." Was all Tal could think of to say.

With a companionable grip on Tal's shoulder, he turned to look back at Vorlin.

"Will you be ok Vorlin?" he asked the quiet Nightwalker.

"Yes, I will lay myself deep in the ground for the day, no sunlight will reach me. It is not quite the comfort of the Coven or a Crypt, but it is not the first time I have had to do it, nor will it be the last I am sure."

Khris smiled at his friend and moved to the main group, Brad was sitting next to Hazel, talking quietly, with the rest of the survivors having their own private conversations.

Hazel had been in a quiet and sulky mood since she had arrived at the Coven and spoken to Tal, and Brad was doing his best to smooth the ground between them.

"Why don't you just say sorry?" asked Brad, completely shocked at the woman's sheer stubbornness.

"Because I am right! He needlessly put himself in danger for what?" she was almost shouting at Brad in a whisper.

"OK so he made a mistake, hasn't he been through enough to make amends for it though? He saved my life and the rest of the people here from slavery, isn't that enough to give him some leeway? There is so much at stake here, not just the Kingdom, but the entire world, why do you have to make one more thing a struggle? Tal certainly feels bad about this, I know you do as well! So sort it out."

Brad got up and stormed away, his face red with frustration. Calming himself down slowly as he walked around the campsite, he paced out his frustration until he was once again thinking clearly.

As his pulse slowed and his mind once again cleared, he found himself thinking of blonde hair. His heart feeling surprisingly empty as the thought of blue eyes and a crooked smile filled his memories.

"Reflecting Brad?" Tal asked, walking silently up behind him.

"Just trying to compose myself. I am not looking forward to tonight Tal, we turn up, at the other end of the Kingdom, we have no idea what people will say to us, where we will be sent, or who we will be facing. And personally for me, I have not seen Cholla for months, will she still want to know me? Is she alive? Has she moved on?

"I really don't like knowing so little Tal, I wish I had your confidence."

"Confidence? I just had Khris trying to reassure me that I would not be removed from the Ranks of the Riders!" joked Tal, trying to make his friend feel better. "At least you have the likely chance that Cholla is still waiting for you, I know Hazel no longer wants anything to do with me."

"That's not true Tal, she is just as miserable as you are with this situation, she is just much more stubborn that you are."

"We will see Brad. Come on, we need to get some sleep before the fun starts tonight."

The two army privates that were stationed on the wall watching the north gate of the city of Sarafell called to their Sergeant. As he left the light of his guard hut to enter the darkness of the night, broken only by the backlighting of the city behind him, he stopped above the entrance to the city, approaching out of the darkness was a group of people, looking travel worn and haggard. Two men in front of the group however, looked confident. One was dressed as a Rider, and moved with a grace that bespoke a quiet danger. The other was a tall man, dressed in a flowing robe and was walking with an air of power.

As they reached the gate, the Rider called up to the Sergeant. His voice was light yet commanding but there was no order given merely a request.

"Sergeant, please open the gate and send word to the command centre that Dragon Rider Khris Risce is here and needs to speak to them urgently."

"I'm sorry sir, but standing orders are that no one enters the city after sunset."

"Who is the ranking Rider here Sergeant?" asked the Rider in a relaxed tone.

"Lord Rayburn sir, he is in joint command with General Peterson." Called down the Sergeant.

"Wonderful, please send a messenger to him and he will certify my identity. We will wait patiently."

The Sergeant paused, not sure what the correct action was. After a few moments, he turned to one of the privates and sent him to carry the message to Lord Rayburn.

It took half an hour for Lord Rayburn to arrive at the gate, he was dressed as usual in his black and red chain armour, the black cloak with the golden dragons stretched majestically across his back billowed slowly in the gentle night breeze.

"Risce? What are you doing here? I haven't seen you for a couple of years! I thought you had run off to the Far West Isles to retire!"

"Gareth! Nice to see you, but sadly no, I have been in the Lost Lands studying the Grey Mages for all those years, not much of a retirement I'm afraid! Now can you open the gate? A cup of tea would go down well for all of us I am sure!"

Khris laughed openly as Gareth sent the privates down to open the large barrier that served as security to the entrance of the city. A loud clang and a creak of wood signalled the start of the swing that slowly opened one of the doors. Walking through, Khris nodded to Vorlin and the party moved through, into civilisation once more.

Tal tried to remain calm as the party moved through the quiet streets. The occasional window would open revealing a curious face, usually in some kind of uniform. It felt strange to him walking through built up streets rather than being caged, chained, or climbing over cooled lava.

He was closer now to his old home than he had been for the past six months. He had been through more in the past year than in the fifteen years previously, yet here he was alive, strong, fitter than ever, and in the presence of one of the most dangerous creatures that ever existed.

Brad walked next to him silently. The wind whistling down the narrow alleys of the city reminded Tal of Dukeray. As he walked, he relaxed more and more until he almost felt at ease for the first time in a year.

Lord Rayburn was walking up ahead with Khris, their conversation inaudible. Looking to Vorlin, Tal thought he might be able to find some trace of concern in the Nightwalkers face, but he was as calm and distant as ever. Giving a silent salute to the man's courage Tal looked at Brad.

"What are you going to do when you see Cholla?" he asked, a slight smile turning the corners of his mouth up.

"Cry? I don't know, probably be spurned because her new guy will be all over her."

Tal chuckled softly. Brad appeared more troubled by this walk to the command post, than he had done the entire time of their captivity, or even the flight through the Grey Mages Lair.

It took about half an hour to get to the town watch building that Rayburn had requisitioned as his command post. As they entered Tal relaxed, for the first time in months he was out of harms way. He, Brad, Hazel and Vorlin were told to sit down and make themselves comfortable, the escapees were led to rooms in an adjacent inn where they could sleep and relax, and Khris was led into a private room by Rayburn.

Tal sat down and Brad followed his example. As soon as he had taken a couple of breaths, Tal felt himself drifting into sleep. The toll of the past few months had taken their toll on him and had just caught up. He looked over to Brad and saw that he and Hazel were already dozing in their seats.

Vorlin looked over to Tal.

"Sleep if you need it, this will be a long night, rest while you can young Rider. You will be woken when you are needed."

It seemed to take no more than the suggestion before Tal found his eyes closing and his thoughts turning to the black nothingness of sleep.

Tal was woken by Vorlin, his hand grasping Tal's shoulder lightly.

"You should wake up Tal, you three will be interviewed any moment."

Looking up Tal, noticed that Brad and Hazel were still asleep in their chairs. He turned to Vorlin, "You are not waking them up?"

"No, you should do that Tal. They both look to you as a leader, it is best not to break that role just yet, they are still highly strung from their ordeals."

Tal was confused, he did not understand Vorlin's logic, but still slightly fuzzy from sleep he came to the conclusion that Vorlin would probably be right anyway.

Moving to his friends, he woke Brad gently before doing the same to Hazel. Brad smiled as he was woken by Tal, as did Hazel at first before she realised it was Tal that had woken her, then her gaze became hard to him once more. At that instant the door to the private room opened and Lord Rayburn came out, motioning to the three Riders he waited for them to enter then closed the door behind them, leaving Vorlin alone in the main room of the town watch building.

Tal had been sitting in the room with Brad and Hazel for a couple of minutes. Khris was standing in the corner behind them a slight grin across his face that the others could not see. Rayburn was seated behind the desk reading a document quietly.

The atmosphere was intense, but Brad and Hazel appeared to be relaxed. But of course, they would be, they were Riders captured in the field and now released and back to serve their country. For Tal however he was a trainee that had broken his orders and placed himself at risk because of it. For Tal it was a dismissal issue for the others, a commendation.

Looking up and facing each of them in turn, he spoke in a soft, fatherly voice.

"Dragon Rider Risce has briefed me as much as he can, but I would like to hear from yourselves what happened as far as you can recall."

Hazel spoke up first, she repeated her ordeal as far as she could remember, starting with when she awoke in the cell. She recounted how the Mages would take prisoners away and how they used the souls of the captured to rejuvenate themselves.

Tal had heard only the brief story from Hazel up until now, and as she told her tale, he found himself in awe of her personal courage and mental strength.

As she finished relaying her ordeal, there were tears threatening to free themselves. She took a breath and completed with the arrival of the group at the gates of Sarafell.

"You are strong and courageous Rider Jensook. The information you have passed on to us will be of value to our effort against the Grey Mages. Tell me though, do you trust this Nightwalker, Vorlin Mansford?"

"Well I'm sure Dragon Rider Risce has given you all the information on him you need to know, I could not add anything else of merit sir." Replied Hazel.

"Yes he has, however I need all my Riders to come to their own conclusions, not those of others. What do you think of him?" said her Lord.

"He rescued me sir, and has not tried to coerce me into anything, nor has he attempted to intimidate me, yes sir I trust him, just not with my life yet."

Rayburn nodded slowly, and then shifted his attention to Brad and Tal. He prompted them to tell their stories and Brad took the lead as he was the ranking Rider. It took him quite a bit longer than Hazel to recount their tale, and he tried his hardest to give Tal the credit he deserved in their rescue as well as the advancement in his skills that made their survival possible.

Tal remained silent the whole time, trying his best to be unnoticed for the interview. As Brad concluded the events that led up to this point, Tal noticed Rayburn's eyes flick to him briefly, and knew he would not get away with remaining on the sidelines tonight.

"Rider Oswin, you too are the very essence of the Riders. Both you and Hazel will receive the merit you deserve for your trials and efforts over the past couple of months."

Turning his full attention now onto a worried Tal, he took a deep breath before continuing. "Tal Parnell, what do you have to say about your actions?"

His mouth suddenly dry, Tal's voice came out hoarse and quiet.

"I'm sorry sir, I went absent without leave, and put myself in great danger, not only that I know that through my lack of training I put Brad in danger too. If you dismiss me over this I will understand sir."

"Is that it?" with a deep sigh, Rayburn set his shoulders and continued. "Tal, you have disobeyed orders several times now. And although it was fortunate that you and Brad were taken together, there will have to be repercussions. You will not be dismissed, this is not the regular army and the Kingdom is at war. Instead, you will be placed under arrest until I or one of my Officers releases you. Use the time to reflect upon what you have done.

"Khris, escort Tal to one of the cells below, and ask Mr. Mansford to come in please. Hazel, Brad, go get some sleep for what is left of the night, I will not assign you any duties for the next few days but I will need you both operational as soon as possible, for that I am sorry."

The younger Riders stood up, Khris moving to Tal and placed his hand on his shoulder. "Use the time son, learn from your mistakes." As they left the room, Hazel walked up to Tal.

"You are the most annoying man I know! But do as your told ok?" she hugged him fiercely and kissed him lingeringly before Risce led him down the stairs to the basement and the cells of the town watch.

Vorlin stood up as Tal passed, his hand on Tal's chest halted him. Offering his hand, he shook Tal's firmly. "Be strong, follow orders, do what is right, and you will still have a rewarding life as a Rider. Do not let this be a negative point in your existence. Be well Tal." He released Tal's hand and walked into Rayburn's office, closing the door quietly behind him.

Brad left the building in a state of exhaustion and shock. He was home, he was safe, and the reason for that was his friend who was now locked up for disobeying orders. Feeling the need for sleep racing towards him again, he moved to one of the inns that had been allocated for Rider use, signed in, and promptly fell into his bunk, sleeping through to midday.

He was woken by a knock on his door. Standing up, he yawned and stretched before opening the door. He wasn't looking forward to the coming days, waiting for orders, making use of his time by simply walking and sleeping.

"Brad?" The sound of the voice asking the question brought his mind into clarity.

"Cholla? How did you know I was here?" Brad was ecstatic and his heart was racing.

"The news that three Riders had escaped captivity has spread through the city already. When I asked my Sergeant, he said it was you, Hazel and Tal. I thought you were stationed at Peters Hold? How did you get here? And what were you doing with Hazel?" The questions flooded from her, Brad could not help smiling, he had been worried that she would forget him, or give him up for dead, worse that she would have found someone else in the months they had been apart. But here she was, outside his room and rambling like a silly young girl at a dance.

He started to explain himself, and where they had been when Cholla kissed him suddenly. Before he could respond, she pushed him back into the room, closing and baring the door behind them.

Vorlin was sitting quietly on a padded sofa reading a book. He was deep into a history of the Kingdom and found he could not put it down. He thought back through his life, the last seven hundred of history was almost correct to his memory, however there were a few discrepancies. The interesting part was the time at the beginning of the Kingdom, no mention was made to the alliance and cohabitation of human and *Seicolantrai*. The early history was passed down meticulously to those that followed the *Honourable Path*, yet this book seems to have missed a great deal of detail of those days. Of course, early record keeping was poor, and his own histories would have changed slightly over the years without a doubt.

Closing the heavy book, he sat back and closed his eyes briefly. He was comfortable. The Rider, Lord Rayburn was seeing to his well being personally, and blood had been provided for him, taken from game found in the plains around Sarafell. He had been taken to the Ducal Keep and housed in a room that had no windows. It was well appointed and he was provided with anything he asked for.

A knock at the door roused him from his quiet musings and he stood, walked across the room and opened it to see the Lord Rayburn and Jakrin Tiersing waiting for him. Although he knew he was a prisoner, he was thankful for the gesture of not locking him up and allowing him his own privacy.

"Are you well Vorlin?" asked Rayburn still standing outside the door.

"Yes thank you. You have been kind in your treatment of me. Please come in and sit down."

As the three sat on the sofas facing each other, Vorlin waited for their questions.

"You were vouched for by Dragon Rider Risce, that means more to me than any answers gained from questioning." Replied Rayburn, "However we need to speak to the King about the matters brought to our attention. You will also have to state your kinds involvement in this and explain your position. Are you happy with that?"

Vorlin nodded to them and waited. Jakrin Tiersing, Lord High Seer of the Brotherhood of Seers, began working on a spell that created a glowing blue disc that floated at eye level. A chime sounded from this disc, and within a few moments, the face of King Amond appeared inside its slowly pulsing blue frame.

"Jakrin, I see you could not help but get involved personally." He said with a slight tone of disapproval.

"Your Majesty, I would have stayed with you in the City of Dragons, but something important came up that required my attention, and now yours."

"Then explain it, and we will see what can be done."

Lord Rayburn reported all that he had heard the past day to the King, leaving out certain parts for Vorlin to fill in afterwards. When he had finished his retelling of events, the King looked tired.

"Riders Jensook and Oswin will be given Honours when you can spare the time Gareth. You may grant them any you wish, but I will grant them the Titles of 'Stewards of the Realm' in recognition of their struggles and service."

"As your Majesty wishes, I will inform them of their titles when the opportunity arises." Rayburn gave brief pause before continuing. "What is your wish regarding the part played by Rider trainee Parnell Sire?"

"This is a tricky situation, although he disobeyed orders, he was perhaps even more so responsible for the information we now have and for the survival of the citizens that were brought back. I will grant him the same honours as the others, however he will not be informed of this until he learns to control his impulses and is deemed dependable."

Rayburn nodded, a weight lifted from his shoulders.

"Your Majesty, there are a few gaps in the story I have told you. Those will now be filed in by Vorlin Mansford, please I beg your patience with his tale, it is a little unusual, but I have had it confirmed by one of the highest ranking Dragon Riders in my Order."

King Amond looked curious but remained quiet for the entire time it took Vorlin to recite his position and story. The Kings expression did not falter once through the recounting, that was until Vorlin stated he was a Nightwalker.

In the ten seconds immediately following the announcement, the Kings face turned from uncomprehending through to outrage. It took Jakrin Tiersing stepping in to calm the King down and let Vorlin continue his history of the two races and their current relationship.

It took a further hour for the King to finish interrogating Vorlin, at the end he faced Rayburn and asked, "You believe what he said is the truth?"

Rayburn nodded once more. "Yes your Majesty I do."

"Then get yourself and all who know what is occurring and come to the City of Dragons immediately, we need to plan our response to this crisis."

All three in the room bowed to the King and the communication disc evaporated as Jakrin released his spell.

Jakrin and Rayburn left Vorlin to his book. When the door to his apartment was firmly shut, Rayburn turned to Jakrin with concern in his eyes.

"I understand that the King needs all present, but I am wary of placing a Nightwalker in striking distance of the King."

"Understandably, but he would be in the protection of you, me, Khris, his bodyguards and let us not forget that Risce has personally vouched for the man.

"I feel it is of minimal risk, and one that is necessary in the current situation."

Rayburn nodded and walked away to organise his return to the Palace.

Jakrin followed Rayburn to the door, shaking hands the two friends parted company. Leaving the Town Guard building Jakrin walked swiftly to the Seers Temple. Entering through the main doors, he acknowledged the Seer at the reception desk who recognised Jakrin and immediately stood and bowed deeply. Returning the bow slightly, he passed the desk and made his way towards the pattern room.

It was a white washed room that was circular in shape and of uniform size no matter which Temple throughout the Kingdom the Seer stood. In the centre of the room was a circular step with a simple symbol of lines on it. Around the walls were other unique designs with the name of the city or town beneath it. Jakrin shut the door to the room, completely alienating himself from the outside world and positioned himself on the raised symbol. He found the design for the City of Dragons and started the spell. The image filled his mind and all else faded around him, a rush of air and a crack of energy jolted his eyes shut and a slight spasm to course through his body. Allowing his eyes to open again he found himself standing in the pattern room of the City of Dragons. Taking a deep breath to clear the after effects of the teleportation, he left the room and moved to his own private chambers to change before his the audience with the King, he had a lot to research and organise before the meeting and he would not have too long before the Riders arrived.

Taking his white robes off, he settled into a clean bath that was waiting for him, gently heating the water he considered what he should do. There would be retaliation from the King, his honour, pride and populace would accept no less.

He had to think of several different options for retaliation that would satisfy the Kings need to protect his people and at the same time progress the overriding aim of the campaign – to completely sever links between this realm and the Demons for the survival of the world.

He started casting a spell, energies jumping lightly from the water of the now cooling bath. A communication disc appeared in the air in front of Jakrin, a chime signalled to his contact that he was required and Jakrin waited for the man to appear.

Eventually a slight man became visible in the glowing disc.

"Lord High Seer, greetings. What can I do for you?" he said in a slightly tired voice.

"The King is going to push for an all out offensive against the Mages and Demons shortly. I don't have the time to brief you fully on the situation however believe me the two *are* linked in this war.

"What I need is for you to set our first option into action and hold it ready for my order. Following that I would like you to assemble a team of five of your best Seers to be made available at any notice, free them from any duties they may currently have and send them to the Grand Temple in the City of Dragons. Do you understand what I have asked?"

The High Seer, second in command to the Lord High Seer, nodded his understanding and Jakrin thanked him before letting the disc slip into nothingness.

His best plan for overriding success was slowly taking shape but he needed to have at least one backup plan. Climbing out of the now cold bath, he walked into his study to lay further plans. Pulling out a selection of maps of the Lost Lands, he lit several candles and settled in, it would be a long night.

Brad was pulled back to reality from the warm comfort of his bed when a knock at his door made him get up. Slowly lifting Cholla's arm from his chest he let her sleep while he walked across the room and left, closing the door so as not to disturb her.

Waiting for him was a Rider with an order from Rayburn.

"Rider Oswin, Lord Rayburn would like to see you first thing in the morning, you are requested to pack for a few days. You, Hazel, and Lord Rayburn will be heading to the City of Dragons. Dragon Rider Risce and Vorlin Mansford have already left and will meet you there. Please be ready outside the Guard House one hour after sunrise."

Thanking the Rider for his service, Brad returned to his room and looked out of the window. At best guess he thought it must be midnight, leaving him about six hours to get ready.

Hearing the rustling of bed sheets from behind him, he turned to see Cholla standing up. He couldn't help but smile at the sight of her walking naked towards him. There was a look of concern on her face as she wrapped her arms around his waist.

"What's wrong Brad?" she asked leaning in to him.

"I have been given orders. I am to go to the City of Dragons tomorrow with Hazel and Lord Rayburn. I should only be gone for a couple of days, but I have only just found you again, I really don't want to go yet."

"It's ok, I will be waiting for you." Said Cholla trying to reassure Brad. She knew he was terrified that she would find someone else, but she could not imagine herself with another now.

She looked up at him, "In the morning right? So we have a couple of hours?" She smiled as his grin spread and she lead him back to the warmth of the bed, worries about the next day forgotten for now at least.

The sun was rising, Hazel had her kit packed and stood, at attention in her full uniform, outside of the Guard House. She had been waiting for half an hour already and still had an hour to wait. She could not sleep, all night her mind had kept returning to Tal. While he was locked up in the basement of that building, he was out of reach for her, and would remain so until he was released. She had days previously to talk to him, to enjoy their time together, but she had wasted it because of her own stubbornness, and now she was feeling guilty. But she would not leave him alone, even if she could not see him, she would at least be close by.

The door opened from the building and Lord Rayburn walked out to meet her. He was dressed and ready to go, but had not brought any gear out with him.

"Wynhazel? Sorry Hazel," he corrected himself at the slight flash from her eyes before she could control herself. He continued on before she could say anything.

"What are you doing out here? There is still another hour before you are required."

"I could not sleep Sir, I thought I might as well be here ready." Hazel lied, trying to cover her real reasons.

"Ok well, I still have some loose ends to tie up before I leave, I will leave you to it until then." Turning, Rayburn started to walk back to the Guard House, but he paused half way back to the door. Without turning, he raised his voice so that Hazel could hear him, "Tal is well, and comfortable. He will be out when he has learned to follow orders, and only he can decide when that will be. Lets all hope it is not too long." He left Hazel in the small square, a tear ran down her cheek, unseen by her retreating commander.

As the hour fled, the streets began to fill up with the remaining populace of the city, soldiers and construction engineers going about their duties, and the general hubbub of city life that could not be quelled with war or dangerous times.

Brad arrived at the square to see Hazel rigid at attention. He could guess her reasons and decided he would let them lie. Approaching, he smiled his greeting and apologised that Cholla had not been to see her yet.

Hazel smiled and said she was sure Cholla had other things that required her attention more than seeing her. Brad was about to say something in return when he saw Lord Rayburn exit the Guard House and make his way over to them.

"Rider Jensook, Rider Oswin. Good morning. I trust you are ready and well rested? I'm sorry I could not give you the light duties I had promised, however the King requires all our attention to form our new strategy, based upon the information you will share with him. We are going to leave the City and head South for a short while until we are met by a Dragon who will fly us to the City of Dragons."

As they followed their Lord, Brad wondered what this would be like. The last time they had travelled by Dragon was with Tal who had sensed the Dragons feelings, something he had not been able to do himself at that point. With his greater experience and his mental training having started, would he be able to sense anything himself this time?

He was in the middle of his musings when Hazel spoke up.

"Sir, should we not bring Tal along as well? Surely he was just as instrumental as us in gaining the information, and as Brad himself has said, without Tal the chances of their safe return with as many prisoners as there were would have been almost nil."

"Hazel, I understand your pain, and yes, in better circumstances Tal would have been with us. His disobedience though requires disciplinary action, and therefore he cannot be allowed to continue as he did before."

Nodding, Hazel continued on in silence. They left the city and walked for an hour until they reached the borders of the Greenhome. They had passed through these woods before, on their passage to the city of Coladan, the Northern area of the forest was given over to the use of the Elves, and Brad remembered fondly their last visit. He was starting to hope that they would have to press on and request shelter with the

Elves once again, until they entered an open area and Rayburn ordered a halt.

They had been out of the city now for about two hours, the last half an hour was spent waiting in silence in the glade. Hazel was standing at the edge of the clearing, her long sword cleaving arcs through the air as she practised her forms.

Brad could hear the swords edge cutting, the swish of the air making a high-pitched whistle. A shadow covered the clearing causing all three to look up, there was a deep sound of beating wings as the great creature slowly descended into the open space between the trees.

The Dragon was a royal blue in colour, its scales shining like the rich colours of night, its fangs and claws the white stars that shone brightly.

"Our host is here, we had best be on our way." Said Rayburn as he slung his pack behind the array of saddles and secured it and then climbing into the front saddle.

Brad was the next to secure his pack and seat himself on the back of the great beast. As he sat he felt the gentle movement of the Dragons breathing and had to remind himself that the creature was friendly.

Hazel sheathed her sword and collected her travel pack. She secured it behind Brad's and then seated herself accordingly.

"This is a good opportunity for both your first lessons in Dragon Sense. Concentrate and focus on the Dragon, do not try and work out what he is saying, nor what he feels for now, just try to become aware of his essence. Using your senses of the environment you should be able to feel the dragon, concentrate on that hard enough and you will feel a deeper understanding of him, this is his essence and that is all I want you to find for now if you can."

Brad and Hazel focussed their senses. Both found it easy to locate the Dragons presence and set about trying to find its essence. Lord Rayburn stayed silent as they both laboured to find the Dragon in their minds.

Hazel gasped as she suddenly felt the Dragon envelop her. Suddenly it was not her finding the great creature in the immediate vicinity but her mind being shared with it. There was an understanding, both being very aware of the mind of the other. The Dragons essence was clear for her to see as much as she was to the Dragon, like two people aware of each other floating in a pool of water but not being able to communicate, so was her link to the Dragon she rode.

As quickly as the understanding arrived, it fled her, leaving Hazel slightly fatigued. Brad was looking back at her as she came round, his face curiosity.

"Are you all right?" he asked, "You seemed mesmerised by something."

"Yes I am fine, I found the Dragon, his mind seemed to be riding with me, I felt so insignificant."

Rayburn was smiling at her. "Do not fret, with practice it becomes more a sharing of minds, but at first the Dragon overpowers your own minds barriers and imposes itself on you because of its latent strength. But that was good for your first attempt. Brad do not feel disheartened, remember Hazel is several months ahead of you in training."

"I'm not upset about that, I'm thinking about Tal, how he managed to communicate with the Dragon out of Coladan."

"Tal has some very strong mental abilities, he picks these things up easily and quickly. He just needs to gain some self-control, and better use of weaponry from what I have been informed.

"Come, we should go."

Rayburn gave a silent request to the Dragon that neither of the other passengers could hear, and with a beat of its powerful wings, launched them all into the air as it started to climb higher.

They circled higher and higher until the Dragon set of in a south easterly direction. Brad felt the same sensation he had felt before, a rush of air past his face and acceleration until things returned to a comfortable state. But this time being daylight, he could see the ground far below as it started to speed up until the dragon was flying at an almost impossible speed. He turned back to look at Hazel, she looked in shock, this was obviously her first time riding a Dragon, and the majesty of the situation did not escape her.

In the distance, a great city was visible, getting closer and closer, Brad soon recognised it as the City of Dragons, great spires reaching high into the air from the palace grounds, and brightly coloured pennants flying from their peaks. As they got closer the dragon slowed, the whole world seemed to lapse back into normal speed and the wonderful creature slowly descended and touched down gently in the palace grounds, in the main marshalling yard outside the Riders Barracks.

As they set foot on solid ground once more, Rayburn walked up to the head of the Dragon. Looking the creature in the eyes, time seemed to pass before the Dragon gave a giant nod of his head, then once more launching into the sky, vanishing into nothingness as Brad noticed the slight air disturbance as it continued to rise.

They departed the square and moved to the Barracks. Inside was a Rider waiting for them, Rayburn nodded to the man and said to Brad and Hazel "Leave your kit here please, it will be sent to rooms for you and you can sort them out later, we are needed in council with the King immediately."

The two Riders complied, and as the three left the Riders Barracks, they were met by a man in a white robe.

"Jakrin, you look awful. I take it you did not sleep last night?" said Rayburn a slight hint of humour creeping in to his voice.

"As subtle and as flattering as ever Gareth. No, I did not sleep, neither did the King he has been talking to Vorlin most of the night and now awaits your presence. He and his advisors are in the council hall, along with Prince Rufus and Princess Kayla. Please follow me."

As the small party moved through the lush grounds, Brad found himself wondering if the people of the City of Dragons were even aware that their Kingdom was at war? There seemed no real evidence of it here, a few more soldiers seemed to be rushing around than before, but other than that, life was continuing as normal.

The man identified as Jakrin was talking to Rayburn and giving him the latest information that had been gathered overnight. Brad was listening as much as he could, but the tone was quiet. There was only one thing he picked up clearly, and it made his spine turn to ice.

"The King has sent orders to all the army commanders. In one month those that can are to assemble a mile to the east of Sarafell, and start to prepare for invasion. The rest of the army will join as it arrives, the estimated time is two months. At this point the Kingdom will invade the Lost Lands, we are taking the war to the Mages, it is out of pure retaliation for the loss of our people, and I think it is made in haste, but no advice from anyone could sway his majesty. We need to make all precautions possible in that time Gareth, because it will be an expensive attack, in every regard."

Chapter 16

Strikes

The King sat in silence.

He had been awake all night, listening to the words of the Nightwalker Vorlin Mansford. A few minutes ago Rayburn, Hazel and Brad had just finished their recitation of events as they were aware of them. Hazel and Brad were beginning to feel as though all they did was to repeat the same chain of events over and over again. It was well past midday by the time they had finished and they were starting to feel fatigued.

The Council hall was not a large room. It was of sufficient size to hold about twenty people – the largest number of advisors that could speak with the King at one time. Today it held the King, the Prince and Heir, the Princess, Jakrin Tiersing, Gareth Rayburn, Khris Risce, and the two young Riders.

The walls were appointed with ornate hangings, royal banners and woven depictions of great battles. Between each, was a regal candleholder bolted to the wall to provide light for late sessions. The floor was covered with a thick, deep blue rug with the Kings personal coat of arms embroidered in the centre. The King sat upon a high backed chair placed on a dais, his son and daughter on a lower level, with his advisors sat in an arc around them. A table against one wall held various maps of the Kingdom and its borders, along with troop deployments and sightings of Mages, undead, Ones of Impurity or Demons.

Eventually the King spoke, his voice soft and coarse.

"I will not cancel my orders for the invasion of the Lost Lands. Yes it will be costly, but I need to show our people that we are not merely hiding out of fear, or hesitating out of indecision. I would hear your advice on how best to capture the Lost Lands and close these Demon Gates."

Lord Rayburn stood and addressed his King, his voice hesitant yet respectful.

"Your Majesty, I commend your desire to show the enemy our teeth, yet I feel that there would be more opportune times. Since however your mind will not be swayed, I would suggest caution.

"We know where the Lair that holds the Gate is, but it is deep within the Lost Lands. Better that we move towards it and construct a stronghold from which we can strike out into the enemy's land. Yes, it will take longer than a single assault, but we can extend our own borders further north and give greater support to our troops."

He moved to the map and tapped a position that was several days march into the Land.

"Here is where I would construct our new fortress, it is two weeks travel from Sarafell, one week from our borders. We can place a holding station at the edge of our Kingdom to house stores and backup troops that we can deploy as necessary. From this point we can strike out where we want and have a strong defensive position to fall back to until we feel it secure enough to construct another fortress deeper into the Lands, thus slowly reclaiming it into our own Kingdom again."

The King paused, as if weighing up his options.

"I would have preferred a single strike, there are too many places to hide in those Lands and who knows where the Mages will run if they feel they are losing. With one strike they will have no time to flee."

It was the Kings daughter, Princess Kayla that spoke up in response to her fathers statement.

"Father, if we are successful then it would be a stroke that could end the war before it truly starts. If we fail though, it would mean the army would have no safe way to retreat, we could lose everyone we send."

There were nods from those seated in the room, each seeing the disadvantage of the single attack.

Shoulders hanging heavily, the King finally seemed to acknowledge the folly of an all out assault.

"Very well. Rufus, please find the commanders of the army and inform them of the new strategy. We will only send one hundred men, and a small company of Seers along with fifty engineers and construction workers. I want a wooden fort created as soon as possible, with stonework replacing the wood immediately after.

"Thank you all for your advice, and thank you for your information.

"Riders Jensook and Oswin, please step forward."

The two Riders looked to each other, worry lining their faces as they stood and approached their King.

"Kneel." They both fell to their knees, their minds wondering what King Amond was about to say. "You two have faced hardship and trials that no person should face, especially those as young as yourselves. In recognition for your bravery and dedication to the Kingdom, it is my honour to bestow upon you both the Title of Steward of the Realm.

"Kayla, the collars please."

The princess smiled as she stood up and produced two red silk collars with crossed swords surmounted with a crown, at the base. The King took them from his daughter and stood before the Riders. Placing them about the necks of the two young soldiers, he spoke to them.

"The Royal Family only award three honours, those of Steward, Guardian and Knight of the Realm. Very few receive these honours, and even fewer are so young. Please wear these collars with pride and remember the gratitude of your Kingdom. Arise."

The two stood, their minds spinning, they had been given the greatest complement that either of them could remember, and both were at a loss for words, managing simply "Your Majesty" as they retreated back from their King.

"Now return to Sarafell, I'm sure you will be required before too long."

They all bowed to the Royal family and departed the room. Rayburn ushering Hazel and Brad out of the chamber and back towards the barracks.

"Ok you two, go get some food I'm sure you must be starving by now. I am giving you the next couple of days to yourself, I will be busy with the King, organising the push into the Lost Lands and there is no reason to send you back alone just yet. Besides you are still owed a couple of days leave, I will send for you when I am ready to head back."

Hazel thanked her Lord and saluted, Brad doing likewise a split second after her. As they left Rayburn's company, Hazel reached up and removed the Collar from her shoulders. She held it in front of her, looking at it. The collar was designed to sit across the shoulders of a formal uniform, the point at the bottom being level with the centre of the chest. It was an honour that many wished they could earn, and such a limited number did that she felt unworthy.

Brad looked at her, sympathy showing in his face.

"Your thinking of Tal again aren't you?" he said, his voice soft.

"He deserves the Title more than I do, yet he is locked up without any recognition of his actions." She looked as though she was about to collapse. Brad rested a hand on her shoulder, trying to give her some small comfort. He knew nothing would lighten her mood until Tal was released, but there was no way he could speed that up, all he could do was lend her support and hope she would bare up.

They spent the next two days wandering round the City of Dragons, looking at the local shops and sampling the taverns. It was nice to sit back and relax, no duties allowed them to spend the evenings listening to bards tales of the war in the North. Though after visiting a couple of inns, they were unable to believe that so many songs had been made about the single conflict with the Mages, and although the Kingdom forces only just managed to escape due to the aid of Jakrin Tiersing, the ballads made the Kingdom troops glorious victors.

All too soon, there was a summons from Lord Rayburn, a Rider found them sitting in a friendly tavern in the market quarter of the City. They were to return to Sarafell immediately, there was an emergency that demanded Rayburn return at once. Wondering what it could be they left the inn and gathered their kit, before meeting with their Lord in the marshalling yard.

The sun had set a couple of hours ago and Vorlin was waiting for them standing next to Rayburn, a scimitar hung at his side and he was no longer dressed in brown robes, but in plate armour.

Two Dragons, one with a Dragon Rider seated upon its back awaited them, and as they approached, Vorlin climbed up behind the powerful looking Rider.

"What is going on sir?" asked Brad as they came to a halt in front of him.

Rayburn, looking very serious in his full plate armour answered their question.

"Sarafell is under attack, one of the Seers there contacted the Lord High Seer less than an hour ago, the Grey Mages have pre-empted us, Sarafell is under threat. We go now to lend aid where we can, a party of Seers and other Dragon Riders are on the way already. Mount up, we need to go now."

The two Dragons approached Sarafell swiftly once more, the earth beneath them sweeping past to disappear into the gloom of night as swiftly as it was seen.

Sarafell was first seen as a bright glow on the horizon, coming ever closer. Brad first noticed how bright the City was and wondered why it had never seemed this obvious to him before. Hazel sucked in a breath and Brad saw why. The light coming so intensely from the city was not streetlights, nor sentry towers shedding light upon the battlefield, it was the city itself. Roofs that were thatch or wooden beam were ablaze streets deep, inside the walls.

Rayburn gave a silent instruction to the Dragon and it banked towards the west wall of the city. Brad looked back and saw that the Dragon carrying Vorlin was descending towards Sarafell, while theirs took a broad swing away from the city.

Calling to Rayburn, Brad asked what they were doing.

"We are going to take a run along the front, but I want the biggest possible sweep so we need to come in from the west. This is so they don't sense us until the last possible moment.

"I don't have time to land you so I'm afraid you will be with me for now."

The Dragon glided away from the city, as it became a glow on the horizon once more, they started to bank, bringing the lights of the city ahead of them again.

Building speed they climbed into the night sky as the battle approached them. Brad could sense the other Dragons around them, unseen but so clear in his mind. They too were flying away and then back into the fray. The sense of the enemy was beginning to spread through their thoughts, thousands of them, like an enormous black smudge on the earth.

From the city, blasts of white heat could be seen erupting into the ranks of the swarming enemy as they approached the walls once more.

Brad was shocked at the sheer number of the enemy that was assailing the walls. There were blasts of magic being hurled back and forth between sides, wreaking heavy damage wherever they landed. Getting a grip on his churning stomach, Brad turned to look back at Hazel, her face was hard and her posture rigid. He had forgotten that she had seen war before, and it had led to her incarceration.

As he turned to face the front again, he saw that Rayburn had ordered the Dragon down, they were approaching close enough to make out single people rushing the walls. Only they were not people, they were skeletons that had been re-animated, they were fallen soldiers and Riders brought back to life to fight for the enemy, there were others that looked as though they had been used for sword practice that still shambled forwards. Brad noticed all this a second before their Dragon opened his fanged jaw and spat an intense jet of flame towards the enemy, incinerating the front rank of the attacking army. Rayburn extended his arm and an arc of blazing light shot straight towards a man in a grey robe, sending him flying backwards, a great smouldering crater in the centre of his chest.

Other Dragons were following the same tactic, this allowed gaps between the enemy lines that the defenders could use to regroup.

Within the city, the population were doing their best to extinguish the fires slowly eating at their homes. There were very few reserve units being kept back noted Rayburn as they banked to turn away from the melee again, most of the forces being used to fill any breaches that appeared in the lines.

An eruption of earth around a group of Mages and the collapse of a large number of undead warriors, was the result of a couple of Seers combined spell casting. Instantly a Dragon altered course and included the fallen in its incineration run, turning both Mages and Undead into smouldering piles of ash that could not be raised to fight against the humans.

The city slowly disappeared behind them as they prepared for another run.

Hazel felt like stone, every extremity slow to move and cumbersome. Her thoughts continuously return to Tal. Was he ok? Had he been released from his confinement?

The Dragon moved beneath her without Hazel noticing. Again and again the strikes at the enemy were made, the three of them alone had been the cause of dozens of mages killed, let alone the number of undead, yet still they pushed on.

The number of deaths rose on both sides, Mages being burned, electrocuted, or cut down, the defenders being dragged of walls by soldiers that would not slow down even for beheading.

Brad was watching with dread as two Riders became cornered by a number of skeletons. As he flew above them he saw Rayburn direct a bolt of energy that shattered two skeletons immediately. The Riders seized the opportunity and fought back, maces tearing their assailants apart.

For an instant, Brad thought they would get out unharmed, until a skeleton managed to run one of the Riders through with a rusty sword as his own head was crushed. The second Rider made swift work of the remaining undead and carried his colleague from the battlefront towards the hospital. Brad thought it was useless, blood was draining from the wound far too quickly.

A screech from above them caused all three to jump and look up together. A huge black beast that resembled a bat was descending upon them, its head beaked like that of a hawk. A Graven. Upon its back was a Mage with a terrible face, dressed in a black robe.

It was almost on them when their Dragon folded its wings, causing it to plummet from the sky. The claws of the Graven missed Hazel by bare inches as she hunkered down to the back of the Dragon. Rayburn turned and fired a bolt of white energy towards the Graven, catching it square in the belly. A scream of pain left its hooked beak as it recoiled and turned away from its tormentor.

Rayburn turned the Dragon as it stopped its fall, and followed the Dark Lord. The Mage had lost the advantage of surprise and knew when to flee, he was heading at full speed away from the Dragon and Lord Rayburn, who was firing bolt after bolt of energy towards the Graven. Each blast that hit, caused the Graven to falter and lose ground, but not one hit the Mage.

It took time, but the Graven was soon no further than a Dragon length in front of them. Rayburn could see the Mage's snarl as he turned to see his pursuer nearly upon him. A bolt of red energy came shooting past Rayburn, only missing when the Dragon dodged agilely away before returning to position behind the Graven.

Brad noticed that though the Graven was smaller than their Dragon, that made it more manoeuvrable in tighter spaces. The dance in the air was complicated and dangerous. The Graven was dodging the jaws and claws of the Dragon as Lord Rayburn tried to blast the Mage riding it, and the Riders and Dragon were dodging the magical blasts returned by the Dark Lord. They spiralled and fell, twisted and clawed around each other until Rayburn managed to catch the Mage with a bolt of energy, his arm blackening as it grazed his shoulder.

The pain was enough to throw the Graven and allow the dragon to latch his claws onto the back of the foul creature, its jaws snapping around the Mage and tearing him in two.

With the loss of its master, the Graven was now vulnerable to attack. Rayburn assaulted it with magical energy, as the Dragon tore at the beast with fang and claw.

Brad looked away from the fray for the first time since the two combatants engaged and saw that the entire time they were fighting so close they had been falling from the sky. Only now that the battle was won did the dragon disengage the Graven, allowing it to fall to the ground below crushing any enemy that did not get out of its way as it thrashed in its death throes.

Rayburn slapped the Dragon on the back of its neck.

Turning to face them he smiled, "Now that was intense wasn't it?! we had best set down, the old boy is tired and I can't blame him! I used up most of his magical reserve in that little affray, we need to get into the city and let him go get some rest!"

301

Turning, the victorious Dragon sped back towards the city, dodging any bolts of energy that were aimed at it from the ground by Mages that saw it's passing. Rayburn occasionally sent back a bolt of his own, taking out one of the enemy, causing the undead in his control to collapse lifeless once more to the ground.

As they reached the relative safety of Sarafell, Rayburn set them down in one of the open parks, allowing the Dragon to return to the sky and depart the battle to rest before it would be needed again.

The three of them rushed towards the north wall, Rayburn intent on finding the commanding officer and seeing what the situation was on the ground.

As they ran, there were bolts of lightening and fire thundering overhead from the Seers placed in the defensive towers. In response to the Seers offensive, black and purple flame tore into the city, striking at random killing soldiers and civilians alike. The street they were following should have led straight to the wall, but a building had collapsed and was obstructing their way. With a quiet curse, Rayburn turned around and shot into a side alley, the two Riders following. The sounds of hand-to-hand fighting were steadily growing louder as they sped up. Emerging from the cover of the alleys and surrounding buildings, they found themselves in an open plaza where the city had been removed to provide clearer access to the walls and to give a good sized killing ground should the defenders lose their hold of the wall.

Looking around, Rayburn tried to see an officer that might be able to give him directions to General Peterson. There was a small contingent of officers that were positioned towards the back of the plaza, messengers were moving to and from the command post, relaying messages and returning with orders. Rayburn moved over to them, all the officers snapping to attention and saluting him as they approached.

"Where is General Peterson, Colonel Ambla?" asked Rayburn as they arrived.

"He is on the wall, my Lord. He gave me operational command of the defence while he took my place in the field."

"Thank you, please continue your defence." Rayburn saluted and left immediately. Drawing his own sword, he moved quickly towards the wall, Brad and Hazel following his example. They mounted the stairs to the parapet and climbed as fast as they could. Messengers and wounded fighters were retreating down the stairs as they ascended, Rayburn not slowing to acknowledge their salutes. Reaching the top, Brad looked out at the battlefield.

He felt insignificant. Whilst in the air with the Dragon, he felt that he could do something for the effort, but now, looking out over the conflict, how could one person make any difference to the surging army that was attacking and retreating then attacking again.

"Keep your focus Brad, it may be your first major battle, but if you survive, it certainly won't be your last, get used to overwhelming odds." Rayburn moved past a group of soldiers that were throwing down a Siege Ladder full of undead warriors, their bodies falling and breaking on the hard ground below.

Archers were firing flame arrows into the ranks of the enemy, the bodies of zombies burning leaving only skeletons that were torn apart by catapults and ballista. A group of skeletons had managed to breach the ramparts of the wall, and were creating a hole in the line of defending soldiers. Rayburn launched into the centre of the fray, his sword breaking the skeletal warriors with each stroke. Hazel copied him followed by Brad, with the arrival of the three Riders, the army slowly managed to fight their way back to the outer edge of the wall and throw off the ladder, once more controlling their section.

Rayburn moved on, not waiting or pausing after helping the Army. General Peterson was up ahead and bleeding from a wound to his side. Brad and Hazel were struggling to keep up with their Lord, such was his desire to reach his friend.

"Peterson, your hurt. Your should retire and let your Colonel take his place on the wall."

"So should you Gareth, yet your still here, sword in hand.

"Here is the situation Rayburn, we have been under attack since sunset. We have no idea how they got so close in such large numbers but they have not let up yet. The Ones seem to be in command but they are not themselves joining the fight, being content to sit back and order the Mages to strike. The Dark Lords are still using Graven but they have lost a couple of their number to the Seers and so are keeping their distance, waiting for quiet moments to launch a sudden strike against our Magicians"

"We need to hold until sunrise, that is only an hour or two away, then we can rest. What are our chances?"

"We can hold until then." Replied Peterson, wincing as he moved into an awkward position.

"Where are the Riders positioned?" asked Rayburn gently, seeing his friends pain.

"They are on the East end of the wall, they are holding well." Said Peterson, a slight tone of envy in his voice.

"Thank you," turning to Captain Reynolds who was acting as personal guard to the General he said, "Captain, get the General to a place of safety where he can get his wounds dressed. And if at all possible try to keep him from returning to the front."

Reynolds looked at Rayburn. He seemed to be struggling in forming a response. Rayburn stood up straight, looking down at the Captain.

"Your response is 'Yes my Lord.', followed by immediate action."

Reynolds reply was tense, just like his facial expression. "Yes my Lord." Taking his Generals arm, he assisted him towards the closest stairs, as they mounted them and started to descend, he looked up at Rayburn, his distaste of Riders clear as he disappeared out of sight.

Turning to face Brad and Hazel, Rayburn signalled them to follow as he set off towards the East end of the wall once more.

Vorlin ducked into a doorway as a group of soldiers ran past him. He had his sword in his hand as he moved through the city heading towards the battle. The Dragon Rider that had escorted him to Sarafell had dropped him off in one of the city parks then soared of into the air to join the conflict.

He had kept to the shadows as anyone that saw him would probably mistake him for an Impure One and call backup. As he approached a sturdy building with bars on the windows, he felt a familiar presence.

With a rare smile, he ran to the door and entered the building. Descending the stairs to the basement he found himself looking at a row of cells, of which only one was occupied.

Tal was sitting against a wall, his crumpled uniform dirty as he looked up.

"Vorlin? Your in armour, how are things going out there?"

"Why don't you come with me and find out?" he asked, a slightly mischievous look in his usually steel eyes.

"I can't leave, I will be punished even more."

"I let you out to help me, that won't get you in trouble."

Tal seemed to consider staying, but he felt vulnerable here. No sky no freedom to move, should this building be struck, he would stand no chance of survival. Nodding, Tal stood and moved to the cell door.

Vorlin placed his hand on the lock and started chanting softly. After a few minutes passed, his words repeating over and over, a series of clicks indicated that the lock had been activated. Vorlin swung the door open and Tal walked out, looking around nervously.

"There should be some chain armour around here somewhere, I suggest you take it and arm yourself with whatever you feel most comfortable with."

Tal did not have to look far, he had seen a soldier place some chain coats in a cupboard opposite his cell and dressed quickly, taking a short sword from the rack next to it.

He signalled to Vorlin and they set off. Leaving the building Vorlin paused, a cross between a snarl and a hiss came from his throat as he looked up. Above them circling was a Graven, the Mage upon its back glaring at them. Tal knew they could sense the danger and threat each offered the other.

After the briefest pause, the Mage wheeled and levelled a thunderous strike towards the pair of them. Vorlin took Tal by his arm and launched them both out of the way of the blast. The energy bolt levelled at them struck the building Tal had just been released from, blowing it apart, the debris striking Vorlin in the back as he shielded Tal from the explosion.

"There, you didn't escape, you were set free by the enemy. Speaking of which we need to get out of here, I cannot fight him while he is on the Graven."

They ran towards the cover of the mass of building that were still standing, energy striking within feet of where they were. Vorlin was almost carrying Tal, their speed faster than Tal thought possible, a roar from above marked the approach of the Graven. Tal turned expecting to see the Mage almost upon them, but instead found a Dragon and its Rider tearing at the Graven, covering it with flame and magic.

Vorlin pulled Tal into the cover of another building that had lost a section of its wall. Inside he pulled off his plate armour to feel his back.

"Are you ok?" asked Tal seeing the Nightwalker test his movement.

"I will be fine, my armour took a lot of the impact, what it didn't will heal in a few minutes. For now, we need to lie low, and I need to take out the huge dent in my plate."

They waited for about an hour, Tal watched how Vorlin stretched out his back, becoming fitter each passing minute until he was back to his powerful self once more. He collected his freshly repaired armour and strapped it back around his torso before collecting his scimitar and moving to the collapsed wall, looking round cautiously.

As he was about to step out onto the street, he paused. Tal was about to speak when Vorlin held out his hand motioning for silence. He thought he heard something, it was faint but he was sure. Cocking his head to one side he listened, the sounds of explosions from the battle washing over him, blocking out the quiet noises he was searching for.

Silence. The battle lulled, there was a reprieve in the sounds of conflict. He listened, waiting. Nothing.

He straightened, then stepped onto the street. It was under his feet, there was a vibration that was not created by battle. Smiling, he turned to face Tal.

"Well, how would you like to make a comeback worthy of mention in the ballads?"

He left the building making Tal follow. Heading in the direction of the south wall, Tal wondered why the Nightwalker was running away from the fight. The he sensed it. Beneath his feet something was moving, and it was big.

"What is it?" asked Tal as they both ran through the nearly empty streets. The occasional soldier noticed them but did not wonder why they were moving with purpose, it was war, and people had missions.

"I don't know, I am several hundreds of years old, and I have never felt its like before. Are you ready for a fight Tal?"

He nodded but did not feel ready, in fact if he was honest with himself, he had never felt more nervous. What were they going to do when they arrived and faced off with this, *thing?*

Tal turned, he saw Khris Risce approaching from another street. Where had he been until now?

"You felt it too huh?" asked Dragon Rider Risce as he fell in next to them. Tal told him that it was Vorlin that felt the thing, and Khris nodded. He looked drained, his energy seemed to be lacking yet he still managed to keep up with the pair as they ran along the paved roads.

"What are we going to do when we catch up to it?" asked Tal as the neared the wall.

"Damned if I know kid, but it will be interesting finding out eh?!" Just as Risce barked a laugh, the three stopped suddenly.

The ground started to shake and they found it hard to keep their footing. The earth and cobblestones in front of them started to break up and fall into an ever-widening crater. Out of the dust came two great legs, shaped like those of a spider, made from bone and covered in a rotting flesh that hung like soaked flags from a pole. A head started to emerge that was of no living thing. Decomposing flesh sagged from it as the eyes emerged over the lip of the hole.

"I can't believe it, it's not possible..." said Vorlin as they looked up at the ever growing creature.

Rayburn arrived at the Riders defensive area. There was an entire parapet crammed with archers, using all types of projectile. The volleys of death being rained down upon the undead army would have annihilated anything else, but here it only slowed them. Out in the field there were squads of Riders doing what they did best. Dealing death hand to hand, those trained with axe, mace, war hammer or pole arm tearing through the enemy ranks with startling speed.

"Captain Erikson, what is the situation?" asked Rayburn as he approached his Officer.

"We are holding well sir, though we are getting through our supplies far too quickly. I'm not sure we can hold for the two hours until sunrise."

"When the arrows are down to half your current level, ask for volunteers to go out and fight hand to hand. That should double the length of our use of ranged weapons. Lets just hope that come sunrise the Mages and Ones pull back their entire army, not just the Ones themselves."

Nodding, Erikson sent a junior Rider to relay his Lords orders to the archers. Rayburn turned to Hazel and Brad, "Can you shoot a bow? Actually it doesn't matter, you can miss them. Go find a couple of Longbows and join the archers anywhere you wish."

The two Riders saluted and disappeared into the stores room to requisition a couple of bows. Rayburn took a deep breath it was going to be a very long couple of hours. He prayed to Telkhan, the God of War that they were given respite come the day. Looking along the wall, he saw that several siege ladders had been successfully held by the enemies one section along. The Army was doing its best to get them cast down, but could not reach it and more undead warriors were spilling over onto the battlements.

"Riders to me!" came the shout from Rayburn. The closest ten Riders downed bows and drew swords, the remaining archers spreading out to cover the newly created hole in the defensive line. Drawing his sword the Lord of the Dragon Riders led the charge against the rapidly increasing incursion of undead.

Brad turned to watch as Rayburn and ten other Riders started to decimate the enemies that were threatening the stability of the wall. A Rider fell to a blow by an axe wielded by a skeletal warrior. Rayburn turned, his eyes catching note of the falling Rider. Falling back he covered the now vacant position of the Rider blocking off a further two zombies from walking over the dead Riders body and into the open. Catching the ghoul's sword on the flat of his blade, a knife rent a deep cut through the neck of his assailant, his head tilting and falling back, holding on only by the torn skin attached to the skull. With a single kick, the reanimated body fell back against the wall and fell over, taking one of the ladders with him.

Looking round Rayburn counted four remain ladders, slowly he shouted his orders to the remaining Riders and they managed to make their way through the attacking forces to remove ladder after ladder until the wall was recaptured by the Kingdoms troops.

Breathing hard, Rayburn released his Riders to return to their part of the wall. Sheathing his sword, he accepted the thanks of the junior officer who he had helped reclaim the wall and turned to return to his own Order. There was a sound of thunder and from somewhere down on the battlefield a bolt of lightening shot upwards to take Rayburn square in the chest, catapulting him backwards to land heavily on his back, unmoving.

Erikson returned to the wall to see his Lord thrown to the ground. Rushing to his side, he noticed Rayburn's armour was blackened by the strike. Stripping him of the armour he checked the grizzled warrior for wounds. His body seemed intact but he was not breathing.

Placing his mouth to his Lords, he gave a breath watching as the chest rose, compressing the heart and lungs, he continued until a tall wiry man in a white robe arrived, relieving him of his task.

Erikson felt the presence of magic, the body becoming surrounded by a soft purple glow. There was a sudden jerk of Rayburn's body, his back arching into the air, supported by his feet and shoulders. With a deep gasp of air Rayburn started to breath again, his body falling limp to the ground. The purple glow started to dissipate and he looked as though he was asleep.

Erikson waited for the Seer to move back from the Lord Commander of the Riders before speaking.

"Will he be ok?" he asked, voice steady but his concern showing in his eyes.

"It is too early to tell, we should move him to a safer position where we can monitor him."

Erikson nodded, and called four Riders over to him. Retrieving a stretcher from the emergency supplies, they loaded the Lord onto it and the four Riders lifted him and made their way back into the city. Fifteen minutes later, they entered the small square surrounding the command post. Where had once stood a guardhouse, now was rubble.

Swearing, Erikson called out a change of orders, making the new destination an inn two streets away. As they started to move, they felt the ground shaking. The Riders carrying Rayburn had to set him down on the ground before they dropped the stretcher.

"Now what?!" raged Erikson as he struggled to keep his footing.

Tal drew his sword, Vorlin and Khris already had their swords ready. The creature that was emerging from the crater was about the size of a two-story house. Its forelegs were sword point sharp and as broad as a cart. As it drew completely out of the hole it looked like a giant bug, its rear four legs were flat like shovels. It had mandibles that look like they could tear a horse in two with a single bite, but the creature was not alive.

"What is it?" asked Risce as they moved back.

"It looks like a Dreydoran, but they died out long before my birth, either as a Nightwalker or human. They were a vegetarian beetle that lived in the Kingdom of Mountains, the Dwarves used their tunnels as the base of their mines. It is how they are so rich in metals. How one got here I do not understand."

"Well it is here, I suggest we try to stop it somehow. I'm guessing that they will be using the tunnel as a means of getting their army inside the walls. They only have one hour before sun up to make us break. Any ideas?" said Risce as they continued to back away.

"One, but you're not going to like it."

Chapter 17

Siege

The earth calmed down. Erikson gave orders for the stretcher-bearers to get Lord Rayburn inside the tavern and stay with him as personal bodyguards. He turned towards where the sound of the ground being torn up had originally come from. Calling for backup from a small squad of Army Soldiers, he headed towards the south side of the city.

"What is your idea Vorlin?" asked Risce as he darted forward between the legs of the beast. They were trying to tie up the legs of the creature to bring it down, but as it was not alive, it's strength was not limited to what its muscles could provide. Each time they got the rope tied the creature would snap it like a thread of cotton.

"We need to get it back into the hole," said Vorlin, as he jumped, clear over the head of the creature his scimitar gouging deep into the bone of the creatures head.

"Oh wonderful Vorlin! I take it your idea goes further, or is that it, plug that hole with the Dreydoran's girth?!" replied Khris, his sarcasm blurring with humour as he dodged a lethargic swing of the creatures foreleg.

"Oh do show some sense Risce, when he is down the hole we will collapse it on top of the thing. The pressure should break the bones apart and destroy the spell."

"Can't we just wait for sun up?" asked Tal his short sword swinging towards the rear legs of the giant bug.

"No," replied Risce. "the main army may fall back as the Ones cannot survive the daylight and they would have no commanders, but the Mage who is controlling this beast will only be controlling *him* and so will be able to direct him however he wants without the aid of the Ones. That means daylight will not stop him.

"Ok Vorlin, how do we get him down the hole?"

"One of us needs to lure him back down there." he said, his scimitar cleaving a large section of bone away from one of the rear legs.

"One of us? You mean me." It was not a question that Risce asked.

With a great swing, Vorlin cleaved the rear right leg at one of its joints, severing the hold the spell had on it. The creature fell back onto the stump losing balance, "You are the only one who can do this Khris, and you know that."

"Fine, how do we lure it down the hole?"

Vorlin left the battle scene. Running to Tal he said "Tal fall back let him think the only threat to the defence of the hole is Khris!"

As the two left the fight, Khris ran back towards the tunnel that brought the Dreydoran to them. The beast turned slowly to face him, advancing slowly on the only threat to the Mages point of infiltration.

Tal watched as the lumbering beast slowly advanced on Khris, the grinning Dragon Rider now looking very serious as he backed up towards the tunnel, his strange looking sword still drawn.

As Risce reached the lip to the tunnel, he stopped and looked back into the hole. Tal noticed him looking back at the deep chasm, and still watched as he stepped into its covering darkness, quickly vanishing from sight.

The Dreydoran followed slowly, each step marching him closer to Khris. Reaching the tunnel the creature slowly descended back into its depths.

Tal could hear nothing but the trembling of the ground as the creature moved up the tunnel again. The minutes dragged on, the dark sky was now a deep blue-grey as dawn approached.

"Stand Fast!" called a voice from behind them.

Tal turned and saw Rider Erikson approaching with a small company of regular soldiers. The two had first met when Tal was in the jail. Erikson had visited him to check he was well on occasion and he had gained a liking of the man.

"Tal, you got out of the jail. Was that before or after it was destroyed?" he asked.

It was Vorlin who answered. "I dragged him out of the wreckage Captain, he did not violate his incarceration."

"And you are?" was Erikson's following question, obviously confused as to who this man was.

"Vorlin Mansford, but this is not the time for introductions, very soon you will have to help you superior out of that hole." As if in agreement to Vorlin's words, there was a deep thunderous explosion from beneath their feet. The group of men were thrown to the ground, their ears ringing as a depression in the street showed the point of explosion and collapse of the tunnel.

Dust rose and started to settle on the floor. As Erikson stood and looked around, he saw that Vorlin had already risen, and was making his way to the entrance of the tunnel.

Following Vorlin over to the edge of the hole, he saw a Dragon Rider, his clothes removed from his body and bleeding heavily emerge from the tunnel.

"The Dreydoran is no more?" asked Vorlin as the man jumped an improbable height and took hold of his arm.

"Yes, I saw the spell fail as the tunnel collapsed on top of him. He will not be re-animated again."

"Good. Then let us return to the wall and give what aid we may." Said Erikson.

Vorlin placed his now rather shabby cloak around Risce's shoulders and then looked up. The sky was ever brightening and the sun was bare minutes from showing itself above the horizon.

"I should take refuge from the daylight. I will join you on the wall at sundown." Waving Vorlin retreated into the shade of an alleyway and vanished from their sight. Motioning them on, Erikson set a fast pace back to the wall.

It seemed to take an age to reach it, but as they mounted the stairs that climbed to the battlements, the sun was visible, spilling its golden salvation across the field of battle. No shouts were resounding, no clang of metal against metal. The daylight had indeed brought reprieve.

"Well at least we can now rest." Said a soldier to Erikson with a smile as he saw Riders studs of rank.

"No, we can't." was his reply as he walked back down the wall. Making his way over to the command post across from the wall he addressed the Colonel in charge. "Colonel, we need to get pyres burning soon and very hot."

Looking up at the Rider, Colonel Ambla took the measure of him, "Ok Captain, but why?"

"There are bodies of Kingdom soldiers and the attacking army at the base of the wall, if they are not all burned to ash, then tonight there is an even larger army that the Mages could animate, and this time they do not have to reach our wall, they are already here."

The Colonel nodded slowly, disliking the thought of a tougher night than the one just passed, he gave the orders required to get the cremation of bodies started.

Tal followed Erikson back to the wall. Piles of bodies, both recently dead and already rotting were being thrown onto the now raging pyres. The smell of roasting and burning flesh was blowing across the city, making Tal gag involuntarily as he walked to the Riders section of the wall. The flames from the pyres reached thirty feet into the air and the smoke given of by the smouldering deceased blackened the light given from the fresh sun.

Seeing Tal approach Hazel ran to him, he arms wrapping around his neck as she kissed him firmly.

"What are you doing here?" she asked, happy to see him but wondering how he came to be released from the guardhouse.

"The building was hit by some kind of magic from one of the Dark Lords, Vorlin dragged me from the wreckage so I joined the fight." He continued the cover created by Vorlin, it might be better for him if everyone hears the same story.

"Thank the gods you survived!" she said holding him tight again.

Brad walked up behind Hazel, waiting for them to release each other before gripping Tal's arm firmly.

"Its good to see you out Tal." He said a broad smile on his face.

He returned his friends grip, thanking him warmly. Erikson nodded to Tal his face grim, "Tal you are under the supervision of Rider Jensook. The three of you stay here, and follow any orders you are given," his voice trailed off to a bare whisper, "I need to find out how Lord Rayburn is."

The room was dark. The windows were covered by heavy curtains that held the light at bay. Upon the single pallet lay a warrior covered in underclothes and a blanket, his greying hair was damp and his skin pallid. Next to him stood a Seer, illuminated by a pale violet glow as he worked magics designed to re-align the warriors energies.

Rayburn had been struck by lightening, his armour conducting the energy round his body and had caused his heart to spasm. A battlefield Seer had set the rhythm of his heart again, but the electrical pulses of Rayburn's body were harder to subdue. The Seer concentrated as another spasm wracked through the Lord of the Riders, causing the veterans back to arch as he cried out in unconscious pain.

The door opened and Erikson entered to see his Lord slump back to the bed. Worry etched his face as Marc came to stand next to the Seer.

"How fares he?" Asked the Captain in a quiet voice.

The Seer turned to face him, the faint glow dissolving from his body. A sympathetic look pinched the wizened mans eyebrows together.

"He is stable, but I cannot seem to sort out his body's electrical pattern. It is strange, if this were any normal soldier, he would not have survived, his body would have simply given up. But Lord Rayburn seems to be able to continue even though he is under considerable stress and discomfort."

"We are hardier than normal soldiers Brother Seer, we have means of containing our spirit within ourselves even when the body would wish to release it."

The Seer nodded his understanding but looked doubtful. He returned his attention to Gareth Rayburn and the light around him bloomed again as he once again focused on his charge. Erikson placed his hand on Rayburn's chest, feeling the slow beat of his Lords heart. He could feel the flesh under his hand tremble as nerve endings twitched with pulses of electricity, he could feel the Seer as he tried to even out the electrical imbalance, he could feel that the Seer was not correct.

"Stop." Pulling his hand away he turned quickly to the Seer. "Stop!" He repeated as he saw the Seer not respond. "Your causing him pain rather than helping. Whatever you may have learned about physiology before, it is not working now!"

The Seer halted his ministrations, looking at Erikson.

"What do you mean?" he asked, for the first time looking uncertain in his own skills.

"I felt his body as it jerked, then your response. His body seemed to fight against it, as though it knew what to do in order to right itself but your arts stopped it. With the greatest of respect brother Seer, I think we need someone that has a deeper knowledge of healing."

The Seer looked to him and shook his head slowly, "With perhaps the exception of the Lord High Seer himself, you will not find any Seer that is better trained in the arts of healing than I, Captain Rider, I am the head of medical research in the Brotherhood."

Erikson stood stunned, he wished that there was a higher ranking Rider here to take over, but the few Major's and the couple of Colonel's that were here were busy organising the defence and preparing for another nights siege.

"If there is only one other person who can help, then I suggest you try to get him here." Erikson said quietly, his face turning to look at his Lord who lay quietly moaning on his bed.

Tal sat on the wall, the cremation pyres still burned ferociously as the bodies of the dead were slowly reduced to dust. It was at least two hours past noon and the pyres had been burning non stop since sunrise. Hazel was sitting next to him her head resting on his chain mail covered shoulder. They had both been dismissed to get some food and change into something resembling fresh clothes. Tal had been restored to the garb of a Rider and Hazel had to wash the grime of battle from herself before returning.

They had sat in silence since Hazel had finished recounting her and Brad's visit to the City of Dragons. Tal had been overjoyed to hear they had been given the Honour of Steward of the Realm, but in his eyes, Hazel saw disappointment that he had not been deemed worthy of the honour also. She could relate, even wanted to give him *her* collar, but that was not possible, so they now sat in silence, simply enjoying each other's company.

Brad was leaning against the wall, sleeping. His soft breathing was almost inaudible over the cracking and roaring of the fires.

There was a loud groan as the cities north gate swung open. Another work party left the city to tend the pyres and throw more bodies on them. It took an hour before their labour was again finished with, and now there were no bodies left for the Grey Mages to re-animate and use to form their army.

"Do you think they are watching us? Are they watching as we burn their army along with our own dead?" asked Tal, his voice as dark as his mood.

"I'm sure they are, tonight's attack will be less about hand to hand fighting and more about magical assault. I hope we have more Seers than we did last night."

"We do." Captain Fen Trillar said as he walked up to the young Rider.

Brad's eyes shot open at his voice, Tal and Hazel shot upright.

"Captain?!" said all three together as they moved towards him. "What are you doing here?" continued Hazel as he gripped all three hands offered to him.

"I got here about an hour ago, extra Riders have been flown in to back up the units already here and Seers are arriving as we speak." He went on to explain how he was now in command of this section of the wall as Marc was busy with Rayburn.

They stood at the ramparts, talking about nothing in particular. The time wore on and soon it was dinner time and the end of their watch. The sky was darkening and the sun was close to setting. They were to eat and return to the wall to wait for the siege to resume. Fires had been built at specific points across the battlefield to illuminate the area, and as the first star became visible, the sun sank below the horizon and a roar of undead voices could be heard from the distance.

Tal looked around. He could see the faces of his comrades, cool calm and collected. The regular army looked like a fighting dog ready for a match, worked up and feverish. Earlier he had requisitioned one of the light, curved blades he now favoured, and currently was feeling its weight in his hand, letting the sword find its own balance.

From above he suddenly heard the cry of an unseen Graven as it circled in the gloom of the night. More than a couple of soldiers, both Rider and Army looked around nervously on hearing the awful sound. There was a sudden crack of lightening, and a flash that illuminated the sky as a blue-white bolt flew downward striking a collection of soldiers, sparks flying from their armour as the energy jumped from one person to the other.

In quick succession, there were a further five such strikes at different points along the wall, before the Seers managed to organise ay type of retaliation.

Several flares illuminated the sky revealing the presence of the Dark Lords as they soared above the city. A quick count from Tal numbered them ten strong. The Seers followed the flares with dozens of quick blasts of fire only catching one of the Graven. It screamed, but continued to fly on, its strength bolstered when its soul was given over to the Dark Lords.

No attack followed from the ground, just blast after blast from the Grey Mage Lords. The Seers had managed to erect a protective barrier over the main concentrations of Soldiers along the wall, giving safe zones for the soldiers where they could take cover from the bombardment of the Graven.

Half an hour passed before the first Dragons appeared on the scene, quickly scrambling the Graven from their attacks and forcing them back to their own lines. A cheer went up from the defenders, directed to the backs of the fleeing Mages, only to be answered by a ghostly roar from the unseen enemy beyond the lights of the beacons.

Silence followed, the only sound was from the wind gusting across the vacant space, making the fires flicker and shedding an eerie moving glow across the field of battle. Tal stood watching, a bow next to him and a quiver of arrows resting on the ground. His breathing was slow, his resolve firm, his hand shaky. Gripping his sword firmer, Tal tried to steady himself. Why was his body giving out when his heart was so set?

A hand appeared on his shoulder causing Tal to jump. He spun quickly to see Vorlin standing behind him, his repaired armour and scimitar looking the worse for wear after the previous night.

"How goes it?" asked the Nightwalker in a quiet voice.

Tal gave him a run down of the previous hour and Vorlin simply nodded and took a position next to Tal looking out across the bleak expanse to the north.

The night dragged, there were no further attacks, no further sounds. The fires burned down to a low glow and the defenders made ready. Still no attack came. The tension in the city of Sarafell was becoming tangible, the soldiers were getting aggressive with each other, brawls starting in the taverns in the few hours off duty that were allotted to each man.

Vorlin waited and watched as the sun began to rise, the black of night becoming the grey of dawn. A soft growl escaped his throat as he moved away from the wall. "I must retire, but this is not good. They are planning something." With a shake of his head, he descended the stairs and once again vanished into the approaching day.

Drew was woken by Richardson. The man had been awake almost constantly since the night before, when one of the Seers had reported that Sarafell had come under siege by the Grey Mages.

"It is our turn to take one of the Seers into the City." He stated bluntly.

Drew rose and dressed. He attached his longsword to his waist and two daggers on his sword belt. There had been no attacks so far, but each day a different Seer was sent into the

City with a different selection of men to minimise the risk to the men.

Leaving the tent, he saw Akarn with another two of his company waiting for him. A small man in his white robe was standing to one side, a selection of papers spread out on the table and several tomes in a small bag were being sorted for him to take along.

When the four Guardsmen were ready, the Seer came over to them. His face was weathered, and his skin was that of a man in his fifties. Seer Fullum was a studious type, and an expert in magical properties, however his solitary nature had halted his career before he could climb the ladder of the Brotherhood of Seers.

"I'm ready Sergeant. Please lead on." Was all the greeting that Fullum gave the Guardsmen before they headed out towards the city.

As the party left the camp, the ruins of the city were clear to see. It was a sight that always dragged Drew's spirit down, the visage of a city where thousands had perished, yet with almost no signs of struggle.

Climbing over the wreckage, they made their way towards the collapsed citadel. Fullum was having more difficulty than the others, his robe becoming caught on any sharp object it could find. Reaching over, Drew helped him to the top of a destroyed building and took his bag from him, allowing him to move more freely.

Fullum thanked him quietly, and gave a grateful smile as he made his way to the bottom of the collapsed roof. They were walking for a further fifteen minutes before they reached the boundary of the citadel.

"OK, where do you want to work Brother Seer?" asked Akarn Richardson as they came to a halt by the wall.

"I want to be as close to the Gate as possible Sergeant, so I guess that would be on top of it."

Richardson nodded and ordered two Guards to stay at the base of the rubble, while he and Drew assisted Fullum to scale the citadel to find the position closest to the Gate.

"It's here. I can feel the Gates energy about thirty feet below us." Said the Seer, his breath short from the climb. "I wont need any assistance Sergeant, so you can stay or go as you wish."

"Thank you Sir, but our orders are to protect you should you need it, so we are here until you are ready to head back to camp." Replied Richardson politely.

"Thank you, but I will need some space to carry out my work, if you could wait by your friends it should be far enough away." Fullum was already unpacking his small bag when Richardson gave his acknowledgement and ordered Drew back down the citadels fallen walls.

Several hours had passed, and Drew found himself practising his sword work with Richardson. Noon had come and gone while Drew swung his sword over and over, exercising his skills and keeping himself busy.

As his blade came down in a sweeping arc towards Richardson's raised sword, there came a shout from Seer Fullum. Halting his attack mid-strike, Drew turned to see Fullum smiling and waving his arms frantically towards them.

Richardson sheathed his sword and climbed back up the wreckage to reach the Seer, "What is it?" he asked looking round for some new occurrence.

"I have found it! I managed to trace the magical signature back from the Gate to its primary instigator!" exclaimed Fullum with the first outwardly dramatic expression that any of the Guards had seen.

"That's just swell sir," said Richardson, "but what does that mean?"

"It means I have found where the power to the Gate is coming from! We can close the Gate!" said Fullum, as though it was the most wonderful discovery he could have made.

"Then unless you have anything else that needs to be done here, we should return to the camp and inform Master Diarmid and Captain Loytan."

"Of course! Of course! Let me get my papers together and we will leave immediately!" said the small Seer, almost dancing around the small area he had cleared to work in.

They arrived back at the camp within an hour, Seer Fullum almost out-pacing the Guards in his desire to reach Master Diarmid with the newly acquired information. As he passed the first line of Guards, the entire camp could hear his calls of excitement, his voice carrying over the rows of tents and alerting both Captain Loytan and Oren to his approach.

Both men exited the command tent and moved towards Fullum. He was talking rapidly, his arms gesturing in a manner that made no sense to either Oren Diarmid or William Loytan. Trying to calm the animated Seer, Oren gripped his arms in a firm grip and told him to hold the explanations until they were back inside the command tent.

Fullum agreed, and they turned back and entered the dim tent. Inside, it was the usual state for the Kingdom commanders at the present time, strategic maps were thrown across tables, lists of troops and inventories were stacked up in each corner. As they entered, Oren moved to the centre table and removed half the maps, leaving only those in the immediate area.

"Brother Fullum, what did you discover that caused you to return with such speed?" questioned Master Diarmid when they were all gathered. Richardson, Drew, Oren, William and Maxtor Fullum stood around the charts as the Seer explained his discovery.

"I started as usual by attempting to identify the essence of the Magic that was used in the Gates. I went through the normal catalogue of the Grey Mages, Black Magic, Necromantic Magic, and even Wild Magic on the outside chance that they had learnt some tricks from the Dark Cousins or even the Elves, but none came up with a match. I was as stuck as we had all been and decided it would be best to just stop thinking, and that is when it came to me! If the demons and Mages had been working together then it could easily be Demonic Magic!"

"The Mages *have* been shown to be the puppets of the demons, it is a distinct possibility." Said Oren "The one question that I can't answer is; how did you identify Demonic Magic? It had left this world years before the Kingdom was set up and I can't think how you would have known about its design."

"That is easy to answer Master Diarmid, I read about it in one of the ancient tomes. Remember the prophecy that was discovered in Coladan? Well after that, I decided to look into the records of the chapel where the priest had recorded the prophecy. The man had been so scared by the ravings of the demons that he had done some research into demonic practise. He had gleaned some small details of the magics that were used to send the younger demon into this plane of existence, and he made records that were kept in the church until the time he died. They were then sent to the library at the Hall of Seers in the City of Dragons as the records were of a magical note and the new priest thought we would have more use of them.

"It wasn't until I stopped thinking that I remembered the main thread that he discovered in the Demonic style of magic, I then tested the Gate and found it matched. From then it was simple to follow the energy back from the Gate to whatever is powering it." Fullum was still excited, though he had calmed down now he was once again working on the mystery of the Gates.

"So where was the power source located Maxtor?" asked Loytan.

"Well I can't be precise, but my calculations would place the source around here." He said placing a finger at a point on the chart between Peters Hold and the Dead Lands.

"That is about a days travel from here. What is the plan Oren?"

"I will discuss this with the High Seer back at the City of Dragons tonight, and will inform you when we have reached a decision." Nodding, Loytan dismissed the rest of the collected Seers and Guards and decided that he needed to sit down. If only he had an ale to calm his nerves.

Drew left the tent with Richardson, both heading towards the camps mess, walking in silence.

The next morning, the sun rose to a hive of activity at the Peters Hold camp. Tents were being struck, fires extinguished, and gear packed onto the back of the horses. Drew was waiting for his Captain to order the company forward. They had a long day on the back of a horse and no one knew what they would discover when they arrived.

Richardson turned to Drew, his face weary, and offered him a slight smile.

"Are you still not sleeping?" Drew asked, concerned for his friends welfare.

"No. I can't settle, each time I try, all I can think of Sarafell. What could be happening there, how the siege could be progressing, how many of my friends could be there." Akarn was starting to talk with a slight slur to his voice. Drew nodded slightly and made an excuse before moving away. Richardson merely grunted in acknowledgement, his eyes heavily shadowed.

Drew slipped behind the command tent as it was being dismantled and found Captain Loytan talking to Master Diarmid and Seer Fullum. Saluting, Drew waited to be called into the conversation. The wait was not long, Loytan gesturing Drew to speak.

"Captain, I'm worried about Sergeant Richardson. He has not slept since he heard news of the attack on Sarafell, he can hardly keep his eyes open, sir."

"OK thank you for bringing it to my attention Drew, we will be stopping tonight before we reach the vicinity of the power source, I will get the Seers to help him sleep when we halt. Until then you will do what you can to keep him moving with us." Loytan dismissed Drew with a salute and then turned to Oren again, the sound of their voices drifting into the distance as he returned to where Richardson was looking into the distance, towards the city of Sarafell.

Lunch arrived finding the group eating travel bread from their packs while on horseback. There had been no stops so far and they had been told there would not be a stop until the sun set when they would get food and rest before starting the closer search the next day.

Fullum was at the head of the column of horsemen, flanked by two Guards. His eyes had been closed most of the morning but he had not shown any signs of difficulty in steering his mount.

Drew turned to one of the Seers and asked what Maxtor was doing. The Seer replied, saying that Brother Fullum was mentally following the thread of the Magic that was supplying the Gate with energy.

As they travelled, the terrain was slowly becoming harsher. The fertile ground was slowly becoming dryer and the soil that was there was becoming thinner, a rock base becoming more visible as they moved towards the Dead Lands.

These lands were well named. They were dead to all life, only small springs of water existed in the depths of the rocky country, and these were usually base camps for bands of renegades and exiles from the Kingdom.

The sun was intense, no shade was available to them and several people were wrapping cloths around their heads, the tail covering their exposed necks. Richardson was swaying in the saddle, and Drew was struggling to keep him attentive.

A crash caused him to turn towards Akarn, and saw his friend in a heap on the floor. The column halted quickly, everyone hearing the fall. Two Guards were at their Sergeants side quickly, and placed him back on his horse before tying him to it.

Loytan approached Drew when they were moving again and spoke quietly.

"This was probably a good thing son. He will now sleep through until tomorrow morning thanks to the Seers, and will hopefully be back to normal for the search." With a slightly worried glance to Richardson, Drew nodded and continued on in silence.

Morning came bright and hot for Drew, his tent oppressively dry. He got dressed and opened the flap letting the warm breeze clear the stale air that was hanging inside. Leaving, he looked round and saw Richardson drinking some water at the edge of camp. He looked very much awake and more alert than he had done in days.

With a sigh of relief, Drew went to speak to him.

"You're looking better." He said as a greeting.

"Thanks, sixteen hours of sleep will do that." said Akarn with a slight smile.

"Indeed. Do you know what time we begin the search?" said Drew, with a genuine smile.

"As soon as were packed!" explained a voice from behind him. Turning, he was faced with the eager face of Fullum. The quiet man had become extremely vocal and friendly since he had discovered a new magical field to study.

The company was packed up and ready to depart before the sun had been above the horizon for an hour. As they set off, Fullum again took point and headed in a straight line. The group had been briefed in their search pattern and they were to head to the centre of the energy source. The thread lead to this area, but the energy source was so broad that Fullum could not pin point its exact location and so he would now rely on the outriders and Guards to search the areas he selected.

The sun made its slow progress through the sky, passing its zenith and marching inexorably towards the horizon. The day dragged and no source of energy could be found, Fullum's senses were overloaded by the power that was based in the vicinity and the entire party were starting to become disheartened. Diarmid called a halt very shortly after and camp was set up again for the night.

No fires were set, Loytan was worried that the Mages would be stationed close by and would see if any fires were lit. The whole group was sat in the dark, eating fried bread and talking in low voices. Watches were set up and slowly, people started to drift from the gathering and retire to their own tents to rest.

The morning arrived just as hot and dry as the previous one. The small group of soldiers and Seers were already combing the countryside, spread wide with Fullum guiding them in an organised search. Drew was on their left flank, examining the country as far as he could see. They were cresting a low rolling hill when Drew saw something that made him halt.

The temperature was causing heat waves to blur the distance, but Drew thought he could see something different. A dark grey mound could be seen protruding from the ground, but any further details were obscured. Drew signalled to the next Guard in the chain, that he was going to examine something before darting off towards the mound.

As he got closer he felt his hopes fade. It was only an outcropping of bedrock, no more than six feet in height. Cursing, he kicked at the thin layer of dirt on the ground and turned to walk away. He passed the rock and only frustration caused him to glance back.

There was something wrong here, he turned and slowly walked back. As he approached, he still could not see anything that would arouse his suspicion. Running his hand over the rough face of the rock, his fingers came across a slight lip. Too regular and long to be natural, Drew pulled back and quickly ran back to the search party.

Within fifteen minutes, the group were stationed at what the Seers deemed a safe distance from the strange rock. Fullum and Drew had walked alone up to the rock, with the young Guard showing the Seer where the lip was.

"Yes! This is it!" explained Fullum running his hand over the rock. "We must proceed carefully, I do not know if there are any traps set within the Magic."

They returned to their superiors to report their findings, and it was decided that Fullum would try to discover what was hidden within the rock edifice.

Camp was set up a good distance from the rock, and Fullum was given an hour to prepare himself before he was required to start his examination of the Magic that surrounded it.

As Maxtor approached he could feel the alien design of the magic, and the lure of it thrilled him. He had to remind himself not to get so engrossed with his new study that his guard would drop and he would make a fatal mistake.

Taking a deep breath, he placed his hands on the rock and closed his eyes. In his mind, he was back at the Hall of Seers, in their library, reading a report from a priest in an isolated village. He went over all the information that he had read, and tried to commit to memory any little detail that might aid him in his study.

The pulse of the Demonic magic differed from the White magic the Seers used and was almost opposite. Where the White magic used, was defined by the energy supplied from the Seer himself, the Demonic magic seemed to be powered from an external source, drawing its energy from some well of power and then pumping it into the spell, like a heart pumps blood to the areas of the body.

Fullum was fascinated by the difference, even the Black magic from the lesser Grey Mages was just White magic used for evil purposes, and the Necromantic Magic drew peoples life energy into the Dark Lord before he then used it in a spell. This was almost opposite to anything he had experienced before.

Like the demons had no magical ability themselves, and relied on other sources to power the constructs they created. Certainly this was a thesis to explore at a later date.

As he followed the threads of the spell, he found the hidden trap, an explosive element that would be triggered on the dissolution of the main power supply. Other than that, there were no hidden tricks that Fullum could discern and so he communicated this back to Oren in the camp and was given the authority to neutralise the spell if he felt comfortable.

Steadying his nerves, he checked one last time for hidden traps, then immersed himself in the flowing mesh that was the Demonic spell. Like an engineer strategically removing the supports of a building to collapse it, Fullum slowly took apart the spell.

Too late he saw his error, as the final thread of supply was cut to the spell, he saw the hidden spell that sealed his fate. The barrier around the now visible cave was destroyed, but so was he. Without a single sound passing his lips he prayed to the God of Magic to speed his soul on its journey. A searing heat like none he had ever felt ripped through his body, burning flesh from bone before his skeleton was reduced to ash that blew away on the dry breeze.

The camp watched as Fullum became immolated in an intense white light, and then was gone, his ashes drifting away in the wind. Silence fell over the watching Guards and Seers as several heads hung in silent prayer as one of their number gave their life for the cause of freedom.

Oren stretched out and could sense nothing from the rock. Before Fullum was assigned to study it, Master Diarmid had gained instruction on how to sense Demonic magic and now he felt nothing.

"I think Maxtor successfully removed the spell covering the cave, even though it took his life. We should not forget his sacrifice, but we must push on and discover what is holding the Gate in Peters Hold open."

Captain Loytan nodded and ordered the Guards forward behind the Seers. As they approached, there was a feeling of unease as they saw stairs descending down into the rock.

Oren was the first to set foot inside the cave, its darkness was almost unnatural compared to the intense light of the day, and he had to push himself to move down, as his own instincts wanted to keep himself in the sunlight.

He must have reached about fifteen feet under ground level when the stairs ended and a small opening faced him. He tried to sense for any other magical presence, but all he could feel was the power source with no spells protecting it any longer.

Walking through the doorway he held up a hand as he was immersed in complete darkness, a white orb ignited above his palm and illuminated an immense cavern with what looked like hundreds of altars. Holding back a feeling of nausea, he suddenly realised what was powering the Gate.

Upon each altar was a child, lying completely still, their skin grey and dry, and surrounded by a faint red glow that thrummed with the same signature that he associated with Demonic magic.

"By the love of the Creator, do not let this be."

Chapter 18

Advancement

Oren retreated away from the nightmarish visage in front of him.

As he ascended the stairs back to the outside world, he could not help but feel tainted by the Dark Magics that had surrounded him a moment ago, the sun seemed dimmer than it had before he entered the cave. He made his way towards the small group of Guards and Seers when he left the cover of the rock, his mind feeling numb.

"What is it?" asked Loytan on seeing the Seers haunted expression.

"I found the source of the Gates power. The Demons, or Mages, are using children – hundreds, possibly thousands of them – their life force is being drained slowly to keep the Gates open."

Apart from a few shocked gasps, the only sound was the gentle breeze washing around the cave entrance. Drew just looked at the others, his mind not being able to understand what had just been said. The rest of the company seemed to look just as lost as he felt, a couple of the Seers had a tear or two in their eyes and one Guard had lost his legs and was now sitting on the floor, vacant eyed and looking to the distance.

"We have to get news of this back to the King, now." Said Loytan quietly.

Oren nodded, and moved away from the party to give himself some privacy to break the news to the King.

Drew stood, he still could not understand how children could be powering the Gates. Checking to ensure that no one was watching, he slipped away from his colleagues and started down the steps to the cave. He had to know what was down there; his mind was racing – what could cause a Master Seer so much discomfort?

The darkness of the cave was oppressing, the small lamp he had ignited on descending only gave a dim light, barely enough for Drew to keep his footing as he neared the bottom of the stairs.

He paused at the base, looking into the depth of the darkness. Taking a deep breath he forced his feet to carry him through the portal. In the blackness his eyes struggled to focus, he could only make out some objects with a faint red glow, but they were too obscured by the gloom for him to make out any details.

Continuing into the dense murk of the cave, his lamps light seemed to be sucked away by whatever lay ahead. Approaching the first line of objects, the lamp gave it shape, it was an altar with a child laying on it, a young girl no older than ten years lay prone upon the stone slab, emanating a red glow.

Horrified, Drew reached out to her with his hand, placing it on her shoulder. The girl was cold and did not react to his touch but Drew saw her chest rise and fall with breath. Himself breathing hard now, fear gripping his heart, he gently shook her, trying to wake her from whatever sleep she may be in. As her body shook on the cold slab, her eyes shot open. Drew found himself drawn to them, unable to break away from the child's gaze. Within her brown eyes, he saw terror, fear and a plea for help that Drew could not answer, only her eyes could move, not even her lips. He fell back, his eyes locked shut as his lamp fell from his hand and went out. A silent scream escaped his lips as he became wrapped in the darkness of the cave.

The sun set again, the enemies fires were lit. Shrieks and howls from undead soldiers echoed across the field of battle. Vorlin appeared at Tal's side without him even noticing the Nightwalker arrive. The defenders were tense, the past week had stretched on with nothing occurring. Scouts had been sent out to find out what the Mages were up to, but none returned. The commanders had been reinforcing the walls again and again, expecting siege engines to be brought to bear at any moment, but the warm nights simply passed with distant challenges and no more.

Tal had been under the supervision of Hazel since he had been freed – a guard he was not too upset about having – and was once more standing next to her on the wall. He had been decked out like a Rider once more, his black chain resting on his broad shoulders, his curved sword in his scabbard. Brad had asked to be stationed at the other end of the wall so he could be close to Cholla, the two had become inseparable over the past few nights.

"This will not last." Said Vorlin quietly, causing Tal and Hazel to jump at his sudden company.

"If they hope to starve us out, they will need to block off our supply route to the south, but they seem more than comfortable to just assault us on three sides. Their numbers will again take losses if they attack now that we have been reinforced. What are they planning?"

Hazel and Tal looked at each other, their expressions showing their discomfort. Throughout the week, reports had been fed back to the wall that Rayburn was stable, but not improving. Jakrin Tiersing had been called to Sarafell, to help with his recovery but had been unable to get away from something he was working on in the City of Dragons.

"This is new." said Hazel, bringing both Tal and Vorlin out of their contemplations.

In the distance a column of fire was stretching upwards, reaching as far up as they could see into the sky, even as the defenders scrabbled to the edge of the wall to get a view of this new tactic – whatever it was! – another two, then four of these columns flared up into existence. Soon there were five columns for each of the three sides of the city, the Riders, Soldiers and Seers were looking on perplexed as a heart wrenching roar echoed across the field, and over the sound of raging fire.

From the light given off by the fire, they could see that the undead army was making its approach again. Calls were sent out by Officers, getting their men back into position waiting for the fighting to start.

Cries from the air signalled the arrival of the Graven once more, immediately answered by the roars of Dragons as their pitched battles again resumed in the skies above the city. The undead army continued its slow approach, catapults and ballista sung from the walls as the attacking army closed within their range. The earth was torn up as fiery boulders crashed amongst the attacking army, bodies being torn apart or incinerated by the assault. Ahead of the ghouls, skeletons and zombies moved with the towers of flame. Their tops indiscernible to those on the wall and they left nothing in their wake other than burnt, and barren earth.

Closer the army came and the bows of the defenders sent a blanket of arrows into the ranks of the undead horde, pinning warriors to the ground. Still closer and the first set of fire arrows ignited the first defensive ring of oil, starting it burning and incinerating the front ranks of undead. The columns of fire aided the defenders as they touched the rings of oil, starting another circular path of death and cremation for the attacking army.

Tal looked at Hazel, the fiery towers close enough to make her squint at the light, the heat causing her to shield her face with her hand. Tal wondered what the Seers had planned to combat the new offensive – whatever it was, he hoped it wasn't too far away.

The burning air was making breathing hard for the defenders, so much so that Tal had to turn his back on the approaching maelstrom, and as he did, he saw a column of Seers taking up position all along the wall. The men of the Brotherhood stood deathly still, the air moved by the flames causing their robes to billow and their hair to become windswept.

Touching Hazel's shoulder, he motioned to the Brothers that were taking up position around the wall. She dropped her bow, there was obviously something about to occur and she didn't think one less archer would make much difference at the moment.

The pillars of fire were about two hundred yards out from the walls when it started. Tal heard a soft chanting from the closest Seer and the air became charged with energy. Flashes of blue and white shot from each of the Seers to points above the city walls, those points starting to link to each other as they increased in size forming a framework.

The chanting continued, and the energy that was being sent to the sky was starting to crackle. The eyes of the Seers had taken on the colour and pulsing flash of the energy that they were harnessing. The columns of fire were about a hundred and fifty yards off the walls, the roar of the fire and the ever increasing heat washing over the battlements causing no small number of the defenders to hunker down behind the wall to get some shelter.

Tal looked up, the Graven were pulling away from the walls, obviously waiting for the fire to do its job.

Silence.

It was sudden and unexpected.

Tal and Hazel looked to each other the air and stood still and there was a feeling of lightness surrounding them. There was a single word that echoed across the city from an unseen Seer, and with a shockwave, the collected energy around the walls descended to the ground and submerged causing earth to fly upwards.

At a speed unknown to Tal with the exception of maybe a Dragon, the energy followed the ground outwards, causing more earth to fly and explode. Tal waited expectantly as the energy reached the pillars of fire then passed straight through without affecting them. Dismay rolled through Tal as he saw the Seers defence fail, a low moan escaped his lips as he drew his sword and awaited the onslaught that was bound to come.

Hazel started to do the same, then halted, her hand gripping Tal's arm.

"Wait! Look!" as she spoke Tal felt the air energise once more.

From behind the line of the columns, he saw the blue-white power rise from the earth and enwrap a collection of Seers that suddenly appeared behind the lines of the undead. In another second they had sent the energy outwards into the night. Screams erupted from the field and from the darkness that was the Mages camp. The Undead army started to collapse, the Mages that controlled them losing their control through death or preoccupation with something else.

Slowly the Fire columns started to disperse, their heat growing less, their size reducing until they were lower than the wall the defenders were manning. As the last company of undead collapsed a single remaining column of fire flared up, its last remaining magical ties causing it to expand rapidly, washing over the wall before vanishing into the night.

Cries of the defenders that had been burned made their way up to meet Tal as the rest of the night descended into a ghostly quiet.

"What happened?" asked Tal.

He was not alone in his confusion either; from all along the walls soldiers were looking to their officers with the same question.

Hazel looked over to the other end of the defences where the column of fire had breached the wall. She watched as the city's reserves raced towards the scene with buckets of water, she saw Seers carrying bags of medical supplies and trying to aid those that had suffered from the explosion. She turned with a gasp as she turned to Tal, "It hit a Rider position!"

Tal had started to move already when Hazel griped his cloak pulling him back.

"We cannot leave our duty until we are relieved, I won't let you get into any more trouble." She said firmly to him.

"But Brad, and Cholla could have been there!" argued Tal.

"It does not matter, if they were the Seers will be helping them, there is nothing we can do!" Hazel held firm, refusing to let him get into hot water and more trouble than he already was. Eventually he relaxed, his sword still gripped in his hand, his knuckles still white against the hilt, the final tension to the situation he could do nothing about.

Hazel slowed her breathing and released her hold on Tal's cloak. Looking around she tried to take stock of the situation. The Graven were nowhere in sight, Dragons and Dragon Riders circled the city ready for further attack. On the field, no bodies were moving, the Seers that had appeared from nowhere, were moving amongst the undead army, capturing any Mages that had been sent in with their units.

From the east and west, Hazel spotted small groups of men in green and brown, searching along with the Seers, they were providing physical protection.

Rangers.

Hazel had only seen the Rangers occasionally, they were almost the equal of the Riders in weaponry, and where the Riders had the advantage of their gifts, the Rangers had some small skill in the use of magic. They were the private army of the Seers, though bodyguards would be a better term.

Vorlin had not moved once throughout the entire ordeal, still standing in the exact same pose when the Order came to stand down.

Tal, Hazel and Vorlin raced to the other end of the wall, to the second Rider position, as soon as they were relieved.

Moving across the blackened expanse, they looked for their friends amongst those being treated without any luck. Calling for Brad and Cholla, they spent the next ten minutes walking round in circles, their voices drowned out by others seeking their comrades.

Tal's heart stopped, he ran away from Hazel towards Brad. She turned, her eyes following him as he raced up the stairs to the top of the wall.

Coming down, Brad looked like he only just managed to get to cover before the fire flowed over the wall, his face and arms were blackened, and his cloak was burnt and torn. Though it was not Brad that made Tal's and Hazel's soul sink, in his arms was Cholla, she hung limp and Brad carried her, tears streaming down his face, his body moved as though it carried a weight far heavier than that of Cholla.

As Tal reached him, he offered to take Cholla from him, but Brad simply shook his head and continued his slow stagger towards the medical teams, not trusting his voice. Hazel reached Tal and threw her arms around him, her sobs being silenced by his shoulder.

Brad fell to his knees, still holding Cholla close to him. One of the Seers approached him, gently lifted the young Rider from his arms and placed her on a blanket, covering her with another one before patting Brad on the shoulder and moving on silently to the next person requiring his attentions.

Tal and Hazel knelt beside Brad, he needed his friends here, and though Cholla was Hazel's closest friend, she was Brad's love.

"I'm sorry Brad." The weak voice caused all three to start. Turning they saw Rayburn standing behind them, he looked weak and very tired.

"Thank you sir." Replied Brad softly, "How are you feeling?"

"Better, the Lord High Seer came as soon as the Mages were repulsed. Made quick work of me, now all I need is rest apparently. Like that will happen." He added with a weak smile. Tal looked at him, his impulsive nature once again asserting itself.

"What happened sir?"

Gareth looked at him, his eyes altering from anger to sympathy.

"A while ago, the Seers started working on a spell that would form a mental shockwave, but it took a lot of work to maintain the level of energy that would be required to stop such a large number of Mages. Jakrin has had most of the Council of Elders constantly working on the spell in shifts to keep it ready for casting. When the Mages made such an all out offensive, he felt it was now or never. The Elders were positioned outside the wall, and Jakrin issued orders for the rest of the Seers to start focussing their energy. He took over the spell and as soon as the Mages were dedicated to their assault, Jakrin launched his own offensive, the Mages either died or passed out to be rounded up. Well that's the short version, but I should be moving on there are lots of people to speak to tonight.

"One other thing, Tal I hear from Erikson that you played a part in the defence against the Dreydoran. Well done, you are cleared of all charges and are free to carry on your duties as a Rider."

"Thank you sir," Tal paused, the realisation of what Rayburn had just said sinking in. "Sir you said?"

"That's right lad, you're promoted to Rider, congratulations." Nodding then turning slowly, Rayburn limped off to speak to another Rider that was injured and receiving the attentions of some healers.

"Congratulations Tal." Said Brad his wishes sincere but his heart not in the moment. Hazel hugged him and kissed him gently, her own congratulations whispered out of respect for Brad.

Taking Brad's hand, Hazel made him stand.

"We all need some sleep. Come on, we can talk and remember Cholla as she would want us to in the morning."

Tal was already awake as the sun rose. He was outside the walls starting pyres for the undead army again. His spirit was about as low as it had ever been, the earth outside the city was scorched and barren, his friend was mourning the loss of the girl he loved, and there were still forces out there trying to bring down the Kingdom because of a manipulated prophecy they believed would bring them to supremacy of the world. The worst part was that the entire situation had been created by an even greater threat that was merely playing games to set the world against itself.

With a deep sigh, he poured oil over a pile of bones and rotting bodies before igniting it. He felt a hand slip into his and turned to see Hazel looking leaning against him. She had said very little since they took Brad back to the makeshift barracks the previous night, her usual confidence seemed to have vanished and Tal saw her as a vulnerable person for the first time.

Holding her close, he did not see Erikson approach until he spoke.

"Rider Jensook, Rider Parnell, Lord Rayburn wishes all Riders to speak to their unit commanders to receive their new orders. Please come and see me at midday, we are taking the fight north."

Brad was sitting on his bunk, the others in his room had been coming and going all morning, he had received commiserations from his friends, and Captain Erikson had requested his company at midday to receive his orders, however he found that he was struggling to even get out the door let alone get to Erickson.

He looked out the window, the sun was nearing its zenith. He shook his head to clear it and stood up. Leaving the barracks he looked up, the sun was bright and the air warm. Too good a day to have such a black heart.

Erikson was in a small room when Brad arrived, the rest of the unit was waiting. Tal and Hazel gave him a weak smile.

Also in the room was Sergeants Gwent and Kendrik, Riders Bryant Lewis, Shan-Yin Hito and both Ilan Brothers, there were five other Riders that Brad had not seen before other than in passing, making a total of fifteen. The Captain, two Sergeants, and twelve Riders stood facing each other waiting to hear what Erikson would say.

"I have been in council with Lord Rayburn and his senior Officers since the siege was lifted last night. The King was consulted and the decision was made to push into the Lost Lands and eliminate the threat the Grey Mages pose to us as well as finding a way to close this Gate you found.

"The Seers are sending three hundred Rangers and one hundred of their Brothers with the Army. We leave tomorrow, several parties of Rangers have been sent on ahead with a select few Riders to find places to set up camp and create fortifications.

"Spend your day as you see fit. Dismissed."

The Riders took their leave of their Captain, Tal and Hazel departing with Brad. They spent the afternoon at the temple of Telkhan, the God of war, praying for Cholla's soul, letting memories of her fill them.

When they left the temple, the sun had set, they had not noticed the time disappearing, nor had they noticed their stomachs desire for food. Bidding each other goodnight, they each slipped off to their respective bunks. The next day would be long, and none of them could guess when the war would be over.

The Riders were trekking across the dry dusty ground that was the Lost Lands. A week ago they had set off with the main army, the Riders were mounted and walking in strict formation, ahead of them were the Rangers, and behind them, the regular Army.

Tal was dirty, sore and tired. The days had been long, the temperature seemed to be ever increasing as the summer approached, and water was rationed. Brad had settled into a quiet melancholy, and no attempts from Tal or Hazel had been able to shake his silence.

At the head of the Rider column, Lord Gareth Rayburn was in full field plate. Although he still looked more worn that Tal had seen him before, his strength was returning. He held his helmed head high and his back straight, the only sign of his close call with death was his pale skin and soft spoken voice.

Each member of the army was quiet in his or her duty, only the noise of horses, armour in movement and wagons rumbling broke the silence. As long as each sentry remained alert for any coming trouble, they could contemplate their own musings while they marched.

The sun passed overhead and once more headed for the western horizon. Tal was counting the minutes until his aching body would have some time to rest and regain its strength before starting off again the next day.

Hazel rode next to him, she looked just as tired if not more so. Her face had been downcast all day and she had kept her own counsel. The column came to a halt. Ahead the Rangers had started to set up camp. Here they would spend a few short hours eating then sleeping before pressing on, and Tal was happy to surrender his mount to one of the soldiers that had been assigned picket duty.

Taking his pack down from behind the saddle, he checked that his Rapier was still attached. Hazel looked over and recognised the sword that had been given to him on the day of his sixteenth birthday all those months ago. "I haven't seen that in a while." She said quietly.

"It has always been forwarded to me where ever I was, this time though I wanted to bring it with me." Replied Tal looking at the elegant weapon.

"It would have been safe at the barracks you know, and your field sword would do you better in battle than the Rapier could."

"I know. But it was given to me when things seemed so much simpler. If I'm not going to survive this, I wanted to have something with me to remind me of the happier times while I can." Supplied Tal as he placed his kit on the ground.

"Don't talk like that, we will get through this! And negative thinking isn't going to help a damn!" For the first time in a week, Tal heard the fire return to Hazel's voice. He looked up and saw her glaring at him, and for some reason couldn't help but smile.

"You're right, and you can stop looking at me like that, you got your point across." He kissed her cheek and told her he was going to find Brad and make sure they were in the same tent before leaving Hazel seething at his strangely changed mood.

"Men!" She breathed heavily and stormed off to find the women's tents.

Tal was asleep when something in his mind woke him, he sat up, fully awake. Standing quietly, he navigated his way past his sleeping comrades and left the tent, wrapping his cloak around himself.

Outside the night was bright, the sky cloudless and revealing the two moons shining vibrantly amongst the countless stars. Unsure where he was going, he simply followed intuition and found himself leaving the inhabited camp. He was questioned by a sentry and made the excuse of not being able to sleep and wanting some time alone. The Soldier was not about to question a Rider further, even if he did appear young, and let Tal go about his business. Walking into the Lost Lands, he made his way deeper until the mass of tents had vanished from his sight.

As he walked a figure became apparent a short distance off. Approaching Tal guessed he was over six feet in height and was wearing a dark coloured robe. The hood obscured the figures features, and Tal thought with regret that he should have brought his sword with him.

"Relax Tal, you are in no danger." Said the man pulling back the cowl of the Robe. Vorlin stood waiting for Tal. The two had not seen each other now since the army had left Sarafell and headed north, Vorlin claiming he had matters to take care of elsewhere for the time being.

"What is happening?" asked Tal, confusion thick in his voice.

"I apologise, I had to place my location in your mind and wake you up to get you here. I do not like to play with peoples minds but it is necessary I assure you."

"Why? What is it?" said Tal, worry now replacing his earlier confusion.

"The Mages are reeling from their lost assault on Sarafell. They are aware that you are heading into the Lost Lands to finish them and have hired a small army of Dark Cousins to stop you. I do not know how yet, but they are on their way and will probably catch you up the day after tomorrow. I need you to speak to Lord Rayburn and organise a meeting for tomorrow night. I have spoken to the rest of the Conclave and have an offer for him."

"The Conclave?" asked Tal his mind racing at all the new information that had just been thrown at him.

"The Conclave is the ruling body of the *Seicolantrai*, the Nightwalkers that you met in the Coven that night after you escaped from the Mages Lair. We each control two of the ten remaining Covens and jointly decide on how we govern our people. That is not important now though, should we survive the coming disaster then I will gladly discuss our methods of ruling, for now, will you speak to Lord Rayburn?"

"I will try." Agreed Tal. Vorlin nodded, seemingly satisfied and told Tal he should head back and get whatever rest he could for the rest of the night.

Shortly Tal entered his tent again, removing his cloak he tried to sleep but it proved elusive and as his mind raced, the moons set and the sun rose. The new day was here and Tal was already exhausted, his mind running while his body struggled to keep up. He sat and ate his breakfast of trail bread, cheese and water. The cheese was past its best and Tal thought this was the last day they would get that luxury, soon it would be just dried bread and salted meats. Finished, he placed his battered plate aside and stood, readying himself for the meeting he must now seek with Rayburn.

He made his way through the array of tents that housed the Riders, eventually reaching Lord Rayburn's private tent. The entrance flap was tied back, obviously there was already a council underway within. Two Riders stood besides the doorway guarding the way. Tal saluted them and when it was returned asked for permission to speak to his Lord. One of the Riders asked him to wait before ducking inside. Tal hated waiting, every time he had to so far, it felt an eternity passed before the reply came.

Entering the relative darkness of the tent, Tal halted and saluted the collection of senior Officer is the room. Dragon Rider Khris Risce nodded with a wink towards Tal as he became aware of him. *When did Khris get here?* Thought Tal, the Dragon Rider was not in the line up when they left Sarafell, and he hadn't been seen since, but then again neither had Vorlin he reminded himself.

"What can I do for you Rider Parnell?" asked Rayburn with a slight smile, Tal became aware that he had just been standing in silence since entering the tent and his face flushed.

"Sir, I have a message for you. Rather a request from Vorlin Mansford." He stated quickly, hoping the others forgave his pause.

"The Nightwalker? Well son what is it?" said Rayburn. Tal noticed Khris lean forward slightly, intent on what Tal was saying.

"He would like a meeting with you tonight Sir, he also gave me a warning to forward to you."

"Why did he not just come to me directly?" Asked Rayburn, curiosity lining his face.

"He did not come into the camp Sir, he called me to him." replied Tal, feeling a little uncertain as to what Rayburn was asking him.

"Called you to him?" countered Rayburn.

It was Risce that answered.

"He has spent a bit of time with Tal now Gareth, and as with me, he has gained a type of mental attuning. This allows him to give suggestions to those few people he can link with. He would not enter the camp as he is not part of the army and would consider it rude without prior notice."

"He is a strange one, if this warning was so important I would rather him have just come and told me." Replied Gareth.

"He is a Nightwalker Gareth, would you really want him to suddenly appear in your tent? You may have taken it the wrong way in the heat of the moment. Plus he is several hundred years old, manners were slightly different when he grew up." Said Khris, an amused look spreading across his face.

"Fine. Well lad what is this message of warning?"

Tal explained about the approaching army of Dark Cousins and that Vorlin wanted to have a meeting at the camp that night. After about half an hour of further questions, Rayburn acknowledged the request and agreed on the meeting.

"How are you going to get word to him Tal?" asked Rayburn, as Tal was about to leave. His brow lining with doubt, Khris spoke saving him the trouble of thinking of a way to pass Rayburn's acceptance on to Vorlin.

"I will let him know, I can get hold of him."

Nodding, Gareth Rayburn dismissed Tal and his staff to prepare for the ongoing journey into the heart of the Lost Lands.

The day passed uneventfully, if uncomfortably. Hazel had been more like her old self, Tal could not help thinking if it only took her getting angry with him to cheer her up, then she would never be upset for very long.

As they settled down for the night, Tal found himself thinking about Vorlin, would he again be called tonight? Would he be needed? He had not mentioned anything of the previous nights adventures to Hazel or Brad, they had enough to be thinking about without him giving them more.

Tal's guess about the cheese was almost accurate, they each had a small cut for lunch but the quartermaster had decided that what was left was far too mouldy to be able to salvage any more from. They were now surviving on basic trail rations and warm water. No fires had been lit since leaving Sarafell, the Mages would probably know they were coming – Tal knew for certain they did – but it was still best not to pin point their position to the enemy, and in such a barren land, even a single fire would be seen for many miles.

Sitting, leaning against Hazel with his arm around her, Tal rested his eyes. Somewhere amongst the Riders, someone was singing a ballad very softly, only the occasional note reaching Tal's ears. Brad was sitting opposite them, finishing his meal. Worryingly silent, Brad still harboured his sorrow at the loss of Cholla, refusing to let himself accept what had happened.

Tal felt exhausted, his exertions the previous night had caught up with him and he could not keep his eyes open for much longer. Kissing Hazel goodnight, he retired from the small gathering of Riders and entered his tent, giving himself willingly to the warm darkness of sleep.

Inside the command tent of the Riders, Rayburn sat and waited. The sun had set and he was expecting Vorlin shortly. He had wondered what agenda Vorlin worked to many times throughout the days ride. Gareth still had trouble trusting the Nightwalker, but Khris had vouched for him, and Rayburn trusted Khris. The argument about the end of the world should the Demons return was definitely a motivator for allies, but he still felt he was missing something of the picture.

The tent flap was pulled back and a Rider entered looking slightly uneasy.

"Vorlin Mansford and Dragon Rider Risce to see you my Lord." The sentry announced. Rayburn's time for contemplations had come to an end and as he ordered the Rider to permit entry, he took a deep breath to steady himself.

Khris entered first, he was in full plate armour, the bulk of which made him appear stocky and the way he moved reminded Rayburn how dangerous this man could be.

Vorlin followed, not in his brown robe, but in heavy chain with a steel body plate. At his side hung a scimitar and pinned to his shoulders was a knee-length riding cloak of black weave. His shoulder length hair was tied back into a short tail, and rather than the scholarly man in his brown robes, Vorlin now stood before Rayburn as a hardened warrior, his sharp blue eyes almost glowed in contrast to his pale skin as he inclined his head to Rayburn in greeting.

Khris gave a slight salute and took a seat in the corner of the tent to let Vorlin and Rayburn discuss what they needed to.

"You desired a meeting? Well you have it, please tell me what brings you here." Opened Gareth, still unsure how to address the Nightwalker.

"Indeed. I am sure Tal informed you of the approaching Dark Cousins?" at Rayburn's nod he continued, "I have ordered some of my kin to delay their progress. At present they will not reach you until tomorrow evening, unless you attack them first."

"What do you mean?" questioned Rayburn, curious now.

"They are not an assault force my Lord. They are about a hundred strong – probably less now – and they come in secret, their aim is to eliminate the leaders and commanding officers of the army, not wage a war. If you take a detachment of Riders from the army, and turn in the other direction, by mid day you can be waiting for them and destroy their threat before they reach the main army."

Rayburn thought about it, and though he still did not like to take military suggestions from a race that up until recently had been little more than an enemy themselves, he had to concede that Vorlin made a good point…if his intelligence was correct.

"Very well, Khris, are you happy to lead such a company?" The Dragon Rider grinned and nodded, giving his answer. "Alright, the company will be sent. Was there anything else Vorlin?"

"Yes my Lord, the thirty *Seicolantrai* that I sent to delay the Dark Cousins are from my own Coven. All are volunteers and we offer you what strength we may give, should your attack on the Mages occur at night."

Rayburn sat back in his chair. Certainly, this was not what he was expecting to hear tonight. Glancing to Khris, Gareth's eyes asked the same question that hid in his heart still, *can we trust him?* The slightest nod gave him the answer he needed.

Standing Rayburn offered Vorlin his hand, and shook it firmly.

"We would be honoured." He said.

Tal and his unit were waiting behind a rocky outcrop, there were three such units spread out around the area, under the command of Dragon Rider Risce, making a total of forty-six Riders.

They had just finished their breakfast when Rayburn had pulled Erikson aside and give them their mission. As the army pressed on to the Mages lair, the selected Riders had turned round and were making their way back along the trail that had been forged by themselves the week previously.

In the distance, they could see something moving, and dust being kicked up. As the approaching people grew closer, Tal could see it was two columns of Dark Cousins, jogging swiftly, across the Lost Lands. Tal was shocked at the speed of their movement, he knew he could not match their speed and stamina.

Erikson gave his unit a hand signal, and those skilled in archery knocked an arrow to their bows and stood ready.

Across from them, another unit was following the same pattern. Tal gripped his sword tighter and rearranged his armour on his shoulders.

The first Elf came jogging into the archer's line of fire. He was dressed in black leathers and wore a cloak of black wool. He did not look to either side, simply following the tracks of the army in the dusty earth.

Twenty Dark Cousins had passed between the two units of Riders before the first snap of a bow resounded. It was quickly followed by another twenty and each arrow found a target. Shouts in a strangely flowing, yet guttural language echoed as the Dark Cousins reacted to the surprise attack. Suddenly further screams could be heard at the back of the column of Elves. The third unit of Riders had made their way behind the Cousins and when the arrows had taken their marks, they struck and quickly started to dispatch those Elves at the rear of the group.

Tal watched from his hidden vantage point, he saw the Dark Cousins at the front turn to the rear and start to make a defensive line to stop the attack of the Riders they thought had ambushed them. When they were secure in their lines, Erikson's unit along with the other sniper group charged down towards the now evenly numbered Elves. When the Riders were only a short run from them they were spotted, in one voice they gave a battle cry that caused the remaining Elves to break. They were quickly dispatched and soon the Riders were alone again in the Lost Lands.

Tal wiped the blood from his sword. He was feeling much more confident with his weapon now, but it was not needed here. The fight had been brief and not one Rider was even wounded, so total was the surprise of the ambush.

Brad was breathing heavily, his eyes shone with an anger Tal had never seen before. When Hazel came over to make sure they were both ok, she pulled back from Brad, his face murderous. She looked at Tal, her concern obvious.

Slowly Brad calmed down, his features returning to his previous withdrawn state as Khris called for the Riders to return to the Army.

"I'm worried about Brad." Said Hazel quietly. Tal could only nod, his own mind wondering what he could do to help his friend. As they moved, he felt defeated. He could think of nothing.

Chapter 19

Assault

The night was clear.

In the cover of his tent, Tal lay awake. Around him, his fellow Riders slept soundly with the single exception of Brad. They had been moving towards the Lair of the Mages for nearly a fortnight now. Since the attack on the Dark Cousins, Brad had not been sleeping well. Each night he had tossed and turned, his mouth twisting in silent screams as he writhed on his bedroll.

By day, he had maintained his dark mood; he shunned Riders company in general and was increasingly quiet with his friends. They could reach the Mages Lair by midday if they pushed, and push they would. The army could not afford to let any of the Dark Lords escape with their secrets.

Tal got up. While his friend was suffering through sleep, he suffered through continuous lack of it. The night was warm, summer was no longer simply approaching. The first of the warm winds from the north had arrived the day previously, signifying that the sun had moved south.

Leaving his tent he walked the perimeter of the camp, trying to calm his mind. He sat on the ground, his thoughts wandering from Brad and his withdrawal, to Hazel and the feel of her hand in his, to the Mages that were waiting just hours away. The weight of the world seemed to weigh heavy on his young shoulders and his spirits were slowly being dragged down to the darkness of despair.

"You worry when you should be sleeping." Came a soft voice from just outside the lights boundary. A dark shape emerged, and Vorlin took a seat next to Tal.

"Not easy the night before a Siege on an underground fortress." Replied Tal, his mind once more remembering his flight through the underground maze following Khris to freedom.

"True, I cannot sleep myself."

Tal's mind stopped racing, suddenly becoming empty. He turned to Vorlin to see the man had a slight smile on his face. The usually stoic Nightwalker had told a joke, and it had taken Tal completely unaware.

Shaking his head to clear it, Tal let out a soft chuckle, his fatigue momentarily forgotten.

"What brings you here Vorlin?" He asked when the Nightwalkers face settled back to its neutral cover once more.

"I was going to wake up Rayburn, and ask him to bring the Riders to the Mages Lair. Though now you can do it, I'm sure he would rather you wake him than me." The Nightwalker sat in silence, waiting for the question he knew Tal had to ask.

"Why do we need to go to the fortress now?"

"Because it is already under siege." Vorlin stood and gripped Tal's shoulder gently. Releasing it, he moved back into the darkness that he first emerged from.

With a low groan, Tal stood. His muscles ached from a hard fortnight riding and the previous days skirmish. Now when he really needed sleep, he had to wake up his Lord and then press on to assist in the assault of a subterranean fortress. This was going to be a long day.

The night was fading. The Riders had been summoned to order as soon as Tal had spoken to Rayburn. Several Rangers had volunteered their services when they saw the Riders preparing, and a few Seers had joined the procession as they left the main army camp.

They were within an hour of the Mages fortress when Tal counted their numbers. There were two hundred Riders, twenty Rangers and ten Seers. The rest of the Army would follow as soon as it could be mobilised. At the columns head was Rayburn and his senior Officers, Tal was directly behind them, in the first rank of Riders, Hazel and Brad flanked him in tired silence.

It must have been about four hours past midnight, and the darkness would only last an hour more before the grey of the approaching dawn would chase it away for another day. Tal looked out ahead of them, there was a faint glow on the horizon, a faint flickering a couple of miles distant.

"What's that?" he asked almost to himself.

"Looks like a fire Lad." Said Lay, his spirit bright despite the hour and looming danger.

"Looks like we found the fortress." Said Kelar.

"Looks like we found a fight." Said Erikson, his hand checking the sword strapped to his waist.

Rayburn called a halt and turned his mount to face his men, his voice carrying deep into the night.

"I know this is unplanned! I know you may feel we are outnumbered without the rest of the troops with us! But we are Riders! We are the best the Kingdom has! And though the odds are stacked against us, we only have to keep a breech open until the rest of the Army arrives, I could do that with half of you!

"So we ride to battle, for our Brothers and Sisters! For the people of this land! For the King! And for the entire human race!" Rayburn finished his speech by raising his sword aloft, moonlight glinting off the blade as he turned his mount towards the besieged fortress and set off with the cheers of his Riders following him.

Tal felt swept along with the passion of his colleagues, his own sword was in his hand, and his horse was carrying him swiftly towards the enemy with Hazel at his side. His heart was pounding, adrenaline giving him a focus he had never known in the sixteen years of his life.

He turned his head to the right, from just behind him, Brad was urging his horse faster, slowly edging ahead of Tal and closing on Rayburn. The look on Brad's face was one of grim determination, Tal knew that he would hold the Mages responsible for Cholla's death, and he worried for his friend's safety.

One hundred yards from the main stairwell to the fortress, half the Riders veered away from the column, and moved into positions surrounding extremes of the Lair while their comrades continued towards the entrance. Ten Rangers and five Seers scattered around the site, providing magical assistance to the supporting Riders.

Rayburn approached the entrance, flames were raging from ventilation holes in the ground all around the area of the fortress, the stairs that led down into the lair itself were bright with the same flames. Leaping from his horse Rayburn was the first to enter the fortress, Erickson's unit following close behind.

Tal's heart missed a beat as he recognised the same stairs he and Brad had fled up all those weeks ago. He felt an exploring sensation in his mind and recognised the tentative touch of a *joining*. He let his mind merge with his fellow Riders and felt the combined senses of the invaders race through him. Focusing on the lead member, he found himself seeing through Rayburn's eyes.

"Lord Rayburn, I am Mikael Tagus. Vorlin has instructed me to aide you in any way I can and to ensure there are no mistakes between our men. We are currently holding this first level, but the Mages have fortified the levels below us, and while we have some skill at using magic, it is not sufficient to break through the Mages defences."

Tal's focus returned to his own body as he descended the steps and came abreast with Gareth Rayburn and the Nightwalker called Mikael Tagus.

"We can handle the hand to hand fighting, but we need your Seers skill to help us get within striking distance of the Mages, and as you no doubt know, dawn is rapidly approaching." The Nightwalker finished.

"Very well. We only have five Seers at present the rest will be here by noon. Are you happy for us to hold the current situation and wait for reinforcements? It will mean that you are stuck here until tonight." Rayburn replied, his voice showing that he understood that if the allies lost their foothold in the fortress the Nightwalkers would be left to the mercy of the Mages or the daylight.

"That is acceptable, we will wait. We are aware of the risks Lord Rayburn, and all here are volunteers."

Rayburn nodded. He called back to the Seers that were coming down the stairs into the fortress. Unlike their usual white robes, they now wore white leggings and tunics, covered in a hardened and bleached leather jerkin.

When they reached Rayburn, he gave instructions that they were to accompany split units of Riders and Nightwalkers and assist in the securing of the stairwells that led down into the heart of the underground fortress.

Although there were five Seers, the first level had ten possible accesses to the next floor. Erikson's unit was assigned a Seer and two Rangers to patrol an area that was currently being held by six Nightwalkers.

Rayburn was led off by Mikael to the area that Vorlin was holding as the command post, while Erikson set off towards his patrol zone with Tal and his unit. As they moved through the Mages Lair, Tal saw the telltale signs of fighting that had resulted in the Mages being pushed back to the lower levels.

Robed bodies littered the halls they transited, some with throats torn out, but most either cut down by various weapons or merely slumped on the floor in unnatural positions. The stone walls were blackened by magical energy as the Mages had tried to repulse the Nightwalkers.

"A real arena down here." Said Brad looking around at the bodies and blood that covered the floor. His face was hard, his eyes constantly scanning the local area for any trouble.

From around the next corner, a snarl resounded followed by a scream and sounds of a fight. A ball of flame came tearing up the hall the struggle was coming from, impacting with the wall ahead of Tal.

The Seers moved to the front of the unit, flanked with the Rangers and a slight blue haze appeared ahead of Erikson's unit. They motioned the Riders forward as they rounded the corner. Tal rounded the bend in the fortress and saw a group of twenty Mages throwing magical blasts at five Nightwalkers. One of the magical assaults struck the blue barrier in front of the Riders, dissipating immediately.

The Nightwalkers were like a blur, moving between the Mages, knives, short swords or claws tearing at the Mages, causing blood to spurt from any limb that the Mages failed to protect. For each ball of fire the Mages sent at the attackers, a Nightwalker gained the opening it needed to finish him, leaving another body twitching on the floor.

A scream of rage from Tal's side caused him to turn, seeing Brad rush forward pushing through the Seers barrier of protection and into the middle of the fray. The Mages were unaware of this new assailant and were taken by surprise. Within ten seconds the Mages had lost three of their number to Brad alone, the Nightwalkers ending the lives of a further seven as their attention was caught by the Rider and his screams.

The remaining Mages pulled back behind an invisible shield that prevented the Nightwalkers and Brad from getting close to them. Turning, they fled down the hallway and down to the lower levels again, leaving their fallen behind as a grim testimony of their attempt to retake the first level.

The Seers lowered their barriers allowing the Riders to move up the hallways faster than they previously could. Erikson approached the Nightwalkers with a stern look to Brad.

"I am Captain Erikson of the Dragon Riders. I have been ordered to assist you in maintaining this area until the Kingdom army arrives to reinforce us."

"Greetings Captain, the Mages keep attacking in groups of about twenty. So far, we have been able to hold them down fairly well, but we have lost one of our number. They cannot keep the same tactics up for long, they are losing their numbers too quickly. We expect some major push soon."

Erikson nodded, agreeing with the analysis after witnessing the Nightwalkers in action. Tal looked round and fell silent. He noticed Brad was wearing a haunted expression and wondered if he had the same look on his face.

"What is it Tal?" asked Lay, all the joviality now gone from his face.

"I have been here before, when Brad and I escaped from the Demons world, this is the way we left the fortress."

"That might be useful, do you think you could find your way back to where the Gate is?" Layland had pulled Tal aside, letting Erikson consult with the Nightwalkers.

"I might, we left in a rush but between Brad and me, we might remember."

Nodding, Layland called Brad over. The young Rider looked a little calmer but Tal was sure that was only on the surface.

"Brad, Tal thought that you and he might be able to find your way back to the Gate room. Do you think you could?"

Brad nodded at once, obviously sure in his own mind.

"Ok, let's go." Layland moved over to Erikson, and whispered into his ear. The Captain nodded and said something to one of the Nightwalkers.

In a couple of minutes Tal, Brad and Layland, along with a Nightwalker and a Ranger were standing at the top of the stairs. No sounds could be heard from below but through the *joining* Tal was aware of several Mages watching the access to the level against the possibility of a further push.

There was an explosion from a few halls away, doors rattling in their frames and sounds of alarm could be heard from below. Four Mages could be sensed moving from their positions at the bottom of the stairs, the other three could be sensed changing position to better cover the access.

Layland nodded and they started to slowly descend with their weapons ready. The Nightwalker was next to Lay with the Ranger and Tal following and Brad bringing up the rear. When they reached the point that they would be seen if they moved lower, Lay started to shift. In a couple of seconds, all Tal could make out was a blurry outline of where he stood. In one fluid movement Lay disappeared into the Mages level. Tal counted to five then saw the Nightwalker move faster than was humanly possible to follow Kendrik onto the second level. At that point a shout was given off and two distinct moans gave away that both Lay and the Nightwalker had taken their targets out.

Tal, Brad and the Ranger followed their colleagues into the Mages stronghold, arriving in time to see the last Mage get cut down by Lays sword.

"Right were in, which way do we go lads?" Asked Kendrik, his figure remaining blurred.

"That way." Said Brad without hesitation, pointing to a hallway that led deeper into the fortress.

They set off at a brisk walk. The Riders sense of the area giving them fore warning if a group of Mages were approaching them, giving them ample time to set an ambush before continuing their march towards the Gate at the very bottom of the compound.

They had moved down two further levels. The frequency of Mages was getting lighter, their main forces being at the levels directly below the Rider controlled area. The few Mages they did come across were getting tougher, strengthened by dark magics that had cost humans their lives. They had not yet come across any of the Dark Lords, or Ones of Impurity, and this was starting to worry Layland, even if he did not voice his concerns to the others.

"How much farther Brad?" asked Layland. Brad had been moving with clear purpose the entire time, Tal had not been sure of his whereabouts from the second level, but his friend seemed to have a map burned into his mind.

"We only have one more level to go down before we reach the stairs that lead directly to the altar chamber." Said Brad, his voice steady but his eyes strangely unfocused.

Layland nodded and moved off in front of the party again, the Nightwalker only slightly behind him.

They had been moving for a couple of minutes towards the steps that led down to the final floor of the complex when Tal called a halt. His senses were stretched out as far as he could and he noted a blackness at the boundary of his awareness.

"What is it Tal?" said Lay coming back to the young Rider. No one there doubted Tal's talent with mental abilities.

"There is something a few halls away. Its alone, but it is coming up as a blackness rather than as a Mage would." Replied Tal, sounding a little concerned.

Kendrik turned to the Nightwalker, his face solemn. "It could be a One, or a Dark Lord. Are you ready?"

The man nodded, checking the grip on his knives.

"Tal link with me personally, I want to know where this creature is." Nodding, Tal focussed on Kendrik, linking with him and allowing him to access the picture of the surrounding area that Tal's senses gave him.

I see him. Said Kendrik, his voice clear inside Tal's head.

Kendrik moved off towards the unknown man, the Nightwalker directly behind him. The rest of the party continued behind the two advance warriors, the Ranger using his small skills to try to cover their approach.

The darkness was moving away from them in a direction that indicated they were unnoticed.

Can we let him go? Thought Tal to Kendrick.

No, we have a trail of bodies littering the floor all the way up. It's a risk that a normal Mage on this level would come across the bodies, if this thing sees them, he will know were here and then he has the advantage. We need to take him out.

Tal understood and readied himself. The party set off after their target, trying to keep their position hidden. Whatever they were tracking was making for the stairs that led to the upper levels. They were slowly gaining on him, but there were too many halls between them, he would very shortly come across the bodies of the Mages.

The dark object turned into one of the halls that the Riders had previously transited. Layland's form solidified and he sprinted ahead followed easily by the Nightwalker. Tal understood, the time for subtlety was past, a roar from two corridors away gave the identity of the darkness. It was not a Dark Lord, it was a One of Impurity.

Tal shivered, he had never seen one of these feared creatures before, and this was not the place he would have picked for his first encounter.

Where would I have picked? He thought, his mood as dark as the object they were now stalking.

Sounds of exertion floated towards Tal as he turned into hall that contained the One and his colleagues. He stalled for just a brief moment as what he saw registered.

Layland and the Nightwalker were moving so quickly Tal found it hard to keep up with their actions. The One was moving faster than either, keeping their attacks at bay even though it stopped him from attacking himself. Tal judged that it would probably be no more than a matter of time before Kendrik or the Nightwalker made a mistake and that would lead to both dying at the hands of the One.

The Impure One himself was like a black shadow, his white skin in sharp contrast to the blackness of his hair and the redness of his eyes. The cloak he was wearing was heavy and he used it as a deflective aid to hinder the attacks of his assailants.

Tal started moving cautiously towards the fight, getting ready to move in if an opening presented itself. Kendrick's sword swung at the chest of the One, it simply found the empty space where he once stood. With a sharp kick, Layland found himself landing hard against a wall, the One flying through the air towards him. Tal ran, he had no choice, if he did not act, then Layland would be dead soon. The Nightwalker sensed this as well, throwing himself at the One with a snarl. Both Tal and Nightwalker realised they would be too late.

With a cry of despair, Tal pushed that little bit harder. Praying he would reach the evil creature before the fatal strike could land. As he neared the One of Impurity, Tal felt a brush of air past his cheek, a knife found itself buried up to the hilt in the Ones side, causing him to falter enough that Layland could duck out of the way.

A second knife flew past Tal, cutting into the neck of the One. The Nightwalker took advantage of the confusion of the creature to tear out his neck, the body of the One slumping to the ground, dark blood oozing from the creature. As it tried to stand, Kendrik took a sword to it, severing the head and then plunging the blade into the creature's heart.

Tal was forced to pull himself up hard as he reached the site of the carnage. Looking at Layland, he saw the Rider was breathing hard.

"That was not easy. I don't want to have to do that again." He said with an exhausted grin.

The struggle had been brief but furious. It had lasted no longer than a couple of minutes, but both Kendrik and the Nightwalker were drained from the conflict, and should either have faced it alone, they would most certainly have been killed.

"Do we continue?" asked the Nightwalker

"We have no choice, we could retreat but then we have gained nothing other than the deaths of a few Mages." Replied Layland.

"It is only a guess, but you should be aware that the concentration of the Ones and quite probably the Dark Lords can only increase from here."

"Understood, we go on." Said Lay, his face strong and determined.

The group backtracked to the point they had reached previously, Tal once again searching ahead for any signs of trouble. They were only a few halls away from the stairs to the next level when Tal called a halt. From the floors above, the alarm had been sounded. Shouts were raised, and the life signs of the Mages could be felt swarming in search patterns.

"They will be able to track us by their dead." Said Tal as Lay readied himself, his face becoming concerned.

"Then we need to move, get us to the stairs Brad." Came Lays response, as he motioned Brad on ahead.

The group moved swiftly, their weapons ready against any unforeseen assaults. They turned a corner and came face to face with a man wrapped in a deep grey cloak, his eyes were dead and his features weathered. The man seemed as shocked as the Riders at the meeting, and it took him a couple of seconds to respond. Throwing his arms up, a bolt of energy was sent towards the party of Riders. The action based on instinct and nothing more, gave Tal and his friends chance to dodge the blast and attack themselves. The Nightwalker wasted no time in leaping towards the Mage, his knives slashing at him, but doing no more than cutting his robe.

Tal ran forward, his sword slicing down as the Mage lifted his arms to retaliate again. The edge of the sword bit deep into the Mages arm, causing him to fall to the floor in pain, Tal finished it quickly with a cut to the Mages throat.

"Quickly done Tal." Said Layland approvingly, "Why didn't you sense him?"

"I don't know, maybe they can shield themselves?" came Tal's response.

Layland looked at the Mages face, slowly the skin started to flake away and turn to dust. In no more than ten heartbeats, the Mage was nothing more than a pile of dirt on the floor.

"Well he isn't your normal Mage by the looks of things but he isn't a Dark Lord. Maybe the more experienced in dark magic they become the more gifts are available to them. It doesn't matter, we have to keep moving just be careful, at least we can sense the Ones of Impurity." They nodded and moved on at a slower pace, knowing that their biggest advantage of knowing what was coming, was now in question.

Brad was once again leading the party, as they approached the last corner in this maze of a level. He glanced around the corner and saw that there were eight of the older Mages guarding the top of the stairs.

"We cant get down, there are eight of those powerful Mages guarding the way." Said Brad, his anger obvious in his quiet voice.

Lay let a fist slam against a wall, at a loss of what to do next.

Rayburn was speaking with Mikael Tagus and Vorlin Mansford when the explosion sounded. He instantly merged his awareness with the Riders close to him, in turn being connected to the web of awareness that ran through the upper level.

Gareth sent out his query to the blast. In moments, he was informed that Sergeant Kendrick along with Tal and Brad had descended into the lower levels. The explosion was a diversion to allow them to slip down and try to discover the Gate room.

Rayburn quickly relayed that information to the Nightwalkers that he was with. Vorlin stepped forward, his eyes seemed distant, "We need to help them, they cannot avoid detection for long. We only have about four hours until the rest of the Kingdom forces arrive, so until then we have to make feinting strikes down to the lower levels to draw attention away from Kendrik."

Moving over to a map of the floor they were on, Vorlin pointed to a selection of stairs that led down.

"Without knowing what Kendrik plans to do when he gets to the Gate room, we can't plan a comprehensive strategy, but trusting he knows that, we can give him some extra cover, allowing him to get there in the first place.

"If we make strikes at these points, lasting no more than a few moments, killing enough of the Mages before retreating that they need to keep reinforcing them, the flow of their personnel might give your Riders enough cover to move down and do whatever they wanted to."

Rayburn nodded, the plan appeared sound enough. He passed the order on to the Riders in the fortress and waited for the first strike to occur. The Nightwalkers, Seers and Riders made pushes into the second level, each time they struck they left a heavy toll of bodies before the Mages made them retreat.

In fact, it was not always an act that they had to retreat, the Mages held a strong force on the lower levels and they were fanatical about the defence of their home.

Kendrik had pulled the group back into one of the rooms that led from the confusing series of hallways that made up the Mages fortress. He was pacing back and forth trying to come up with an answer to the situation. If they waited for backup, the Mages would find them without a doubt.

"What are we to do?" asked the Nightwalker.

"I don't know, any ideas are welcome."

Tal was just about to speak when he felt massive movement from this level and the one lower.

"Something is happening." He said simply.

"Show me." Said Lay, his voice steady. Tal let his senses reach Layland, the movement of dozens of Mages and several Ones of Impurity caused him to draw his sword, the rest of the party copying his example.

"There is a large force of Mages being led by Ones of Impurity heading towards us. If they know were here, we are finished. Get ready."

Very shortly, the sounds of feet running up the stairs and along hallways could be heard getting louder. Tal's heart was racing as the company spread out in an arc behind the door.

Closer came the sound of boots on the hard floor. His breath held until it burned in his chest, Tal's sword tip came up, ready to fight for his life. As the echoing sound reached the door everyone visibly tensed. Sweat beaded on each of their foreheads, with the exception of the Nightwalker who had a dangerous glint in his eyes.

The Mages did not stop. The sound of footfalls continued passed the hiding place of the Riders. As they vanished into the distance Tal sank to the floor, his breath exploding in a ragged gasp as he struggled to compose himself.

"I don't understand." Said Brad, not willing to move from the spot he was rooted to.

"There is something else at play here. That is not a routine move of forces, that was an assault force." Said Layland, "If there were forces like that moving up all the other stairs as well, then there could be a serious attempt at the first level, and with our current level of manning, it's probable the Mages will succeed."

The Ranger who had remained quiet throughout the whole incursion spoke with a gruff voice. "We have two options, go back and try to help, or head down to the Gate room. But make the choice fast, if we sit for too long, we die."

Layland looked to the Nightwalker, his eyes asking his opinion. With a slight shrug, the man gave all the answer Kendrik needed.

"We won't make a difference up top, we have to go on." He said, his voice tight with anger. Leaving the room the party crept to the corner before the stairs again. Layland blurred his form and slipped round. The fluttering torches on the walls gave the hazy outline of Layland a spectral quality as he vanished from sight.

A few moments later, sounds of bodies slumping to the floor could be heard. Tal rushed round ready to back up his Sergeant, but four Mages were lying on the floor with their throats cut, and the stairs were open to them. Signalling the others, Tal moved up to Layland who solidified again.

Lay smiled at the young Rider, he had rushed round, without any real protection and not knowing what he would face in order to help his friend.

Stepping onto the stairs Lay looked round, everyone was tense and he saw that the strain was starting to affect the men. As they moved down he blurred himself motioning the others to wait until he had inspected the hall at the bottom. Slipping down further, he looked left and right, there were four directions he could take from here, two of them doubling back on the stairs. Moving to the right, he turned the corner, the sound of his heel scraping on the floor caused a Mage that was guarding the stairs to turn.

Kendrik did not have time to worry about detection. In one fluid movement, his sword sliced the Mages neck, nearly severing it. Falling to the ground, his life's blood spilling onto the floor the Mage let out a gurgling sound that caused Lay to wince at its volume.

From behind, the sound of a body collapsing caused him to turn rapidly, his heart in his throat. A second blurred figure was standing behind the Mage, his sword invisible but the blood giving it form, as it protruded from the mans chest.

The Mage on the floor behind Lay slowly turned to dust, followed moments later by the Mage held upright by the invisible sword. As the Necromancer decomposed around the blade, the Rider slowly regained his form.

Tal stood with a hard expression on his face his sword lowering slowly.

"Now just when did you learn to do that lad?" said Lay, a slightly amused look on his face.

"When we left here last time, it sort of just happened. I guess I remembered how I did it." Replied Tal, his voice as hard as his face.

"What's wrong Tal? You're not your usual self right now." said Kendrik softly as he approached the Rider.

"It's Hazel, she is still up top. Whatever forces are being sent up, they will be attacking her."

Layland nodded, he could understand Tal's fear for his girl. He had felt the same thing a fair few years ago. He sent Tal to get the rest of the group, and they started to move towards the final stairs that led into the altar room with the Gate.

Layland wondered what he was going to do when they arrived. He prayed to any God kind enough to be listening that something would present itself in time.

Hazel flinched, a bolt of energy exploded into the barrier erected by the Seer she was with, sparks crackling over the surface and dancing like lightening. The Mages had made a push up into the first level, backed by the strength of the Ones of Impurity. So far, they had only succeeded in regaining the stairs, but they were going to take the level, it was only a matter of time. The Riders had been told to delay the inevitable for as long as possible.

Back up was only two hours away. One of the Seers had been bright enough to wait until one hour before dawn and then alert the main army as to the situation, they had then set off as fast as they could. Hazel could have kissed that Seer, he had given the army enough time to be fresh and cut down the time before they were reinforced.

Each time the Mages cast their assaults it took something out of them. They needed to draw back and regroup. That usually let one of the Seers attack them from behind the safety of the shield. Rarely it came to anything other than a stand off, unless one of the Ones became involved, then there was an all out struggle which had an even chance of leading to casualties on either side.

As the Mage retired to the rear of his assault group one of the Seers with the party let fly with a bolt of lightning that was deflected by another of the Mages. The stand off persisted. Hazel had done nothing more than provide an extra body since the push started. She felt as though she should force through the safety of the shield and take the fight into the hands of the Mages themselves.

Every time she hefted her sword to charge, she heard the command of Lord Rayburn. *Stay behind the safety of the shields, we can only delay the inevitable, there is no need to throw lives away.*

The Mages fell back. The routine was not new, they would fall back and a fresh party would push forward, gaining a little more of the level.

Preparing for the new group, Hazel took a deep breath. The worn group stepped aside; from behind them came a group of four pale skinned Ones. The Seer stepped back, before the Ones had only fought singularly, as the leaders of strike forces. This was the first time they would fight in unison.

In one shockingly fast move, the Ones had closed the distance to the shield of the Seers, testing its strength with their claws. The Seer was frozen with fear, holding the shield was the only thing he was interested in at that moment. The lead One placed his clawed fist against the barrier between the Riders and his own men and started to push. The Seer found himself being pushed back by the force exerted by the One of Impurity, his feet sliding along the floor as he struggled to hold the barrier against the undead General.

The One drew back his fist and levelled a punch at the very centre of the wall. With lightening crackling over the surface, the shield gave way in an explosive fashion. The Seer was sent flying backwards into the Ilan brothers who collapsed under his weight. The Ones stood two abreast in the hall, looking at the Riders who were now defenceless.

Hazel, Kelar, and Shan-Yin Hito spread out covering the hall themselves. From behind Mathew and Martin laid the body of the now dead Seer on the floor and placed their swords next to him, drawing their bows.

Two arrows flew between the Riders to strike the Ones square in the chest. They stumbled back, but showed no other sign of the impact. In quick succession four further arrows sped past, leaving three cloth-yard shafts sticking out from the chest of the front two Ones.

A dark laugh emanated from the throat of the Impure Ones, the sound sending a chill down the corridor to the Riders. Placing their bows on the floor, Mathew and Martin collected their broadswords and stood just behind the other three Riders.

The two sides stood facing each other, none moving, both waiting for the first move to be made. Hazel's thoughts drifted to Tal briefly, wondering how far he had got, hoping he was still safe.

The lapse of concentration was almost fatal. The Ones sensing the momentary slip made their move. The first two Ones struck fast, pushing the Riders back easily, the second two merely walking behind their unnatural brothers, not needed for this trivial task.

"Hold them! We must hold them!" Came the call from the back. Erikson had arrived from the second front he had to maintain. Two Nightwalkers flew directly into the fray, their knives tearing at the Ones viciously. A snarl from the two Ones at the rear was all the warning the retreating Riders had before the fight expanded into carnage. Four Ones of Impurity and a squad of Riders and Nightwalkers slashed at each other, small wounds being s scored by each side, neither gaining any advantage.

Slowly, the Riders were losing ground if not the fight. The Ones were outnumbered but their power was greater. One of the Nightwalkers got close enough to take a large gouge out of one of the Ones sides, dark blood oozing from the wound. With a quick counter strike, the One snapped the neck of the Nightwalker, his body falling limp on the ground.

Pull back, retreat to the main entrance! The command was from Rayburn. Throughout the level, the Mages had been making similar pushes; most had been successful, with the Mages and Ones overrunning the Riders and Seers.

Their last hope was to retreat to a defensible position and to consolidate their forces. Outside the daylight was getting brighter by the minute, the Nightwalkers were now trapped in the fortress, the allied forces needed to hold the entrance halls, not only to ensure their assault had a chance to succeed, but to give the Nightwalkers any chance of survival.

Hazel and the Riders pulled back, each fighting furiously, swords blocking claws and slashing in retaliation. Her arms were burning with exertion, they had a long way to defend themselves before they would reach any kind of reinforcements, and she was sure that before they got there, more Mages would join the attack.

Wiping the sweat from her brow, hazel pulled back allowing one of the Nightwalkers to step in and give her a few seconds of respite before she would be engaged again. With a deep breath, she lifted her sword said a quick prayer to Telkhan the God of War, and gave a quick thought for Tal before entering into the melee once again.

Chapter 20

Answers

Colonel Ambla climbed off his horse. His men were worried and he did not blame them. They had passed the outer sentries a few minutes back and were now moving towards the main entrance to the Mages fortress. General Peterson had set up a command post just this side of the sentry ring, and Colonel Ambla had been sent in to gain intelligence from Lord Rayburn and to reinforce where he could.

His brief conversation with the sentries had lowered his spirits. At first the call from the General had filled him with optimism, the Riders had set off late in the night to aid an assault by the Nightwalkers of all creatures. But the Riders alone did not have the numbers to hold the level, and when the Mages and Ones had retaliated with a greater force, the allies were forced to pull back and concentrate on holding the first few halls and the main entrance to the lair.

The Colonel started to descend the stairs and was met by a tired Rider. The woman had several cuts and her right arm was in a make shift sling. Colonel Ambla saluted the Rider, who could only nod in greeting. She led him and his men down one hall and into a room that had Lord Rayburn and about ten Nightwalkers inside. Checking his sword subconsciously, Ambla walked over to Rayburn and saluted. The Lord of the Riders returned the salute and shook the Officers hand, grateful to see him.

"It's good to see you Colonel, we are sorely outnumbered at the moment but we only have three fronts that need to be held for now. Nightwalkers are assisting where they can, but with the daylight, it is safer for them to remain closed here. I need to you send fifty men to each of the fronts to relieve my Riders. The Seers are going to increase their presence as well. Where is General Peterson?"

Colonel Ambla gave the Generals location, and ordered his own men to go and relieve the Riders that were fatigued from hours of conflict. Rayburn left the Lair and took in his first breath of fresh air for what seemed an age. The light was almost painfully bright after the dim light of the subterranean fortress where the only source of illumination had been torches and the fires that blazed in furnished areas of the compound.

As Gareth arrived at the command post, Peterson greeted him warmly. Rayburn explained the situation to the General and where he had posted Colonel Ambla and his men. Offering his friend a seat, Peterson poured some freshly brewed tea and joined him. Rayburn needed to relax and Peterson could not think of a better way at the moment. Whilst they were discussing the different options available to them, the High Seer made himself known. He was a slight man, with an almost timid personality, but his intellect was well known for its acuteness and his magical skill was second only to the Lord High Seer's.

He informed them that he had sent thirty of his Brothers along with an equal number of Rangers to relieve the Seers that were still alive inside the fortress.

The conversation became a lengthy discussion on tactics and strategy. The three men in charge of the offensive knew that whilst they had to hold the entrance to the fortress at all costs, they were now in a much better position to accomplish this, and that in itself gave Rayburn a reason to relax slightly. It was going to take a while to get the army into a solid position ready for a concerted push into the depths of the fortress, and all three knew they would have a lot to plan until they were ready.

Sergeant Layland Kendrik snapped the neck of a Mage that had left a room they were passing. They had been walking past the door when a the Mage had left in a hurry, the man flew straight into Lay, knocking him flying, his sword spinning across the floor. The two fell into a heap on the floor, arms and legs flailing as they wrestled. Every time the Mage tried to focus his mind to create a spell, a heavy clout to his temple by Layland scrambled his thoughts and once again he lashed out blindly, trying to best his opponent.

Rolling on top of the Mage, Kendrick used his greater strength to end the struggle with a loud snap, the man falling to the floor and starting to turn to the dust that was becoming common at the lower level. Retrieving his sword, Lay worked his jaw, the Mage was not a wrestler – and Lay wished he had taken more time to study the style now – but he had managed to land a solid blow to his chin that now throbbed dully.

"At least there are no bodies to disclose our presence here." Said the Nightwalker as he helped Layland to his feet.

"How far off the Gate room are we Brad?" asked Lay, nodding to thank the Nightwalker.

"Not far, only a couple more halls." He replied, his voice still dark and strangely distant. The party pressed on.

The halls were becoming increasingly populated, with groups of Mages moving in hurried pace, causing the small group of insurgents to dive into any room they were close to, in order to hide when such a party came into contact with them. Several times the rooms they hid in themselves had several Mages in, and the rooms quickly erupted into carnage as whatever the Mages were involved in became quickly forgotten in the slash of steel.

"Why haven't we come across more Mages?" Asked the Ranger, his concern showing at the major lack of numbers in this level. "Surely we should not be able to move for the foul creatures down here?"

"I think most have been sent up to retake the upper level, and then posted close by to ensure that we cannot take it again. I think we got lucky and the main strength of the Mages passed us before when we were hiding in that room. Even so, lets not get overly confident shall we?" answered Lay, his eyes still searching the halls for trouble, his senses still reading Tal's mental search just in case the young Rider missed anything.

The five men moved cautiously through the halls, feeling the effect of the constant fighting wearing at their muscles. After two more turns and another confrontation with a group of four Mages, Brad halted the company. In a whispered voice, he indicated that the door down to the Gate room was around the next bend and along the hallway.

Lay nodded and blurred himself. Looking around the corner, he noted the number of Mages and Ones guarding the door. Cursing to himself, he ducked back and un-blurred to speak with his comrades.

"Well I knew there were two Ones, but we also have a further eight Mages guarding the door. I wouldn't be surprised if a couple were Dark Lords either."

The group seemed to hold their breath, it had been hard enough to take a single One of Impurity, and the powerful Mages were enough trouble in number before adding the Dark Lords into the equation.

"What do we do?" asked Brad, his voice concerned, showing emotion for the first time Tal could remember since they had left Sarafell.

"We can't take them straight on, we would never survive. I think we should try to attack from both sides." Turning to the Nightwalker he raised an eyebrow. "Unless you have any objections, you and I should probably try to get to the other end of this hall, when we are in position I can call to Tal and Brad. Tal and I can try to sneak up on the position and take out the two Ones while we are blurred. If we are lucky, we might be able to kill a couple of the Mages as well before they realise what is occurring. When we start, the rest of you will have to do your best to close the distance and assist us."

When no one objected, Lay nodded, gave Tal and Brad a slap on the back, and turned and headed back into the depth of the compound with the Nightwalker following silently.

Tal turned to Brad and the Ranger, his face expressing the worry he was sure they all felt. This could easily be the end of the war for them, and Tal might never see Hazel again.

Closing his eyes, he searched for Kendrik. Feeling the familiar sensation of his mind, Tal quickly *joined* with him, giving Lay a reference point that he could use to steer himself to the other end of the hallway.

The time seemed to drag for Tal, each minute that passed seemed to last for an eternity. He noticed Brad suffering the same worry, the lines in his brow deepening each time he looked up and down the hall. The Ranger pulled out his knives and tested them, flipping them in his hand and checking the edge over and over. His short sword came out of his scabbard repeatedly, the weight being felt and the balance examined.

Tal's mind was still searching when he felt two Mages approaching from the other direction, heading towards the Gate room.

His hand hefted his sword, and he noticed Brad stiffening at the same instant. Calling silently to Lay, Tal asked him where he was.

We are making slow progress, we keep encountering Mages, just hold there until we are ready.

Tal sent that they would be fighting Mages themselves very shortly and to hurry in case those that were guarding the Gate room head the struggle. A quick affirmation was the only reply that he received, so Tal took lead of the party and headed up towards the corner the Mages were about to round.

Blurring his form, Tal waited for the first Mage to turn. He could feel them as the Mages approached, at least these were not the more powerful of the Mages that could take them by surprise. A thought hit him at that moment; there could be more than just the two that he could not sense. He considered turning back and trying to find a room to hide in, but there was no time. The first of the two Mages was about to turn the corner.

Moving to the outer wall Tal made a gamble, he would be able to see how many they would be facing, but if the Mages were paying attention they would also see his blurred outline against the stone walls.

Luck had favoured them, there were only two Mages, but they had troubled expressions on their faces. Clearly, something had upset them. Were they rushing to report the number of piles of dust lying around the labyrinth of halls? Tal could not risk them getting to the Ones a few hundred yards away. Pressing himself against the wall, he waited, his breath held deep within his chest as they passed him without noticing, all their attention focused on getting whatever message they were carrying to their superiors.

Slipping his knife from his belt, he crept up behind them. Where were Brad and the Ranger? Right now it did not matter, pulling his blade up to throat height, he steadied his nerves and pulled the mans throat back, slicing it with one powerful cut. The man gurgled and fell to the floor, Tal holding him tight. The second Mage turned and looked on in confusion as his colleague laid bleeding and suffocating to death on the floor. Two knives appeared from nowhere to embed deep into the second Mages back, he let out a scream as he turned toward his tormentor, allowing Tal to use his knife to silence the man.

Tal saw the Ranger and Brad only a short way down the corridor, they had hidden in a room until Tal had dispatched the first Mage and confused the second. Tal rushed passed the Rider and Ranger, still blurred to see if the scream had attracted the attention of the guards.

As he slipped his head round the corner, he saw a One give a hissing command to two of the Mages. They bowed to the nightmarish creature and set off in a rush to investigate the scream.

Tal, sent a message to Brad through the *joining*, he waited until his friend acknowledged before hiding in a room at the end of the hall just before the corner. He spotted Brad and the Ranger picking up the bodies of the Mages and pulling them into the room they had just hidden in, closing the door just before the other Mages turned the corner.

Tal watched as the two more powerful Mages walked up the hall slowly, eyes looking for the slightest thing out of the ordinary. When they reached the room that Tal was hiding in, he held his breath again, his heart racing.

Blurred, they could not see his eyes behind the slight crack in the door and walked past, their attention looking for something solid, something wrong. Opening the door Tal stepped out softly, both his knife and sword drawn this time. approaching behind the two men he stalked them slowly, stepping at the same time they did to keep the sound of foot falls to a minimum.

Half way up the hall, the two Mages stopped, Tal could feel their eyes narrowing. In a raspy voice that spoke of an age extended beyond its natural years, one of the Mages spoke.

"Is that blood?" he said, pointing to a dark slick on the floor.

Before the second could get his reply out Tal thrust his knife through the back of the Mans neck, erupting from the front of his throat with a spray of blood that turned to dust before it hit the floor.

The second Mage found his own neck just as punctured with Tal's sword, both dying without uttering a single further warning.

Tal sent a mental call to Brad, and then collected his weapons from within the piles of dust that he had created. Tal sent the summery of the action to Layland, telling him he probably did not have too much time before the Mages were noticed as missing. Lay acknowledge, saying they were nearly in position.

Tal once again checked the door to the Gate room, the two Ones of Impurity, and now six Mages were still there, none looked overly concerned yet that the other Mages had not returned.

Tal was weighing up their chances of success when Lay's voice entered his mind.

We are here. Are you ready?

Tal said they were and duly started his walk up the hall towards the enemy. His mind link with Lay letting them reach the door at the same time. Silencing his mind of all the nagging fears that were screaming at him, he gripped his sword tighter and stepped round the Mages, scared that each time he passed one that he would be discovered. But they were too focused with looking up to the far end of the halls rather than looking opposite them. Halting in front of the Ones, both Tal and Kendrik paused waiting for the Mages to be looking away.

In the space of a heartbeat, Tal swung his sword with all the force he could muster. If he did not kill the foul creature now, he was surely dead. Time slowed as the sword passed through the air, just before contact with the One, Tal was sure the dire creature turned to face him, its eyes focusing on him and realising what was occurring. The beasts' mouth opened but it did not matter, with a spray of dark, thick blood, the creatures head was severed from its body. Tal watched as Kendrik reproduced the assault on the other One of Impurity.

The Mages spun, eyes wide at the surprise attack, and not immediately seeing any enemy they looked outwards from the door. Seeing the Ranger, Rider and Nightwalker approaching they assumed these to be the threat and started to throw deadly bolts of magic down the halls. One found his chest punctured by the Rangers knives, falling back to the floor and writhing in agony.

The Nightwalker was involved in the melee almost immediately, closing the distance between the combatants and him in unbelievable speed. Slashing at the throat of one of the Mages he instantly reduced one to dust. Tal and Layland dispatching another Mage each in the seconds following their initial attack.

There were two Mages remaining, one throwing a second bolt of energy down the hall towards Brad and the Ranger. As it thundered towards him, Brad realised that he could not dodge the bolt quickly enough. Using his sword as a makeshift shield, he closed his eyes, taking the blast square on the flat of the blade.

Feeling the bolt hit the metal, he found himself propelled back, a searing pain flowed through his chest as he hit the ground hard. Trying to stand he felt the pain spread and he could only lay on his back, his eyes closed in pain.

Seeing his friend take a blast to the chest, Tal left the fight, Kendrik and the Nightwalker struggling with one Mage, both finding themselves being pressed back by the man. The Ranger had dispatched the other remaining man in grey robes and went to help the Sergeant and Nightwalker.

Tal found threw himself to the floor next to his friend. His tabard had been burned away and his chain was red hot. Taking his knife, he cut away the leather straps that held the armour in position, using them to throw the glowing metal away.

Looking at his friend, he could see that he had been lucky. His sword had taken most of the heat from the blast and was now only a lump of molten metal on the floor. The remaining heat had burnt away his top tabard and turned the chain mail into a branding iron, but Brad had been protected by the thick leather vest that was worn underneath to stop the leather chaffing the wearer.

Tal saw that although he had suffered heavy burns that would take a long time to heal, as long as Brad was careful from now, he would survive. Comforting his friend, Tal looked to the fight. The Mage was wearing a slight smile, his face looking leathery, young yet old, powerful. The three attackers were struggling, each time a sword or claw looked like it was about to connect with the Dark Lord, a slight hand gesture and the strike would be deflected without so much as scratching the Mage.

Tal removed his own tabard, rolled it up and placed it under his friends head, giving his shoulder a gentle squeeze he stood and ran to help his sergeant. Thinking back to the first time he had met Layland, Tal remembered that the Rider had saved his life in the woods, and again in his tavern room when the Dark Cousin had tried to kill him. Later, he had even endangered his life to try to stop Tal from being taken by the demon. Now Tal could repay the favour and help save Layland's life.

With a roar of defiance, Tal threw himself at the Mage his sword angled directly to pierce his skull. With a dry, and echoing laugh the Mage twisted a hand, and Tal's sword was moved to the side, Tal followed it and tumbled to the ground.

Layland, the Nightwalker and the Ranger continued to dance with the Mage. Whilst they were attacking he could not get the time to focus a counter attack, but he still knew that all he had to do was keep these self-righteous humans and Seicolantrai engaged and before long someone would come along, then the balance would shift and he could easily kill them.

The Ranger sliced at the man's head, his sword only finding air. He was feeling drained but knew he could not stop. As the Nightwalkers claws slashed towards the Mage, the Ranger concentrated. As the Mages hand moved once more to deflect the attack, the Ranger used all his meagre ability to manipulate the Mage instead. His hand being held back allowed the Nightwalker to take a gouge from the man's arm. Pain and shock caused the Mage to turn to the Ranger, but the man in the dark hunting leathers had overstretched himself, and had passed out, falling to the floor unconscious.

Kendrick saw the Mage pause, and thrusted, taking the twisted creature through the eye with his sword.

The Mage's mouth dropped in shock, and he fell, becoming dust as he slumped to his knees then falling back to the ground. Running to the Ranger, Layland knelt checking the man's vitals. His pulse was strong and his breathing steady, his own breath exhaling in relief, he looked over to Tal who was picking Brad up. The young Rider with his friend in his arm's, was a sight that in other circumstances could have brought a tear to Kendrik's eye. However, now was not the time for such emotions. Lifting the Ranger himself, Kendrik moved to the door that led down to the Gate room.

The Nightwalker opened it and looked down the long flight of stairs. With a nod, Kendrik urged him inside, taking one last look up and down the hall, he stepped onto the final set of stairs.

Inside, the Nightwalker shifted aside to let to two Riders pass before closing the door and pushing the latch shut. A faint red glow surrounded the door as the metal bar locked into place. In a couple of seconds the red surround to the door spread into the centre, covering the entire surface and starting to pulse slowly.

"I assume that means we are now locked in." said the Nightwalker softly.

Lay nodded in agreement, checking his senses he confirmed that he could still feel what was occurring on the other side of the door.

The Nightwalker took the lead and started down the stairs. The Ranger was still unconscious, and Brad was lapsing in and out of consciousness. As they descended, Tal could hear voices coming up the stairs, two men were chanting their voices not changing in either tone or pitch.

Laying the Ranger on the floor, Layland signalled the Nightwalker. In hushed whispers, he outlaid the plan he wanted followed.

"This couldn't be better, you and I will go down and I will kill the first Mage, I want you to try to keep the second alive, but do not let him cast any type of spell."

Nodding the *Seicolantrai*, followed Rider down as he started to blur into the dark flickering light of the stairs and Gate room. Tal stayed with the Ranger and Brad, ready to defend them if he needed to. Reaching the base of the stairs, the Nightwalker paused, obviously waiting for Layland. A slicing sound reached Tal's ears and a scream followed. The Nightwalker disappeared from sight and a heavy thud could be heard. Curses were shot at the invaders, and Tal felt magical energies building.

"You were fools not to kill me straight away like you did with Yure. Prepare to die *mortals*." The raspy voice spat with hatred.

As the energies reached a climax, Tal realised that the spell would be designed to kill both Lay and the Nightwalker. Launching himself down the stairs Tal was determined to kill the man before he could release the spell and doom their efforts to secure the Gate.

He hit the bottom of the stairs, his feet moving. As he rounded the corner he feared he might be too late. The Nightwalker was standing in front of the Mage, still and waiting. Tal thought he had simply accepted his fate. The Mage was laughing, his eyes alight with lightening as his body crackled, his hand creating a focus for the energy. Just as the Mage looked at the Nightwalker, a second short of releasing the magic that would annihilate him, the fist of the Nightwalker flew up into the stomach of the Mage, propelling him backwards.

Tal's eyes lit up as he felt the energy dissipate with the thundering blow levelled by the *Seicolantrai*. The Mage hit the floor next to the altar, his eyes going blank. Layland walked over to the man and grabbed his legs, Tal indicated where they Gate was when he came through it, and said that anything that happened here was visible from the other side.

Dragging the Mage out of sight of the Gate, Tal went and brought Brad and the Ranger into the main chamber.

"Now, let's see what we can find out. Wake up Magician!" said Lay with a sharp slap to the Mages face.

Master Diarmid was sitting in the cave, the children that were laying on the altars had not moved, nor given any sign that they were aware of the Seers and Household Guard. The days had been long for the Seers, extra men had been sent from the Hall of Seers in the City of Dragons, and still they were working nearly around the clock to try and sever the Demonic Magic of the Gate.

So far, the way the magic was sewn together was a mystery to the Seers. In their studies they had covered their own magic or White Magic, the Wild Magics used by both races of Elves, and had touched upon Black and Necromantic Magics used by the Grey Mages and other rogue magicians.

However, the Demonic Magic was completely alien to them, its order was more like chaos, and they had yet to find a way to interact with it.

Oren stood, he had spent most of the day, every day, for the last weeks in the dark and oppressive cave. He could see the strings of energy coming from the children, he could see the spells that kept that energy flowing, but he could not do anything that would disrupt it, each new idea fell through, and the Seers were starting to doubt they would ever manipulate the spells.

Returning to the light of day, he moved back to the camp that had set up around the cave. A group of engineers had done good work in rigging the landscape around the cave with traps and fitting basic fortifications. Entering the tent that had been put aside for the use of the Seers, the most senior of his Brothers were gathered around a centre table with several heavy tomes held open.

"Any luck?" asked one Seer; He was a short and rather rotund man of middle age, his white robe tied with a white rope around his ample waist.

"No, Brother Hale, each time I follow the threads of the Magic, I sense something hidden in the chaotic patterns. I do not know what that something is, but after the loss of Brother Fullum, I do not want to make any rash decisions.

"The power for the spells is coming from an external source, and just as the Gate is held open with the life energy of the children on the altars, something is powering the spell that sets the link up and holds the children in stasis. For all I am aware, it could be the life energy of the children themselves, so if we cut the threads, we might unwittingly kill the children too."

The rest of the Seers just turned back to their books, it was the same answer day in day out. No one could distinguish between the chaotic swirls that held the spells together, and no one wanted to risk the lives of the children.

"Is anyone working tonight?" asked Oren to the assembled Seers.

"That would be me." Replied Adept Seer Hale. He looked weary, but then again so did everyone else in the tent.

"Ok, wake me if you find anything of interest, I need sleep." Master Oren Diarmid left the tent and winced at the bright light. He had not slept for nearly three days; the daylight hours were spent in the cave studying the spell constructs, his nights were spent studying ancient tomes in the Seers tent. He watched the Household Guard change the watch again and again, and sleep had passed him by continuously.

Going to his private tent, he collapsed into the pallet that had been assigned to him and not even the bright flickering of sunlight through the tent flap could stop sleep overtaking him.

Master Diarmid, wake up.

The words rang through his mind gently, bringing him back to wakefulness.

He got up and stretched as he left the tent. The sun had set a while ago, the stars were bright and the moons cast a soft light over the camp. Still shaking off the effects of sleep he walked to the cave. He knew that was where Brother Hale had called from, and he also knew he would not have been woken unless some breakthrough had been made.

Descending the stairs, he saw that there was a bright light emanating from the cave and his brows gathered at the difference. Normally the Seers did not bother with any illumination other than that of a torch or two as it was not needed.

Entering the cave proper, he saw that there was a whole series of torches set throughout the massive expanse. At the far end, a group of Seers were standing around a selection of altars all talking rapidly to one another.

Hurrying to reach them, his interest now piqued, he saw them notice him and quiet down, standing aside to let him reach Brother Hale.

"Brethren, good night to you all, what have you found?" he said formally as he reached the collection of white robed men.

Adept Hale stepped forward and explained what they had found.

"Master Diarmid, I was trying to separate the threats of the Demonic Magic again and something struck me as odd. I wondered why it all seemed so chaotic and I decided to check each of the energy patterns coming from the altars. It took several hours to just do a small section so I got help from some volunteers. It was at about sunset that we made the discovery." He paused as if trying to work out the best way to explain it to Oren, his eyes clouding over and his hands twisting as he puzzled it out alone.

Eventually Master Diarmid tried to urge him on, "Yes?" he said, reminding the Adept that he was still there.

"Ah well, the reason that we could not work out what was what, is that the energy from this group here isn't going to the Gate. It is not even leaving the cave. The energy is going to a focus point at the centre of the cave, and then splitting towards every one of the other altars. The chaos we registered was seeing the threads of spells flowing against each other. These children here," he made a gesture indicating about twenty altars, "are powering the spell to focus the life energy of the others and directing it to the Gate."

Oren considered this, he then stepped away without saying anything and felt each of the energies leaving the altars. Sure enough there were two elements, one was the energy from the child, the other was a spell that was drawing the energy from the child, and the energy powering *that* spell could be traced back to the altars that Brother Hale had discovered.

Yes! This was the breakthrough they had needed, now they could study the master spell and work out a way to break that, hopefully that would close the Gate and allow the children their freedom.

Morning came bright and clear and Drew was just about to go on watch. He had been lucky, other than his first appointment in the City of Dragons, he had always been assigned day duties. As he left the tent he shared with three other Guards, he noticed that a group of them had gathered around the entrance to the cave. Jogging to the gathering, he asked another Guardsman what was occurring.

"The Seers think they can close the Gate."

Drew was shocked, they had been here for so long he had almost given up on the hope that they could free the children. Drew found his own company and stood next to Sergeant Richardson, waiting for whatever news may come.

A few minutes later, Master Diarmid emerged from the cave and stood upon the rocky entrance, enabling him to see the assembled camp. Raising his voice he addressed the crowd.

"Gentlemen, we had been working all night when a possible solution came to the attention of one of my Brothers. We now feel we have a good chance of closing the Gate once and for all, but due to the magics involved I would ask you to move to a safe distance from the site. We will start our castings in about half an hour, so please make sure you are clear by then. Thank you."

James R. Kitney

Drew smiled, the thought that the Gate might be fully closed, that the children might be freed and that he might get back to civilisation ran through his mind, causing a feeling of surprising exaltation to run through his body as he moved away from the Seer's preparation.

The Seers were ready, inside the cave they were all spread out among the altars, each one monitoring the magics that surrounded a selection of the children. At the centre of the room, Oren stood with his eyes closed and his face cast down slightly, his mind concentrated on the main spell that focused the energies from the select children. If that spell was cut, then there would be no energy to fuel the more complex spell supplying the Gate and hopefully that too would collapse.

At the given time, he touched his own gifts and started the casting that let him manipulate the threads of the Demonic Magic. He tentatively let his own spells submerge into the weave of the Mages'. Finding the one thread that pulled energy from the few, he cut it with the gentlest of his own magics, watching as the construct of the Demonic spell collapsed around it.

Waiting, and expecting some kind of backlash, he monitored the energies gathered in the room. As he watched, he saw the life energy from the twenty altars return back into the children, the hold of the spell over them crumbling and dissolving into nothingness.

With the disappearance of the source of energy, the spell that drew the life energy from the rest of the altars slowly collapsed. With a feeling of relief, the oppressiveness of the cave slowly vanished. It felt lighter, fresher all of a sudden, when Oren opened his eyes, he saw the rest of the Seers were smiling at him.

"You did it Oren, you cut the spells." said Hale, his own mouth curled up at the edges.

Master Diarmid collapsed, his eyes closing as the relief washed over him.

It was done. They closed the Gate.

Drew was outside when he felt the energies being worked. The hairs on his arms standing on end as the feeling of pressure increased until he thought he would explode. He was starting to question whether the distance they were at was indeed safe. Then as fast as it built, the sensation lifted, leaving them disorientated and bewildered.

While everyone was shaking off the effects of the magic, Drew ran to the cave. He had to make sure that the children were ok, maybe then he could get the thoughts of them out of his dreams. When he reached the stairs, he slid to a halt, Master Diarmid was unconscious and two of the Seers were levitating him out of the cave.

"What happened?!" asked Drew, fearing the worst for the Seer.

"Don't worry young man, Master Diarmid is ok, he is just overcome by the pressure of the past weeks." Replied one of the Seers.

"But it worked? The spell has been stopped?" pressured Drew, his eyes still slightly worried.

"Yes, the spell was cut. Now please, we have to get Master Diarmid to his bed." The Seers sent Oren on floating towards his tent, following behind to ensure his comfort.

Drew shook his head. Oren would be ok, he was a powerful Seer, but the children below would need support after this horrible event. As he entered the chamber, he saw Brother Hale moving from one altar to another trying to rouse the child lying upon it. Moving to the Adept, Drew spun him round.

"What is going on?" he said urgently.

Brother Hale turned his face showing a great sadness.

"I don't know. The spells have been cut, the life energies of the children are no longer being drawn out of them. There is no reason why they should not be coming out of their coma." Turning away from drew he continued to try to rouse the youths. Their eyes opened briefly, alarm showing clearly, but so soon their faces became heavy and their eyelids closed once more, returning them to their unnatural sleep.

Drew fell to the hard floor, a strangled sound escaped his lips as he sobbed against the cold rock.

Chapter 21

Retreat

Tal watched the Mage fume silently.

For the past day, they had been locked inside the Gate room, out of sight of the demons that could view them from their own world.

The Ranger had regained consciousness after a couple of hours. The Seers personal guard had woken to the screams of the Mage as the Nightwalker had worked on him. They needed information, and Layland had given the Nightwalker approval to get that information in any way he could.

The interrogation had not been gentle and the Mage had found it wiser not to try to escape by using Magic. With a more acute sense of magical energy, the very instant that the Mage had started to focus his thoughts to cast a spell, the Nightwalker landed a heavy blow to the side of his head, destroying any concentration the Mage had.

Tal had feared the man would rather die than give up his secrets, but when it was clear that the Nightwalker could inflict pain and keep him alive, the Mage had finally conceded and spoken.

The room was a place of the Necromantic Arts, the heart and soul of the Grey Mages lair. It was the place where those that were strong enough, were given the secrets of Necromancy and given the tools to capture the life force of others to lengthen their own sorry lives.

The man they held was a Necromancer, one level above the Grey Mage, one level below the Dark Lords. He had been assisting the Dark Lord that they had killed in worship to the Master.

The question the Nightwalker had asked next was obvious, *who was the Master?* It sent the Necromancer off on a fanatical speech.

"The Master is the original Dark Lord! The man who first created the Grey Mages! Zailon Uran! Remember that name Nightwalker, for he shall be your master and lord! He disappeared three thousand years ago, with a prophecy that when he returns he shall conquer this whole world and we shall be elevated to the status of gods!"

The tirade continued unstopped for an hour on the purity of the Grey Mages, how their knowledge set them above the rest of the mortals that cower clinging to life, too scared to take the life they so desperately desire and move forward with the glory of the Mages.

The end of the zealous sermon came from the Ranger who had tired of the mans sick devotion, slammed his fist square into the Mages face, breaking his nose and causing his eyes to roll back in their sockets. As he slumped to the floor, Tal turned away, the blood pooling on the floor running thickly.

"Ensure he lives, we may need more answers, and a pile of dust will do us no good." Said Layland. The Ranger knelt next to the unconscious Mage and checked him over.

"He will live, he will just look that much uglier." He said in a flat tone.

A thudding came from the door at the top of the stairs, sounds of a ram being used against the door.

"They wont give up will they?" asked Tal, his senses telling him that there were Mages and Ones of Impurity behind the door, probably Necromancers and Dark Lords too. The attempts to get into the chamber, started about twenty minutes after they had sealed the room, and had continued through the past day without any signs of success. From what Tal could sense, they had tried by physical means, and had attempted magical force, but neither had resulted in the opening of the door to the chamber.

"No, they wont quit until we are dead and out of their holy place." Said Layland, looking at the Necromancer lying prone on the floor. His blood seemed to stay fluid while he was alive, how did that work? Why did it not turn to dust as it left the body?

The Nightwalker was watching the blood with an intense interest that made Tal remember that none of the people in the room had taken any form of sustenance since the day before.

Looking up, the Nightwalker spotted Tal watching him, smiling slightly he spoke in a gentle whisper.

"Fear not young Rider, I am not suffering any blood lust yet. Take a moment and just listen."

Tal wondered what he could mean. His eyes followed the blood as it ran from a pool by the Mage towards the centre of the room and the altar. As it collected at the base of the altar, Tal watched it.

Tal, Layland, the Nightwalker and the Ranger were now sitting or standing in silence watching the blood. With the exception of the slow, rhythmical pounding on the door, no sound could be heard in the room.

Then Tal heard it. A quiet drip, then silence again. Minutes passed, then again came the soft drip.

"Where is that coming from?" asked Tal after he had heard the drip several more times.

"From the altar." said Layland, sounding slightly confused.

"No, not from the altar, from *under* the altar. There is a space below it." said the Nightwalker. He stood and moved over to the cold stone slab, only Layland's whispered warning about being seen through the Gate followed him.

Reaching the altar, he knelt and waited, again he heard the drip, louder now he was closer to the altar. Standing, he placed his hands on the side of the rock, feeling the cold stone against his skin. Applying pressure, he tried to push the altar, but nothing moved, walking to the others side he repeated attempt to move the massive stone table. When no success was forthcoming, he knelt and studied the dark stone. It took him several minutes of examination but then he saw it, a faint line running around the top of the stone.

He motioned for Tal to come to him. Using Tal's strength, the Nightwalker counted to three and together they managed to lift the top from the altar, letting it fall to the ground with a heavy crash. What they had revealed took all of them by surprise. When the top started to move, Tal had come to the conclusion that it was not just a sacrificial altar, but also a sarcophagus, maybe the resting place of Zailon Uran. But what they found was more confusing still. A steep flight of stairs led down, the blood dropping from a lip at the base of the altar onto the stairs about six feet below the floor level.

Layland told the Ranger to keep an eye on their unconscious prisoner and joined Tal and the Nightwalker at the top of the stairs.

"Well if we don't go down, we wont know what is there will we?" said Layland, some humour creeping back into his voice again.

Jumping over the sides of the altar, he landed lightly on the steps and started down. The Nightwalker followed his lead, not even pausing to check back on the Mage. Tal steadied his breathing and then followed a few paces behind.

The steps were only a short flight and led to a cavern just under the Gate room. As they reached the bottom, all they could see was an array of dim red lights spread hundreds deep.

Hazel swung her sword, the arm of a Mage being severed at the elbow. His scream echoed down the corridor before she could silence him.

The fighting had been non stop for the past day. There had not been a stop to the push that their commanders had ordered, merely a few hours respite while they were relieved to rest before being sent back in. All the while, that recovery time was becoming less and less as they pressed further into the lair. Each level they took require more soldiers to hold it and secure it, and those soldiers were taken from the reserve that had previously been used to allow those on the front line to get some rest. Now the rotation was six hours fighting with two on the upper levels and then three off for rest outside of the subterranean fortress.

They still had two floors to take before reaching the bottom at best guess. Hazel's party under Captain Erikson had just taken a Mages fortified position. The element of surprise could not be theirs, and so each hallway or corridor was a full on struggle between the Mages and the Army.

Seers and Nightwalkers worked alongside Riders, Rangers and the Kingdoms standing Army. All groups were taking losses in digging out the Mages, but Hazel was glad that the Nightwalkers loyal to Vorlin had joined the struggle. Without their aid, the Ones of Impurity would surely have swung the battle in favour of the Mages and the struggle would already have been lost.

As the remaining group of Mages fled under the Riders constant attack, the battle trained Seers threw magical energies down the corridor after them, whilst holding their own protection. The Riders retreated back behind the pulsing blue shield as the Mages retaliated with powerful bolts of lightening. They were now holding an intersection further down the hallway, their numbers reinforced with a half dozen extra Mages and a One.

Hazel heard Erikson report the situation back to Colonel Nisen, with the order sent back to hold the position until a Nightwalker could be sent to assist with the One of Impurity.

Holding the position, with Mages and Seers trading spells, Hazel let her senses wander. She could feel Tal was beneath her, but with only this level and one more to capture, she wondered why his life sign was so small. Had be been injured? Was he a prisoner and just a few breaths from death? She shook the thoughts from her head, this would not help Tal or her, she had to concentrate on the current battle. They had passed a few bodies of Mages at the higher levels, and she was aware how competent Tal had become, he did not need her worrying about him.

Her musings came to a halt as Erikson ushered her aside, letting a Nightwalker move to the front of the barrier. It was the Nightwalker that had first met Rayburn when he entered the lair, the black haired man named Mikael Tagus appeared even more stern if that was possible, now that he approached the One. The Seers barrier moved forwards. Mages blasts bounced off the shield yet it did not falter. As they walked behind the Nightwalker, the Riders readied their weapons, ready to assist with the deadly One.

Barrier met barrier, and energies crackled. The two opposing sides stood facing each other, the One and the Nightwalker barely a meter apart. Mages and Seers struggled to push their barrier through the others, breaking the spell and removing the protection it offered.

Hazel waited anxiously. These struggles could last ten minutes or ten seconds, the contest ending in an instant if one person lost concentration or tired. As magics pressed against each other, Hazel watched and could see the Seer holding the barrier start to falter.

Seeing one of their Brothers start to fail, the other Seers took the strain of the barrier, continuing to fuel the spell with their own power. The force of two Seers was taking a toll on the Mage, sweat became visible on his brow as one of his comrades relieved him.

Hazel noticed something in that instant, a realisation that took her by surprise.

She turned to the Seers, her voice just loud enough for them to hear.

"They can't work together! Only one person can hold the shield!"

Looking to the Mages, they noticed that there were two that were waiting by the shield holder and not adding their power to the single one that was straining. Was this a weakness they could exploit?

The Seer that had to rest was the strongest of the three, and as he registered what Hazel's observation meant, he threw what little energy he had left into the barrier. The Seers shield shattered the Mages construct in one swift move. The Nightwalker expecting the shift in balance flew straight at the One, hurling him down the hall opposite. The Riders flowed into the junction, quickly dispatching the Mages that were drained from their magical struggle, while the Seers confronted the six remaining Mages.

At such close quarters, shields became useless and it was magical ability alone that counted for anything in the fast paced melee. Lightening flew back and forth, being deflected by each magic user before their own attack was launched at opponents. The Riders split into two groups, one moving to help the Nightwalker in his vicious battle with the One, the other darted between the energy blasts created by the Mages to engage them hand to hand.

It did not take long to break the Mages, the surviving couple retreating further into the lair, leaving just the One as their opponent. It had backed into a smaller corridor that limited any opponents to two abreast. Mikael Tagus was slowing, his face still dark and strong, but the effort obvious in his eyes.

From the behind the Nightwalker, Rider Bryant Lewis loosed an arrow that sped past him, taking the One in the centre of his chest. The One was startled enough to pause as the slight shock washed over him, allowing Tagus to tear out his throat. The One slumped to the floor, his face a snarl as a blankness settled in his eyes.

Erikson was breathing hard. Shaking off the blood from his sword, he watched as some of the bodies crumbled to dust, while others stayed limp on the ground. With a quick mental thought, he sent their discovery to the other Riders in the area, maybe the information would save more deaths to the Allied Army.

Lifting his head, he motioned to the group and they pressed on further into the lair.

Tal walked amongst the altars, his hands brushing the cold stone. Laying atop the cold slabs, were people of all different ages and races. There were men, women, Elves, children and Dwarves. Some alters lay unlit, the bodies atop them old and gaunt, and their lives long since ended.

"What is this?" he asked softly. Above them, they could still hear the pounding of energies and battering rams on the door to the Gate room. Layland and the Nightwalker were wearing the same confused look as Tal.

"I'm not sure," said Lay "but I think we should let Rayburn know."

He concentrated, focusing on the Riders above. The closest company was only one level up, it was Fen Trillar and his unit.

Captain Trillar. Went the silent call.

Who is this? Came the reply, his unit stopping behind a shield of Seers as the Mages blasted the barrier with ferocious energies.

It is Sergeant Kendrik. Myself, Rider Parnell, Rider Oswin, and a Ranger and Nightwalker are below you, locked in the Gate room. Beneath it, we discovered a large cavern with hundreds of altars. Join with me and take a look, pass the image back to Rayburn and find out his instructions for us.

Trillar *joined* with Layland and observed the view of the cavern. The Sergeant could feel the dismay of the Captain above as he left the *joining* to relay the report to their Lord.

It took several minutes before the Captain came back to Lay, Tal was beginning to think that they had been forgotten about.

Sergeant Kendrik. Lord Rayburn has been in discussion with the High Seer and he says this is not the first such discovery. In the Dead Lands, a group of Household Guards and Seers, discovered another such prison. It was being used to power the Gate at the heart of Peters Hold. They managed to destroy the spell closing the Gate, but they were unable to wake the people that were being used as a source of energy.

Kendrik tried to make sense of what he had been told.

So what are our orders? He asked eventually.

Hold the room, if we can close that Gate, then there will be no way for the demons to access our world again, for the time being at least. Maybe we can then work out how the Gates originated and whether it was through the Demons or the Mages. We will get to you as soon as we can.

Layland sent his acknowledgement.

Thank you, hurry, but be careful, there is a large group of Mages and Ones trying to gain entry to the room, if they get in, we will not be able to hold.

Retreating up the stairs, they left the evil place.

Back in the Sacrificial Chamber, they replaced the top of the altar and crossed to behind the guessed position of the Gate. Brad was awake but his pain was obvious. The Mage was also conscious again.

The two of them were arguing about the purpose of the room. The Mage was defiant that all the living sacrifices below were just a gift to The Master, to give him the strength to return, and that the thought of Demons in their Lair was just a lie to deceive him.

"You fool!" rasped Brad, "We have *been* to the Demon world! We escaped through the very Gate in this room and fled through *your* Lair!

"Don't you remember the dead found all those weeks ago? You held a Rider in captivity, she escaped and there were Mages dead right up those stairs!"

The Mage snarled, his lips curling up to show yellowed teeth.

"You have been duped Mage, your entire prophecy is a sham of the Demons to retake this world and make it theirs again. They have an invasion force, millions strong, just the other side of that Gate, ready to attack us and eliminate the humans from this planet. If that happens we all die, you, me, even your all-powerful Dark Lords."

"Lies!" screamed the Mage. Brad shook his head, the pain in his chest taking its toll after his passionate argument. He slumped back to the ground, his brow becoming damp with sweat.

Tal sat down next to Brad, helping his friend. They were all thirsty and hungry. However, until they were released by their own side, they would have nothing. With one floor left to go, Tal guessed that they still had several hours before they could be set free.

The Mage was glaring at the young Rider, when a huge cloven hoof stepped from thin air to land in the room just in front of the altar.

The Mage gave a squeal of fear as he saw a Demon appear from nothing to stand at about ten foot tall and just as broad in the centre of the Room.

"Now do you believe us?" said Brad with scorn as the Mage scurried on his knees to hide behind the Allies.

The Demon slowly turned as the Nightwalker and Lay moved in front of the two younger Riders. When it saw them, it gave a guttural growl, its fangs dripping with saliva as it took a step towards them.

Four knives flew past Lay from the Ranger, to stick into the leathery hide of the creature causing it to give a below of pain.

As it reared back, clutching at the knives the Nightwalker flew towards it. His own knives slashing at the beasts calves, cutting deep. It fell to the floor hard, the muscles in its legs severed.

Lay, Tal and the Ranger rushed forward and dispatched the Demon with several heavy cuts across the neck.

Kendrik looked at the Portal, the invisible entry to their world was letting more Demons in. Smaller than the previous one, they stood only five feet tall but were stocky, and each looked dangerous.

Trillar, hurry, Demons are entering through the Gate.

Trillar was pushing down the final corridor. There was a large contingent of Mages and Ones in this alley, and the Seers could not break through their shields.

They had been reinforced from the Army and they had gained the assistance of other Seers and Rangers. Half way down the corridor was a door that was shut. The Mages were doing their best to get in to that room, but it was barred from the other side. Trillar was waiting anxiously for the Seers to overcome the Mages that were there. It would only be a matter of time as the Seers outnumbered the Mages and they had the advantage of being able to work together. But the Mages that were here were the strongest they had faced so far, and Kendrik and his small unit were stuck behind that door fighting off the Demons that were now invading their world through the Gate.

At the other end of the hallway, another contingent of allies were attacking the Mages from the other side. The Mages were stuck between two forces that were increasing in size. They had no way out but they were not giving up.

The struggle of magic continued, unseen forces battering each other in the hope one would overpower the other. At the sound of approaching men, Trillar turned to see Colonel Nisen walking towards him. He had with him a good-sized number of Riders, Soldiers and Seers.

"What is the situation Captain?" asked Nisen as he arrived.

Trillar saluted and explained their present circumstances.

"The Mages are trapped down that corridor. There are about twenty of them with a further ten Ones of Impurity. Captain Reynolds is down the other end of the corridor. He has a contingent of Riders with him, their Captain and Sergeant were killed but they refused to stop their assault. Seers are pressing the Mages hard on both sides, but so far, they are holding.

"Sergeant Kendrik, Riders Parnell and Oswin along with a Ranger and Nightwalker are through that door that the Mages are trying to break down. Demons are coming through the Gate but they are coping, for now."

The Colonel nodded, his eyes closed, Trillar could see the Colonel weighing up the situation with the new numbers. Eventually he opened his eyes, and sent half the Seers that arrived with him to support this side of the offensive and the other half to Captain Reynolds.

"We have a further five units sweeping this level. The upper levels are nearly empty of Mages with just a few pockets of resistance left. They will break before too much longer, then maybe we can talk our way to that door."

Trillar turned to the Colonel.

"Unlikely Sir. So far all the Mages we have encountered are fanatical, they would rather die than give up."

"Maybe so, if they felt they still had a cause worth protecting. Take that away from them, we may break their spirits." The Colonel nodded and seemed satisfied that everything was under control. "Carry on Captain, keep myself or Lord Rayburn up to date with the situation."

Fen Trillar acknowledged the order with a salute and turned to watch the Seers continue to assault the Mages protection without much luck.

Colonel Nisen turned and walked back through the Lair, towards the surface and the fresh air. As he walked through the halls, he saw all around him, the signs of battle and death. His lip curling up in distaste, he nearly missed the Mage that walked round the corner in front of him. With one swift move, he spun the Mage around and snapped his neck. Shaking his own head, he cleared his thoughts and reminded himself that he was still in enemy territory, no matter how many Riders and Soldiers were patrolling the area.

Leaving the musky tunnels of the Mages Lair, he looked up; the sun was high in the sky. It was around midday and he had to inspect the outer sentries. Walking over the baked and dry ground, he squinted, his eyes not yet adjusted to the brightness outside the halls.

He reached the position where one of the sentry units should have been stationed, and looked around. The company were not on station and he could not see them anywhere,

Stretching out his senses, he could sense the other units at their positions, it was strange that none of them had noticed anything occurring here.

He searched at the edge of his senses and found something. One Rider was leaving the area he could search quickly. Calling to the two closest Rider units, he asked for half their number to follow the lone Rider, and set out to keep him within range.

Tal was breathing hard, the demons were steadily entering their world, and it was taking all five of the small company to kill what arrived.

"Why are they only coming through one at a time?" asked Tal.

"I don't know, how big was the gate when you looked through it from the other side?" asked Lay, his sword taking a slice out of a Demons chest.

Tal thought back to when he had escaped through the Gate into this very room. Try as he might however, he could not remember anything of detail about the flight from the Demons world.

Brad was struggling with his sword. Standing behind the portal, he used all his strength to slash at the demons legs when they appeared. Calling to Tal his voice was coarse.

"It was only just bigger than us! They can only send one through at a time, and they are limited to the size of the Demon!"

"Then we can hold! We have to keep fighting at all costs." Said the Nightwalker as his knives flashed in the flickering torchlight.

The pounding on the door above them faltered for a minute, and Tal wondered if they had managed to break it down. *No sense worrying, I can't do anything about it even if they have.*

His sword flashed and the demon fell, another stepping over the body of the dying creature. His muscles were burning from exertion, and the footing in the chamber was becoming treacherous, thick with slimy blood and littered with bodies.

The Mage was still cowering behind the portal, not even trying to escape, his eyes wide with fear. A continual whining sound was all he made, as Demon after Demon came into the room, only to be cut down by the Riders and their allies.

Screams could be heard from the top of the stairs, something new was occurring outside the door, but Tal still could not spare the time to think on it, a new Demon, the size of the first climbed slowly into the room, taking his time to squeeze through the Gate. Bellowing a challenge, he swung a razor sharp claw at the Nightwalker who retreated out of range.

Open the door! We have secured the area! Came the call, resounding inside Tal's mind.

Brad signalled that he had heard, and started to move away from the Gate and circle towards the stairs slowly. The Mage was faster and seeing his only protection heading towards the escape ran towards the steps himself.

The Demon saw the man fleeing and quicker than his size would credit swiped the Mage up in his claw. The Necromancers screams were silenced with a single bite of the creature's jaws. Blood sprayed across the beast, as he continued to consume the Mage.

Their attention held by the grisly sight, the small party watched as the Demon seemed to swell, growing larger. The life of the Mage was being consumed, as was his spirit. Tal wondered if the spirit energies of all those that the Mage had consumed over time were also being taken by the Demon.

The fiend was now over fourteen feet tall, and had to crouch to stand within the chamber. Regaining their composure, the allies struck hard, swords and knives biting deep into the flesh of the creature. Each time they made contact barely more than a scratch was left.

A second Demon had come through the Gate, his head taken quickly by Layland as he circled round to the read of the larger foul beast. Brad turned to face his friends as he reached the bottom of the stairs. They were starting to lose the control, more Demons coming through than they could keep up with.

His face hardening, Brad turned to the steps and started to drag himself up them. He had to get to the top and let the others in as quickly as he could if he was to help his friends survive. A day ago he would have gladly died, so great was his loss with the death of Cholla, but seeing the evil in this Lair, seeing the horrors that would become loose on the world if they failed, he knew he could not die and leave the world to the mercy of evil creatures. He had to live, he had to ensure that Cholla's death was not in vain.

Hand over hand, he crawled up the steep stairs, his weight being supported by the cold stone walls.

A scream from below shuddered through him. Who was it? Faster, he must move faster. He was so close to the door when he slipped, his burnt chest slamming into the stone steps and causing pain to flood through him. His vision blurred and he feared he would pass out. Pushing to his hands and knees, he forced himself on. Using the last of his strength he threw the latch on the door back, the glow surrounding it fading as he pushed it open. Light entered from behind the door and he saw Riders and Soldiers, Seers and Nightwalkers standing ready in front of him. He was taken by two Seers as his vision failed and darkness overcame him.

Tal twisted as the large Demon swung at him, he cut at the head of one of the smaller five feet tall beasts as he passed it and took a chunk of flesh from its arm, but it did not slow it and he was forced to give ground. Tal watched as the Nightwalker flew in close to the large beast, he slashed at the thing with both knives, and was rewarded by a good spray of blood from the creature as he cut veins. The lumbering monster turned violently and caught the Nightwalker with his arm, sending him across the room to hit a wall. Tal heard the air expelled from his lungs as he tried to stand, but he was taken unaware by two smaller Demons, his own throat becoming the target this time.

Ruby red blood seeped from the Nightwalker, and a scream of loss and defeat left his mouth. The two Demons that had taken his life started to grow themselves, almost reaching the same size as the largest among them. Layland, with a scream of rage, ran straight at them whilst they were still evolving. With a stroke as powerful as it was fuelled by hatred, he decapitated one of the demons and thrust the sword with all his strength into the eye of the second, plunging it deep, right up to the hilt so that the blade exited the creatures skull the other side in an eruption of bone and bloody mess.

The two dread beasts fell to the floor, their nerves causing them to twitch as their blood seeped to the ground, mixing with that of their own kind already flowing freely across the stone slabs.

Layland drew his knives, and turned to slash repeatedly at another Demon that was bearing down on him. The thing fell in a limp tangle atop the two just despatched by the Rider.

Tal was the last remaining combatant with a sword in his hands. The demons were coming in faster now and they could not stop the flow any longer. He felt the hopelessness rise within him and was almost ready to give up. A bolt of lightening threw the largest Demon against the wall and continued to slide over his body, burning his skin from a deep red, to a blistered black before letting him slip to the floor dead.

Other bolts of lightening filled the room, killing Demons with each strike. Riders flowed into the chamber, the Seers covering them and dealing death to anything that the fresh soldiers and Riders missed. Tal, Layland and the Ranger limped over to Captain Fen Trillar. The Rider looked as Tal remembered, hard brown eyes with short dark hair, yet a face that could be young or old.

"Its good to see you alive Tal, we were not sure you would make it for a while, though it looks like you will have a few scars to show for your courage, and Brad will spend the next few months recovering from the nasty burns he has received.

"Sergeant Kendrik, congratulations, your actions have allowed us to stand a good chance of closing what we assume is the last Gate to the Demons world. What gave you the idea to try this in the first place? And how did you manage to plan this so well?" said the Captain, respect bright in his eyes when he addressed the Sergeant.

Kendrik winked at Tal tiredly, "Honestly Sir, I did not have a plan at all, and I did not get the idea until we were all standing at the top of the stairs on the first level, I just asked a favour of a distraction from my Captain to see how far I could push."

"Then you are a reckless young Rider, Layland, but you always have been. Thank you for staying alive." Replied the Captain with a slight smile. Layland saluted and moved across the room, collecting his sword and slicing his way through one of the Demons that got through the Seers wall of lightening. Approaching the altar, he flipped the top off and revealed the stairs to Captain Trillar before leading the three remaining original combatants out of the carnage of the sacrificial chamber and back up towards the light of the lair proper.

"You seem to be very friendly with Captain Trillar." Said Tal as they reached more friendly ground.

"Yes, like I found you, he found me when I was one of the Children."

"I have heard of these Children before, but no one has ever explained what they are to me." Said Tal interested in what was just said.

409

"No they wouldn't, that explanation is usually kept for when you are promoted to Sergeant, so you will have to wait I'm afraid." Layland waved away the slightly hurt look of Tal and took a water bottle from a soldier at the top of the stairs. Passing it to the Ranger, he got another two bottles and gave one to Tal, taking a long drink, he used the rest of the water to rinse the blood of the Demons from his arms and face, examining his own cuts and wincing each time he saw one that would leave a scar.

"Well there goes my good looks." He said with something that Tal expected was only half a joke. Shaking his head, Tal followed the Rider as they made their way upwards towards the daylight and the chance of some food and rest, and maybe the chance to see Hazel.

Colonel Nisen reached the single Rider that he could sense, the man was barely alive, laying on the parched ground his body blackened and left to rot. The units he had called arrived shortly. He told two Riders to carry their fallen colleague back to the camp and with the remaining eight and four Rangers he started to search the area to try to discover what had happened to the unit that should have been stationed on the ring of sentries.

The small group of soldiers spread out, and over the space of an hour, they discovered little that gave any reason for the missing unit. They were just about to head back when one of the Rangers gave a shout. The Riders froze and felt the surrounding area. There was a prickling of magic that they would have missed had the Rangers abilities not been available to them. Between the allies and the ring of sentries, suddenly were a group of ten Mages.

Gathering the men into a stronger formation, the Colonel headed straight for the enemy. They had appeared no more than a stones throw from the position where the missing unit had been posted.

When they were almost within sight of the Mages, the Riders and Rangers drew bows and nocked arrows. They waited, lying prone on the ground. The minutes seemed to drag on and on, the Riders feeling the Mages approach through their *joining*.

The first sign they had that the Mages were getting close was the rapid speaking, they were not trying to hide their position, just get away as quickly as possible from the Lair. When they were close enough to make the Riders bows effective, the party rose from the ground and drew their cloth yard arrows back to their cheek. The Mages ahead of them saw too late. With the snap of bowstrings they paused, squinting to the low sun to see what the sound was. When the first fell to the ground, an arrow planted square in his chest, the others panicked but it did little good, within seconds the rest of the arrows found their targets.

Approaching the fallen Mages, the Colonel checked them for life, and when satisfied that they were safe, gave the Riders and Rangers orders to maintain this area and ensure no Mages escaped.

Walking back towards the main encampment, he headed to the field hospital. There was a reason that unit went missing, and the only one who could explain it was in that tent, and Nisen was determined to find out where his missing men were.

Chapter 22

Hunt

Tal was lying on the hospital bed.

He had been cleaned and examined, all the larger cuts had been stitched and any dirty wounds had been flushed clean. He looked like an embalmed corpse, there were so many bandages on him, but his spirits had been lifted with some food, water and a visit from Hazel.

He now lay listening to her as she gave him a running commentary on the last few struggles within the Lair. The Mages had been routed, and were in full retreat. The Ones of Impurity always fought to the death, but the Mages they left behind were not always as fanatical, many starting to surrender when it was clear that they had lost and any further attempts of defence were futile.

Next to Tal was Layland who slept with a slight smile on his face, the Ranger lay across from Tal also sleeping heavily. Brad had been taken to a private tent with a Seer that was skilled in healing. He had not emerged for half an hour and Tal thought that the Seer must be worried about him to still be in there. On the other side of Tal, lay a Rider that had been brought in about an hour ago. He was covered head to toe in bandages that made

Tal feel grateful to have at least most of his skin showing. The man had received the attentions of a Seer, but he had still not regained consciousness.

Colonel Nisen had been at his side for the past ten minutes, not speaking but continuously looking at the man's face. Tal thought he could sense the Colonel willing the Rider to wake, there was something that he needed from the wounded man, and it was important.

Without looking away from the Riders face, Nisen managed to silently get the attention of a passing Seer. The Colonels face was worried and his voice held that concern heavily.

"Brother Seer, this man may have information that is vital to the elimination of the Grey Mage threat to the Kingdom. Can you tell me how long he will be unconscious for?"

The Seer looked sad, he had obviously seen a great many men in bad shape the past couple of days and it was taking its toll on him.

"I'm sorry, we have done all we can for him, we have managed to help his body, but his mind and spirit are up to the Gods. Only they can know when he will awaken…or if he will." With a slight bow, the Seer moved on, his head hanging low as he moved from bed to bed, offering what help he could.

Tal looked at the Colonel, he knew something had occurred at the perimeter, but so far, he had not been able to figure out what. His face still locked to the other Riders, the Colonel spoke his first words to Tal and Hazel since he had arrived in the tent.

"There were units of Riders and Rangers stationed all around the perimeter of the Mages fortress. I was doing my inspections of these positions when I came across one that was not there. I searched the surrounding area, looking for a reason that the post had been abandoned. At the edge of my awareness, I felt this one Rider, faint but there none the less. When I reached him, I found him like this. I had him brought here as soon as I came across him, and proceeded to search the area physically.

"Near the area that the unit had been positioned, there suddenly came into being, ten Mages. The party I was with killed them all, and a new post was set up to watch for further fleeing Mages, but where they came from, and how they got that far away without being noticed I do not know. We searched for escape routes, but found none. This man is the only member of the original unit we found, and he is the only one that can tell us what happened, and if any Mages escaped or not."

With that, the Colonel sank back into the silence that had consumed him previously. Tal asked if Rayburn was aware of this or not. The Colonel shook his head, without speaking. Finding himself unsure what to do now, Tal asked if he should go speak to Rayburn for the Colonel. A very slight nod was all the acknowledgement he received.

Swinging his legs off the bed, Tal stood, stretched his still aching muscles, and left the tent. Hazel followed him, catching up to him quickly and walking next to him like a personal bodyguard. She seemed reluctant to let him out of her site after the trouble he appeared to keep finding.

Descending the steps that led back into the fortress, Tal left the fading light of day and once more entered the artificial torchlight of the Mages fortress. Walking the halls that lead to the command centre of the allied forces, he wondered what he was going to say to his Lord.

Approaching the guarded door that held the commanding officers, Tal requested entry and waited while the guard disappeared inside to ask Rayburn's approval.

"What are you going to tell him?" asked Hazel quietly.

"What I was told? I have no idea really. I guess I will just pass the information on and leave." said Tal. Hazel smiled, Tal used to be a quiet boy full of insecurity, but with the trials of the past few months, even when he had no idea what he was doing, he managed to sound full of confidence, if not answers.

The guard returned and held the door open for Tal and Hazel. As they entered, Tal looked round and suddenly realised that he had neither weapons nor armour and that should they get attacked he would be dead before he could even react.

Noticing his hesitation, Rayburn put his nerves at ease.

"Don't worry Tal, the upper levels have been cleared out, and even the lower levels are almost empty now. You are completely safe here. Now what is it you wanted to see me about?"

"Colonel Nisen Sir." Said Tal, pausing and trying to figure out what he was going to say next.

The pause must have been longer than he thought because Rayburn cleared his throat, looking at Tal with slight impatience.

"What about him Tal?"

"Oh, well he is in the hospital sir," Rayburn's impatience turned to concern at the mention of the hospital. "he is waiting for another Rider to wake up. He was inspecting the perimeter units when he noticed one was missing." Rayburn sat down, concentrating on the report Tal was making.

When the full story had been recited, Gareth took a deep breath and looked at the maps of the area that were pinned to the wall.

"I think we should assume that a good sized force of Mages managed to escape, to completely eliminate a unit of Riders and Rangers like that." Calling one of his Majors over to the map, he pointed a finger to an area and asked him to organise a search as soon as he could, to try to pick up any tracks that might have been left by fleeing Mages.

Turning back to Tal he smiled, and asked him to send Colonel Nisen to see him personally to fully explain the situation. Tal saluted and turned to leave as Rayburn called him back one last time.

"You did well Tal. I'm glad I promoted you to Rider." He then turned, and with his officers, started to plan further searches of the area. Tal found that despite his tiredness and aching joints he was smiling broadly. Leaving the dark halls he found his spirits rising.

The Mages had been routed and were fleeing, the Gate was being closed by Seers and the Demon threat had been stopped. He was still alive and he was a fully-fledged Rider that had played a pivotal role in the Kingdom's greatest threat that he had ever known. He had girl standing next to him that he cared for deeply and knew she felt the same, he then thought about Brad and Cholla. His smile faded as he realised how much it would hurt should anything happen to Hazel. He found himself rushing back to the hospital tent, he would pass on Rayburn's message then find out how Brad was.

Drew was on sentry duty.

The night was settling in and he had until midnight before he was relieved. Richardson sat next to him, his pike being used as a support. The camps moral had been sapped since the Seers failed to awaken the children after the severing of the Gate to the Demons realm.

It had felt like an eternity ago that they had waited outside the entrance to the cave expectantly, only to have Master Diarmid collapse after closing the Gate and the children remain in their comatose state.

Now they waited, guarding the site of the cave while the Seers tried repeatedly to break whatever hold the Demonic Magic had over the children on its altars. They had been reinforced to a total of fifty Guardsmen now and had about twenty engineers making better fortifications and defences around the area.

Staked walls had been placed and reinforced, pit traps and other progress hindering surprises had been laid in the ground surrounding the defensive position and Drew began to wonder if he would ever see a populated town again.

Stores were brought in weekly by wagon, along with updates in orders and any relief's.

A torch was burning brightly from the entrance to the cave. Brother Hale was entering the mouth and descending the steps again. He seemed to be hit hard when the children did not wake, and was spending almost every moment awake within the confines of the dark cave, working on attempt after attempt to set them free.

Midnight arrived and Drew's relief turned up. Richardson handed over the watch to the oncoming Sergeant, and he and Drew headed towards the tent they shared with their company. The days were dragging, and Drew found himself wondering what the rest of the Kingdom was doing and how the war was being felt in other parts of the land. Surely, something must be happening elsewhere, or this would be the most uneventful war in the history of his homeland.

The sun rose once again and Tal found himself feeling more refreshed. Hazel was sleeping against him, as they sat at Brad's bed. Their friend had woken briefly when they arrived back from seeing Rayburn, but fell into a deep sleep shortly after, and had stayed there until both Tal and Hazel had fallen asleep.

Tal gently woke Hazel and stood, placing his chain armour over his shoulders and strapping his sword to his waist. Leaving her to get herself ready, he left the tent and found Captain Erikson preparing his travel kit by their shared tent.

"Captain? What's happening?" asked Tal, curious.

"Ah you're awake, good. How are you?" said Erikson without answering Tal's question.

"I'm ok sir, feeling better than last night anyway." Replied the young Rider.

"Excellent, are you up for travelling?"

"Yes sir. Where if I can ask?" pressed Tal, desperate to know what was occurring.

"Tracks were found last night by a group of Rangers. About a hundred Mages have managed to escape. The Rider that Colonel Nisen brought in woke only briefly last night, but he did say that these Mages could not be sensed and that they were the most powerful that had been faced by all accounts.

"We are to take horses and track them down with the aid of the Rangers and eliminate them. Are you up for it?

"I am sir." Replied Tal, his energy level raising as adrenaline found its way to his system once more.

"Good. Tell Hazel and Layland what is occurring, and meet here in half an hour. Horses have been arranged for us and we will be off as soon as we are all here. Leave Brad here, as I understand it, he is still in bad shape."

Nodding, Tal left immediately to tell Hazel and Layland. From what he had heard, the Mages that had escaped sounded like Dark Lords, and with a hundred of them loose, no chances or delays could be taken in tracking them down.

The Riders were saddled and ready to leave in less than the half an hour ordered. This was to be a tracking mission only, they were to locate the Mages and when they had made contact, notice was to be sent via the Rangers to Seers that would then take over the attack.

Layland and Tal rode with stiff muscles, bandages hidden under their uniforms, but their awkwardness obvious to anyone that looked at them for more than a second. As they headed out into the Lost Lands once again, Tal hoped they could remain hidden from the Mages if they did come upon them, for the twenty Riders and two Rangers would make easy picking for one hundred Dark Lords.

The days passed and the company was still following the tracks in the dry and barren land. The Mages were moving quickly, from the information relayed by the Rangers, they were no more than one day behind the foul creatures - but the same had been true for the past day and a half.

It made no sense to Tal, mounted Riders and Rangers should have been able to overtake the Mages travelling by foot, and yet somehow they remained ahead of them, getting no closer. Captain Erikson reasoned that they were increasing their speed with dark Magics but could not guess how long they could continue to do so.

They were heading east towards the Kingdom and neither Rider nor Ranger could guess to their destination. It was assumed that they were just running for now and when they reached more habituated areas would try to vanish from sight. The theory did not sit well with Tal, there was more at play here than they knew and Tal was sure there was reason and direction to their flight.

His muscles were still drawn, and hindering his movement, but the wounds he had received were healing quickly. Faster than they should have done in all fairness, but he placed that down to the care of the Seers back at the camp.

The night was drawing in, and the Rangers could no longer follow the tracks at and reasonable pace so Erikson called them back and set up camp. He was looking at the map of the area that Rayburn had provided him with before leaving. The entire area was desolate with no landmarks. This used to be part of the Kingdom of Dragons about nine hundred years ago, until a renegade group of Magicians took it by force from a King that was weak at the time. Over the next hundred years, the land itself had shunned the Mages, becoming a dry, dusty wasteland. Yet still, this had not dislodged them and so they endured.

Until now.

"Where are they going?" mused Erikson to himself.

Tal and most of the other Riders were looking at the map in silence. There was a slight change in features a day's hard ride in front of them but Tal could not work out what it was.

"What is that?" he asked pointing to the grey area on the parchment.

"That? Its just a stone mound, its been there for as long as I have been alive."

From the darkness of the sky an immense flash soared overhead, giving the illusion of day to the company.

"Get your kit together, we're moving!" Called Erikson, as his men rapidly surged into activity.

Tal's body screamed for rest as he mounted his horse once more. The Rangers took point again as the party pressed forward, moving as quickly as the rapidly darkening night would allow.

The sound of hooves echoing through the night was deafening to Tal, his heart racing and pounding in time with the beat of the horses hoof fall. Focusing he added his conscious to the *joining* and searched ahead. The tingle of Magic was strong in the air, something had happened ahead of them, but they had no idea what.

Erikson passed the update back to the Riders that were stationed to act as relays all the way back to Rayburn and push forward, his own horse catching up to the Rangers mounts.

The push lasted almost completely through the night. The horses were foaming when they finally reigned in. They had to rest them frequently that night, the previous days ride, added to the frantic night-time rush was taking its toll on the poor animals and they could not ask more than they were getting.

With two hours to sunrise, the Riders took a rest. They were exhausted, travel worn and hungry. They had not eaten that previous night and rations were thin as it was with their mission set to last an unknown time.

Taking a swig of his water, Tal looked in the direction they were heading. In the pale moonlight, he could see an imposing tableau framed against the horizon.

"Is that the rock face from the map?" asked Tal between long drinks from his flask.

Erikson nodded. He stood next to his horse, focused on the large growth of rock. "The light must have originated from there." The Captain gave his men ten minutes then called for them to mount again. Pushing towards the rock in the slowly approaching grey of dawn, Tal found himself troubled by the panorama – it was oddly sinister in his mind.

It took a further two hours to reach the mountain of stone. The sun was just above the horizon and the day opened bright and warm.

Erikson dismounted and approached the giant chunk of rock slowly. His hand never strayed too far from the hilt of his sword as he jumped onto a slightly jutting platform of stone. Layland followed him close behind, Kelar, Tal, and Hazel following along with the rest of the Riders.

The Rangers remained on the broken and dusty ground, constantly patrolling the edge of the large mass of granite, keeping their eyes open for any signs of trouble.

As the Riders crested the top of the stone, they stopped dead. Into the top were carved two distinct patterns, one at each end, and the rock along the top of the small mountain was heavily scorched and blackened.

"This was not here last year when I passed it." said Layland quietly to the others. "We best report this, it looks like the teleportation patterns used by the Seers, but I don't know why the light was necessary unless distances larger than the Kingdom were involved."

Erikson nodded and relayed the news back to the command post in the Mages Lair. They waited for several minutes for the reply, fearing that their prey had escaped for good. One hundred Dark Lords free somewhere in the world, no longer confined to the small corner of the Kingdom, and desperately trying to fulfil their false prophecy that could destroy the whole earth.

The word came back from Rayburn to hold the edifice, and await himself and the High Seer. Less than half an hour later, Tal looked up to see the great wings of a Green Dragon beating silently as it descended onto the ground next to the mountain.

Lord Gareth Rayburn and High Seer Librensca climbed down from the back of the gracious beast and made their way to the top of the mound. The Riders saluted their Lord when he arrived, Rayburn quick to wave away any formality in such a circumstance.

High Seer Librensca headed straight for the centre of the scorch mark which was positioned over one of the patterns. Examining the burnt surface he walked back and forth across the top of the stone. It was large enough to hold the hundred

Dark Lords easily but the scorch mark was the product of only one design. The rest of the dark colouring was just the residue from that one point of high exposure.

He returned to the Riders who were just finishing their description of events to Lord Rayburn. He nodded and explained that they also had seen a bright flash but it was based on their horizon and only just reached them.

"What can you tell us?" asked Rayburn as the High Seer stood next to him.

"By the feel of the area, both patterns were used by the Dark Lords. The one here was the reason for the intense light, the magical energy left as trace residues hints at a great use of power. I would guess that where ever these Mages teleported to, it is not any land close to us, probably much further away than the Kingdom of Mountains as well." He paused waiting for the news to sink in before continuing.

"The other pattern was also used. This one however was only used like those in our Temples. It would have been used to transport them within the Kingdom somewhere, but where I cannot say."

"Thank you High Seer," said Rayburn. Turning to his Riders he continued, "Gentlemen, thank you for your service and dedication over the past few days, I will send some fresh Riders out on Dragons to replace you and you can return to one of our camps to refresh yourself. Others will carry the search on for the remaining Mages for the time being." With that he saluted then turned and left, the High Seer following as they made their way back to the Dragon that waited for them before taking flight and flying back towards the Mages Fortress.

"What's for breakfast?" asked Tal as they stood in silence.

Drew was waiting on duty, night was just pulling in and he was again looking forward to getting his head down after eating some of the stew that had been prepared for dinner.

Richardson was resting with his back against the wooden parapet of the makeshift walls. They had been discussing the last time they had been able to drink good ale without it being watered down or stale.

A flash of light that illuminated the sky briefly had stopped their conversation mid way, and they now stood watching the horizon where the light had originated from, waiting. A loud and ear shattering crack echoed across the Dead Lands and died, being cut off suddenly as darkness settle once more over the encampment.

"What on earth was that?" asked Drew as they stood looking out into the empty night.

"I don't know, but I don't think we're the only people to notice it." replied Richardson, nodding towards the number of lights being lit within the tents that made up the camp within the walls.

Soon the entire camp was up and looking out over the walls. The Household Guard were turned out swiftly, Captain Loytan arriving in full armour in barely five minutes. Richardson reported to Loytan what had occurred and was told to maintain his post until further notice.

Leaving the staked wall, the Captain moved to the tents shared by the ten Seers that were now stationed with them and entered to see them all up and dressing themselves.

"Any idea what that flash was gentleman?" he asked when they noticed him.

It was Oren that answered.

"We know it was magical, but at the moment that is all, apart from one other worrying piece of information. We were woken by the gathering power before it was released, when it was, we managed to identify the style of magic." There was a brief pause from Oren as he weighed up his next words. "It was Black Magic, identical to the variety that the Grey Mages use, and it was close."

Loytan cursed. He wished he had more men here if that thunderclap was anything to judge the strength of those that had cast it by. He turned to leave the tent and prepare his men for an attack telling the Seers to prepare for an attack.

He went to the Engineers tents next, they were milling around in mild confusion, unsure what to make of the situation. In quick words, he explained the situation and asked them to prepare the couple of catapults they had constructed. They nodded, looking slightly apprehensive, but Loytan could not blame them, they were not soldiers, but civilians that had volunteered to help the army against an invading threat. Not being able to spare the time to comfort them, he returned to the walls to organise their defence.

Calling his Lieutenants into his private tent, he outlined the probable source of the light and asked them to get their units into place and be ready for attack at any moment. They saluted and left, professional beyond reproach and not showing the least hint of fear. He wished he was as confident as they, but he had seen too much in the past few months that made him doubt he would be ready for this.

Leaving the tent, he saw the Guardsmen getting ready. Bows were placed against the wall with quivers of arrows propped up from the ground to provide easy reach. Swords, spears, shields and other weapons of war were readied, and no few men were saying a quick prayer to Telkhan the God of War.

Taking a deep breath Captain William Loytan drew his own sword and hefted his shield, walking to the wall in the direction of the light. Saying a brief prayer of his own, he kissed the shield that had saves his life on dozens of occasions over the years and prepared for a fight that was more in the realms of Seers and Mages than Soldiers.

They did not have to wait long. Within the hour, a cry came from overhead. The dark, menacing sound that belonged to legend. The Seers passed word to watch the skies, and to keep their heads down. The cry was from a Graven.

Wings sped above them, the beating of leathery hide passing unseen in the darkness above. Torches had been staked outside the camp, giving areas of illumination spread around like glowing orbs in the night. Nothing moved, but the presence of the Mages could be felt.

With the realisation of the Graven came the equally terrifying realisation that they were facing Dark Lords, not just ordinary Mages.

A scream from outside the walls brought the distance of the Mages to within a hundred yards. One had obviously slipped and found a pit trap. The Mage would probably now be staked through by any number of a dozen sharpened logs placed inside the pit.

In silent action, the Guards let loose their arrows, the snap of bow strings the only signal that they had been released. Drew could hear the arrows arcing through the sky, but nothing else, they either missed anyone out there, or those they hit died in silence. Drew did not think it was the latter.

The Seers were ready within the walls, at the centre of the camp by the cave. All had their eyes closed and heads bowed. Their minds were focused on the energies surrounding them, waiting for any change that would indicate that the Mages were preparing any spell. They had split into two groups of five, Oren Diarmid being the weaver of the power of one group, and Brother Hale in control of the other party's magic.

The minutes dragged on and another scram signalled that one of the Mages had been careless and found another pit. With a heavy creak of wood, one of the catapults sung out, a large boulder being thrown to the distance of the last cry. The defenders could hear the solid rock crash into the ground, but no cry was given from the Mages that would betray any target had been struck.

The Graven cried out again, blood lust clear in its call. A scream from the defenders caused Drew to turn quickly. From the wall next to him, one of the Guardsmen had been snatched by the Graven, its claws piercing his armour and silencing his cries as he disappeared up into the night.

Silence surrounded them, the tension almost heavier than his armour. A crash showed the body of the Guardsman that had been carried off torn up, his head missing and allowed to drop from above them, back into the camp.

Master Oren Diarmid called back to Borders Edge, he contacted the ranking Seer there and requested any aid from the City of Dragons that he could get.

The silence of the night pressed on. As sun rose, there was no sign of the Mages and no sight of the Graven. They were alone in the Dead Lands, but Drew wondered for how long?

"Why didn't they attack last night?" asked Loytan. The Captain was worried by the lack of activity of the Mages. He was pacing back and forth in the camp. He had slept for a couple of hours when the sun rose, but could not rest while the enemy was out there somewhere hidden.

Oren sat in his tent, the Master Seer had managed to get just as little rest as the Captain, and was sipping a cup of coffee, trying his hardest to stay alert.

"If I had to guess, I would say that they were testing our own ability. The trip they made would have required a fair amount of magic to create such a flash. Though I do not know why it suddenly cut off like that. It should have died away gently, not suddenly stop. Either way, it is highly probable that the mages would be tired after the transport, we get tired moving from one city to another. I would suggest that they arrived and were not sure what to make of this camp. They tested us briefly and now rest, waiting and gathering their strength for the real battle."

"When would that be? How long would they need to rest for?" Loytan asked, his face concerned.

"They would probably be able to attack tonight if they could rest all day." Answered Oren looking worried.

"See if you can get any time scale for reinforcements." Said Loytan as he walked out of the tent, leaving Oren to send his thoughts to Borders Edge and again request help.

Tal had fallen into his tent as soon as he had arrived back at the camp outside the Grey Mages captured fortress. Although the sun had been bright, it was not a bar to sleep for the exhausted young man.

After sleeping for the whole day, he was feeling better, waking in time for dinner. He guessed it was about five or six hours after midday when he finally shrugged out of his tent and made his way to the mess tent. Hazel was already up and eating when he sat down.

He kissed her gently on the top of her head and she spun to look at him, smiling brightly.

"You're up early." He said, sitting down next to her before taking a bite out of his small piece of bread.

"There was some kind of emergency, most of the Girls in my tent were called out and told to prepare for travel by Dragon. Lord Rayburn got a call for help from a small company that was defending a cave, with altars like those you found in the Gate room here. They were under attack from the Dark Lords and needed reinforcing before night set." She finished her soup and sat back with a contented sigh.

"It looks like the Mages have had their time then, I just wish we could have caught up with the rest of them." said Tal, taking the last of his bread and soup. "Who managed to hold them to call for help?"

"It was a small group of Household Guardsmen. They managed to hold them off for the night somehow, but they probably only have an hour before the Mages attack again."

Tal stopped suddenly, it was a thousand to one shot he knew, but he was beginning to discount the existence of coincidence.

"I have to get there." he said suddenly, taking Hazel by surprise.

"What for? Rayburn has taken more than enough Riders and Seers to tackle the Mages, and you have faced more danger than most Riders have during this war, let someone else deal with it for once." She said, hearing the determined set to his voice and fearing for his safety again.

427

"My friend might be there." said Tal simply.

"Be realistic Tal, what are the chances that one person out of the whole Household Guard is involved with this?"

"He is there, I know it." Tal stood and left the mess tent. Hazel ran after him, determined that he would not go, or at least that he would not leave her behind again.

They headed to the command rooms inside the fortress. The stairs that led down becoming familiar to them both after the countless times they had traversed them. Arriving at the Riders command room, they requested entrance and an audience with the Rider in charge in Rayburn's absence.

They were admitted and Colonel Nisen greeted them briefly before asking what their need was.

"Colonel, I need to get to the camp that is defending against the Mages." Tal said confidently. Then waiting on his officers comment.

"I see. Why?" Asked Nisen, not giving anything away with his voice or body language.

"I have a friend on the Household Guard there, I need to make sure he is ok."

"How do you know this?" Asked the Colonel, his head tilted slightly as he posed his question.

"I just know it sir. Please I have to get there before it's too late."

"This is beyond your skills Rider Parnell. Dragon Riders and Seers have been sent and they can deal with this, your friend will still be in the same amount of danger whether you are there or not. Keep yourself safe this time and I will let you know any information as it becomes available." Nisen turned to a Rider that Tal had not noticed in his haste to get to the Dead Lands.

Dragon Rider Khris Risce saluted the Colonel and left, saying that he had matters to take care of and would speak to him when something new came up. It had been a long time since Tal had seen Risce in full dress uniform, the Dragon

Rider had a set of eight closely spaced silver crescents on each shoulder over his cloak, and his black chain armour glinted in the dim light.

The Colonel saluted his superior and Khris gave Tal a slight wink as he left the room.

Tal tried to forget about Khris and returned to Nisen to plead his case once more, but found the Colonel looking at him with hard eyes.

"Forget it Parnell, I will not request a Dragon for you so you will have to put up with it. Now get some more rest, if you're ready for battle, I will have duties for you in the morning." The Colonel dismissed him and returned to his reports and mapping of the fortress.

Tal and Hazel left the Colonels office and started back towards the dimming night. The sun was setting now, he thought of Drew and wished there was something he could do, something that would help his friend.

Hazel was smiling at him, happy that he had been stopped from another suicide mission. Tal was about to say something that would have wiped the smile from her face, when he saw Khris standing at the edge of the camp, just inside the illuminated ring of the camp.

He gave a wry smile that Tal struggled to see, then beckoned with his head before disappearing into the darkness.

With a vicious laugh Tal followed the man rushing to catch up to him, Hazel trying to scold him softly as she followed him towards the edge of the camp.

Leaving the bright camp, Tal's eyes struggled to adjust to the setting darkness of the night. He called to Khris softly in fear of attracting other people's attention but no one answered. Moving further into the rapidly darkening night, he tried to listen for the Dragon Rider, but all he could hear was Hazel's disapproval.

Then he heard something. A great breath was let out slightly further away from the camp. Smiling at Hazel in the dim light given off by the now visible stars, he rushed forward to see a Dragon waiting for him, Khris was nowhere in sight, but Tal knew it was thanks to the Dragon Rider that he now had a ride to get him to the Dead Lands.

"Thank you Khris!" said Tal softly, approaching the magnificent creature, hoping that Khris could hear him. Climbing onto the back of the creature, he looked at Hazel.

"Are you coming or not?" he asked her seriously."

"Of course I am, you always get into trouble if I'm not around!" she said in an angry voice, but she climbed up behind him and wrapped her arms around his waist.

Tal patted the Dragons neck and spoke softly to it.

"Thank you for this. Do you know where the Riders have been sent?"

The Dragon raised its neck, and Tal could have sworn he felt an affirmative sense from the gigantic being. Before he could contemplate his own senses too far, the Dragon spread its wings and launched itself into the air.

"Hold tight Drew, we're coming." Said Tal to himself as the Dragon set of towards the Dead Lands and the Dark Lords.

Chapter 23

Brothers

Drew waited anxiously.

The sun was setting, and everyone had been informed the Mages could launch an attack tonight. The entire camp was tense, tempers flaring at the least provocation. Friend turning against friend as the day pulled closer to night. The Seers had set up magical protections into the wooden walls, lacing it with some spells to try to reflect any small magic that happened to strike them.

The cave had been locked by a spell from Oren Diarmid, a last ditch attempt to keep the Mages from using the children of Peters Hold as power for their demonic Gate.

Captain Loytan had been walking up and down the lines since the sun was close to setting, ensuring that each man was in place, and that their nerves were as steady as they could be in such trying circumstances.

More torches had been set outside the perimeter of the camp tonight, and the engineers had managed to cobble together some explosive projectiles for the catapults, using barrels and oil.

Their request for aid had been acknowledged, and the King and Lord High Seer had promised reinforcements were being prepared by mid afternoon. Loytan just hoped that they would arrive in time.

The upper most limb of the sun vanished below the horizon and the flat, open ground of the Dead Lands were cast in a rich crimson colour. *Fitting.* Thought William Loytan as he stood still, waiting for the carnage that was surely about to follow.

The silence in the camp was almost deafening in its totality. A slight whisper of a sigh that was the evening breeze, was the only sound drifted across the small band of defenders.

A creeping dimness overcame the small, fortified position, the night settling it finally. The two moons of their planet were nearly full, casting a ghostly blue cast to anything that they could illuminate. As the defenders said their last prayers, that wicked cawing, echoed across their heads, sending shivers of apprehension across the Guardsmen as they watched the skies above them.

"Steady!" called Loytan, hoping his firm voice would bring his troops back into control of their fears. *If only I was as confident as my voice.* He thought wistfully.

A single globe of flame appeared in the distance, appearing no larger than that of a small ball. It hovered in the air, illuminating a man in grey robes standing behind it. This one object captivated the attention of the whole of the camp, watching it with concentration that almost made their heads ache, waiting for the moment it was released to see how it would affect them.

The time passed and the tension built. The only visible sign of the enemy was the bright ball of flame in the distance. With a gesture to the Engineers, Loytan gave the order to prepare one of the explosive barrels and a catapult. With silent movements, the civilians checked the range and the force on the launching arm and loaded a single barrel of oil. When all was ready, they turned to Loytan, awaiting his order to fire.

Captain Loytan held his hand up, a firm order not to launch. He needed to buy as much time as possible for the reinforcements to arrive – he could not afford to start the battle any earlier than was necessary.

A high-pitched screech echoed from above, and great wings flew down taking another guardsman from the wall and carrying him upward, vanishing into the night. A second cry from the dark skies gave the return of the creature. All the defenders readied themselves, waiting in fear that they would be next to fall to the claws of the Graven.

With a screech that would send a shiver down the spine of the hardest of warriors, the Graved descended. With a blast of pure light, Oren reacted, the beam taking the foul creature square on its exposed belly. Reacting from shock the Mage wheeled the beast and flew away, retreating from the camp.

Loytan was still watching the ball of flame as Master Diarmid attacked the Graven. At the instant the blast was released, the burning orb vanished. Maybe the Mages did not realise that there were Seers within the Camp? If this was true then perhaps it would grant the defenders a last minute reprieve, and allow their reinforcements to arrive.

He was not given any further time to hope however. Within ten minutes, the Mages must have come up with a new strategy, for one instant there was nothing but torches staked into the ground outside the fortifications, the next, flaming bolts of energy were being hurled towards the encampment.

As they struck the walls, the magic strengthening that the Seers had given them lit up, shining bright blue as they dissipated the spells of the Mages. Oren cast down lightening from the skies above the now known position of the Mages. Most of the bolts struck the earth and went to ground, but the slow Mages that had not moved were caught in the high-energy strike. It then became a battle between their own strength and that of the five combined Seers under Oren's direction. Shields glowed red around the Mages as they struggled to withstand the power of the Seers, and as one magical barrier gave way, the Mage within screaming as he writhed under the lightening.

Catapults crashed, their missiles, flying towards mages and exploding as they struck the ground, spilling their oils over a wide range and burning brightly. Another couple of Mages were caught by surprise, their shields only covering attacks from above, the oil covering them and burning them with intense heat. Arrows were released but most collided harmlessly with the protection of the Mages.

From above them, the sound of the Graven could be heard. Waiting for attack, Brother Hale summoned energies to him. Sensing rather than seeing the flying nightmare, he launched another bolt of light towards the creature, but the Mage controlling it had already fallen for that once and would not do so again, swerving aside as the bolt passed harmlessly past him, reacting with a strike of his own.

Brother Hale felt the power surging towards him and shivered in spite of himself. Had he not the combined energies of five Seers to command, he would have been sorely outmatched by the dark magician above. The flaming ball thrown by the Mage struck Hales hastily constructed barrier and swamped the Seers in flames, the heat washed over them but the shield held off the worst of it.

As the flames died down, Hale used his energies to change the flow of air around the Graven, creating a strong cross wind that threw the beast well outside of the walls of the camp.

Oren saw the dark mount wallowing in the turbulent air and launched a vicious assault of his own, leaving the creature smoking slightly as it limped back towards its own lines. A cheer went up from the defenders that was swiftly quietened by the reaction of the Mages.

A flurry of magical blasts was levelled at the barriers, several sections being destroyed, the magical protection of the Seers not holding under the repeated battering of the Mages.

Guardsmen were flung back into the compound, bodies torn by the attacks leaving them lying prone on the floor or writhing in agony as their lives slowly ebbed away.

Drew was drawing his bow back, releasing arrow after arrow at the wicked men attacking them. For every ten he loosed one would strike and injure a Mage. He was sweating heavily, the entire camp being surrounded by fire from attacks of the Mages.

Thunder roared as a section of wall next to him was blown apart and he was thrown sideways, crashing into another Guardsman. Climbing to his feet, he shook the ringing in his head away and returned to a still standing part of the wall. Arrows were spread all over the floor, and he took any he could find, trying to ignore the burning parts of his skin, and the level of fatigue that was rising within him.

Richardson was next to him, his own bow singing as he released arrows again and again. A cry from above saw a pair of Graven circling, the Seers trying to attack them without success. Air gusted back and forth, buffeting the creatures and stopping them from attacking, but they were still a threat, still raining fire down on the camp.

Richardson aimed for one of the beasts, his arrows doing little good against the land walking Mages. Drew followed his line of thought and took aim, both released together, two arrows flying upwards towards the Mage on the Graven's back. The Mages was killed instantly, two feathered arrows protruding from his side sending him toppling from the beast. A strike from Oren immolated the dread animal.

They were killing Mages, but not at a rate fast enough for them to live through this, Drew realised. He fired again at the second Graven but found that avenue closed to him, the arrow reflecting harmlessly from the creature's chest as his rider used him for a shield. The Mage lunged at Drew and Richardson; his anger peaked by the Guardsmen.

As the Mage swooped, Hale sent a gust of wind across his path, the Mage forgetting all other threats in his desire for the Household Guards. As the wind took him, he lost control of his mount, the Graven spiralling out of the sky and unable to correct itself. Hitting the ground hard the Mage was thrown from the creature and was set upon by the Guards. With the rider dead, the Graven was vulnerable, Drew and Richardson charging the beast with long spears, shedding its blood across the floor. As it launched into the air again, Drew knew that it would not pose any threat for this struggle; it was too badly wounded to take any further involvement.

Loytan surveyed the field. Half the defensive walls had gone and the catapults were both destroyed. His number was less than twenty. They needed the reinforcements now.

The Mages were simply holding back, using Graven to attack while their main numbers threw spells from a safe distance. The only success the Kingdom men had was the occasional arrow and the spells of the Seers.

A roar bellowed challenge from the sky once more, the Seers looking up, ready to launch another volley of light against the newcomer, but they saw nothing. Then suddenly in an explosion of light and fire, the lines of Mages were torn into by an entire company of Dragons, Riders and Seers. Magic and fire were hurled at the Mages destroying dozens in the first strike until the surprise was lost.

In short order, the Mages numbers had been decimated. The defenders cheering and rallying to the new arrivals and watching as the battle changed from them to the new much deadlier foes.

As the struggle wore on, the Mages were starting to slip, their singular strength not being able to cope with the Dragons and Seers. Graven and Dragon fought for the supremacy of the sky, flame and claw tore at leathery hide. Mages and Seers fought from the backs of giant mounts, energies flashing past the twisting and speeding forms.

A shiver ran down Drew's spine as he heard the howl of a Graven above him. Turning and looking up, he saw the creature descending on him. Pushing an unaware Richardson aside, he then threw himself out of the path of the creature. The claws grabbed at the earth, gouging the ground beneath it. Swinging his sword at the beast, he struck the wing.

The head turned in an instant, the Graven's eyes dark and merciless. No damage could be seen from his contact, and the Mage on its back laughed a deep and empty chuckle. Drew retreated as the Graven stalked him, hoping that someone would react and help him.

As if in answer, a bolt of light struck at the Mage, it skittered off his shield, but he launched the Graven back into the sky, choosing to fight from a position of power rather than be contained within the Seers range.

Drew collapsed, his heart racing and his energy spent. Brother Hale approached him, and helped him to his feet. Drew rested against the Seers ample size as he was led to the Seers area. He could not fight any longer anyway, his last reserves drained by the Graven.

The creature above them circled, waiting for the chance to strike. The Seers kept blasting at the foul abomination, but it gave no opening for them to exploit. Drew noticed that the Seers were tiring, they were using their energy too quickly trying to keep the Mages at bay. Brother Hale looked close to fainting, his bearing gently swaying as he used blast after blast. The four Seers that were giving him their strength were already supporting themselves against the entrance to the cave, their breathing deep and the bodies trembling with each attack that Hale made.

Oren was launching ranged attacks, doing his best to keep the few Mages that were still assaulting the camp at bay. He failed to notice when Brother Hale and his party fell to the floor unconscious. A cry of exhilaration could be heard from above the defenders as the Graven dove once more for Drew.

What have I done for them to take such interest in my death? He thought as he closed his eyes and waited for the inevitable, his strength no longer great enough to withstand the doom that was descending.

Tal saw the battle approaching rapidly.

The ground sped past as he saw the night illuminated with fire and magic. As the Dragon slowed, he saw the struggle between the Mages and Graven and the Dragon Riders and Seers. Dodging the attacks that were thrown up by the Mages, he urged the Dragon higher to dodge the combat, he had to get to the camp and see if he could locate Drew.

Circling the main conflict, he saw the small camp, battered and shredded by magic. The men at the walls were barely standing, one Seer remained, casting magic and deflecting what he could away from the defenders. A Graven and Dark Lord were above the ravaged defence, flying round and round as if waiting for something.

He felt more than saw Drew. He was sitting on the ground by the entrance to a cave, his head on his chest, Seers around him were falling exhausted to the floor. A cry by the Graven signalled his triumph as he launched himself into a vertical dive, straight for the collection of defenders on the floor.

Tal screamed in anger, Hazel behind him holding his waist as the Dragon sped towards the Dark Lord. He was not sure that they would make it in time, the Dragon was fast, but there was so much distance between the two.

Drew heard a roar and looked up, defiant to at least stare his own death in the face. The Graven descended like an executioners axe, fast and with no mercy. As the creature was barely twenty feet above him, great claws speared the thing and dragged it upwards again. Drew watched in wonder and amazement as he saw his childhood friend upon the Dragons back. Using its sleek neck, the Dragon reached around the frantically beating wings of the Graven, and took the Dark Lord from his seat with his fangs, tearing the man in half and spitting him out, a roar of victory bellowing from his throat as the Graven writhed in his clawed grip, slowly dying as the claws dug further into it.

Watching as his friend in the black and red of the Riders soared upwards filled Drew with awe. Gone was the woodcutter's son, now he was a man of the Kingdom and from the way he held his seat, a highly competent Rider. Drew stood and watched as Tal's Dragon let the limp form of the Graven fall from its grip to tumble to the ground outside the ring of walls. Banking Tal started to head back to the conflict, his arm raised in greeting to his lifelong friend.

A look of shock and horror spread across Tal's face, and Drew's brows creased in confusion.

"No!" Came a call from next to him. Drew turned to see Brother Hale struggling to stand, his body still sagging heavily. A sudden force knocked Drew sideways, the air being thrown from his lungs. A sudden burning in his chest caused him to try to scream but nothing came out. He looked down to see the claws of a Graven piercing his chest and the ground moving rapidly beneath him as he was being carried away and upwards, just like so many of his friends that night.

You got me then, you finally got me. Thought Drew as his vision fixed on Richardson. He sent him a silent goodbye then turned to see Tal, his Dragon chasing after him, but he could see them dropping back. The Graven had already been travelling fast when he had snatched Drew, and Tal had to turn the Dragon before he could give chase.

Looking at his friend, Drew wished he could have had one day to catch up with him, but that was not possible and as the life fled from him, a single tear ran down his cheek, drying in the wind before it could even fall to ground.

Tal screamed as the Graven fled into the distance, vanishing into the night with his friend. Hazel was holding him close, she knew that it was too late. The Graven had pierced his chest with a talon and Drew had gone limp in the creatures grip.

Tal felt the Dragon slow under him, he tried to urge him on, but only got a sense of finality back. With tears streaming down his face, Tal watched the rest of the fight as if through a telescope, away from the conflict.

The Dragon flew, fought and killed Mage after Mage, its anger and hatred obvious. Soon there were no Mages left, the night was once again quiet and the Riders set down on the ground.

Strewn around the floor were bodies of Mages and Graven, torn and shredded by teeth and magic. The ground was rough and burnt and the small fortification was almost completely destroyed. The traps that had been set had claimed a good number of the Mages but most had just been sprung as the battle started and now stood empty.

The Dragon Riders and Seers dismounted. Although the Dragon Riders looked battle tired and worn, they still stood powerful and dominant. Tal and Hazel dismounted and approached them. Rayburn was in the centre of the Ranks of the senior Riders, the golden bar across his shoulders standing out is a sea of silver crescents and bars.

"I must confess I'm surprised to see you here Tal. I would have thought Nisen would have kept you at the Lair after all you had been through. What brought you here? And with whom did you ride?"

Tal looked up at his Lord, the tears had dried on his face, but his eyes were still bright red. Rayburn notices and his face softened slightly.

"What is it Tal?" he asked in a gentle tone.

"My friend sir, the one I came to the City of Dragons with, Drew. He was here, I could feel it. I asked to come but Colonel Nisen would not allow it. I was leaving the command post when I saw Dragon Rider Risce, he called me aside and I followed him. When I got to where he should have been, he had left, but a Dragon was waiting for me, I guess he called it for me. I came to try and save my friend sir, and I did once, but I didn't see the second Graven until it was too late, he was taken by it sir, I saw it kill him." Tal had to stop talking as tears threatened to surface again.

Rayburn placed a hand on Tal's shoulder, looking at Hazel he asked her the same question.

"He was determined to come sir, I came to stop him getting into even more trouble that he would find if he were by himself."

Nodding, Rayburn turned his attention back to Tal.

"I remember Drew Tal, and as long as you do not forget him either, then his memory will keep him alive in our hearts. He did a great thing here today, his sacrifice kept the Gate to the Demons realm closed, and I'm sure that meant more to him than his own life. He has saved the world, as have all the other Guardsmen here that died in the name of the survival of our planet.

"You should head back, I'm sure the Dragon that bore you here will do the same for your return, go to the City of Dragons and I will see you there when this mess has been cleared up." Rayburn gave him a weak smile and turned, heading towards the remaining Guardsmen that were at their posts.

Hazel placed her arms around him and hugged him close, she knew how it felt to lose someone close to you. She had lost Cholla, her closest friend here, and she had constantly worried about losing Tal. She could sympathise with him, he had not just lost a friend, he had lost his brother, so close had they been since childhood.

Leading Tal gently, she moved to the Dragon, letting him mount first, Hazel climbed up behind him. Holding him close, she spoke normally, hoping the Dragon would understand her.

"Can you take us to the City of Dragons?" The Dragons giant head bobbed in a type of nod, acknowledging her wish.

Tal sat there quietly, he could relate to Brad now, his dark mood that seemed to bloom forth with the death of Cholla. He felt that the world was somehow darker than the night would allow. As the Dragon beat is huge wings that carried them into the air, he glanced around.

Across the battlefield flames still burned, kept alive by wood and oil. Smoke rose into the sky and the whole area had an oppressive feeling, as if it would never be clean again. They left the camp behind them, Tal not glancing back as they sped away. Better to forget this place ever existed that to linger on the pain and suffering it had cost so many people.

Loytan looked around at the carnage. Of the fifty Guards that he had with him two days ago, he was lucky if ten were now still living. The Seers were exhausted, only Oren was still conscious, and he was not in much better shape than his Brothers. The magical exertion that the battle had demanded was enormous for ten Seers and they all showed the result of it.

Loytan was struggling to cope with the feeling of failure that rested across his shoulders. It had been the Seers that had really provided the defence and the retaliation to the Mages, his Guards had only been able to kill the already near dead Mages and in turn be killed.

The Lord of the Dragon Riders approached the camp. For all his bearing and strength, it was still obvious he had been in a battle. He was dirty with the grime of war and his eyes held that haunted look that only soldiers could hold after such a night.

Saluting, he waited for Rayburn to speak first.

"Hello Captain," he said simply. "I'm sorry we could not get here any quicker, we only found out shortly before we left. If there were anything we could have done to get here quicker, rest assured we would have done it."

Loytan merely nodded. "Thank you my Lord, I know you would not have left us here."

There seemed little else to say. The Seers that had just arrived were already seeing to the wounded, and by the morning, more reinforcements would be there to set up a better fortification around the cave, ensuring that it stayed out of Mage control until the children within could be released from the spell that held them.

Rayburn turned to a Dragon Rider with a bar of silver that ran down the length of his shoulder. Waiting to make sure that he was out of earshot of the Guards and Seers, he spoke softly.

"If your happy sir, I will return to the City of Dragons to report to the King and his advisors."

The Dragon Rider nodded and shook Gareth's hand. The two parted company and before long Rayburn was once more speeding through the night on the back of a Dragon. His mind asked a single question the entire trip, *where did the other Grey Mages transport to?*

The question was echoed by the Dragon, both wishing desperately that they had the answer. In that one question lay peace and safety once and for all for the Kingdom.

Richardson stood, his face covered with his own blood. He had been pushed aside by Drew when the Graven attacked, after that it was all he could do to stay alive, where Drew had gone was not known to him until it was all over.

He had collapsed with grief, he had taken the boy under his wing, protecting him as much as he could. Being a soldier was a dangerous life, but Drew had so much potential, he should have been in the City of Dragons protecting one of the royal household, not out in some dead part of the world, facing massive odds with little chance of survival. He was only sixteen, and should not have died. *He* should not have let Drew die, he had let him down.

Turning away from the carnage, he turned his attention to the wounded. He had to help where he could, he had to keep busy. Too many had died as it was, if he could help keeping anyone else alive he would. The night wore on, and as the sun rose, Richardson was still numb, his mind still trying to come up with things to do to keep busy. How long would he have to do this for? How long until the pain let him be?

Chapter 24

Homecoming

A knock resounded on the door.

Tal hopped across the clothe strewn floor to open it. Standing outside was Brad, his blonde hair tied back in a neat ponytail and his green eyes bright in the morning sunlight.

Summer was here in all its glory, the bright rays of the sun illuminating the corridors of the grand barracks in the City of Dragons. With the warmth of the light heating his body, Tal hurriedly strapped his rapier to his waist, and stepped out to meet his friend.

Tal was dressed in his best uniform. The black chain mail of the riders, covered with a black tabard with the red dragon at its centre framed his shoulders, and his lightweight cloak with the red border at the bottom was pinned to his armour. It was his personal preference to wear the Rapier that Captain Fen Trillar had given to him on his sixteenth birthday rather than his usual light curved blade.

Brad wore an identical uniform, a longs word strapped to his waist instead and the collar of a Steward of the Realm was sitting around his neck under the cloak. He looked every inch the returning hero that was sung about in ballads, and Tal just

444

hoped that he might look half as good when they were sitting in the Great Hall of the Palace.

As they left the barracks, Tal asked Brad where Hazel was. His friend gave a slight smile, "She said she was going to call for you, but couldn't bare to turn up and see you dressed in field gear again, so she sent me instead."

Tal gave a gentle punch to his friends shoulder, it was good to see him a little brighter and happier after the loss of Cholla, but he didn't have to keep dragging up the events of the night in the Greenhome spent with the Elves all those months back.

With a feigned look of hurt, Brad set off towards the Palace. There had been the usual welcome home speeches and festivals laid on by the Royal Family on the return of the armies, but this was a private recognition by them for the selection that had made personal sacrifices or shown exceptional bravery and courage. Tal and Brad were informed that they were to be promoted to the rank of Sergeant for their efforts in escaping from the Demons realm, and Hazel was to be offered the medal of courage for her work on the front line in the original push into the Lost Lands.

The war, although brief had been vicious and punishing for the armies of the Kingdom. Hundreds of Soldiers, Riders, Rangers and even Seers were being lost each day on the battlefronts, and the loss of an entire city counted dozens if not hundreds of thousands of civilians in the total cost of lives taken by the Mages and Demons.

Arriving at the entrance to the Palace, they were surprised to see so many of the local populace waiting outside, cheering them as they were ushered inside by the Household Guard. The crowed cheering the heroes of the war, and though they were unaware of the specifics of anyone that entered today, they knew that they had risked death a hundred times or more for their safety, for that they owed them their support.

As the procession of armed men and Seers walked through the high vaulted halls with large stained glass windows that gave a warmth to the palace that Tal had never witnessed before, a voice called out to him and started to push back through the crowd that were moving in the direction of the Great Hall.

Sergeant Kendrik looked much like Tal remembered that first night he had met him in the woods outside of his home city of Dukeray. The one difference was that he had two medals pinned to his tabard this time.

"What are those baubles Lay?" asked Tal, ducking the resulting backhanded swing from his friend.

"You ill educated youngster, show some respect to your elders! These are the Riders Medals of Courage and Valour. Do enough stupid things and you might end up with one yourself some day!" he said with the wry grin that seemed to follow him everywhere.

Tal laughed and pointed out that it was not so long ago that Layland had refused to be called his elder.

"Fine you got me lad, but you will be the one getting mocked by fledglings soon enough! So make the most of this poor Sergeants plight whilst it is not your own!" Layland replied with a slight wink.

"So what are you here for Lay?" asked Brad as they approached the entrance doors to the Hall.

"Ah Brad, that would be telling!" he answered in an infuriating fashion before laughing and darting through the lines of people ahead of them, leaving Tal and Brad stuck in the queue waiting to enter.

"He gets more childish each time I see him." Said Tal with an open laugh.

Brad nodded, the grin on his face showing his agreement.

When they finally got inside, Tal searched the Great Hall for Hazel and found her standing against one of the side walls in the area set aside for the Riders. He walked over to where she was waiting and gave her a gentle hug and a light kiss before the Director of Ceremonies called for order and for the guests to be seated.

As the Hall settled and became silent, the Director of Ceremonies rapped his steel bound wand three times on the solid stone floor, resulting in echoes around the chamber.

"Lords and Ladies, gentleman and women of the Kingdom of Dragons; King Amond and the Royal Family!" The assembly of people stood and saluted their King in one fashion or another as he stepped into view from behind a curtain at the head of the Hall, followed by Prince Rufus, Prince Allin and Princess Kayla. The Royals took their seats with the exception of the King who gave his acknowledgement to their respect by an inclining of his head. The Director of Ceremonies gave another rap with his wand and the gathering of subjects released the salute.

"Please be seated." Spoke the King as they all settled back into their chairs.

Next to the Royal family, were the high ranking commanders of his forces. Lord Rayburn, Lord High Seer Jakrin Tiersing, Lord Commander Denholm and various others lined the wings of the dais.

"This past period of months may have seemed short for a war, but they will be felt for many generations to come. The loss of a city, the loss of the *population* of a city was a cost that no one would have thought possible, but we were proved wrong. The cost that each member of the Kingdom forces paid was high, too high to be acceptable. Moreover, each of you here, has paid a price greater than most. You have personally taken the well being of this Kingdom to your heart, and through great bravery, fortitude and courage, you prevailed.

"The people of this land owe you their gratitude, the people of this world owe you their thanks, but more importantly, I owe you my love.

"You and your colleagues have closed the Gates that threatened invasion from the Demons and the destruction of the whole planet. You thwarted an ancient enemy of the Kingdom in the Grey Mages and stopped their necromantic preying on our citizens, and you did all this with the zeal and determination that credits you among the best men and women that have ever lived.

"Thus today is for your glory, for your recognition and reward, and to give you my personal appreciation for all you have done!" The King stood silent and waited for the applause to subside before continuing.

Lord Gareth Rayburn, Lord Commander of the Order of Dragon Riders, stepped forward. He saluted his King, taking the centre of the dais.

"The first order of business is to address promotions. Each person that gains it should be honoured, for it was your bravery and determination that helped us to victory." Tal waited, listening to the first few names being called. They were of trainees that had fought through the struggle, and were being promoted to full Rider status. The crowd applauded the young Riders as they left to take their seats, the next set of names were for the Sergeants.

Tal waited for his and Brad's name to be called out, and then standing, they both approached the dais, marching in time. There were a further five Riders that were also to be promoted, and as they all reached the raised platform, they mounted it together. Reaching their Lord, they saluted and he pinned the studs of rank to their cloaks, marking them as Sergeants in the Order of Dragon Riders.

Again the crowds gave applause as the newly promoted Riders left the stage. The names for promotion to Captain were read as they returned to their seats, their faces beaming.

"Layland Kendrik," Tal's heart missed a beat. *That* was why he was here! Lay was being promoted to Captain. Tal and Brad watched as the grinning Rider walked past them with his ever-present grin and a quick wink.

The same pattern was followed for the rest of the promotions and after a short time, Rayburn announced that the following Riders were to receive the Medal of Courage.

As Hazel's name was read out, Tal felt his heart swell with pride. She stood and started to walk towards the dais as the rest of the names were called out. Tal was so intent on watching her as she mounted the couple of steps, that he had stopped listening. Brad was standing and pulling on Tal's arm.

"Tal he called our names!" said Brad as he started to move towards the stage, his approach a lot less graceful than previously.

Rayburn was smiling as he pinned the medals onto their tabards, Tal and Brad's faces showing bewilderment. Waiting for their Lord to dismiss them, they waited in silence. A voice from behind called out Tal's name for a third time.

Turning, the young Rider felt his nerves racing as he saw that it was the King that had spoken.

"A short time back, you did great service to men of this Kingdom when you led them to freedom from the captivity of the Demons. At the time I was unable to reward you for your selflessness," Tal flushed slightly remember that he had been arrested and placed in a cell for disobeying orders, he was glad the King did not bring that up here. "I am not unable to do so now."

An attendant stood behind him and handed him a collar. Tal's mouth almost fell open as he recognised it, it was the same collar that was being worn by Brad and Hazel. *Steward of the Realm.*

He fell to his knee as the King approached. The attendant unfastened Tal's cloak and stood back, allowing the King to drape the collar over his shoulders. After reattaching the cloak, the attendant disappeared from the dais again, and the King took Tal's hand, bidding him to rise.

As soon as Tal had returned to the line of Riders that had received their medals, he noticed that Hazel had a tear in her eye that she was struggling to hold back, and Brad had a grin as wide as he had ever seen. The guests applauded vigorously, but the Riders that were aware of Tal's trouble over the past months were standing and cheering, all decorum and propriety forgotten.

The King and Rayburn were smiling and when the crowd had quietened, the Riders were dismissed.

The rest of the military orders were progressed in the same manner, even the Seers were given the recognition they deserved. The ten that had defended the cave in the Dead Lands were given Royal Recognition with the honour of Guardian of the Realm. The honour was given for the act of its own name. The collars were of a blue silk that met in the centre with a shield, upon which was embossed the same crown that sat above Tal's crossed swords of the Steward of the Realm title.

The ten Seers were almost in tears as their desperate stand was recreated by Jakrin Tiersing for all to see.

With the ceremony complete, the King gave some last words of gratitude and retired with his family.

Tal was leaving the Hall with Hazel, Brad and Layland when Rayburn caught up with them. Pulling them aside, he again congratulated them on their honours, but his face turned serious as he asked them to come to his office at sundown, before disappearing with Jakrin Tiersing and Cyran Denholm.

"What was all that about?" Asked Brad as their Lord was quickly swept away into the crowd.

"I don't know, but I would be surprised if it was good tidings." Replied Layland as he said goodbye to the three of them and vanished himself into the mass of the Kingdom forces.

The sun was sinking beneath the horizon and gave the City of Dragons a silhouette that was almost artistic in its beauty. Tal, Brad and Hazel were walking to the Palace of Dragons to make good their appointment with Lord Rayburn. They were still unsure what he wanted with them, and why was it so secretive that he called them at sunset?

Reaching the entrance to the Palace, they found themselves face to face with Vorlin Mansford, the tall nightwalker was dressed in his brown robes again, his bearing more like that of a monk than a vicious warrior.

"What are you doing here?!" asked Tal. He suddenly blushed furiously, not sure whether he had seemed rude or overly excited to see the man.

"I received a request from Gareth to see him tonight, so here I am." Said the Seicolantrai as he passed through the main doors to the Palace.

"Well that explains why the request was for sunset." Stated Hazel. The four of them were walking through the vaulted corridors towards Rayburn's office. After their initial meeting they had lapsed into silence, the echoing steps from their uniform boots resounding ahead of them.

The door to Gareth Rayburn's office was ajar when they arrived. Knocking, they entered when permission was given.

"Please close the door." Said Rayburn, his voice serious. Hazel closed the door and stood next to Tal. Inside the room were Rayburn, Tal, Hazel, Brad, Vorlin, Lay, Khris, Jakrin Tiersing, and Oren Diarmid.

"Gentleman I have called you here tonight to discuss something very serious. As you are aware, we have been in a struggle for the very planet. The Demons and their puppets the Grey Mages have been beaten, but they have not been eliminated. The people that were used to power the two Gates are still in a magically induced coma, from which we have not been able to wake them, and at least fifty Dark Lords have escaped and are out of our reach.

"With the chance of them reopening the Gates if they manage to regain control of our people, we have to take precautions. The nine of us have had closer dealings with the Mages and Demons in one way or another throughout this conflict, and because of our unique positions the King has given us certain privileges. Those of us who are sworn to Kingdom Services – with the exceptions of Jakrin and myself – are no longer bound to our Orders, you are free agents under direct command of myself and the King. You will have any funding you think is necessary for you to accomplish your duty but there is one condition.

"You are not to be discovered." Rayburn let this information sink in. Tal and Hazel looked confused, Brad showed no emotion, Layland was grinning as usual and Khris seemed to be contemplating. Oren asked the question that was on everyone's mind.

"What is our duty then?"

Rayburn turned to Vorlin, "The Seicolantrai that are loyal to you have been given the Mages Lair to make your own, I would ask that you allow one of us free access to all that is contained there, and I would like to request that it be Oren."

The Nightwalker nodded slowly, "Of course, but why?"

"We need to ensure the protection of our Kingdom. Within that fortress might be the answer to releasing our citizens and ending the threat once and for all, so I would like Oren to try to discover a way to achieve that. The rest of you are to disappear into the Kingdom, spread yourself out and keep vigilant for any resurfacing of Grey Mages or Demons. There is still a high chance of a secondary attempt to overthrow us, and the King does not want them to get the element of surprise they had this time.

"All the information you gather will be sent to myself who will liase with Jakrin and present your findings directly to the King. Vorlin, you have done so much for us, for the old alliance between Seicolantrai and Human, I would be honoured if you would join us in this undertaking."

Vorlin Mansford seemed to ponder the offer, his head bowed slightly. After a very short time, he gave a deep bow. "The honour is mine Lord Rayburn. Maybe through this I can start to close the wound that was opened centuries ago."

"Then we are all gathered under a single banner, the Order of the Dragon is created, and it must never be spoken of unless to a true and proven member."

Rayburn continued, giving out regions for each of them to investigate. The meeting continued late into the night, each of them receiving instructions on how to relay information back to Rayburn and Jakrin, and how to collect new orders.

Tal held Hazel's hand, he had thought the war was over with the final battle in the Dead Lands, but he was now coming to understand that it had only just begun, and he did not like the thought of a prolonged struggle with the Mages. The Kingdom had been sent into chaos in the last ten months, and if the war stretched on for years, it could come to affect all those he loved.

He could not let that happen, he *would not* let that happen. If the Mages tried anything he would do whatever it took to protect the Kingdom, his family, and Hazel.

—

The Dark Lord walked over the frozen floor. Deep in a cave within a mountain covered in snow, he placed his hands on a wall of solid ice, deep within this mass of frozen water was The Master.

He was waiting, the Dark Lord told himself. Waiting for the right moment to come forth and step back into this world. If he required anything, he would come to the Mage in his sleep, as he had done ten years ago when he ordered the collection of the humans to power the Gates. It had taken a decade, but he had achieved the Masters wish, it was only bad luck that had led to the discovery of them and the destruction of His plan.

Well it did not matter; there were other plans that were in motion. And in a few minutes, the Masters Steward would be brought forth to lead them until He deemed them ready for His return.

Leaving the resting place of Zailon Uran, he made his way back to the Ice Temple. It had been created by the Master before he withdrew from the world for the purpose of creating the Dark Knight if his followers required him.

Upon the Altar was a human. The man, if he was old enough to be called that was tied hand and foot to the frozen altar. The solid slab of ice was directly above the resting place of the Master, and blood was dripping from the mans chest and running down holes drilled through the altar. As it reached the ice that contained Zailon's body somewhere within, the blood turned from a red to a black, the colour spreading back up the ice towards the human. The dark blood touched him, and his entire body arched in pain. His naked skin started to darken, changing from a light hue to a deep grey that was almost black. Eyes shot open and the brown pupils flared red before dimming back into darkness.

The mans mouth opened in a silent scream, his lips curled back in agony as his teeth shattered and fangs grew from his bleeding gums. As the transformation slowed and finished, the man slumped back on the altar, his eyes closed, his body no longer bleeding but heavily muscled and healed.

The Dark Lord untied the creature's hands and feet. He was no longer a man; his form had been taken by the Dark Knight, twisting it to his own purpose.

Standing back, the Mage spoke quietly.

"Wake up my Lord, the Master has need of you." The eyes of the Knight opened and he sat up. Looking at the Mage his eyes bore deep into the mans heart, he could see the devotion to their Master and its conviction.

"What is my name?" He asked of the Dark Lord.

"Your name? You are the Dark Knight, I do not know your name." He said slightly worried, should he know the Knights name?

"I have forgotten my name over the millennia, what was the name of the form I now hold?" His voice was deep but not raspy like the Mages were, tired with years of extended life, it was smooth, soft, but carried a threat with it that was unquestionable.

"The mans name? It was Drew my Lord." Said the Mage, his head bowed.

"Drew," the Knight paused; he was slowly reliving the life of the man that he had taken the form of, his memories becoming the Knights own. "that is acceptable. Listen well Mage, we are going to rebuild my Masters army, and we are going to free him so he can lead us to victory and domination over the humans once and for all."

End

Printed in the United Kingdom by
Lightning Source UK Ltd., Milton Keynes
142154UK00001B/1/P